Acclaim for THE FIVE ACTS OF DIEGO LEÓN

"A story that begins in revolutionary Mexico and travels to Hollywood during the film industry's transition from silent films to talkies, *The Five Acts of Diego León* breaks greater silences—taboos of race and sexuality, of reinvention and assimilation—in a fantasy called Hollywoodland."

— Sandra Cisneros, author of *The House on Mango Street*

"With its colorful narrative and historic sweep, *The Five Acts of Diego León* has both a story line and characters that a wide readership will surely enjoy."

— Oscar Hijuelos, author of *The Mambo Kings Play Songs of Love*

"Fresh, surprising, and delightful. There is nowhere this gifted writer can't go."

— Luis Alberto Urrea, author of *The Hummingbird's Daughter*

"Novelist Alex Espinoza swiftly moves the plot of *The Five Acts of Diego León* from rural Mexico to Hollywood as his protagonist Diego León, leaves his intended at the proverbial altar to pursue his dream of becoming a star. Set against a backdrop of key historical events of the early 20th century, *The Five Acts of Diego León* captures all the contradictions, illusions, and disillusions Hollywood serves on a gilded platter."

— Norma Cantú, author of *Canícula and Cabañuelas*, Murchison Professor in the Humanities, Trinity University

THE FIVE ACTS
OF DIEGO LEÓN

THE
FIVE
ACTS
OF
DIEGO
LEÓN

ALEX
ESPINOZA

LARB
LIBROS

This is a LARB Libros publication
Published by The Los Angeles Review of Books
6671 Sunset Blvd., Suite 1521, Los Angeles, CA 90028
www.larbbooks.org

Screenings were previously published in *Huizache, The Magazine of Latino Literature*. Vol 1, No 1. Fall 2011.

ISBN 978-1-940660-58-5

Library of Congress Control Number: 2019948613

Designed by Tom Comitta

*For my mother, María Luz Espinoza Carbajal (1927–2007),
who taught me to question everything,
to forget nothing, and to live without fear or regret*

Every man is a revolutionist concerning
the thing he understands.

—George Bernard Shaw

ACT I

SCREENING

The Bride of Blood/ La bruja de sangre (1933)
Director: Dalton Perry (English), Ruben Salazar
(Spanish)
Cast (English): Fay Carmichael, Margaret Dillon, and
Jean Jacques Fantine
Cast (Spanish): Alicia Prado, Veronica Aragon, and
Tino Guerra

The Countess, a sinister, blood-sucking ghoul, is terrorizing the Hungarian mountainside when honeymooning newlyweds Emil and Greta arrive in town. Diego León plays Emil in both the English and Spanish production in this, his first major role for *Frontier Pictures*.

SCREENING

Far From Home (1933)
Director: Dalton Perry
Cast: Lester Frank, Eloise Kendall, and Susana Mills

When misguided youth Johnny Romano (Diego León) comes to the small town of Webster, Ohio and is wrongly accused of a string of robberies, a local lawyer named James Dryden represents Romano much to the displeasure and anger of his neighbors and friends.

1

San Antonio de la Fe, Michoacán, Mexico
February 1911

YEARS LATER, DIEGO WOULD remember the lit torches, the shadows wrapping across crumbling walls and stone buildings, the glowing faces of women clutching crucifixes, and the cheers from the old men as they raised withered fists in the air the night the revolution came to San Antonio de la Fe. Most of all, though, he would remember the feel of his father's hands, remember the dirt and grit beneath his fingernails when he reached out to touch Diego for the last time.

"If I die out there," he said, with no fear or pity or passion in his voice, "you will be the last León. You alone will carry on our name."

Diego was proud of his father, but he did not want him to go. Without his father, who would plow a ditch around the field to protect it from flooding? Who would teach him when to plant the corn? How would Diego learn these things now? His mother, clutching the rifle's neck, pleaded for his father to stay.

"Let the others go," she said. "We need you here. Think of your son. Think of me."

The other men were already on their horses, some of them shouting, "Death to Díaz! Long live the revolution." Of Díaz, Diego knew only this: He was the president of the country, and he was very rich. When people in San Antonio talked about him, they spat on the ground, cursed his name, and called him a devil. They said he had ruled Mexico for a long time and had taken everything away from the poor and given it to the rich. But then the people called for revolution, and men like his father were rising up against him.

As the men made their way out of town, their cries mixed with the sound of hooves clopping down San Antonio's only paved road. The women tossed bundles of food wrapped in flour sacks at the soldiers as they paraded by. The men caught these and tied them to their saddles, cheering and firing their guns in the air. The loud cracks echoed through the street, and the horses whinnied and shook their manes.

Luis Vara, whom the others called el Barriga because of his large belly, whipped his horse's flanks, and the animal galloped toward the rest of the troop. He turned and shouted his father's name, said something about marrying a city woman, and told him it was time to go. Diego clung to his mother's skirt and looked at his father, hoping he might not listen.

When he at last broke away from Diego's mother, she let out a cry. He watched his father put on his hat and drape a bandolier over each shoulder, and his face was stoic, almost expressionless. He mounted his mare and the horse snorted and neighed, puffs of white mist blowing out from its damp nostrils. Seeing him coming, the troop took off once again, and the people waved good-bye from the sagging doorways of their shacks. Just before he disappeared around the bend, Diego's father turned and saluted them. But his mother didn't see it—she had already looked away.

In that moment, just as his father rode off, into that darkness and violence which knew no beginning and knew no end, Diego León was only a boy. He knew nothing of the world then. He couldn't understand why men like his father—men like the one he himself would one day become—were always forced to make these choices, always forced to make sacrifices that shaped destinies and altered lives forever. He was just a child, frightened, unsure, confused. He could not imagine the many faces he would be called to wear—a soldier, a thief, a lover, a villain, a king, a husband, a father—or the name by which he would be known and remembered. Not his birth name, his father's name, but a false name. A name he would spend his life inventing, then becoming, only to lose himself in the riddles and the lies.

2

June 1912

IT HAD BEEN over a year since his father left, and still there was no word. Each day, his mother grew uneasy, restless. One afternoon, Diego found her in the middle of their cookhouse, head bent down in prayer before an image of the Virgin Mary painted on a thin piece of tin. A tallow candle resting atop a wooden bench burned, small and solitary, and the flame stirred in the breeze.

Unlike their house, which was built of brick and clay, the cookhouse had no walls, just a flimsy thatched roof. It was the wet season, and through the strips of dried palm fronds Diego could see the sky above, the clouds rolling by, white and massive, like strips of torn cotton. The roof always leaked during the heavy rains, muddying the dirt floor, dampening the posts that held it up so much that the wood would swell up from the moisture only to split during the warmer, dry months of September and October. Diego had awoken early to gather twigs for the fire, and he placed the bundle he collected near the dugout in the center of the cookhouse.

"Mamá?" Diego asked. "What is it?"

Watching the candle burn, she sighed and shook her head. "I can't take it much longer. I wish I knew where he was, if he was fine."

Diego lowered his head and remained silent. He'd learned by now there was nothing he could say.

"What should we do?" she continued, speaking more to the Virgin than to him. "Go back to Morelia?"

"What is it like there, Mamá? Tell me about the city," he insisted, hoping to distract her.

"I'm sorry," his mother said, hugging him. She blew the tallow candle out and rose. "The city feels like a world away. It's big and there are lots of people there."

"How many people?"

"Well, thousands," she said, smiling.

Diego asked, curious, "How many is that? Is it more than here in San Antonio?"

"Yes," she told him. "Many more. Yet, out of all those faces, I still managed to meet your father, someone who would offer me an entirely different life."

Two years before Diego's birth, she explained, his father had left San Antonio for Morelia to find work. He got a job selling trinkets on the street, and each day he would stand on the sidewalk in front of Diego's grandfather's notary business peddling his wares.

"Your grandparents hated him," his mother said. "A lowly peasant. They wouldn't dream of their daughter falling for such a man. I did it to spite them, really. We married, and I followed him to San Antonio, and then you came. It's been hard, of course, but I don't wish I'd chosen another life. Otherwise I wouldn't have you. I thank God every day for you." She wiped her tears on her dress. "Go out and gather more wood. Quickly, before the rain comes."

Outside, the sky was darkening, and the air smelled of damp earth. Chickens pecked at the muddy ground, and a sow rolled around in a tuft of wild grass. Diego followed a narrow dirt path leading up a steep hill and out into a wide clearing behind their house, gathering twigs that would keep the fire going well into the night. At the end of the path, he turned and looked down the hill. In the distance was the lake, Pátzcuaro, the weak sunlight bouncing off its surface, glimmering like ribbons of glass. Diego looked across the water and could make out some of the other villages—Tzintzuntzan, Tocuaro, Erongaricuaro—along the northern shore, strung there like beads on a necklace. Before him was San Antonio, his home, his birthplace, so small that outsiders tended to forget its existence among the bigger villages. Here was the main avenue, which started at the lakeside and passed through the town. Two summers ago, his father and a few of the other men cobbled the road by hand with bricks that everyone had given money to buy. He could remember the day vividly—his father kneeling, scooping out handfuls of dirt with his coarse hands, and spreading it in the gaps between the bricks, the August heat, the flies buzzing in the cool shadows of opened doorways. His father had taken some mud and placed it in Diego's hand.

"Here," he had said, bending down, guiding Diego's fingers. "In between. Spread the mud there. It'll bake under the sun and harden."

He looked at the avenue now, at the houses along its sides, one next to the other. Beyond, there was the tortilleria, the wood-carver José Tamez's shop, the grocer's store where the women could buy soap for the laundry or sacks of bleached flour and cubes of sugar. Diego looked still further, beyond the plaster church, beyond the town's small zócalo where people gathered on Sundays after Mass, beyond the cemetery where his father's family was buried, their bones mixing with the red clay soil of the land, toward the wide green hills of the countryside. Cicadas hummed in the huisache trees, and the wind rustled, the air warm and heavy with the coming rain. And where was his father? he wondered. Had he been killed? Was Diego indeed the last León?

Every Saturday, Diego and his mother traveled to Pátzcuaro. Even though the city was several kilometers away, his mother preferred the marketplace there over the one in San Antonio because it was larger, because they sold bolts of fabric, fine soaps and oils, and newspapers and magazines from Morelia, things you couldn't get in their village.

Since his father left, his great-aunt Elva had started accompanying them, because she said traveling alone through the countryside was unsafe for a lady like his mother. Tía Elva was one of the last remaining full-blooded P'urhépecha indias.

"My mother refused to marry a Spaniard, and my late husband was full-blooded too. Even though all three of my daughters are P'urhépechas they moved to Mexico City, cut their hair, and rejected the old ways," she once told Diego. "Your father's mother, my sister Eulogia, married one of the mestizos who moved to San Antonio years ago to buy up land to build haciendas. She was taken in by their lighter skin and sophisticated ways. But she was india. So your father's half and half. Your mother, well, I'm not sure what she is. You'll have to ask her."

One such Saturday, his mother mounted the burro, and Elva led them out of town toward Pátzcuaro. It was past eight, and they would likely reach the city by noon. From where he sat behind his mother, Diego could see the glistening skin of the lake. The fishermen were out, their wooden canoes bobbing up and down as they drifted toward the middle of the water. They raised their nets, the long arms extending like the wings of a magnificent bird, and dipped them in then out. To Diego, it looked like a dance, the way they all moved together.

They soon came into a field dotted with prickly pear cacti, their wide green paddles reaching up into the sky like hands in supplication. Diego thought about the cochinilla, the insects that arrived in the spring and attached themselves to the paddles. Elva once told him that the females liked to feast on the cactus fiber. He watched the old woman press her fingers across the white clusters, crushing the insects. They released a bright crimson tint, which she dabbed on her mouth, then leaned in to kiss the back of his hands and arms, leaving faint impressions of her lips behind. They lasted the rest of the day, fading away little by little.

Elva held the burro's saddle with her hand as she guided them, singing in P'urhépecha. More than once, Diego had heard Elva speaking the language to herself while she worked, mixing the words with Spanish. They were so strange, so different, and Diego liked their sound. He asked her to teach him, but his mother didn't approve. He had some of their blood, she said, but he wasn't one of them. He was different, she insisted. He could grow up to be whatever, whoever, he wanted.

They arrived in Pátzcuaro and followed the main avenue into town and toward the marketplace. It was teeming with vendors selling fruits, vegetables, spices, and flowers whose fragrant buds mixed with the scent of fresh tilapia the fishermen had caught that morning. They passed the ice vendor, the large square blocks dripping water, dampening the walkway where customers shuffled about. Under a blue tarp, his mother purchased strips of fabric, a lace handkerchief, and a new pair of shoes and knitted socks for Diego.

"Aren't they nice?" she asked, bending down to show him the shoes.

Elva reached out and felt them. "Very nice," said the old woman. "And expensive, no doubt."

"Nothing is too much for my son," she said. "We have to make sure you have nice things for when your father returns. Come along. We'll get you a bag of candy."

His mother led them through the maze of stalls, past bundles of herbs drying in the sun, wicker baskets full of baked bread, and slabs of meat hanging from iron hooks where children with smoke-stained faces swatted flies away and shouted prices.

On their way out of the market, they passed the rail station. His mother pointed to the train that had just arrived. The engine hissed steam into the air as a whistle blew and a crowd of people climbed out from the wooden cars and onto the station's planks.

"Look," his mother told Diego. "That train there. You see it?"

Diego nodded, chewing on a piece of guava candy.

"It's coming from Morelia," she said. "We should board it. Take it into the city."

"What about my father?" Diego asked, looking at her now.

But his mother didn't answer.

∃

May 1913–November 1914

IN LATE MAY, a troop of revolutionaries rode into town, toting treinta-treinta rifles. Their shirts were dirty, their trousers rags, their leather sandals thin and worn away. They were in shambles, their wide-brimmed hats filthy with the dust and grit of other fields and chaparrals extending far beyond San Antonio de la Fe and Pátzcuaro and Michoacán. One was injured, his leg covered in bandages caked in blood. He was carried into town on a cot and laid to rest inside the church; in case he died, they said, he would be near God.

The men were hungry, and the women, including his mother, gathered together what they had to feed them: a few eggs here and there, a stack of tortillas, beans, chiles, pieces of bread, enough coffee to make one pot. As the men ate, they talked about the battles they had fought, the mayhem and the slaughter, the fatigue and filth. It was hard to outrun the federal troops with their new weaponry, their faster horses, their better supplies, information and conditions. After eating, they gathered around a fire near the zócalo, drinking tequila and telling stories well into the night. Diego followed his mother to a group off to the side who were quietly cleaning their guns and smoking cigarettes.

"Excuse me," she said.

One of them removed his hat and bowed his head. "Antonio Felipe Méndez at your service, señora." The man strapped a gun to his holster. "And how old are you, son?" he asked Diego.

"Seven," Diego said.

"Seven." The man whistled. "You're nearly old enough to join us, eh?" He gripped his holster.

"My husband—" his mother cut in. "The boy's father . . . his name is Gabriel León. He followed some of the others out. We haven't heard anything from him in two years. Can you—"

"I'm sorry, ma'am, but we're scattered. It's a real mess out there. I wish I had news of him."

"Of course." His mother thanked the soldier and said to Diego, "Come. Let's go back inside. It'll be dark soon."

A few of the men had removed their hats and placed them on some of the boys, the brims falling over and covering their eyes as they chased each other around the fire pit. Diego wanted to join them, wanted to pretend to be a fighter protecting his village and his family.

"Can I stay?" he asked his mother. "Please? I want to play, too."

"Not now," his mother insisted. "We're going home."

Early the next morning, they rode off, on to Guanajuato to join another group of insurgents from Jalisco. Diego heard that the injured man had lived through the night, but his leg still bled. Elva said he would be lucky if he lived to see another day.

A week later, Diego's mother told him to stay away from the other children. When he asked why, she said they were sick.

"How many of them, Mama?"

She hunched over the mortar and pestle, grinding cloves of garlic. "Enough to make me worry." She turned to him now. "Promise me you'll be careful. I don't know what I'd do if you got sick."

"I'll be careful," Diego said.

"Of course you will." She reached out and stroked his face; her fingers carried the scent of garlic and onion. "I never have to worry about you."

Diego did as she said and stayed away from the other children. He kept close to her side. But the next day, he began to cough, and that night, he woke shivering, his teeth chattering so loudly that the sound woke his mother. She covered him with blankets and lay close to him, blowing on his hands and feet with her breath, but nothing helped. He was so cold. By morning, his forehead burned, and it hurt his eyes when she carried him out into the bright sunlight of the cookhouse. Elva insisted she had seen this before. She shook her head and sighed. "Those men," she said. "The troops who were just here. They reeked of disease. No doubt they brought this."

"I tried keeping the children away from them," she explained. "But no one listened. They think an old lady doesn't know anything."

Some said it was the mosquitoes that swarmed around the nearby lakeshore, especially during the warmer months. Smudge pots had been brought in and placed around the perimeter of the church grounds to keep the bugs away. Still, by the end of the week, more children fell ill, and the sickness spread to some of the adults. By then, the rash had appeared on Diego's chest and soon it covered his arms and his legs.

The fever was so high that it caused him to sweat and see things, strange shadows lurking in the corners of the house and outside in the meadows, crouching behind trees and bushes, circling about in the cornfield. Hands passed over his body. He saw threads of white smoke. He caught the scent of burning herbs. A red feather brushed across his hands, eyes, and the back of his head. He could hear his mother's voice, far off, distant, her cool lips against his forehead when she kissed him. Then her voice faded and fell away and the sound was like a pebble cascading down the side of a well, the tapping growing fainter and fainter until it was no more, until it was only Elva's voice that he heard, breaking through the wall of the fever, as she placed damp cloths on his forehead.

"Listen to my voice," she said. "Stay here with me. Listen to my voice. Please."

There was nothing else to do but lie there, drenched in sweat, his head throbbing from pain, his body aching at the slightest move or twinge. When Elva tried lifting his arms up to towel his back, he cried out. When she placed cloths soaked in alcohol and marijuana on his stomach, he writhed. She stayed with him. Day and night. Elva never left Diego's side. He watched her shadowed face. The wrinkles and folds etched into her skin appeared as if they'd been carved from stone.

"Can you hear me?" she asked. "Diego? Can you hear me?"

He nodded, tried speaking, tried looking up at her, but everything spun. The ground rocked and quivered. He watched the shadows grow and move across the walls. They took the shapes of jaguars, snakes, eagles in flight.

"Look," he said to Elva, pointing. "A toad. There. On the wall."

"And a monkey," said the old woman, smiling. "Swinging from a branch. Look at his long ch'éti."

"Ch'éti?"

"Tail," said Elva. "Ch'éti is tail in P'urhépecha. The language of your ancestors."

Because they were P'urhépecha, it was in their blood to tell and to recall, Elva told him, to see and to imagine things beyond, past that and into eternity. In between sleep and waking, she told him stories full of magic, of battles, of spirits that robbed people's souls, of animals that could speak. There were brave warriors and wise priests with the ability to see into the future, to look to the stars and predict tremors and eclipses and droughts. There were noble kings who ruled the lands from large temples, their stone steps leading up to the heavens where the gods lived. There were marketplaces under vast blue skies, and everywhere there was peace and no one ever went hungry. Everyone had what they needed. She told of Curicaueri, the god of fire, how he and his brother gods settled along the shores of Lake Pátzcuaro, how the P'urhépecha were the descendants of these spirits who taught them how to shape clay, how to weave, how to carve wood, and when to plant and harvest. These, she said, were his people, his kin.

And he saw them come to life. In his fevered dreams, his ancestors were men with scaled skin, eyes yellow as corn, wearing robes adorned with bright feathers and shells, with jewelry made of iron and brass and gold on their necks and arms and fingers. They were beautiful and, as Elva spoke, he watched them form a circle around his bed and dance and chant, and they called him "son" and "brother" and blessed Diego and swore to protect him.

"Here," Diego said, pointing. "They're here. I can see them. Standing near you, Elva."

"Yes," she said, soothing him, her hand pressed on his forehead.

"The spirits are here. They want you to see them. They want you to know they will be with you. Always."

She talked on well into the night, as his fever climbed higher and higher, his skin grew hotter, his eyes peering into that world of the spirits, of the ghosts of his past. Elva held a candle up to her face. She told of the fierce P'urhépecha warriors who were so strong they fought back and beat the Aztecs, the most hated of all the tribes in the years before the Europeans arrived. She told of Cortez and the Spaniards, who came on ships, destroying everything, laying waste to the great cities. She told of Eréndira, the young princess and daughter to the last ruler of the P'urhépecha, who trained an army of men to ride horses and fight against the invaders.

"This is what you're made of," Elva said just as he felt the fever consume him. He saw flames surrounding his bed, and the spirits stood watch, whispering, pointing at Diego, beckoning him to come, to join them in the darkness.

"Your blood is the blood of the gods," he heard Elva's voice say as he drifted away, further and further.

He was many things, she said. So many wonderful things. Then her voice faded away, and he heard only the roar of the unseen fires.

The fever broke a few days later and didn't return. When Diego was strong enough to lift his head, he asked for his mother.

"She fell ill right after you did," Elva explained. "You were too sick to notice, and even if I had told you, you wouldn't have understood. Your fever was so high. You were hallucinating. Seeing spirits."

"But where is she?" he asked, glancing around.

"It was terrible. So many people . . . Your mother . . ." she said, pressing his head to her chest, gripping his hand. "She's gone. She died."

He didn't understand. How could this happen? Diego wanted to scream and cry and shout out her name, but he still felt very weak and tired. Instead he closed his eyes and let Elva hold him in her arms and rock him back to sleep.

A few days later, when Diego was stronger, Elva told him to get dressed. He wore the socks and shoes his mother had bought him the last day they went to the marketplace in Pátzcuaro even though he had already outgrown them. Elva bundled him in blankets and led him by the hand to the cemetery. A handful of crooked crosses jutted up from the ground as they made their way to a fresh mound of earth adorned with bouquets of carnations and lilies. A marker was staked in the ground, and his mother's name was carved into the wood. What would become of him now that there was nothing and no one to root his spirit to the earth? he wondered. Elva said not to worry, that he would see his mother again, in one form or another, and he tried very hard to believe her.

She would be his caretaker, Elva explained to Diego. Until his father returned. When she spoke of him, of his coming back, Elva would point vaguely toward the distant mountains. And Diego imagined his father there, just beyond the craggy ridges, down below, in a wide valley where wildflowers and grass grew, sheep and oxen grazing freely and uninterrupted.

"What if he never comes back?" he asked Elva. "What will become of me then?"

"Hush," Elva said. She stood over a large copper colander, boiling goat's milk, which steamed and foamed, the warm scent making Diego hungry. "You just concentrate on your work and stop thinking about all that nonsense."

Elva had killed a chicken from the coop that morning. Diego watched her snap the animal's neck then cut its head off, which she flung into the pigsty for the two sows to fight over. It was his job to pluck the feathers before taking the knife Elva kept nailed to a wall of the cookhouse and skinning the carcass. The feathers were tough, but he had managed to remove most of them. Now he placed the chicken on the wooden table, took the knife, and held it over the dead animal's breast. Elva stood over Diego and placed her hand on his.

"Así," she said, guiding the point of the knife and jabbing it in until the chicken's skin broke. "No," Elva said when she saw Diego turn away. "You must see it. You must look. No matter how disgusting you think it is."

He turned back around and watched as she led his hand down, the knife making a straight incision down the chicken's belly. Now, she said, he needed to separate the skin, slowly, patiently. Diego's hands felt moist and sticky, and his arms were smeared with blood as he took the chicken and crouched down on a straw petate to continue his work, removing the innards.

She finished boiling the goat's milk. She took two clay mugs and filled them both and handed him one. Elva rolled hot tortillas from the griddle near the fire and sprinkled them with salt and told him to leave the chicken for now and to come and eat. Diego watched her chew; the bones beneath her thin and wrinkled skin still looked strong, he thought, and Diego wondered how it was that such an old woman as this could still rise each morning at five, carry heavy bundles of wet laundry on her crooked, spiny back, chop blocks of wood, splitting logs with much force, cook and clean and feed and look after him. She stood beside him, her white hair wrapped in a black rag, sweat glistening her face, breathing with her lips parted. She was missing all her front teeth, and he could see her gums, smooth and bright pink, and her mouth reminded him of that of a newborn.

"Elva?" he asked.

"Yes, Diego?"

"Are you my mother now?"

The old woman sat down, bunching the fabric of her woven skirt between her legs. She was barefoot, her toes knotted and coated with dust. "Well, no, but you're my son for now. I must help you. I must teach you things."

"Teach me what?"

She pointed to the chicken. "Well, how to skin animals, of course. When to plant. When to harvest. How to—"

He interrupted her. "Are you going to teach me more about the P'urhépecha?" He finished his milk and tortilla.

"I will," Elva said.

Sadness filled him in the days after learning of his mother's death, a terrible loneliness. Diego wondered why she had left him. Maybe she was with his father now. Maybe they were together, living in the mountains somewhere, waiting for the war to end before coming back for him.

But why had they abandoned him? He asked Elva this one afternoon when they were out in a wide field dotted with mesquite bushes, gathering twigs for the fire pit. He watched her, stooped over, her arms reaching down, deep between tall blades of grass and weeds and wildflowers. The gray mountains, veins of snow lacing their sides, circled them, keeping watch, cradling the whole valley. An eagle soared across the sky, and when its screech pierced the silence, Elva straightened her back and held a hand up to cover her eyes from the sun.

"No one abandoned you, Diego," she said. "Your father's still out there."

"He could be dead. Like my mother."

"You father's not dead."

"How do you know?"

Elva laughed. "He's very stubborn. He always has been. Your grandfather raised him to be a farmer like him and his father before him, but Gabriel didn't want that life. So, he went off to the city. And now he's gone off with the revolutionaries. Always looking for one thing or another. Always being called by something. When he left for Morelia, people thought he'd never be seen again. Well, not only did he come back, but he brought your mother back with him."

Elva said she didn't think his mother would survive that first year. Such a fine lady, she said, living this life. She grew up with servants who took care of her. But she was stubborn, just like his father, she explained. And she was smart, quick to learn. Elva had taught her many things.

"Like what?" Diego asked.

How to grind corn for tortillas, how to milk a cow, what to do when a scorpion or snake invaded the house. Elva and the other women showed her what plants were poisonous, showed her how to make a balm out of animal fat and sprigs of mint, which rocks were the best for scrubbing the laundry, how to drape the wet clothing on the branches to prevent them from snapping. And she taught them things they never knew. She urged them to boil their water and when they asked why, she told them about small creatures, so tiny one couldn't see them with the eye, swimming inside, carrying diseases that made people sick. She talked about wide paved avenues and trolley cars, railroads that brought the riches of the capital and, still further, the cities of the north, los Estados Unidos. She showed them magazines and newspapers advertising a hand-cranked washing machine, voyages on big ships to faraway places, women in elegant evening dresses and fancy hats.

"I thought she was a little full of herself," Elva said now as she gathered more twigs. "But she was brave. Strong-willed. She cared for your father." Elva gathered the large bundle of spindly mesquite twigs, wrapped them together in a burlap sack, and tied this with a strip of twine. She heaved it onto her back and held it. With her free hand, she took Diego's. "Come. It'll be dark soon. We have a ways to go."

They traveled through a flat meadow and into a thicket of tall oak trees where the air cooled and dampened. Diego loved the vastness here, the shadows, the stones furry with bright jade moss, and the silence. It reminded him of a church, so still, so sacred.

"And you will teach me things, right?" he asked. "Like you taught my mother?"

"Yes," the old woman said. "I told you already."

Elva taught him the P'urhépecha words for everything: fish and cotton, cinnamon and water. "Kóki," she said when they were out washing clothes and there came, from a small rivulet, the sound of frogs croaking. "Listen to the song of the kóki." Elva pointed to the sun. "Tsánda," she said. "Janikua." She showed him the thin clouds skirting the sky. "Anhatapu." She pointed to the trees around them. She taught him to sing the pirékuas, P'urhépecha songs. His favorite was "Canel Tsïtsïki," which he started singing now as they walked on. She hummed the tune, and he cleared his throat and raised his voice, which was high and strong:

Tsïtsïki urápiti, xankare sesi jaxeka, ka xamare p'untsumenjaka
Ji uerasïngani sani, ka xankeni nona mirikurhini ia . . .

"Very good," she said, smiling. "What a lovely voice you have!"

Diego said, "I'm glad that you like it." And he felt proud then, felt himself part of the words, which were ancient and wise, the tongue of his father, his ancestors. He imagined his voice lifting up and being carried off by the gentle winds that blew, reaching his father who was far, far away, guiding him back home.

¤

That November of 1914, Elva celebrated her 75th birthday. Their neighbor, Narciso Méndez, killed a goat, and the women helped his wife, Rogelia, make birria and tortillas. Everyone in San Antonio gathered to celebrate. The men drank pulque and stood around the fire pit, and Diego remembered the revolutionaries who had passed through the year before, bringing the disease that killed his mother. He saw the church and remembered the injured man lying inside, crying out in pain all through the night as the statues of the Virgin and Christ looked on. The revolutionaries had forced the man to drink tequila. To help with the pain, they said. He got very drunk and shouted at Diego and some of the other children, many of them dead now, like his mother. Was the man still alive?

The small church, with its two rows of pews and one candelabra, was open, and some of the women went to confess to Father Solís, who traveled on horseback to the different villages in the area to hold Mass and give Communion. Some children ate sweets and played, Diego among them, and they ran around the church, chasing one another. As night fell, everyone gathered to toast Elva.

"My birthday wish is for Diego to sing to me. Flor de Canela," Elva told the crowd. "Canel Tsïtsïki," she said to Diego. "Do you remember it?"

He nodded. He focused, sang the words to himself in his head:

Flor de canela, I sigh, I sigh because I remember you
I sigh, I sigh because I remember you
Do not suffer, do not cry, for I will be waiting for you

The other children watched him move toward the old woman who sat on a bench near the fire pit, a long rebozo woven of golden yarn wrapped around her head and shoulders. Someone had placed a fresh bouquet of flowers in Elva's hand. She sipped pulque and smoked a cigarette rolled from marijuana leaves, which she said helped ease her stiff joints. Diego removed his hat and he took Elva's hand. He cleared his throat. He took a deep breath and began to sing:

Tsïtsïki urápiti, xankare sesi jaxeka, ka xamare p'untsumenjaka
Ji uerasïngani sani, ka xankeni nona mirikurhini ia . . .

Except for the occasional giggle from one of the children, the people were silent with appreciation. Elva listened intently, taking long, deep puffs from her cigarette, her eyes low and red, glowing warm and bright in the firelight. He continued to sing, watching the embers drift up into the darkening sky, and he imagined them to be his voice. This filled him with a warmth that was painful and lovely all at once. Everyone gathered around him, and Diego sang on and on:

Axamu uerani, axamu k'arhancheni, nokeni jurákuakia.
Ji uerasïngani sani, ka xangeni nona mirikurini ia
Axamu uerani, axamu k'arhancheni, jikeni eróntakia.
Ji uerasïngani sani, ka xangeni nona mirikurini ia.

When he finished, they applauded. Narciso gave Diego a sip of pulque, which he drank quickly and immediately spit out. Elva threw her head back and laughed loud, and Diego felt happy that he had brought her such joy.

Afterward, Elva said, "You were wonderful. You have a gift. Like all of the P'urhépecha. From the gods. They have blessed us, you especially. Given you the ability to sing."

"And my father?" he asked. "What was his gift?"

"I don't know," Elva said. "You'll have to ask him when he returns."

"Will he ever?" Diego barely remembered him.

Elva responded, "We can only hope."

4

July 1915–June 1917

FOUR YEARS. GABRIEL LEÓN was gone four years. There had been a heavy rainstorm the night before, and the roads and the fields were badly flooded on the day when he and Luis Vara finally returned to San Antonio.

Luis hugged Diego and kissed Elva. He had lost much weight, and he was now thin, his round belly completely gone, his trousers and shirt loose and baggy on his body. His father frightened Diego. He was like an apparition, a spirit. His hair was tangled and matted, his fingernails and toenails thick and yellowed and curved like a dog's. He wore tattered rags, a hat woven from strips of palm fronds, and a pair of flimsy leather sandals. His hands trembled as he ate the plate of beans and tortillas Elva served. He gulped the coffee down quickly, even though it was hot. He sat hunched in the corner of the cookhouse for most of the day, watching the puddles of rain outside. There was a new scar running across his left cheek, a deep gouge splitting his skin.

"What happened, Gabriel?" Elva asked, reaching out to touch it.

"Nothing," his father responded, pushing her hand away.

"He was captured," Luis said. "Tortured. He was found chained to . . ." He stopped now, glanced over at Diego. Luis cleared his throat before continuing: "I won't say more in front of the boy, but I had to bring him back or he would have died."

His father remained silent for a long time, chewing his tortillas. Finally he spoke. "Where is Amalia?" he asked Elva. "Did she return to Morelia?"

Elva took a deep breath and reached for the clay jug on the crooked wooden shelf near the washbasin. Diego knew she kept it full of pulque and took drinks from time to time when her nerves acted up. She looked over at Diego, who fixed his eyes on his father. She took a drink from the jug then walked it over to Gabriel. He took a long drink.

"Two years after you both left, a troop of fighters came to San Antonio. Afterward, many children, including the boy, got very sick," Elva explained. "Then some adults became ill. Amalia got it, too. The boy recovered. She didn't."

Luis sighed and muttered something under his breath.

"She's dead?" his father asked.

"Yes," Elva said. "We buried her in the cemetery. Near your parents." She reached out and took his hand. "But the boy was spared. And you're both alive. We thought you died. It's a miracle."

His father set the jug down on the table. Diego caught the scent of fermented alcohol mixing with the smell of wood smoke and toasting maize as his father charged out of the cookhouse and into the street.

"What a tragedy," Luis said, removing his hat and looking at Elva, then Diego. "I'm sorry, son. I'm so sorry for all of this."

He went with his father the next day to Mass, and after everyone left, they stayed. Gabriel lit a candle and said a prayer for Amalia. His hands trembled and he cried into the sleeve of his shirt.

"I'm sorry," he muttered. "I'm so sorry."

Diego didn't know what to say. He wanted to reach out and pat his father on the shoulder, but something stopped him. Instead, he watched the candles flicker and burn away to nothing.

On the fifth of February of 1917—a month after Diego's 11th birthday—the country rejoiced but just for a brief moment. The land, Luis told him, had a new Constitution that guaranteed many rights for workers, such as paid holidays and better wages. Things will get better, he said. The fighting will cease. But Elva knew the truth.

"This isn't anything to celebrate," she said one day as Diego stood a few feet away from her, feeding the chickens. "The men are still abandoning their plows and pickaxes and still following the revolutionaries."

"Who's fighting now?" Diego asked her. He wondered what was left to defend.

Elva squinted. "Let me think. I can't ever keep track of it." She paused, counting with her fingers. "Madero, Villa, and Zapata against Díaz. That's how this started. Then it was Zapata and Orozco against Madero, wasn't it? Then Huerta turned against Madero and had him and Suárez executed, I think. Then Carranza, with Villa, Zapata, and Obregón, kicked Huerta out. Now we have Carranza's Constitutionalist army fighting the rebels. It's all a mess. Why are you asking?"

Diego shrugged his shoulders.

She glared at him. "Don't go getting any ideas about charging off like your father did. He left, and look at him. Back now two years, and he's still not right."

It was true. In the time since his return, his father had grown more and more distant. With each passing day, Diego sensed him drifting further away. Gabriel León, Elva said, had lost hope, had given up.

"His will had been so strong before he left," she said. "And whatever happened to him out there pulled that will from his spirit and cut it loose, and now it's lost, wandering the earth without a purpose, without a home. It's a very bad thing."

The next morning, he worked the plow alongside his father and Luis Vara. He was bored, the task exhausting, so he sang to keep his mind occupied, to ignore the fatigue and the hunger. Once in a while, Luis whistled along.

"Diego has quite a voice," Luis said to his father. "Don't you think?"

But Gabriel remained quiet as he worked, not seeming to notice.

Xúmu, Diego thought, looking at the thick fog veiling the trees and mountains in the distance. *Karichi*. He watched the goats. *Tsíkata*. He saw a group of chickens pecking at the ground for worms. *Karhasï*, he remembered, was the word for worm. *Kúchi*. *Kúchi* was P'urhépecha for pig. He glanced around. Where were they? Where were the *kúchi*?

The fields had gone fallow while his father was away, so there was no money, no food, and even the animals were growing desperate, hungry; many of them had simply collapsed. *Tiriapu*, Diego repeated to himself as he held a few kernels of corn. Seeds, like food, cost money, and there was no money, so there was little food. What measly crops they planted and harvested were sold for a few pesos to buy coffee or flour or beans. What little corn was left, they ground up for tortillas or fed to the animals.

"Sing to us some more, Diego," Luis urged him now.

"No," insisted his father. "We have to concentrate on plowing the field."

"Gabriel," Luis protested. "Let the boy—"

His father turned to Diego now. "Go to the house. Get me some tortillas. I'm hungry."

"Yes, Father," Diego said, then turned and ran through the corn-fields toward the house. *Taati*, he said to himself. *Taati* was full of *ikiata*. His father was full of anger.

He knew why his father was mad: the land refused to yield any-thing beyond a few diseased ears of corn. They came from the fields tired, dirty, the handles of his hoes and sickles faded and splintered, worn not just from hard work but anger and resentment. All he did was work, and nothing came of it, he would say to Elva. They barely had enough to eat. When she told him not to lose hope, to be strong for Diego, his father merely shook his head and glared at him. What would be left of them, he wondered, as he made his way back home to fetch his father some tortillas. *T'upuri*. That's what would be left of them. Nothing but *t'upuri*.

Nothing but dust.

In preparation for the feast of the town's patron saint, which would be held on June 13th, Father Solís announced that he would be organizing a performance of the *Dance of the Old Men* and needed four boys whom he would teach the steps to. Diego said he want-ed to learn it, even though Elva told him he shouldn't. His father would not approve, she insisted. But Diego ignored her and asked

Father Solís if he could participate. When he said yes, Elva sighed and shook her head.

"Stubborn child," she said. "Just like your mother and father. Always doing what you want."

In the weeks before the festival, Father Solís had Diego and the rest of the boys practice for an hour each day. There were three other dancers—Ignacio Flores and the twins Mauricio and Mateo Avila—and they didn't like Diego and took turns making fun of him when Father Solís wasn't paying attention. They called him stupid, a bad dancer, and Ignacio pushed Diego one afternoon as they walked home, causing him to fall over a rock and scrape his knee. Then the three boys laughed and ran off together, leaving Diego lying on the ground, bleeding, angry. When Elva asked him what happened, and he told her, she called the boys rude and ill-mannered and told him to quit.

"No," he said. "I don't want to."

He didn't care. He liked it too much. Father Solís had taught him the steps, taught him how to bend his legs and crouch and shake his arms while the violinist named Gonzalo played. The dance would start with Diego and the others walking into the center of the clearing, holding on to their canes, hunched over, their knees trembling. They would pretend to stumble and fall then form a straight line with the canes held out before them. Then came Diego's favorite part: the heavy stomping of their feet. He found he liked the way his movements blended with the music of the violin. He felt himself part of the song, part of something ancient and meaningful. After they rehearsed, the music stayed with him the rest of the day and, at night, when his father lay snoring just a few feet away, Diego would hum quietly, would imagine dancing under the bright blue moonlight, an audience of owls and white-haired coyotes looking on from the trees or from behind bushes.

Elva said she would use some of her money to buy his costume when Diego's father said he had none. Then he grabbed the last bottle of pulque from the shelf and walked to the back house.

"Aren't you going to eat?" Elva asked.

"I'm not hungry," Gabriel said, and vanished.

The old woman shook her head. She turned to Diego. "You'll need a mask," she said. Elva handed him a few pesos and said, "Go see José Tamez. Tell him I sent you."

Old José Tamez was skilled in the art of taking lumps of misshapen resin from candles or a hunk of dried and brittle wood and giving it a life, a meaning, a purpose. Diego found him outside his shop off the main avenue. José sat on a crate with a hunk of wood between his legs. A lit cigarette dangled from between his lips, and he wore a hat with a wide brim. He looked up when Diego approached and said hello.

"You're León's boy, aren't you?" José asked.

"Yes." Diego handed him the pesos. "I need a mask. For the *Dance of the Old Men*."

"That's what I'm making here," he said, lifting the hunk of wood, splintered, its edges sharp and jagged.

"From that?" Diego asked.

The old man took his cigarette and placed it on the ground. "Hard to see, I know." He laughed, and his teeth were bright white and perfectly straight. "But use your imagination."

Diego stood there, waiting. After a few moments, the old man spoke.

"You young people," he said. "No imagination." José waved toward a set of opened doors. "Go. You'll find something."

Elva said José came from a long line of wood-carvers and used tools that had been passed down from father to son over many years—knives to cut and smooth wood, gouges to scoop out the insides of hunks of wood like the flesh of a piece of fruit, chisels to form lines and wrinkles across the faces of the masks he made. In the courtyard, the old man's bench stood like an altar, its many jars of paint and pigments and varnishes like the chalices and vessels Father Solís used at Mass. A yellow glow filled the patio, lighting the area just enough for Diego to see that, on the walls, a series of shelves and niches had been pecked out with a chisel. On each shelf was a different carving of an animal. There was a burro, a horse galloping through a field of wheat, ducks with ruffled feathers, the veins of each plume so delicately etched they looked real. A dog played with a stick, and a cat stayed busy batting a ball of yarn, one string of the yarn undone and wrapping around its tail. On another shelf there were keys of different shapes and sizes. There were crosses and Holy Spirit doves sandpapered smooth.

And then there were the masks. Some had forked tongues sticking out of opened mouths, their heads crowned with horns or spikes. Others looked like old men, wearing wide grins, their teeth chipped or missing. In the setting sun, the shadows of his carvings danced and leapt across the walls and floor. All around him, the figures elongated, their bodies stretching and bending and contorting. The forked tongues of the masks wiggled around like those of hissing snakes. The eagle's wings fanned out, and its beak swelled almost to the size of Diego's head. The monkey's arms reached out, and he imagined them wrapping around his body, its hands tightening around his neck. The tip of the rhino's horn rested just above the doorway, swallowed it whole, trapping him inside. They circled around Diego, stalking him like prey, and he remained there, motionless, scared of making any sudden moves. He felt as if he'd fallen down a deep well, the daylight absent, only darkness and shadows, when he felt a tap on his shoulder.

"You saw them, didn't you?" the old man said, laughing.

"No," Diego said, still afraid to move. "I . . ." he began then looked closer now; the figures had stopped moving.

"The masks are here," said José, leading him to an overturned trunk strewn with more carvings of animals and birds, saints and crosses, arms and mouths. "All you have to do is pick your face. Pick the one that suits you."

There were five of them, all rowed neatly, one next to the other. Their noses were sharp points that appeared not human at all, but more like those of ferocious and unnamed beasts. Creases ran across their foreheads and rows of crooked teeth were set deep within twisted smiles, pulling their cheeks upward. They were painted pink, mimicking skin, and strands of yarn were glued to the tops and sides of each head. He was afraid to touch them, to run his finger over their lips and brows. Their eyes were narrow slits, without pupils, only hollow eye sockets that stared upward, looking past the straw roof and up to the sky, at something so large, so ominous that Diego recoiled.

"Which one?" asked José. "Any of the five."

But Diego couldn't decide.

After some time, José said, "Very well. I will pick for you." He took one, wrapped it in newspaper, and handed it to him. "Good luck, young man," he said.

"Thank you," Diego said, and he tucked the mask under his arm, turned, and left.

He had carefully laid out the outfit the night before and, on the day of the festivities, he took his time dressing, handling the outfit with gentle, delicate touches, as he fastened the cotton trousers around his waist, pulled the shirt over his head, and draped the gold and blue serape across his chest. Diego placed the mask inside the morral, which had been hand-knitted with bright yarn and fabric, and slung the bag over his left shoulder. He regarded himself now in the outfit Elva had purchased, and Diego knew that it was important for him to take good care of it, to not dirty or ruin it. He felt resplendent in the outfit, noble, like a warrior or priest. If his father came, he would notice Diego and be proud of him. The embroidered designs along the hems of the pants and cuffs of the shirt were like bright strings of sugar laced together so delicately, their patterns forming roses, hummingbirds, and butterflies. He clutched his straw hat— the long strips of blue, red, and yellow paper glued around its rim so that they hung down along the sides and front—and the cane Elva had fashioned from a sugar stalk, grabbed his things, and ran off to the church.

Elva had made sure to tell his father and Luis about the festivities the day before. Luis had nodded and said he would surely make it.

"What do you say, Gabriel?" he asked Diego's father.

Gabriel swatted the air with his hand.

"Please," Elva had insisted. "There'll be food and music, Gabriel. The whole town will be there. It'll cheer you up."

"No, Tía Elva," he said. "Nothing can. Nothing ever will." Gabriel sighed and looked over at Diego. "I'll try to be there, Son."

The town gathered at the lake's edge and followed the priest up San Antonio de la Fe's single crooked street, past the houses, to the church. Diego could see the statue of San Antonio from his place in the procession. A group of men, including Luis Vara, carried the statue into the church and set it down near the altar as Father Solís began Mass. Luis stood to one side, his hat off, listening to the priest. Diego looked around, but he didn't see his father.

After Mass, the congregants filed out of the church. Outside, the air carried the scent of damp hay and burning wood, of boiling milk and cinnamon from the colanders of hot atole a group of women stirred with large copper spoons then poured into clay mugs for people to drink. He found Luis talking to a small group of men.

"Where's my father?" Diego asked him.

Luis sighed and scratched his mustache. "He was in the field at the foot of the hill clearing out the brush when I left, son. I don't think he's coming, I'm sorry."

"There you are!" Elva said, approaching Diego and Luis. "The others are changing now. Come quickly. They're about to start. Where's your mask?"

He reached into his bag and brought it out. The mask was an ugly thing, he still thought. It looked sinister, its wood-carved skin ravaged, weathered. It appeared to mock him. Father Solís emerged from the church and walked over, gathering the other boys and Gonzalo together as the crowd made space in the center for them.

"Very good," he said, clapping his hands. He helped the others adjust their outfits and straighten their shawls. "Elva," he whispered. "Help the boy with his mask."

"Here," said Elva, turning to Diego. "Let me." She took the mask and placed it over his face. He felt her hands reach around back, tie the twine together, securing it. She smelled like corn and smoke, and he wondered if this was what his mother had smelled like before God called her up to the clouds. He saw through the mask's slits that Elva was pointing off in the distance at something.

"Look," she said. "Look."

At the edge of the courtyard, his father was leaning up against the wall, smoking a pipe. Just as he was about to run to him, Father Solís grabbed Diego by the shoulders and placed him alongside the other boys who were already lined up as Gonzalo began to play. Diego's breathing quickened. It was uncomfortable and hot underneath the mask. He felt his forehead dampen and his cheeks itch. His heart beat faster and faster as he began to dance, and he imagined it swelling up, threatening to burst forth from his chest. His palms moistened, making it difficult to grip the cane.

They took small steps, forward then back, their leather huaraches squeaking over Gonzalo's violin. The crowd gathered around them, laughing and clapping. He concentrated on their cheers, and when he imagined his father joining in, smiling and waving, the fear vanished. *But will he know which one I am?* he wondered. *My face, it's hidden behind this mask. How will he know me? Will he see me?*

He looked out onto that world now, and the things he knew transformed before his eyes. And the sun shone brighter, striking the crowd gathered there in such a way that they glowed, and Diego wondered if he was seeing their souls inside their bodies. The edges of their shabby homes and the sagging columns and the crooked street seemed to soften, straighten, and expand. Everything was reaching out, fighting to be noticed, and he felt the same way. He stepped farther out, toward the front of the crowd, so close to the group that several of them reached out to touch him. One of the other boys tried pulling him back, but Diego was too quick. Then someone, a lady carrying a bag woven from straw shouted, "Let him. Can't you see that he just wants to dance?"

He moved farther still, into the mass of people, which gradually parted for him. He improvised, shuffling his feet in a different way, swinging the cane up in the air. The more he moved, the louder the crowd cheered him on, the more they applauded, and the happier he felt. Surely his father was noticing him now, Diego knew. He weaved in and out, circling around their legs, around a goat with dirty white fur standing next to a young girl. The crowd continued to cheer and a woman took him by the hand so they could do a little dance. But just as they began, Mateo Avila stepped into the clearing and chased Diego around until he was back where the others stood, no longer dancing, but watching the spectacle. They had removed their masks and were glaring at Diego.

"Very good," Father Solís said to the boys once they finished the performance and the crowd dispersed. "Especially you, Diego."

The other boys watched him now, fists balled, mouths puckered, eyes glaring at him.

"Thank you, Father," he said. "I'm glad you liked it."

A week after the Feast of San Antonio, Diego stood outside, boiling gristle and meat from a slaughtered goat. They would use the animal fat to make candles and soap. Diego watched the pot, the pink chunks of flesh swirling inside, stirring it with a wooden spoon. It was always best, he knew, to boil this outside because of the smell.

His father walked over and sat a few feet away, in the bright afternoon sun, watching Diego. The scar across his face seemed deeper, darker, and more intense than when Diego saw him the day he returned with Luis.

"I know I haven't been myself. Ever since I came back," his father said.

Diego stayed silent.

"I'm sorry. I don't know how I'm supposed to raise you on my own."

Diego slowed his stirring and focused on his father's words, on the body of that mutilated animal.

"I left for the city then ran off to fight in the revolution because I thought I could change my destino." His father sighed and looked around. "I thought I could make something of myself. I thought I could become someone important. I sought my fortune in Morelia and failed. I brought your mother back and we had you. I followed the revolutionaries because I believed in their cause. It turned out to be a lie." He laughed. "Then I come back to find that your mother is dead. I try and try, and I can never change any of it. Why can't I?" Gabriel approached, crouching next to Diego.

And he wanted to love him, to understand him, this man called his father. Diego watched him now, and Gabriel began to cry. He said there was nothing else he could do, that there was nothing left to seek, that this would be his life.

"You'll die here if you stay," he said. "Just like I will. Just like all the Leóns have. Your mother would have wanted more for you. I want more for you." He rose, stiffened his shoulders, and cleared his throat as he wiped his tears away. "This isn't the place for a boy like you. I'll send you to the city. To live with your grandparents. I have no other choice."

"But why?" he asked him. "Why are you doing this?" Diego stopped stirring and let go of the spoon. It fell to the ground, and he stepped away from the colander.

"Because you won't survive this life if you remain here. I want you to make something of yourself. I can't do anything else for you. I don't have the means. But they do."

Gabriel took the boy by the hand and led him back inside. He took a pickax and walked over to the spot on the ground where he slept. He dug and dug until he unearthed a tin box. Diego watched him reach in and pull out a roll of money and a stack of papers.

"Here," his father said. "This is a letter your grandmother wrote to your mother." He placed the envelope in Diego's hands. "I don't know what it says, but it has her address on it."

He told Diego to tell them who he was: their daughter's son. Make them know you, he said. Make them know *us*.

A few days later in the church, Diego knelt before the statue of Christ crucified. Elva lit a glass votive and arranged it in the candelabra among the others. Soon he would be leaving on the afternoon train to Morelia; he was nervous and Elva told him to say a prayer.

He hadn't said good-bye to his father; Gabriel had risen early that morning and left for the field. In truth, it was better this way, he thought. What would he say to him anyway? The man had made it clear: he couldn't be Diego's father and didn't want him around anymore.

"I'm a burden," Diego said to Elva. "That's why he's sending me away. Because I'm a burden and he doesn't love me."

"That's not true," Elva said. The church was drafty, so she wrapped her shawl tighter around herself. "Deep inside, he does. You can't feel it. Like God's love. Your mother's. But just because you can't feel something doesn't mean it's not there."

"I don't want to go," he said. "I want to stay here with you."

Elva put her arms around him. "I'm not long for this world. I'll be going soon. Your father will be fine. Your mother will always be with you, too, guiding you."

"Will I ever see you again?" he asked.

"Of course you will," she said. "If not here, somewhere else."

"Where?"

"Back there. At the beginning and the end of all things," the old woman said.

Diego looked up at Christ, feet nailed to the cross, a flimsy cloth made from the leather hide tied around his waist. He saw the figure's rib cage, each bone a narrow strip, one on top of the other like rungs on a ladder leading up to his hollow chest, his neck, then to his face, which wore the weight of sin and despair and agony. There were the gaunt cheeks, the desiccated skin, the plaster thorns of his crown piercing fake flesh. He was only a thin strip of flesh, naked, so hard to reach. He could appear as anyone, anything, Elva said—a cloud of smoke, the petals on a flower, an insect, a stray dog, a white dove, a bearded old man. "Don't let the image on the cross fool you," she told him. "God is everywhere. God sees everything. God is everyone, and everyone is God."

"You go now. But you'll be back," Elva assured him. "Maybe a little different. A little changed. But you'll come home again."

ACT II

SCREENING
Crazy for Miss Cavendish (1939)
Director: Dalton Perry
Cast: Eloise Kendall, Janette Stewart, Catherine Hammond, and Victor Allen

Set in a prestigious all-girls prep school, this film stars Diego León as a shy and bookish language teacher from Andalucia, Spain who falls for a beautiful new English instructor. Diego León is Mr. Vega.

SCREENING
PANAMANIA (1940)
Director: Sid Stanley
Cast: Eloise Kendall, Gayle Turney, and Stephen Evans

In this flashy musical extravaganza, beautiful socialite Amanda Grayson, along with her two friends, sisters Myrna and Verna, aspiring singers and dancers, cruises down on a luxury liner to Panama. Stars Diego León as Enrique Pel and Eloise Kendall as Amanda Grayson. Cameo performances from Elpidia Baca and Martin and Margarita Moreno. Musical numbers include "Shuffleboard Shuffle," "The Panama Tango," and "Adios, Amigos!"

1

Morelia, Michoacán
June 1917

DIEGO WATCHED THE COUNTRYSIDE unfold outside as the train traveled down the tracks. There were endless green fields with tall grass unfurling in the breeze, humps of oxen grazing in the distance, and rows of tiny shacks and houses clustered together. He wondered if he would ever see it again. His father and his father's fathers had been born and raised in San Antonio de la Fe. They never knew another place. For as long as anyone could remember, Elva once told him, the Leóns had lived in San Antonio, had forever been tied to the land. It would end, though, with him.

Most of the other passengers slept, waking when the train arrived at the station. They rose and collected their things, stretching, rubbing their eyes. Diego looked at the people outside—the men in their suits and ties and hats, the ladies in dresses and jackets, the boys on the corners selling toys and wooden whistles.

"This is Morelia?" someone asked.

"Yes, it is," another responded. "Finally."

Diego stepped off the train and followed the crowds. There were people everywhere, jumbling and bustling about, hailing taxis or boarding trolley cars that coasted by on rail tracks threading throughout the avenues. Diego walked cautiously, clutching his valise. He followed a crooked alleyway with houses squeezed together, flanking either side. It wound upward and, hoping to get a better view of the city, Diego climbed to the crest. He soon found himself atop a low rise with all of the city of Morelia below. In the distance, the cathedral's twin bell towers rose up into the sky. Somewhere among it—the old buildings with their elegant arches and graceful columns, the large homes, unlike any he had seen before, the expansive and shaded plazas—lived his grandmother and grandfather. Diego trembled, afraid he'd never find them. He clutched the valise and walked down the hill, cautious. The people he passed looked at him with suspicion. Maybe they thought he was a beggar, because a few of them held pesos out to him. After he accepted one, a police officer strolling by walked over and told Diego that, if he was to beg, to please do so around the corner, in front of the church, where the rest of the city's vagrants were permitted by the municipal authorities to gather and solicit money.

"But I'm not a beggar," Diego explained. He handed the officer the letter his father had given him. He pointed to the address. "There," he said. "I need to go there."

The officer squinted, trying to make out what was written on the envelope. He shook his head. "I know this address," he said. "This is the home of Licenciado Sánchez. Licenciado Doroteo Sánchez. What kind of business does a dirty peasant like you have with him?"

"He's my grandfather."

"He's your grandfather?" The police officer laughed.

"Please, I'm telling the truth. Will you help me?"

The police officer sighed. "Very well," he said, handing him the letter. "It's not that far. I'll escort you." The officer reached out and snatched the peso Diego had been given. "For my troubles," he said.

Verdant laurels and ash trees lined the sidewalks, providing shade from the hot sun and perfuming the air. The police officer led him through a park with stone trails and bandstands, down streets where shops sold extravagant gowns and suits and ties. There was the constant rush of trolley cars and the clopping of horses' hooves. Diego saw bars, a few houses where women in tight dresses leaned in the doorways or waved at passersby through opened windows.

There were dance halls, rooms full of games, restaurants, and large hotels. The women paraded by in fancy hats and dresses, the men in striped plus fours and silk spats over their shoes, well shaven and groomed, nothing at all like the men of the countryside, Diego thought, nothing at all like his father. The city was noisy with movement; people boarding trolleys, darting across the crowded avenues, avoiding honks and shouts, and screeching tires. Finally, they turned down a quiet street where there were many two-story houses made of plaster and adorned with iron and glass.

"Here you are," said the officer, stopping before a white house set toward the back of the plot, away from the sidewalk. "Go on."

In front of the house, giant clay pots held plants and flowers of vibrant colors and strong smells—hibiscus bushes, bougainvillea vines, roses and lilies. A stone fountain trickled water, and a sundial sat on a large table, casting shadows near the imposing front door. He took a deep breath before knocking, and soon there came the sound of footsteps from the other side. The locks were unfastened, and the hinges groaned as they squeaked open. The woman was older, her gray hair pulled back tightly in a bun. She wore dark clothing—a sweater, a long blue dress, thick stockings, and black shoes with low, wide heels. She looked sad, lost, far away.

"Yes?" she responded, eyeing Diego curiously. "What do you need? Quickly. State your business. I haven't got all day."

He remained silent, unable to speak; he was so panicked.

"Are you looking for charity?" She gripped the door's handle. "Speak, or I'll notify the police."

"No," Diego managed to say.

"Go away. Just go away and take your begging somewhere else. We haven't got anything here for the likes of you."

Diego's voice quivered when he spoke. "I'm sorry. I'm sorry."

"Why?" She sighed now, folded her arms. "Well?"

Finally, he spoke again. "Grandmother?" he asked. "Are you my grandmother?"

"What did you say? What did you call me?"

"Are you the mother of my mother, Amalia León?"

"Amalia." She whispered it as though it were a name she hadn't heard in a long time. She gripped the gold crucifix around her neck. "Who *are* you?"

"I'm Diego. Amalia's son." He handed her the envelope.

She looked at it then reached out to him. The woman cupped her palm underneath his chin and regarded him, as if he were not at all a person but a thing. Then she pulled her hand back, straightened her shoulders, and cleared her throat.

"And your father? Something must have happened. Is he dead?"

Diego lowered his head. "No," he said. "But he sent me away. He told me to come here. He said he couldn't take care of me."

The old woman shook her head. "Very well," she said. "Come along inside. I don't want the neighbors thinking we're taking in vagrants." She led him through the door. "Quickly. Quickly."

Inside, the house was vast. The tile floors shone brightly in the afternoon sun. The living room was filled with clay pots, couches with pillows, and sitting chairs with intricate scrolls and designs etched into their finely polished and fragrant wooden backs. A thick tapestry hung from a long metal rod on the wall alongside an oil painting of a young man wearing a suit of armor. A collection of antique pocket watches and magnifying glasses were arranged in locked cabinets. Glass figurines covered the top of a credenza made of dark wood with iron inlays. When the grandmother had him sit down, Diego couldn't believe how soft the cushion beneath him felt, and he had to fight the urge to let himself go and fall asleep. The grandmother ordered a servant to bring him a glass of warm milk and two slices of sweet bread and roasted almonds that she carried in on a silver tray. Diego ate, swallowing the milk in deep and long gulps.

"Slowly," she said, her voice tense. "Slowly." She took a seat across from him, in a chair with a high back. She sat erect, her hands folded neatly on her lap. "Diego?" she asked. "You say your name's Diego?"

He put the milk down. "Yes."

"Wipe your mouth before you speak." She gestured at a lace handkerchief before him.

He dabbed his lips with it then passed it back. "Thank—"

"No," she interrupted. She waved a hand at him, flinging her thin wrist, the bones beneath her skin jagged. "Keep the thing. I don't want it back. How old are you?"

"Eleven. What . . . what should I call you? Grandmother?"

"Doña Julia. Call me Doña Julia." Her face was gaunt, the flesh pulled taut over her sharp cheekbones. Her mouth was small, the lips very dry and pale. Her eyes were two dark brown pits that seemed to devour all light, and Diego found he couldn't look directly into them. They were crowned by a pair of uneven and bright white brows that rested—very heavy and sagging uncomfortably—along loose and flaccid ridges of skin.

"Doña Julia?" Diego asked. "Can you tell me about my mother when she was younger?"

"She was very pretty." His grandmother rose and walked over to a wooden secretary. She pulled the front drawer out and removed a photograph in a pewter frame that was heavy when she placed it in his hand. "Here she is. It was taken her last year of school," his grandmother said, her voice tender, her eyes filling with tears. He saw her smile when she placed the photograph before him.

It was hard for Diego to believe that this woman in a white dress with ruffles along the neckline, pearl earrings dangling from her earlobes like small drops of milk, was his mother. In the photo, she neither smiled nor frowned. She was beautiful in a way that would forever be difficult for him to describe. His grandmother took it from him, walked back to the secretary, and placed the photograph inside. From another drawer, she removed a telegram.

"Two years ago, I received a wire from *him*." Her voice changed; it was cold, hard. "From your father telling us that your mother had died." She shook her head. His grandmother sighed then placed the telegram along with the letter back in the drawer and closed it. "There's a part of me that still won't admit it, that still wants to believe she's alive even if it means she's living up there. In the hills. With those savages. You said he sent you here?" she asked, composing herself once more. She sat very regal in her chair, hands once more folded and in her lap.

"Yes," Diego said.

"And what does he expect us to do with you?" She reached for a lace fan, unfurled it with a snap, then folded it again. "What are *we* to do with you?" She reclined, tapping the tip of the fan against the back of her hand.

"Let's see you," the old man said to Diego, walking inside the living room from the entryway. "We need to take a look." He wore thick spectacles, and a gray mustache with pointed tips. He hardly had any hair left, and the patches of bald skin on his head appeared smooth and unblemished. They talked about him as if he were invisible.

"You say he showed up this afternoon?" The old man leaned in closer, adjusted his spectacles.

"Yes," the old woman said. "I have no idea how. He had the letter with the address."

"He can *read*?" the old man asked, stunned.

"I don't have a clue." His grandmother walked across the room. Heavy clear bottles crowded the top of the credenza, and she poured some of the amber-colored liquid into a glass and handed this to her husband. "There's nowhere left for him to go," Doña Julia said. "*He* sent him here."

The old man shook his head. "What unnecessary suffering. All of this could have been avoided if only—"

His grandmother interrupted. "What should we do with him?"

The old man took a long drink. "We'll do our best to take care of him, to educate him and refine him. What other choice do we have? He's still our blood."

"Thank God he inherited our light skin," his grandmother said.

"Yes. There's that. You checked for lice?"

"I had one of the maids do it. I was stunned when she told me he was clean."

"Have them run a hot bath. Then take his clothes and burn them. Give him his mother's room."

"Very well," said his grandmother. She tugged on her long neck-lace. "Go upstairs," she said to Diego. "Your room is at the end of the hall. The maid will bathe you, then you'll eat afterward."

"Yes, Grandmother."

"Doña Julia," she corrected him.

"Doña Julia."

"You can call me 'Grandfather,'" the old man said.

"Yes, sir," Diego responded before turning around and leaving the room. He walked slowly and stopped at the foot of the wooden stairs, listening to them.

"Why indulge this?" his grandmother said. "Why let him call you 'Grandfather,' Doroteo?"

"He's still our grandson," the old man responded. "Despite everything, he's the son of our only daughter. We can culture him, teach him to be a good and moral citizen."

"Peasants have no morality," his grandmother told him. "Still, I suppose you're right. He *is* blood."

They were quiet for a short time before his grandfather spoke again. "God is testing us. Looking to see if we can be charitable. Can we, Julia? Can we show clemency?"

She sighed. "I guess we can. But I don't have to like it. Or him."

Diego crept up the steps and into the dark mouth of the long hallway.

"You'll be schooled," his grandfather said to him the next morning in the courtyard.

"Yes, sir."

"You can call me Grandfather. How old did you say you were again?"

"Eleven. I'll be 12 in January."

He didn't look up from his newspaper when he addressed Diego. He sipped coffee and smoked a cigarette. "You'll attend Mass each Sunday with us."

"Yes, Grandfather."

Doroteo folded the newspaper and looked up at Diego. "Come here," he said. "Sit." He rose now and pointed to an empty chair across from his. "You should eat." He rang a bell, and a servant appeared. "Give the boy some oatmeal. Bread. A glass of milk," Doroteo said to the woman, who nodded and went back inside.

"Thank you, Grandfather," Diego said, keeping his head down.

"Sit up straight," the old man said. "And look a person in the face when you address them, child."

"Yes, Grandfather." He sat up, pushing his shoulders back, and raised his head.

"After you eat, I want you to return to your room. Someone will be in to take measurements. I'll have them go out and purchase some new clothing."

"Yes, Grandfather," Diego responded. The servant returned with a bowl of warm oatmeal, two pieces of sweet bread, and a glass of hibiscus water.

"Very well," the old man rose now, whistling as he strolled back into the house.

That Sunday, they took him to Mass. His grandmother wore a black dress with white gloves and a lace mantilla over her head. His grandfather donned a striped suit and a top hat and held a cane. Diego wore a new shirt, the collar tight and itchy and stiff, and a pair of thick wool trousers with buttons and suspenders. His black shoes were uncomfortable, and his grandmother had instructed one of the maids to wash and comb his hair and to scrub his hands and beneath his nails. His fingertips hurt now, as he fought the urge to run them through his hair. They arrived at the church and took seats in one of the front pews. Diego tried hard to contain his excitement; the church was massive. There were swooping arches and columns and pilasters with gilded edges. Ornate iron candelabras swung from the high ceilings, supported by thick chains bolted to wooden beams. There were huge stained glass windows, statues of saints resting atop tall pediments, a baptismal font made entirely of silver, and an organ with many brass pipes and a choir that stood nearby, singing. Diego felt small and insignificant sitting there, among such grandeur and opulence. And there were so many people crammed inside the pews that seemed to go on and on, row after row. This was nothing like the church in San Antonio—small, intimate, each individual voice distinguishable when the congregants prayed or sang. There were two lines for Communion, and it took a long time before Diego reached the front. The priest hardly looked at him and muttered the words "Body of Christ" so quickly that Diego didn't have time to answer him before moving on. When the priest ended the Mass, and everyone rose from their pews and made their way out, the crowd was vast, deep, hundreds of feet shuffling forward. Diego felt disoriented, dizzy, overwhelmed, and he was relieved once they were outside and he felt he could breathe again.

Several people stopped to say hello to his grandmother and grandfather as they stood on the steps near the main entrance.

"You say he's your grandson?" a young woman with hair the color of corn silk asked his grandmother.

"Yes," Doña Julia said. "He's been away. Living . . . abroad."

The woman was so exquisite, her face smooth and flawless, lips bright red, her eyes so wide, like an animal's, he thought. She wore an elegant pleated dress made of soft fabric with large gold buttons that shimmered and danced each time she took a breath. The top flap of her purse was open and, as she talked to his grandparents, gesturing excitedly with her hands, a lace glove tumbled out and fell on the ground near her feet. When he reached out to grab it, she jumped, startled.

"Give it back," his grandmother snapped at Diego, taking the glove and handing it to the woman. "My apologies," she said.

"The boy," his grandfather said, clearing his throat. "Like my wife said, he's been living abroad. Europe. His ways are . . ." and he waved his hand.

The young woman smiled. "Yes," she said. "Well. Curious little fellow, isn't he?"

"What's wrong with you?" his grandmother asked as they walked away. "You had no business taking her things. She's a very important person, the daughter of a powerful politician. If I ever catch you doing that again, I'll—"

"Don't be so hard on the boy," his grandfather interjected. "It's not his fault. The people he was raised among, they're backward. We'll straighten him out. Now, let's try to enjoy ourselves."

They strolled though a park and plaza where vendors sold toys and pinwheels and kites made of bright paper. There were figurines of glass and clay, so many small and beautiful objects that glimmered and shined. His grandfather purchased a leather belt and a vaquero hat, and he gave Diego money and told him to buy something, whatever he wanted. He used the coins on a wooden whistle and two pieces of squash candy. He was chewing on the last piece and standing with his grandfather, who was reading an announcement nailed to a post, and watched when Julia stopped to talk to a man and a woman. A parasol was hooked over the woman's arm, and the man wore a waistcoat with a frock jacket over it, and a white cravat tied around his neck. A few minutes later, a boy about Diego's age with light brown hair joined them. His grandmother said something and pointed across the street. They waved at Diego and his grandfather, but the old man was too busy reading the announcement to notice.

The first three months there, his grandmother left Diego alone during the mornings. Every day his grandfather closed his office and returned to the house for a long lunch. On the first day he was told he would be eating with them instead of taking his meal in the kitchen with the servants, Diego learned of Javier Alcazar and his mother, Carolina. It was Doña Julia who spoke of the family first.

"I saw Carolina Alcazar again this morning." She looked over at his grandfather.

The old man sat at the head of the table, taking spoonfuls of his soup. "And how is she?"

"Fine," his grandmother said. She finished her soup, and one of the maids, a young woman with a long ponytail, walked over, removed the bowl, and placed it on a tray. His grandmother dabbed the corner of her mouth with her napkin and looked over at Diego. "We saw them last week in the plaza, remember? They waved at you. Javier's about your age. You two should meet. He would be a good influence on you." She stared at him from across the table, in a way that made him feel uneasy.

Diego held his spoon, his hand trembling slightly. "Yes, Doña Julia," he responded, lowering his head.

His grandfather pounded on the table, rattling the dishes and cups, startling the maid. "Head up, son. Head up," he said, his voice elevated. "A refined gentleman always speaks with confidence."

"I'm sorry, Grandfather." He adjusted himself, straightened his bow tie, and looked them both directly in the eyes. His grandmother shifted her gaze back to the table.

"Take these away!" she ordered. The maid came over and quickly began removing the dishes.

His grandfather said to Diego, "Carolina's husband is a very wealthy man named Manuel Alcazar. He was in love with your mother at one time. They almost married but—"

"She ran off with that peasant," his grandmother interrupted. She sat back in her chair and folded her arms. "Doroteo, don't start."

The old man ignored her and continued: "Carolina was once an opera performer. She has a beautiful voice. She gives lessons from her home to some of the children of the more affluent families."

Diego cleared his throat before he spoke. He tried not to look at his grandmother. "What kinds of lessons?"

"Singing. Dancing. That sort of thing." The old man lit a cigarette and squinted at Diego through the smoke. "Does this interest you?"

"Yes," he said smiling confidently. "Very much." He felt his heart beating faster. "Back home I danced in some of the festivals."

"Good." His grandfather smiled and nodded very sagely. "Would you like to take lessons from her?"

"Doroteo, don't," said his grandmother.

"This could help him," he explained. "Boost his confidence. Refine him. He'll learn about the opera. Learn oration."

"I think this boy's incapable of such—"

His grandfather interjected. "Julia, I'll do what I please with him." He turned to Diego. "We'll talk to Carolina."

"Thank you, Grandfather," Diego said. "Thank you."

The old woman's face was flushed, but Diego didn't care. Doroteo had made his decision. Around the house, his word was final, absolute.

Javier and Carolina came to visit that September, a week before Diego was to start school at the primaria not far from the house, the same one his mother had attended as a girl. His grandmother was in the kitchen, lecturing one of the cooks about the meal she had prepared the night before, and Diego sat at the mahogany piano, pressing his fingers against the black and white keys, pretending he was giving a concert, singing one of the songs Elva had taught him. He didn't hear them walk in; he turned and found them standing in the entryway. The mother wore a long tweed skirt and a shawl over her shoulders. Her hair was pinned back and adorned with flowers. Javier wore a pair of pressed black trousers, a blue jacket with gold buttons, and dark shoes.

"You're Diego, correct?" asked the woman. "The one who is living here now?"

"Yes," he said.

Diego rose, walked across the room, and extended his arm. "It is a pleasure to meet you."

Carolina removed her glove, took his hand, and shook it. "My, what good manners you have, young man." She then turned to Javier, unbuttoned his jacket and said, "Why don't you two go outside for a while? Get to know one another."

Javier looked at Diego and smiled.

Diego said, "I can show you my grandmother . . . I mean . . . Doña Julia's birds."

Diego led him through the glass doors into the back courtyard where his grandmother kept the wicker birdcages. Inside, parakeets hopped from one end to the other, their plumage fluffy and vibrant, their small eyes darting back and forth. Javier walked over to one of the cages and regarded the birds.

"Are their feathers soft?" he asked.

Diego shrugged his shoulders. "I don't know. I'm not allowed to touch them."

"Why not?"

"Doña Julia says she doesn't want me upsetting them."

Javier laughed. "Why do you call her that?"

"She doesn't want me calling her grandmother."

Javier walked over to one of the stone benches and sat. He looked up at Diego and said, his voice lowered, "Some of the kids at school say your grandmother's a witch who eats children."

"Do you think it's true?" Diego asked, sitting next to him on the bench. "Do you think she'll eat me?"

Javier laughed again, his grin wide. "Probably," he whispered. "You better beware."

They chased each other around the courtyard and hid behind the clay pots and wooden posts of the trellis. Diego was just so happy and relieved to have someone else to play with that he forgot about his grandmother and Carolina inside the house. It felt like they had been outside for only a few minutes when Carolina came out and called Javier over. "I lost track of time. We've been here over an hour. We need to go."

"Can I stay?" Javier pleaded, stomping one foot on the ground.

"No." Carolina handed Javier his jacket. "But Diego's starting school next week with you. You two are going to be in the same class. You'll have plenty of time together."

Javier leaned in close and said to Diego, "Be careful. Your grandmother. Lock your bedroom door at night."

"I will," Diego told him.

"I'll see you at school," he said. "Try to survive until then."

"We'll start your lessons soon," Carolina said. "I have a great feeling about you, Diego."

"Thank you," he said. "Thank you, señora."

"Carolina," she said, crouching down, looking at him directly in the eyes. She smelled of lavender. Her hair caught the sunlight. She was beautiful. Then she kissed him on the forehead and was gone. Diego couldn't wait to start his lessons.

He had never seen so many children gathered together in one place. They carried satchels filled with books and colored pencils. They scribbled on the concrete with thick pieces of chalk that dusted their fingers. They played on wooden seesaws and pushed one another on swings. Diego's stomach turned and his hands trembled as he watched them through the slats of the iron fence circling the school grounds. He was obligated to wear a uniform—black trousers and shoes, a shirt and bow tie, and a sweater with the school's crest on the front—and he tugged at the collar of his shirt nervously.

"Don't be afraid," his grandmother told Diego, bending down to adjust his bow tie. He was taken aback by the tone of her voice, by her gesture; she was almost genuine, almost affectionate. She led him through the gate to his teacher, a pudgy lady with a nest of curly brown hair. She smiled at the teacher, and Diego realized that it was the first time he had ever seen her do so.

"After your classes end, you'll go with Javier to his house. Carolina will start you on your lessons today," she said. Then she turned around and waved.

His teacher gave Diego a strange look when he instead looked to her.

"It's fine," the teacher told him.

He waved good-bye.

He followed the teacher across the school courtyard, which all the classrooms faced. She led him down a tiled hallway, up a flight of steps, pointing with a bony finger to a playroom full of wooden blocks, the floor scattered with puzzle pieces, balls, and felt puppets. There was a library with many books, and a salon with tables and chairs where they ate and assembled. There was more of everything here—more teachers, more rooms, more children. It overwhelmed him. Diego was glad then when at last they walked into the classroom where Javier sat in a circle with a group of other boys. Behind them there was a map of Mexico and large charts with numbers and letters.

"You're still alive," Javier said, jokingly, as Diego sat beside him.

"Yes," Diego said.

"My mother told me you'll be coming to our house today after school. I'll show you a new train set my father brought me from Mexico City."

"My son doesn't take after me in this regard," Carolina said to him that afternoon as they sat on the plush sofa in her sitting room. The window curtains were pulled back, and the afternoon sunlight streamed in through the glass, falling on the floor in long, bright beams across the study. There was a piano, a small easel holding sheets of music, and a gramophone in one corner of the room. The top of the piano was crammed with pictures of Carolina in elegant costumes and dresses as well as a strange wooden device with a pendulum. When she saw Diego looking at it, she asked him if he knew what it was.

"No," he said, approaching the piano.

"It's a metronome." She adjusted a small metal weight at the base of the pendulum before moving it from side to side with her finger. It produced a series of small clicks. Carolina clapped her hands, faster, then slower, keeping beat with the clicks. "This helps us keep a rhythm when we're composing music. Together. With me," she urged him.

Diego did so, and they clapped along, their beats in steady synchronization with the metronome.

"Very good," she told him, smiling. She wore a sweater draped over her shoulders, its arms hanging loose on her sides. "Come here," she said, taking Diego by the hand, squeezing it. Her touch was warm, calming. They walked over to a trunk in the middle of the library. "I had one of the servants pull this down from the attic last night. This is where I keep the things of my former career. I don't normally show these to the other children I tutor," she explained. "Would you like to see inside?"

"Yes," he told her.

Inside there were advertisements for extravagant operas with her name on them, wigs and funny hats, wooden canes and suspenders, pamphlets and newspaper clippings, and more photographs of Carolina in lavish costumes.

"I was a diva," Carolina said. "Do you know what that is?"

He shook his head. "No."

"A diva is a great singer. Powerful. My voice had the strongest pitch and widest range in the company." Carolina closed the trunk and led him back to the sofa. She sat very close to him and placed her arm around his shoulder. "You're special, Diego."

"No I'm not, señora," he said. "I'm not special at all."

"Of course you are. Why would you think such a thing?"

"I know it," he confessed. He kept his head down and felt tears welling up in his eyes. "I've heard it."

"Oh?" Carolina asked. "Where did you hear this, Diego?"

He took a deep breath before he spoke, his voice quivering. "My father. He sent me away because I was nothing more than an inconvenience. And Doña Julia. I heard her tell my grandfather that she doesn't love me. That she can't. Just like my father."

Carolina squeezed his shoulder. She sat back and placed his head on her chest. "You're anything but an inconvenience. You're special, Diego. A wonderful boy."

"But how can you be so sure?" he asked.

She laughed and sat up. She looked him in the face, wiping his tears away. "I was shy as a girl. I was misunderstood. My parents wanted me to be a nun. I grew up faithful, very obedient to them and to God. But then something happened when I was around your age."

She told him that she discovered her voice. But here, she said, it wasn't just her ability to sing, but a calling, she explained, a realization that she had a purpose in life that would not involve the church and God.

"I saw myself," she said. "I understood myself. It was as if I was suddenly standing in a very bright room with a thousand pairs of eyes all on me. Everyone noticed me. And I wasn't afraid. I felt confident. Sure of myself. It was wonderful."

"But I'm nothing," he said.

"No," she said. "You're not nothing." She paused and took a deep breath. "You must have faith in me and in yourself, Diego. Can you? Can you have faith in yourself as I do in you?"

"Yes," he said. If Carolina believed in him, maybe his grandparents were wrong after all. He raised his head, pushed his shoulders back, and looked her directly in the eye. "I can."

"Good. Then let's begin your lesson!" Carolina said, rising now, clapping her hands.

She gave him speeches to memorize, and when he told her he couldn't read very well, she helped him by reciting them first out loud herself then asking him to repeat her words. Over the next few weeks, he improved. His favorite speeches were those written by Cicero, and reading the epic poems by Homer and Virgil because they were filled with wars and battles, gods and monsters, and journeys to the underworld. Just like Elva's stories, he thought. Carolina made for Diego a toga by stitching together strips of fabric and cloth. She made a sash and tied this around his waist and fashioned a crown by weaving together a few leaves and twigs she found outside in the garden. He stood before her, atop a stone bench in the courtyard, reading from the *Aeneid*. He was concentrating hard on the words, letting the speech and emotions overcome him when he heard someone giggle. He looked out and there, standing behind Carolina, was Javier, laughing and shaking his head.

"Hush," Carolina said to him.

"But he looks like a girl," Javier said. "Wearing a dress."

"It's a toga. It's what the Romans wore," she told her son. "Never mind him, Diego." She clapped her hands three times. "Continue."

But he couldn't because Javier kept on snickering and laughing. Diego stopped now, jumped down from the bench, and removed the leaves in his hair.

Carolina rose. "Look what you've done," she said to Javier. "You ruined his concentration."

"So," he said, folding his arms.

It was all Diego could think to do. He moved toward Javier and pushed him until he fell back and into a plot of dirt, muddying his trousers and shoes, his face and arms.

"Stop," Carolina shouted. "Both of you." She reached out, grabbed Javier, and made him stand. "You both apologize to one another. This minute."

Javier sighed, wiping away streaks of mud from his face. "I'm sorry," he said.

"I'm sorry," said Diego, looking down at the mud where Javier's handprint had remained.

"Go inside and get cleaned up," Carolina said.

"Will you help me?" Javier asked.

"I'm with Diego right now. Go."

He walked away, his head lowered.

She turned to Diego once they were alone and said, "There are always going to be boys like Javier in this world, boys who'll make fun of you, who'll ridicule you. But you must not let them distract you. Don't let them lure you away from your dreams. I never gave up on mine. Even after I married."

There were times, she said, moments in the day when she caught a glimpse of the woman she used to be. There was a way her face looked, a feeling that would overcome her, she admitted, and she would be back to being that woman anew, the opera singer. Up on the stage again, singing, making the audience happy.

"What do you seek?" she asked. "More than anything in the world, son? What do you want? What is your destiny?"

Diego was confused. "I don't—" he stammered. "I don't know. I want my father and my grandparents to be proud of me. I want my mother in heaven to remember me."

"They will," Carolina said. "If you work hard enough. If you stay true to yourself." She rose now. "We are through for today. I will see you tomorrow." Carolina turned and went inside. A few minutes later, Javier came back out. He stood across from Diego, his head down.

"I'm sorry I said you looked like a girl," he said.

"That's fine." Diego put the book down and walked over, careful not to step on the hem of his costume. "I do look silly." He untied the sash and removed the toga.

"Now you look fine," Javier proclaimed, pointing to Diego's shirt and bow tie. "Now you look like me." He walked over to the side of the house, pulled back a tangle of wild weeds and vines until a small iron gate came into view.

"What are you doing?" he asked Javier.

"Let's go," he said, beckoning him.

"But your mother."

"My aunt's inside talking with her. Come on now. Let's go to the zócalo and feed the pigeons," Javier urged him.

Diego heard Carolina's voice inside the house.

"Quickly," Javier insisted. He turned the knob and the gate creaked open.

Diego ran out after him, a few feet behind, catching up to Javier at the corner. They walked along the narrow street, their arms draped over one another's shoulder. At the zócalo, they bought a bag of roasted garbanzo beans and stole a piece of bread from one of the bakers when he turned to help another customer. They sat down on a bench, eating the smoked garbanzo beans and feeding crumbs of bread to the flock of plump gray pigeons.

"My mother hates me," Javier said, breaking off chunks of bread.

"No, she doesn't," Diego said, reaching for a handful of garbanzo beans. He watched the sun descend behind the buildings, the shadows of the elegant arches supporting the portico lengthening out. The sound of gurgling water from the nearby fountain was soothing. "She loves you very much," Diego told him.

"She wishes I'd turned out like her. That I enjoyed singing and dancing and all that stuff." Javier sighed and tossed more crumbs at the pigeons. "I don't like it. I never have. I never will. But I'm glad you do. I'm glad she cares about you so much. Do you know why?"

"No. Why?" Diego asked.

"Because we're like brothers," Javier said. "We'll always be friends."

This made Diego smile. He had someone now. He had a friend. A brother.

When the bread and garbanzo beans were gone, they rose and left. The sound of church bells gonging and a man in a hat playing a tune from a wooden flute filled the air. The laughter of a handful of schoolchildren faded away as the two boys walked the short distance back home.

2

April 1922

HIS GRANDPARENTS' FIRST PRIORITY was to mold him into whatever they felt necessary in order to secure a position for him within the affluent citizenry of the city, thereby preserving their place as a prominent Morelian family even after their deaths. After all, as Diego was coming to learn, Mexico was a nation built on the notion of legacy, of families passing down wealth and power and land from one generation to the next, over and over again. They planned to let their half-indio grandson inherit the money, the house, and the business. Better that than to leave it all to the government or the church or to charity. No one would know his true pedigree, though.

He was ordered by them never to mention his father and his P'urhépecha lineage. Diego would stop using his paternal last name, León, and would instead use his maternal one, Sánchez. His father, they told him, was a banker. A wealthy Frenchman. Diego was born there, in the southern part of the country. Somewhere near Nice. His mother died there. He stayed with his father until he too died of influenza. They made Diego memorize these details, over and over, until his real father, until San Antonio de la Fe, Elva, and his entire life before his move to the city faded away like long threads of smoke. With the exception of Carolina, who had learned about Diego's existence from his grandmother years before he came to live with them, no one knew the truth. And certainly not his grandparents' rich and powerful friends—bankers, merchants, politicians—whose respect they had worked so hard to maintain. By the time Diego reached sixteen, most of the memories of his past had altogether vanished as he tried to become someone different, someone who would please his grandparents.

Since Diego was to inherit the family business, he spent more time with his grandfather as he grew older, learning from him how to notarize court documents and certificates. As a young boy, he had browsed through the large wooden bookcases in the office, thumbing through the ledgers and stacks of papers, smoothing out the crinkled birth certificates and land deeds. Now, he sat next to his grandfather, watching him record a set of papers. Everything was assigned a number and logged in, stamped with an official seal, and left to dry overnight before being passed on to the owner or stored away in the large vault in back. Diego found the solitude of the office comforting and grew to admire his grandfather, enjoyed watching as his ink-stained fingers moved expertly back and forth from ledger to document then back again.

"You see that spot there?" Doroteo said one afternoon. They were inside the office, and the old man pointed out the open door, to the sidewalk crammed with pedestrians. The day was warm, but under the shaded portico, the air was cool as Diego leaned his head out.

"Where?" he asked, adjusting his bow tie.

"Right there. Right by the column. The cracked one."

"Yes," said Diego. The column was plastered with bulletins and flyers. "I see it, Grandfather."

"That was where your father used to stand. The first time I saw him he had on a pair of dirty trousers. You know? The kind peasants wear, made of simple white fabric with a drawstring around the waist. And he wore a white shirt. And one of those pointed hats made from a palm. He was barefoot. Quite a sight, son. I say this because I want you to know how lucky you are. You'll never have to worry about being poor. All this will be yours once I die."

"I'm so grateful to you and Doña Julia for that," Diego said, turning to him.

The old man sat in a chair, his small body lost among the tall stacks of ledgers and crates full of papers and documents, all of them waiting to be catalogued and notarized and filed away. Suddenly he looked at Diego, his gaze stern. "Promise me that you won't let this business, everything I've worked for, fail," he said.

"Of course not," said Diego. "I promise, Grandfather."

"You're all that's left of our family. You have to stay focused," he said. "Continue to study. Part with things that distract you, if need be."

"Like what?"

"Like your friends. Like all that time you spend with Carolina singing and dancing. It's time you give up such childish pursuits. What kind of a life will you have if you follow that, huh?"

"But I like it, Grandfather. It makes me happy. I don't find it gets in the way of my work here or my studies."

"I know," he said. "But you're old enough now to begin assuming more of the responsibilities around here so that you'll be well-prepared for *this* job, for *this* life." His grandfather rose, loosened his tie, and removed his jacket. He walked over to Diego and put his arm around his shoulder. "I know you enjoy it, but I think it's best that you end those lessons. Think of your future."

Diego looked out the door, at the cracked column where his father once stood. He imagined him there, holding a tray full of cigarettes and lottery tickets, lost among the faces of the masses, a poor peasant, so desperate, so hungry and tired. After all, Gabriel had sent him here to make something of himself, to use his grandfather's influence to chart another course for his life, hadn't he? And Diego had no reason to defy his grandfather, to ignore his advice. The man had given Diego everything he needed, had sheltered him when he arrived on that day many years before. Where would he be without Doroteo? He remembered San Antonio de la Fe, the cold and damp house, the overgrown fields and dying animals, the stench of rot and decay. Doroteo was right: Diego was fortunate to have escaped that destiny. He owed the old man his life. Who would he have become had he stayed there?

"If you say so, Grandfather," Diego told him. "Whatever you think is best."

¤

The next afternoon at Carolina's, before his lesson, she hugged him in a way only a mother could.

"Five years," she said. "Diego, it's been five years. You've come so far. I'm so proud. You've learned quickly. Everything I've taught you. And you've rekindled my love of performance again. For that, I can't repay you."

"Thank you," he said, releasing himself from her hold and rising now. "You've given me so much." He was about to tell her of his plans to end the lessons with her when she pulled out an envelope from her pocket and handed it to him.

"Here," she said. "Open it." Inside there were two tickets to an opera that Saturday at a small theater near the main plaza.

Diego leaned in and kissed her on the cheek. "Thank you."

"I figured you could see if Javier wants to go with you. Convince him, will you? It's *Faust*. I think he would like it. Do you remember *Faust*?"

"I do," he said. "It's the one where Professor Faust makes a pact with Mephistopheles, a devil determined to lead him astray. This is the best present. Thank you very much."

"Thank you," Carolina said. "For all that you've given me."

He would not tell her of his decision. Not just then. But soon.

Compared to the other buildings in the center of town, the theater was badly in need of repair. The plaster was chipping and breaking off, the columns holding up the main arches crumbling from years of neglect, the tiled ceiling fading. As they entered, Diego handed his ticket to an usher, who bowed and tipped his hat in a dignified way to the two boys. Everything around them darkened. What little light there was from the street was now gone. The lanterns along the wall emitted a low and weak glow. Sound was muffled, and the people walking into the theater moved slowly, so slowly, and the swish of their arms, the stomping of their feet on the ground, the tilt of their heads, all seemed choreographed, in perfect synchronicity.

Diego and Javier made their way down the main aisle of the theater and from their seats near the front, Diego could feel the warmth coming from the stage lights that would soon dim, pulling him further into the world of Faust, a world where the devil walked and communicated with man, where someone could conjure up evil spirits and learn the true value of knowledge and the dangers of obsession and excess. He held his breath, waiting for the start.

"How long is this?" Javier asked, slumping in his chair as men and women filled in the seats near them.

"I'm not sure," said Diego. "I promise you'll enjoy it."

"I hope so."

The lights in the theater faded, reducing them all to shadows, to unidentifiable figures, and the performance began. He nudged Javier repeatedly, tried getting him to concentrate and focus on what was happening throughout the performance. Diego was afraid to blink, and his breath was caught in his throat, his heartbeat quickening. Now and again he would lean over and whisper to Javier, "This is where Faust conjures up the evil spirits," or "This is where Mephistopheles first appears," or "What a fool Faust is."

It wasn't until the lights came on, until everyone around them rose to applaud that he realized Javier had slept through the entire performance.

Outside the theater, the church bells rang ten times. "It's still early," Javier said, yawning and stretching. "Let's not go back home just now. Come on."

Diego followed him.

With electricity, Morelia became a different place at night. Light posts lit up once darkened streets and alleyways, illuminated the gardens, the walkways twisting through the parks, turned the plazas and public courtyards into places to gather and pass the time. Organ-grinders filled the air with music, couples held one another on benches, vendors hawked trinkets and paper parasols, and boys sold newspapers and lottery tickets. Electric signs flashed on and off with quick and rapid precision. Everything—the wooden trolley cars, taxis, bicyclists—pulsed with movement. They wandered around for a while, Diego still talking about the performance, not paying attention to which direction they were headed.

"Where are we going?" Diego finally asked Javier as they began moving farther away from the lights of the city center.

Javier stopped, turned, and faced his friend. "Don't ask impertinent questions!" He laughed loud. "Just come on now."

After some time, Javier stopped in front of La Pulquería Santo Remedio. The bar was the only thing on the narrow street that was lit, a square of golden amber among the rows and rows of black, squat, menacing buildings and broken sidewalks. Diego heard coughs and shouts and low music playing from a gramophone as they stepped inside.

"A pulquería?" Diego asked. "Have you been here before?"

"No," Javier said, "But let's give it a try. What's the worst that could happen, huh?"

Inside, the pulquería was no bigger than his bedroom. A long wooden bar occupied much of the space, and men in rumpled jackets and dirty shoes—some in leather huaraches, the skin around their heels cracked and chalky white—slumped on wooden crates, taking sips from the cups they called tornillos because the ridges resembled those on screws. Others sipped from large tan bowls made from dried-out gourds of a calabash. These were the jícaras, called *urhani* in P'urhépecha, Diego remembered. Rowed neatly on wooden shelves behind the bar were large clay pots with the fermented drink. They were all the same, red clay in color with a wide handle and pointed spout. Spaced throughout the jugs there were several urns shaped like grimacing monkeys. The bartender, a skinny man with no hair, stared at them. He pointed to his face; there was an empty hole where an eye should have been.

"I may not be able to see as well as I used to ever since that scorpion bit my eye and it fell out," he told them. "But I know you two can't be in here."

"Sir, please," Javier said. He reached into his pocket and pulled out a wad of bills, his hands steady. "Surely we can work something out."

One of the drunken patrons looked up, squinted, and said, "Let them stay. Let them stay." He raised his tornillo to both boys and went back to resting his head on the surface of the bar.

"Ah," said the bartender as he reached out and snatched the wad of bills Javier held out. He turned, grabbed two tornillos, and filled them with pulque. "But don't sit here," he said, pointing at the bar with dark, chubby fingers. He waved in a direction toward the back of the room. "Go over there."

Diego and Javier grabbed their tornillos but didn't move.

"What are you looking at?" he said. "Go. You need to sit back there. In case the police come. If they find two young men like you in here there will be trouble. I can't afford any more fucking trouble." They turned and sat on the crates in a dark corner. From there, they could see only the backs of the patrons, hunched, leaning forward, each hovering over his tornillo. A stray dog with matted fur wandered in from the street and strolled up to each man at the bar as if it were looking for someone it knew until the bartender yelled, "Get out of here, you bitch!" and hurled a brick at it. It yelped and ran off. "Every night that mutt comes in here. Always at the same time."

Diego and Javier watched it all, afraid to move or flinch.

"What are you looking at?" the bartender yelled at Javier and Diego, who remained seated on their crates, their tornillos still in their hands, the pulque untouched. "Drink up and get out of here."

They hesitated, afraid to drink.

"Now!" the bartender shouted. "I don't need to be babysitting you two all night."

Javier was first. He took one long gulp and swallowed, then slammed the tornillo on the ground. Then Diego closed his eyes, took a breath, and swallowed. It was sour, and the taste made his eyes water for a moment. He remained like that, with his head tilted back, looking up toward the bar's ceiling, the rusted corrugated roof riddled with bullet holes. The night sky was a series of black dots among the dirty sheets of silver. He breathed again, felt the liquid slide down his throat and settle in his stomach. Pulque could induce visions if you consume enough of it, Elva once said, and this was why the indio priests and seers drank it. As the sour taste slowly began to vanish, Diego craved more. Maybe if he drank enough, he thought, he would see what life waited for him ten, twenty, fifty years from then. Would he be married? Would he have children?

"Go on, get out of here," the bartender shouted. "Leave the cups there and go."

They both stood and were about to leave when, from the front of the bar, they heard shouts and curses. A struggle was breaking out between two men. The bartender and a handful of the less inebriated customers rushed over, trying to get between them.

"Stop it!" someone shouted.

Diego saw two men fall to the ground, rolling around and punching one another.

"Separate them!" the bartender shouted. "Now!"

Javier and Diego stood near the bar, and they couldn't see who had thrown the tornillo. It hurtled across the room toward the shelves, behind the bar, breaking three of the clay jugs, sending pulque pouring out, soaking their jackets and trousers. As the fight got bigger, some of the drunker patrons managed to lift themselves from their seats and stumble out. Another fight broke out between three men, and suddenly there was blood on the floor, and the bartender had stopped shouting now and was kneeling on the floor next to a man with a wound in his side.

Diego and Javier stumbled over the tangle of men and bodies, the wide puddles of blood and pulque. Then Javier reached out to grab one of the broken jugs with some pulque inside just as the bartender began to rise up from the ground.

"Hey! Filthy fucking thief!" he yelled before slipping and falling back down. His shouts and curses followed them as Diego and Javier ran down the street, their bodies dripping pulque.

Once they were a safe distance away, Diego and Javier sat on a park bench and took turns dipping their hands inside the broken jar, sipping up as much of the pulque as they could, the sticky liquid trickling down their chins and between their fingers.

"Were you scared?" Javier asked Diego.

"Yes," Diego admitted. "Weren't you?"

"A little." He tossed his head back and laughed. "But I knew nothing was going to happen to either of us."

When they were finished, they tossed the clay pot in a bush.

By the time they reached Javier's house, Diego felt quite drunk, dizzy and giddy. Javier swaggered some as he led him to a window at the side of their house.

"It's late," Javier said. "You should stay here. Quiet," he whispered, as he opened the shutter and placed one leg in then the other.

Diego stumbled getting through the window, but Javier caught him and led him through the dark room to his bed. He lay down as Javier lit the oil lanterns. He watched the flames bathe the walls orange. Diego felt confused, hot, his skin moist with sweat. His head spinning in the soft glowing light, Diego watched Javier undress. Javier's naked body—his thin arms and smooth legs, his back and chest untouched and free of scars or bruises—was beautiful. His skin radiated a kind of warmth. It stirred a new feeling, though he couldn't be sure if it was the pulque or something else. When Javier turned around to face him, Diego looked away. He unrolled the sheets and the blankets so Javier could crawl in. Their bodies pressed close to one another in the small bed, everything was quiet and still; nothing moved except for Javier's steady breathing. Diego couldn't form the words to express what he was feeling. He prayed in the dark, wondering what was happening to him, until he fell into a deep and heavy sleep.

3

June 1923–December 1925

JUNE MARKED THE END of their last year in school, and it came with little fanfare. Diego was grateful. He felt no desire for celebration. Now that he had stopped his lessons with Carolina, he just wanted to live his life. Perhaps he would move out of his grandparents' house, rent an apartment somewhere near downtown, close enough to the office so that he could walk there every morning. Javier decided to attend the university, where he planned on studying politics and philosophy. Though Diego felt a great deal of sadness at the thought of not seeing him every day, he knew they would still keep in touch.

The days immediately following the end of school were humid, the skies over the city filled with thundering clouds that burst open with rain. The wetness coated the air, his skin, the documents he notarized. The city during these months was unbearable—stuffy, crammed with noise and heat. Since Diego finished school, the old man had been leaving him by himself in the office. Diego came in each day at eight in the morning and didn't leave until well after six in the evening. The days were long, monotonous, uneventful, and there were still more documents, still more forms and grants and declarations to catalogue and stamp and file. On one particularly humid day, he walked across the office and watched the rain pour down and gather in puddles outside. The city was empty and gray and quiet.

Diego returned to his desk and the forms waiting, unassuming, indifferent, to be catalogued, notarized, and filed away. It was the same thing, day after day, he thought, and the stacks of papers never seemed to end. He looked at his grandfather's desk, his empty chair, the armrests and seat worn away, the wood faded, the faint impressions of his thighs blending with the grain. His own chair would look like that one day. But what could he do about it? And was that such a bad thing? No, he told himself, it wasn't. He cleared his throat and tried focusing on his work as the rain outside fell and the air around him dampened and grew heavier still.

Come autumn, he told himself. When the rains vanish, the steam evaporates. The air would cool down. Come autumn, Diego thought, things will be different. Something would happen. He could feel it. He truly could.

He was with Javier, and they were in Diego's room. It was a hot summer afternoon, and Javier had taken his shirt off. He lay on the floor, his chest glistening with sweat. He was beautiful, but Diego resisted the urge to touch him; such impulses, he knew, were wrong. Over a year had passed since the night they had slept together. Diego could still feel the thick syrup coating his tongue. Ever since then, he craved being alone with Javier in a way he never had before. They had always been close, like twins, Carolina would say. "The two of you are always together. You sound alike, dress alike. You even look alike. I'm having a hard time distinguishing you from one another."

Javier asked Diego, "Do you know what a faggot is?"

"Yes, I do," he responded. "Men lying with other men. The Bible says it's a sin, an abomination."

"Fuck what the Bible says." He rose and walked over to the window.

"Don't let my grandmother hear you say that."

"Who gives a fuck about the Bible?" he asked. "About church. Rules and regulations. It's all such bullshit."

Diego felt a surge of excitement. It gave him a thrill to sense Javier's anger, his wild spirit. Javier had taken to cussing lately. More and more, he had taken to noticing some of the girls around school, confessing to Diego when they were together about the things he dreamed of doing to them. They were seventeen now, nearing eighteen, and Doroteo had told Diego that changes were coming. You'll start shaving, Doroteo said. And your attention will be drawn to certain things. Diego had wanted to ask his grandfather what those certain things were. Watching Javier there now, sensing the heat and energy radiating from his body, he knew, though.

"Sometimes I hate it here," Javier said now. "Sometimes I wish I could run away."

"Really?" Diego asked. "Where would you go?"

"Mexico City. Or north. The United States. Just us two."

"That would be something," Diego said, knowing it could never be. He had his grandfather's business to attend to. Besides, Diego knew that what he was feeling for Javier wasn't acceptable. Neither here nor anywhere else. He would be strong, though. He would resist.

In December of 1925, his grandparents told Diego that Emmanuel Pacheco—a wealthy banker—and his wife, Lupe, were coming to dinner that evening and that Paloma, their daughter, would be accompanying them. His grandmother had the cooks prepare an elaborate meal of tomato bisque, duck mole, and fresh baked mango pie. Doroteo opened two bottles of imported French wine he kept in the cellar, aging for "the right occasion," he would say. Lying on his bed when Diego arrived home that afternoon was his best dark brown tweed suit, freshly laundered and pressed, the creases running down the leg sharp and precise. A white undershirt hung from a hook in his bureau and, on the floor at the foot of his bed, sat his shoes, freshly polished. The knock at his bedroom door startled Diego.

It was one of the servants, Jacinta. "Your grandmother asks that you bathe," she said, lowering her head, avoiding Diego's gaze. "The tub in the bathroom down the hall has been drawn. She also requests that you shave."

"Jacinta, tell my grandmother not to worry herself," he said, irritated. "I'll do everything within my power to look absolutely respectable."

A bouquet of fresh flowers adorned the center of the buffet, and a thick tablecloth covered its entire surface. Napkins were arranged near each seat, and the best plates and saucers, the ones his grandmother kept in a trunk in the kitchen, had been brought out, the silverware polished, and the candles lit. The dining room glowed warm, a yellow light bathing everything.

"Why such a fuss?" Diego asked Doroteo as he entered the sitting room where his grandparents were, awaiting the guests.

"Paloma was away in Europe for some time," his grandfather said. "Studying at a very prestigious girls school in Spain. She has few friends here. We hope you can make her feel at home."

"Yes," he said. "Of course." He wanted to please the old man but wasn't the least bit interested.

There came a knock at the door, and Jacinta answered and led the family to the sitting room. Emmanuel Pacheco wore a dark suit, a large bowler hat, and white gloves, which he handed to Jacinta before walking over and giving Doroteo a firm pat on the shoulder. Emmanuel was a short, stout man with a lumbering walk, a thick, unruly mustache, and blond hair. Lupe was a tall and slender woman. She had dull light brown hair that was swept up in a simple bun. The gown she wore seemed too big, as if she were a little girl playing dress-up with her mother's clothes. While she and his grandmother exchanged pleasantries about the weather and the house, he watched Paloma. She was tall, like her mother. Paloma wore a shawl draped over her shoulders, which she clutched with her left hand as she extended her right to shake his grandmother's. Her shoulders slumped forward, and her face was plain, no eccentricity to it. It was a face that would never inspire a man to write a poem about it, sing a song about it, or fall in love with it.

"My, how you have *grown*," his grandmother said to her. "The last time I saw you was when you were just a child playing dolls with your cousins." She led Paloma by the hand and walked her over to the parlor where Diego stood near the fireplace. "This is my grandson," his grandmother said, introducing him to both Paloma and her mother.

"Charmed," he said, bowing slightly, taking each of their hands and kissing them. Paloma's stare was vacant; there was no sparkle, no vibrancy in her small eyes. He turned away from the woman as Emmanuel lumbered over with his grandfather, both of whom had lit pipes. The sweet smell of tobacco filled the air.

"Your grandfather tells me that you've been helping him with the business since you left the preparatoria," Emmanuel said.

"That's correct," Diego said. "It's been nearly two years."

"I imagine then that you'll be taking over soon," he said. "Doroteo says you're very bright. A very good and dependable young man."

"I can only hope to be as bright and dependable as my grandfather," he said, smiling.

Emmanuel pointed to his left temple. "Let's hope better, because your grandfather's mental capacities are a little foggy." Everyone laughed as they moved over to the dinner table to eat. Paloma sat next to him, and there was a toast.

"In Europe all the boys and girls are allowed to imbibe almost as soon as they're able to stand on their own two feet," Paloma said, her voice soft but not unpleasant.

"So enlightened, those Europeans," his grandfather said.

"Diego was born there, you know?" his grandmother said, taking a spoonful of bisque.

"In France, correct?" Lupe asked him.

He cleared his throat. "Yes. France. Near Nice. That's where my father was from. It was where he and my mother settled after eloping." He glanced over at his grandmother, who nodded approvingly.

"I just adore French culture," Lupe said. "So sophisticated. Wouldn't you agree, dear?" she asked, looking at Paloma.

"Yes," she said quietly, stirring her spoon in her soup. "Certainly."

"She's so shy," Lupe said, apologetically.

Paloma adjusted herself, straightened her back, and lifted her head.

She and Diego sipped their wine silently as the conversation turned to politics, to the ever-present tension between the church and the government. From the moment his father returned to San Antonio after the revolution, Diego had never become interested in politics. Fighting, killings, and corruption . . . it was all so meaningless, so destructive.

After the main course, dessert, and coffee, his grandparents and Emmanuel and Lupe went into the parlor to sip brandy.

"Son," his grandfather said. "Why don't you take Paloma outside to the courtyard? It's a beautiful night."

"Very well." He rose, extended his arm out, and she took it.

They sat down on a stone bench, and Paloma tightened her shawl around her shoulders. She looked up at the sky, at the fading blue light turning to black, the few stars glittering in the sky like specks of sugar.

"How have you adjusted since you returned from Europe?" he asked, fumbling for conversation.

She shrugged her shoulders. "Fine. I suppose." She ran her fingers through her hair, which she wore short and parted to the side.

"Why did you return?" he asked.

"I was through with my schooling, and my parents wanted me back."

"I see."

She fussed with the tassels on her shawl and slumped back down again, her back curved, her bony shoulders jutting forward like two horns. "How old are you?"

"Nineteen. I'll be twenty next month. You?"

"Eighteen."

They were silent. He was relieved when he heard his grandmother calling their names. Back inside, he stood with his grandparents and Emmanuel and Lupe in the foyer.

"It was nice meeting you, Paloma," Diego said.

His grandfather cleared his throat and jabbed him in the side. "Isn't there something you'd like to ask Paloma?"

Diego tried not to show his anger. He had always been obedient to the old man, but this was just too much. They all stared, waiting for him to speak. "Paloma," he said, his tone reluctant, "would you like to go for a stroll with me tomorrow? Say, six in the evening?"

The girl said nothing, only looked down at the tips of her shoes.

Lupe shook her gently. "Paloma," she said. "Diego's asked you out. What do you say?"

She shrugged her shoulders again. "Yes," she said. "Fine."

"There," Emmanuel said, clapping his hands, his palms and fingers plump. "That settles it."

She was from a good family, his grandfather reminded him

after they left. From good stock, he would say. As if she were cattle, as if she were a thing to be bred. Paloma Pacheco would secure a good position for him among the elite of Morelia. The marriage of a Sánchez and a Pacheco. Finally! As much as the thought excited his grandfather, it terrified Diego, made him feel weighed down. Imagine it, his grandfather urged him, pouring Diego a glass of cognac. Doroteo had taken to inviting Diego to sit with him in the parlor to drink and smoke tobacco.

In between sips, his grandfather laid out the merits of his seeing Paloma. She's a good girl, he said. Wealthy. You would never have to worry about money again.

"But what if I don't love her?" Diego asked him that night. The cognac had gone to his head. He thought about Javier, wondered where he was, what he was doing.

"Love?" His grandfather chuckled and swatted the air with his hand. "You grow to love someone. It happens little by little."

That was how emotions worked for the old man and others of their generation. Love wasn't something felt deep within the blood, a mystery of the heart. A man married not for love. A man married to secure for himself a good place within the ranks of society. Love was incidental. If it was lacking in the marriage, his grandfather said, there were other ways to acquire it.

Perhaps it was the liquor that was blocking his ability to follow the conversation, but he didn't fully understand. "What other ways, Grandfather?" He took the last sip of his cognac and felt it burn his throat as it slid down.

Doroteo glanced around to make sure they were alone. "Young ladies," he whispered. *"Friends."* He winked. "Pay them visits. Keep them around. Hidden but close by. Keep them for many years." Then he raised his glass and nodded. "Even the most honest and morally straight man among us keeps a mistress."

"Have you ever?" Diego asked him now, setting his empty glass down.

And just as his grandfather was about to answer, Doña Julia walked into the parlor. "It's late," she said to them both. "Doroteo, you should rest." She leaned in and kissed him on the forehead.

Diego couldn't bring himself to watch. He looked away.

"Thank you, my love," his grandfather said. He rose and followed her out.

Over the next several months, Diego had little choice but to spend more time with Paloma, when he really ached to be with Javier, whom he saw less and less now that his friend was enrolled in classes at the university. He took Paloma for long walks and to the symphony, which helped distract him from imagining a life with her. During a theater performance, Diego watched, enthralled, and the urge to get on stage stirred up inside of him again.

"I used to perform, you know?" he said to Paloma.

"Your grandmother told me," she said. "What were you in?"

"Pageants at school. I was in *Julius Caesar*. I was the lead in *Macbeth*. I studied with a very renowned opera singer."

"Fascinating," she said, her tone flat.

What would it be like married to such a person? he wondered. It was true what his grandfather had told him, that he would have everything he'd ever need, that his children and his children's children would be secure. And Emmanuel Pacheco liked Diego. Each time he stopped by to pick up Paloma, Emmanuel would greet him with a hug and a handshake, his robust face lighting up. He would invite him to sit and have a drink. He doted on Diego, gave him advice and his opinion on money matters and stocks and bonds. More important—and unlike Doroteo—he listened to him. Like a true father, Diego thought.

But there was one thing that Diego was sure of: he was not, nor could he ever be, in love with Paloma Pacheco. Quite simply, he found her dull. Diego spent their dates trying as hard as he could to engage her in one way or another. He took her dancing, to dinners, to church parties and socials with other people their age. No matter what he tried doing, he could never draw her out. He yearned for the kind of partnership and excitement he knew was possible with Javier, his closest friend.

One night, as they stood in front of her house saying good-bye, he took her hand and kissed her on the cheek. He was about to leave when she spoke.

"Despite what you may think, I do like you," she said.

"Oh?" he asked, turning around now. He really didn't care one way or another.

"Yes," she said. "And my father says you would make a fine husband." She lowered her head, trying to be coy. "You must forgive my awkwardness. It's just that I have little experience with boys. I get nervous." She approached him now, took his hand and brought it up to her face. "You can kiss me," she whispered, assuming he wanted to. "On the mouth."

He closed his eyes and pressed his lips to hers. He tried to but felt absolutely nothing, and then it was over.

"Good night, Diego," Paloma said, climbing the steps to the house.

"Good night, Paloma."

The following year, they announced their engagement.

4

June 1926

PLUTARCO ELÍAS CALLES—elected president of the republic two years earlier, in 1924—was, like many of the radicals and intellectuals around Morelia, a staunch atheist who harbored little sympathy for the Catholic Church. On June 14, 1926, Diego read in the newspaper that Calles would actively enforce Article 130 of the 1917 Constitution, stripping the church of much of its power. Priests no longer could hold public office, were required to register, and were not allowed to wear religious garb in public. Individual states were allowed to regulate the number of priests in specific regions, leaving entire areas completely void of clergy. Schools were secularized, and priests and nuns were regularly arrested. As a result, many began to flee to the United States.

Shortly after Diego read the newspaper article, he noticed the unease around Morelia gradually begin. Those opposing the church began nailing leaflets on posts around the city calling for control of the church by the government. Young people stood on the street corners and sidewalks shouting, handing out *Libre Morelia* leaflets announcing meetings to inform the wider public of the dangers and corruption inherent within the Catholic Church. After all it was the Benedictine and Franciscan monks in robes who had blessed the Spanish conquistadores, they charged, the very ones who then turned around and enslaved or slaughtered the indigenous. They told of the accounts of the priests in Nueva España, of their condescending view of the "native beast"—his savagery, his animalistic urges, and the murderous and treacherous tendencies coursing through his blood. The church, they proclaimed, had, from the beginning, manipulated the government, destroyed lives, shattered the nation's faith.

The priests preached that it was the end time, that it was foretold that an era would come when a godless government would rule over this land, condemning generations of souls to an eternity in hell. Their sermons stirred up feelings of resentment and suspicion in Diego, his grandparents, and their closest acquaintances. They prayed in secret, late at night, by candlelight. The saint statues and crucifixes and rosaries were hidden away, brought out only when they were in the company of those that could be trusted. The air in the city was charged with a sense of instability, with nervous energy. Diego could see it in the way people walked, their steps quick and frantic, in how they eyed one another with erratic and suspicious glances.

At the university, Diego knew students were banding together in between courses or after school and congregating outside the church's gates to protest. They wore hats emblazoned with red stars, cursed, and caused commotions wherever they went. Hearing of all of this, Diego thought about the warring tribes before the Spaniards arrived, the Conquista, the French occupation, the fight for independence, the revolution, now this, and what was yet to come. An endless cycle of violence in Mexico. It was in their nature to wage war over false ideologies. They would die that way. What a waste.

Diego was excited about meeting Javier for a cup of coffee. But when he showed up to the café that afternoon with Esteban Rosales, Diego became quickly annoyed. Esteban's father owned and ran a small printing press that some of the more radical newspapers and daily circulars used. Esteban's parents were atheists whose anarchistic beliefs were in direct violation of those of the Catholic Church and the country. In their preparatoria, Esteban Rosales had had few friends and was known around the school for being something of a misfit, an odd boy. He had been a skinny and frail teenager with messy hair and long legs. Now, he was more filled out, his hair cut and combed neatly. He wore a thin mustache and long sideburns. He strolled into the café with confidence, smoking a cigarette and holding a stack of books.

"Do you two know each other?" Javier said.

"I'm not sure," Diego said, feigning ignorance as he glanced at Esteban.

"Julius Caesar," Esteban said.

"No. Diego."

Esteban laughed. "I meant the play. *Julius Caesar.*"

"Yes," Diego said. "Of course. I remember now." Diego had been angry because he wanted to play the lead but instead was given the part of Brutus. In the end, though, he was glad he got the role he did because, as Carolina had explained, Brutus was a much more complicated character, far more challenging and interesting. Esteban Rosales had been cast as one of the senators who conspired, along with Brutus, to assassinate Caesar. There had been rumors around the preparatoria about Esteban and his ways. Some of the boys had talked about seeing him with an older man, the two locked in an embrace and kissing each other.

Javier and Esteban went on and on, gossiping about their classes at the university, talking about the current climate between the government and the church, which they saw as evil, controlling, an oppressive institution that needed to be eradicated.

"Isn't that a bit extreme?" Diego responded.

"Hardly," Esteban said.

Diego soon felt excluded, and he finished his coffee and stormed off. The two of them hardly noticed he was gone, not until they looked out into the street and waved good-bye to him.

A few days later, on his walk to his grandfather's office early in the morning, Diego saw Esteban. Esteban wore a pair of argyle stockings pulled up to his knees, baggy tan knickerbockers, a striped shirt with a high collar, a bow tie, and a yellow vest that fit very tight over his lean body. Pinned to the vest was a patch in the form of a star. He stood near the plaza's central fountain holding a stack of leaflets. The few pedestrians out at that hour paid little attention to him, but when a woman did stop to take one, she looked at it, shouted something to Esteban Diego couldn't hear, and shoved the leaflet back at him.

"Hello, Diego," Esteban said.

"Hello," he said. "What have you got there?" He pointed to the leaflets.

Esteban handed him one.

Across the top, *Libre Morelia* was written in big bold letters. It was an announcement condemning the Catholic Church. It talked of its corruption, its greed, and its dangerous influence over the lives of everyone—from politicians to the rich to the very poor—in the republic. There would be a meeting, it went on to say, a gathering of "like-minded" individuals, to discuss and come up with ways to resist the church and fight back.

"You should come to the meeting," Esteban said. "My father says it's important for people our age to involve themselves. He says we'll inherit this country and that if the church continues to grow, all will be lost."

"Do you believe it? Do you think the church is corrupt? That it's bad?"

"I do," he said.

Despite himself, Diego imagined Esteban doing the things the others had gossiped about. He envisioned him bent over with a man behind him. He wanted to ask him if the stories were true, wanted to know what it felt like to be with someone in that way.

"What do you say?" Esteban asked now. "Javier's coming, too."

"Really?" Diego nodded. "You two are close, aren't you?"

"Sure. Well, we're . . . friends."

"Friends," Diego repeated.

"So, tomorrow then?" Esteban said, after a pause. "Meet us in front of the university. By the main gate."

He was still holding the flyer when he arrived at the office. His grandfather was already there, standing over his desk, squinting at an old document with faded letters and smudged ink. He picked it up carefully, the document so aged and delicate that it looked as though the slightest stir, the softest breeze, would disintegrate it, turning the fibers to dust.

"Land deeds. Old. Very old," his grandfather said, sighing. "Sometimes I fear. What will be left when all these traditional things vanish?" He placed the document inside a slim folio with a leather cover and a buckle. His grandfather then noticed the leaflet in Diego's hand. "Where did you get that?" he asked.

"Esteban Rosales was handing them out," Diego said, removing his hat and sitting at his desk.

"It would be better if you avoided the likes of that boy and his family. How could someone not believe in God?" he asked, shaking his head. "They claim the church is evil. They're the evil ones."

"I shouldn't have stopped," Diego said.

"Those people," Doroteo said, "the whole lot of them are dangerous. They have wild ideas. And that boy gives me the strangest feeling."

"Don't worry, Grandfather. I'll make sure not to befriend him."

"Good," the old man said. "No bad influences, no distractions. You must stay focused. Just like when I told you to quit your lessons with Carolina. Remember?"

"Yes, Grandfather."

"And look how that turned out for you. You and Paloma are engaged now and about to be married. You'll have a home and a family soon. I'll be a great-grandfather." He clapped his hands and went back to work.

Even though their lessons had officially ended just after his sixteenth birthday, after that talk, Diego had continued seeing Carolina and continued, though informally, with their afternoon meetings. "I'm seeing Javier. Studying with him," he would tell the old man. "I'll go to the office with you next week. Once we pass these exams." The excuses stopped working, though, once he completed the preparatoria; then he gave in and stopped seeing Carolina, assuming his rightful role as his grandfather's heir. Still, there were times he caught himself humming a melody, daydreaming about performing a soliloquy to a theater full of people, reciting lines from a play he memorized years before. Diego had worked so hard to change, to mold and shape himself into a new man, the person his father and mother and his grandparents had wanted him to be. He had worked so hard to reject those things that distracted him. But why was their pull so strong? Why couldn't he forget? Why did the musical notes, the melodies, the words, the feeling of performing, haunt him so?

Despite his grandfather's warnings, he couldn't resist going to meet Javier and Esteban the next day. Diego was surprised to see that, like Esteban, Javier wore a beret emblazoned with a red star. Javier's arms were crossed, his pose relaxed. He leaned up against the iron bars, talking to Esteban. He was smiling and nodding his head. Esteban stood very close to him with his left arm extended out, gripping one of the gate's metal slats.

"Javier," Diego said, approaching them. He glanced at Esteban, who let go of the fence and composed himself, adjusting his jacket, and straightening his posture. What had Diego interrupted? "Hel-lo."

Javier turned to him and smiled. "Hermano. So glad to hear you'll be joining us."

"We should go," Esteban said.

"Very well," said Diego, following them.

They led him through the city, then down a series of alleyways and empty lots until they were standing in front of a large brick building crowned with a single smokestack that jutted from its roof like a slim gray finger. No smoke billowed out, but a heavy layer of soot and ash covered its sides. A row of tall windows adorned the front of the building, and they were very dirty and some of the glass panes had been shattered, leaving black squares. Diego thought of his grandfather's chessboard.

Inside, the place was cavernous and drafty. Toward the back of the single vast room, there was no light, and the dark corners and splintered doors appeared menacing and sinister. Thick cobwebs clung to the columns and posts. There were chunks of wood, broken bottles, old rubber tires, and rusted sheets of tin with jagged edges and bent nails that stuck out from their sides like claws. Everything smelled of petroleum and dust. Gathered inside were mostly boys his age. Every now and again, he would spot girls in black berets, mingling, their hair in pigtails.

Diego followed Javier and Esteban as they made their way in, saying hello to some of the boys and girls. They referred to each other as "brother" or "sister" and saluted Javier and Esteban as they moved toward a long wooden table stacked with posters and leaf-lets, the ink still drying. The group gathered and sat atop empty wooden whiskey barrels or old crates. The chatter died down and they all looked up now, toward the front, where Javier and Esteban stood behind the table.

"Hello, Brothers and Sisters," Esteban shouted.

"Hello, Brother Esteban," some shouted back.

"Hello, Comrade," a few said.

"We are gathered here," Esteban began, "in solidarity against the injustices and atrocities brought about by the Roman Catholic Church. Our countrymen have suffered long enough under this oppressive regime that has, systematically, subjugated and destroyed many. From our brothers and sisters in the fields and valleys, to our brothers and sisters in the mines and smelting plants, to our brothers and sisters in the factories and textile mills, to our brothers and sisters in the shipyards and rail yards, we stand here today as comrades united against tyranny and injustice inflicted upon the working man by those forces and institutions in power."

Then Javier spoke. "The Catholic Church?" he shouted.

"Down!" they shouted back.

"The bourgeoisie?" he shouted.

"Down!"

"Organized religion?"

"Down!" They threw their fists in the air.

"Corrupt politicians?"

"Down!" they shouted louder.

Esteban spoke again now, making grand and elaborate proclama-tions against entities of power, against foreign companies which, he claimed, were slowly seizing control of the country's petroleum re-serves, its businesses, its precious minerals, everything. He made ref-erences to Karl Marx, Oswald Spengler, Leon Trotsky, and Vladimir Lenin. He talked about José Vasconcelos, about how they—the young idealists who had grown sick and tired of the greed, the cor-ruption, and manipulation—embodied his theory of la raza cós-mica, a cosmic race that would incite an uprising, bring about a new order, a new social structure whose core principles would be egalitarian, would remove social class, and would give back to the poor what had been rightfully theirs. Esteban, that shy and awk-ward boy, the one they said had intercourse with men and fellow classmates, spoke proudly, his voice filling every square inch of that massive room. Javier stood there, almost transfixed, it seemed, his eyes wide, unblinking, muttering, "Yes, yes," now and again. But Diego felt confused by it all, couldn't identify with their insipid ideals. He wanted nothing more than to leave them there, such a pretentious and juvenile bunch, filled with an agenda that had clearly been spoon-fed to them by their radical parents.

Before the meeting ended, Diego had to endure "accounts and news" from various members. Comrade Gómez-Alaniz reported that a local priest was heard criticizing the government. A rally would be planned, Esteban replied, pointing to the leaflets and posters on the table. Someone said they would notify the authorities. Comrade Mejia said a group of nuns in one of the nearby remote villages had barricaded themselves inside a schoolroom and held several children hostage. The nuns were caught and arrested. Everyone cheered and clapped. Javier told of a group of local businessmen who were planning on donating large sums of money and supplies to a handful of priests scattered around the area in order to aid them in what they called "the cause."

"We need a list of names of those places of business," Esteban told him. "We need to rally and protest these businesses in league with the church." When it was done, when each comrade had spoken, Esteban turned to Diego. "I would like to take this opportunity to welcome a new member," he said. "Comrade Sánchez."

"Welcome, Comrade," some shouted.

"Welcome, Brother Sánchez," others said, rising and patting him on the shoulder.

He smiled and played along, saying, "Thank you. Thank you. It's an honor."

As the meeting broke up, Esteban stayed behind while Diego followed Javier outside.

Javier lit a cigarette. "You should get home."

"Since when do you smoke?" Diego asked.

He shrugged his shoulders. "I can't tell you exactly when I started. I just did. I do a lot of things you don't know about."

Diego smirked. "Like associate with this lot? With Esteban? I remember the rumors about him in school. That he was a faggot?" Diego raised his voice, and a few of the boys inside heard him.

"Would you shut up?" Javier said, pushing Diego. "He's good.

He's a good person. He's my friend."

Diego pushed Javier back harder, and he stumbled and fell. "A good friend? I bet. What sort of mischief are you getting into with your good friend, Javier? Are you two—"

"Shut up," he said now, rising, brushing the dirt from his trousers and jacket. "I know what this is about. You're jealous that I have new friends at the university and you don't. All you have is your boring life and your precious fiancée Paloma who you probably don't even like. They're forcing you to marry her, and you're too much of a coward to question them."

"I'm leaving," Diego said, turning and starting to walk away.

"Go back home then," Javier shouted. "To your grandparents. To your pampered life, and your meaningless job. That's all you'll ever know,"

Diego broke into a run, Javier's voice following him all the way back.

Two days later, when he knew Javier would be out, he went to see Carolina. She answered the door, a surprised look on her face. It was late morning, and she still wore her robe.

"Hello," she said.

"Hello. I wanted to talk. Is now a bad time?"

"Not at all," she told him. "Come in." Carolina went into the kitchen then returned, leading him out to the patio. A few minutes later, a maid came out carrying a pot of boiling coffee, slices of fruit, and warm rolls of sweet bread.

She poured them some coffee. "I love mornings like this. Sitting out here. So peaceful." She reached out and squeezed his hand.

He didn't realize how much he had missed their time together. He sat there admiring her. Carolina was beautiful in that bright morning light. Her face was free of lipstick and rouge. Her forehead was wide and strong, her eyebrows arched and perfectly symmetrical, as if they had been painted on her face by a delicate and patient hand.

"What would you like to talk about?" she asked. Carolina knew him well, probably better than anyone else, except maybe for Elva; he still wondered about her from time to time.

He sighed. "What, um, what do you think about all this commotion? What's brewing between the church and the government?"

She sat back in her chair and crossed her arms. "Well." She cocked her head to one side. "I suppose that, if you take away a person's faith, a person's need to believe in something else, no matter how intangible, what follows is inner turmoil and chaos. Fanaticism."

"Whose side are you on?" he asked.

She shrugged. "Does it matter? I think this whole mess, just like the revolution, is more than just sides," she said. "Lines will be drawn. There'll be battles and fights and death. It'll end badly. Then, years from now, it'll start all over again. The people know nothing about sides. They're just caught in the middle. The church has too much power, has influenced things in this country far too long. On the other hand, like I said, it's dangerous to take away a person's faith, what they believe in."

"I see it the way the church does," he finally said. "My grandparents, they—"

"Oh, but," she interrupted, "the church is just another form of control, another way of keeping you, us, under its thumb with its rules and moral codes."

"It's what I believe," he said, sighing. "It's what helped me become who I am now."

"And who are you now?" She rose and walked over to a wire cage lined with straw. It was where Carolina had kept a white rabbit with red eyes like rubies and a nose that constantly wiggled. The cage was empty, though. It had remained so since the day four years before when a cat snuck in and ate the rabbit.

"I've grown. Changed," Diego said.

She regarded the empty cage. "It's ending now, isn't it? Our time together? You'll marry Paloma soon. Start a family. You won't have time for me, and all of this will end."

"It ended a long time ago," he said, remembering the conversation with his grandfather years before.

"I know," she said. "I just didn't want to accept it." She turned to face him now. "Does any part of you miss it?"

"What?" he asked.

"The performing. The singing and dancing. All those things I taught you."

"At times. I think about it now and again. But what am I supposed to do? Throw everything I have away just to go chase an impractical dream?"

"You're absolutely certain that this is the course you want your life to take?" she asked him. "That you want to marry this girl and inherit your grandfather's legacy?"

"Yes," he said.

"You're positive?"

"Yes," he said once more. "Why do you sound so incredulous?"

Carolina reached out, placed both hands on his shoulders and told him she thought he was making a grave mistake. "You're good. Not great," she said, taking a sip of her coffee. "But you can be. I believe it's your destiny."

"I haven't performed in several years now. Haven't sung a single note. Have hardly danced."

"You never lose it. It's always in you."

"But my grandfather," he said.

"What about him?" she asked, throwing her hands up in the air. "Why follow his advice? So that your life will be like his? Sitting there in that empty house surrounded by all those old relics? You have a chance. Don't waste it."

"I don't want to," he said, and Diego could feel himself growing angry. "All I have is here."

"No," she said. "It's not. You have a talent, one I believe is meant to be shared. You should at least give performing a try. Otherwise you may be passing up a great opportunity."

"What do you propose I do? Start meeting with you in secret? Practicing more speeches and taking more voice and dance lessons?"

She shook her head. "No. There's only so much I can do for you. There comes a time when every pupil must leave his teacher."

She told Diego that she'd recently talked with some friends of hers from her art school where she had trained as a vocalist. Ana and Juan Brenton married soon after school and lived in Europe for many years, but they had recently returned to Mexico City with the intention of opening up a small theater house. They were gathering a troupe of actors and performers, and Carolina was convinced they would love him.

"If you want I'll write them about you," she said. "I just know they'll want to work with you. Or you could at least audition."

"But I can't," he said. "My grandfather. I made a promise."

"I think you should ignore your grandfather," she said. "You could be making a terrible mistake."

He watched how her face changed when she said this. Carolina looked around, regarded the patio, the large house looming before her, filled with exquisite pieces of furniture, with pictures, with memories of her and Manuel and Javier.

"Sometimes I wonder," she began to say, her voice quivering, "what would have happened had I not—"

"No," he interjected. "I can't. I'll stay here. I'll work by my grandfather's side. It's what I must do. I'm sorry."

With that, he put his coat on and left. He couldn't listen to her fantasies a moment longer.

5

January 1927

THE MARCH DATE THEY set the year before had felt so far away then. Now, it was less than eight weeks before the wedding. His grandmother and Lupe and Paloma handled all the planning. Diego was relieved. He didn't want to think about it more than he had to. It all filled him with an anxiety he couldn't quell no matter how many cups of cognac he drank. Since the summer, the house had been full of activity, with Lupe and Paloma spending hours planning the menu and deciding on the flowers. His grandmother became another woman. She was more animated, smiling regularly and giving Diego the odd kiss on the cheek or hug. She complimented him sometimes, even when there was no one else around.

As the date approached, Diego began to feel as though he were standing in a room crowded with people, and the walls of the room were closing in. Wedding rings were purchased, a conference with the priest who was to wed them scheduled, the guest list finalized and the invitations sent out. His grandmother hired more servants and cooks to help with the task of planning the meal and the reception. She floated from one part of the house to the other, scolding the maids when they failed to fold the table linens right or yelling at the cooks when she tasted something she didn't like. One day in

February, he sat in the parlor, watching all the commotion, feeling the entire world spinning beneath his feet, careening out of his control. Doroteo walked into the room and sat near him, regarding Diego.

"Are you ill, son? You look terrible."

He took a deep breath before speaking. "I guess I'm just a little nervous."

His grandfather laughed. "That's natural. You should have seen me on the day I married your grandmother. I was a frightful mess." Doroteo reached out and patted him on the shoulder. "It'll pass. Paloma's a sweet girl. You two will be very happy. Trust me. I know what is best for you."

Work did nothing to keep his mind off the wedding. Instead, he found himself altogether uninterested in the endless task of notarizing and cataloguing. The old documents no longer felt important. They were flimsy, transparent, unreliable. Everything in his life felt this way now. On the days when his grandfather left him alone in the office, Diego closed up early, wandering aimlessly through the streets of Morelia. He bought cigarettes from a street vendor one afternoon and began smoking, drifting from one plaza to the other, watching people, hoping for something to happen. He thought about Javier, imagined him waving at him from across the plaza, walking over and sitting next to Diego. They would share cigarettes and talk and make plans again. Diego would take Carolina's advice, and he and Javier would move to the capital together. Diego would join Ana and Juan Brenton's theater troupe. He would become a famous performer, and Javier would be very proud and they'd be happy.

Then the movie houses came to Mexico, and one opened up around the corner from the office. It was in an old building that was dilapidated and falling down. But then there was a ticket booth and a marquee lit up by electric bulbs that flashed and moved in rapid succession. The lines soon began to wrap all the way around the corner and out into the sidewalk, a few feet from the office's entrance. One day, instead of wandering around again, Diego took a place in the line, leaning against the cracked column where his father once stood. The line inched forward bit by bit until he was before the ticket booth. He paid the attendant inside and stepped into the lobby.

He would never forget the silence, the way in which the theater cut off all sound and movement from the outside; the silhouettes of the people around him settling down in their chairs; the click and whir of the projector; the snapping and cracking and sputtering of the film as the celluloid strip worked its way through the rivulets and channels of the camera. Soon, a little man with a striped vest and a bowler hat walked onto the stage. He sat at a piano and began playing music from a stack of sheets placed before him.

And, just like that, the moving picture began. It involved a pretty heiress, an evil baron, and a kidnapping. Diego would never forget the thrill of it all, a chase scene involving many horses, a majestic castle, and the pretty heiress by her father's side, clutching his hand as the mustachioed old man took his last breath and died a dramatic and poignant death.

Diego was riveted. He remained in his seat long after the film had ended. It was only once he was outside, once he was back at his desk in the notary office, that Diego realized that he hadn't thought about the wedding the entire time he was sitting inside the theater house.

A few newsstands around Morelia began selling magazines solely devoted to the "moving picture business," as they called it. These featured pages and pages full of glossy black-and-white pictures of movie stars like Charlie Chaplin, Mary Pickford, Louise Brooks, and Ramón Novarro, who was also from Mexico. The articles told of lavish poolside parties, of veritable nobodies hopping off trains from all over the world and finding themselves instant movie stars. He kept these magazines under his bed—pulling them out at night, when the house was quiet and free of all the wedding nonsense— and stared at the pictures inside that showed wide avenues flanked with palm trees, rolling verdant hills, and the sunshine which, he learned, always shone every day, year after year. Hollywood was paradise, and Diego wanted to go, to get lost in the masses of people who were flocking there to become stars, to toast their skin under a warm sun that was constant and rejuvenating, to stroll under the shaded branches of orange and grapefruit trees, to go to the fancy restaurants and dance clubs the movie stars went to. Most of all, he dreamed of becoming a famous film actor himself. He stared, night after night, at the picture of Ramón Novarro and told himself that he too could become like him, that young boy from Mexico. A nobody who became a somebody there. In paradise.

With the wedding only a few weeks away now, Diego found himself spending more time inside the theater. He lied to his grandparents, told them he was going to the church to pray in the evenings after dinner. Instead he went to watch more filmstrips, some of them over and over again. He saw chases, a dance by a woman in a veil and an elaborate headdress. There were pirates on large ships, an old hunchbacked man playing with a group of orphans. He saw Paris and ancient Egypt and Babylon, Greece and Italian villas. The thrill, the pursuits by bandits, the police officers and bank robbers, it all made him think of other things, further away, far from Morelia, Mexico, his grandparents, Paloma.

There were nights when he would watch Doroteo, slumped in a chair, a drink in his hand, his eyes tired and wasted by years and years of notarizing, of documenting the lives of others, not his own. He imagined himself old, in that very chair, nodding off, just like his grandfather was. Paloma would be by his side, hair graying, eyes empty and void of love or passion or all other things that made life worth anything. He wanted to be brave like his mother, who risked everything to be with the man she loved, to seek out, to live the life she truly wanted. But he wasn't that person. He couldn't do that now or ever. There was the wedding. There was a suit he still needed to buy.

He hadn't seen Javier at all, not since their fight after the meeting. Paloma's maid of honor, her cousin Irma Salas, had enrolled at the university and told Diego that Javier was in some of her classes. He got into the habit of asking Irma from time to time if she had seen him, how he was doing, what he looked like. Through her, he learned that Javier and Esteban were still very close, that they were always together, that they spent the majority of their free time between classes handing out leaflets and organizing meetings.

"That place is such a breeding ground for liberals and atheists," Paloma told her cousin one day. "I don't know why you continue to attend."

"I'm looking for a husband," Irma said. "That's all."

"Well," Paloma said, gripping Diego's arm. "There are plenty of other, far more respectable places to find one. Just ask me."

Diego couldn't bear the thought of Javier missing the wedding, which was only two weeks away. He put his coat on, adjusted his hat, and took several deep breaths before walking over to his house and knocking on the door. One of the maids answered.

"Doña Carolina and Don Manuel aren't here," she said, letting him in. "But Javier's in his bedroom. He has company."

"Thank you," he said, glancing up the stairs.

He thought about leaving, but he couldn't. He just had to see Javier. They needed to put things right. Diego climbed the steps one at a time, his hand squeezing the banister, the wood cool against his warm, damp skin. The hallway was dark except for the shafts of dim white light seeping out from the bottoms of the doors. He came to Javier's room and stood there. He raised his hand, balled up in a fist, and was about to rap it when the door creaked slightly open, enough so that he could see inside, could see Javier with his shirt off, his arms wrapped around Esteban's torso. They were locked in a tight embrace, their eyes closed, their lips pressed together, kissing. All Diego could do was look away. The dark wooden floorboard creaked when he stepped back, and Javier saw him standing there. Diego's breath was caught in his throat. Before Javier had a chance to do anything—fumble for his shirt, walk over, slam the door shut—Diego turned away and ran down the steps and out of the house as quickly as he could. Those two perverted heathens deserved one another, he thought when he arrived back home. Such a vile and putrid act. Two men with each other. What a disgrace. He wasn't like that. He had Paloma. They would have children. Lots of them. They would be raised Catholic. God-fearing. There would be a place for them in heaven.

A week before the wedding, he stood there looking at his suit and hat, perfectly pressed and tailored to fit him. He thought about Paloma. Such a kind and loyal fiancée.

"Sometimes I think we should just run off," she said. "Have a quiet ceremony. Just us two."

Dear, sweet Paloma, he told himself now, his hand touching the new fabric, the thick tweed trousers, the silk tie, the top hat.

He didn't feel the same way at all. He wanted nothing more than to escape. It was the wedding announcement, the name "Diego Sánchez" printed in the newspaper, which made it real for Diego. If he married her, there would be no turning back. For it was now legitimized in print, as official as the documents he notarized day after day. *Diego Sánchez. Son of a wealthy Frenchman. Diego Sánchez would marry Paloma Pacheco, daughter of one of the richest and most powerful men in the state.*

How had this happened?, he thought as he regarded his wedding suit and hat. Who had he become?

He kept the valise under his bed, and two days before the wedding he touched the handle, felt the worn leather buckles and snaps. The night before they were to be wed, he packed. He rummaged through his clothing, tossing woolen socks and undershirts, trousers and a belt in the valise before securing his toiletries in the front compartment. He placed a crucifix between the pages of one of the Hollywood magazines he had collected. He reached for them now, first making sure the crucifix and chain were safe, before arranging them at the bottom of the valise and snapping it shut. His hand shook as he held the pen. It took several tries, several deep breaths, before he could focus long enough to tell them what he was doing and why.

It sounded so illogical, so unclear, when he read it back, before sealing it in an envelope and placing it in the pocket of his jacket. He asked to be forgiven, told them he was grateful for everything they had done. He told them not to worry, that he would wire them once he arrived in Mexico City. I must do this, he wrote, underlining each word. I simply must. I won't be gone forever. Only for a little while.

The sun had not yet risen when he dressed and placed the letter on the table in the foyer before sneaking out of the house, valise held tightly in his hand, his passport, money, and the address of Carolina's friends in his front pocket. He opened the door, inching it slowly, the hinges squeaking only slightly, and placed the valise on the front stoop, turning around one last time, the shadows of the furniture menacing. He saw the wooden secretary, remembered the photograph of his mother, the one his grandmother had shown him when he first arrived that day so many years ago. Diego left the door open as he crept back inside, stepping carefully down the darkened hallway toward the secretary, pulled the drawer down, reached in, and took the photograph. Once out of the house, he breathed a deep sigh, unbuckled the snaps on the valise as fast as he could, and placed the photo inside. He stepped out into the street and kept walking. He refused to turn back.

Carolina had been surprised to see Diego a few days before. "What brings you here?" she asked, leading him into the parlor.

He wiped the sweat from his forehead with a handkerchief. "I'm sorry. It's just that—"

She poured him some brandy, which he took and drank in one, big gulp. "Easy," she said. "You must be nervous."

"Yes," he said, placing his glass down. "I'm going to be married in about three days." Diego chuckled.

"Of course," she said. "So, what brings you here today? I would have imagined your grandmother was keeping you very busy with the preparations."

"Yes, well." He laughed. "A while back, you said you knew some people. In Mexico City. That they were opening up a theater company."

"Yes. Why?" She leaned in close. "Have you changed your mind?"

"No." The lie came so easy, and it was as if it were one he had rehearsed in his mind, again and again. "I'm taking Paloma there. I thought I might visit them. See if they could recommend some operas for us to see."

How could he admit to Carolina that he'd been wrong? That he didn't want to be Diego Sánchez anymore. That the thought of living this life filled him with a dread that plagued him day and night? That new feelings had begun to stir inside of him? That something, a great desire, now tugged at his flesh and bones, the feeling growing stronger and stronger. Something was calling to him, pulling him away. He had tried everything he could to ignore it, but he found he simply couldn't. He had no other choice but to give in to it.

"One moment," Carolina said, walking out of the room. She returned shortly with an envelope. She wrote the address down on a slip of paper and handed this to him. "I'll wire them. Tell them you're on your way."

"Very well," he said. "Please don't tell anyone I was here either."

"But—" she began to say then stopped. She stepped forward and hugged him, stretching tall, so that her arms wrapped around his shoulders. Carolina looked into his eyes, tears gathering, and he could tell now that she knew everything. "Be careful," she whispered. "Write to me when you get there. I won't say a word."

He kissed her on the cheek. "Thank you," he said. "I'll never be able to repay you. For this. For everything."

The address was folded in his pocket. He would tell them he was Carolina's student and do his best so that they would offer him a spot in their troupe. He would become someone else. He would become himself again, a León.

Diego arrived just before the all-aboard, so there was no room in the overhead racks for his valise. A porter took it and stored his belongings with those of the second-class passengers.

"My apologies," the man said. "I hate to have to do this. Those people don't own anything but the clothes on their backs, so there's always room in the overhead compartments there."

"It's fine," Diego said, tipping him. He loosened his bow tie, removed his gloves, and sat. Riding across from him was an American journalist. He carried with him a leather satchel, a notepad and pencils, and one book he had been reading for much of the first leg of the voyage. Its title—written across the cover in English—was *The Traveler's Guide to Mexico, 1927*. The man, though American, spoke fluent Spanish, and Diego heard him tell another passenger how he was on assignment, reporting on the escalating violence between the church and the state.

"Interesting stuff," he said. "Awfully violent."

"You don't know the half of it, mister," said the passenger.

The reporter just laughed. Behind a pair of gold-rimmed pince-nez, he had large blue eyes and a full head of bright blond hair cut short, almost down to his scalp. "Hello," the man said when he caught Diego looking. He had a wide chin and ruddy cheeks.

"Hello," said Diego.

"Reynolds," he said. "Walter Reynolds." He extended his hand across the carpeted aisle separating them. "Pleasure."

"Diego," he responded. "Diego *León*." He smiled. It felt good to say his own name.

Through the wooden planks of the floor, Diego felt the train groaning to life, the engines pumping steam, the gears shifting and grinding. Soon the great giant wheels lunged forward, pulling them away from the station. At that moment, he knew his grandparents would be waking, would find his note. He imagined them standing in the foyer, shaking their heads and sighing. He imagined Paloma clutching the letter to her bosom and weeping, Irma sitting beside her, consoling her. There was a pang in his chest and it mixed with the moaning train, the hissing and banging of its multitude of gears and whirring machinery. Sacrifices. That's what he was doing, what Carolina once told him that all great artists faced. Sacrifices.

"My fire was extinguished before it ever had a chance to burn bright because I didn't sacrifice enough," she once said. "You need to remember. You need to be willing to follow the impulse no matter how outlandish it may seem, no matter what you think your life will be."

The train gathered steam, gained momentum, and they moved forward, and he felt the skin of the land peel away from his own, revealing a fine layer of new flesh just beneath the surface, unblemished.

He slept most of the day and into the evening. He woke to the sound of the air whistling through the windows of the cars. The sun was beginning to rise, and he looked at his pocket watch: it was nearly six in the morning. They had been traveling for almost 24 hours. Diego rose and stepped into the aisle and walked through the dining car, past the sleeping berths, and into the second-class cars. It was true what the porter said; the poorer peasants and indios seemed to travel with everything they owned on their backs, perpetually uprooted and dispossessed. Some had brought along their farm animals, and they darted back and forth along the aisles and rows. Their chickens huddled together for warmth in cages with floors lined with hay. A goat chewed on strips of paper. A potbellied pig, tied to the back of a bench, snorted and sniffed the air as Diego passed. *Kúchi*. He laughed, remembering the P'urhépecha word for pig.

"*Kúchi*," he said out loud. "*Kúchi. Kúchi*." He raised his voice, but no one stirred.

The people hunkered down on the benches made of splintered wood that was nicked and scratched and dull. They crumpled coats or folded their arms underneath their heads for pillows. Many of them now slept—men with their heads thrown back, mouths open, as if waiting for something to fall in, a husband and wife curled up on the rough wooden bench, holding hands, a young girl in pigtails and frayed leather sandals alone, clutched a stuffed bag beside her. A few rows away, a baby whimpered softly, and his mother roused herself. She unbuttoned her dress, searching, until she revealed the pointed and purple tip of her nipple. The baby suckled it, and the nipple was so dark it glowed from the yellow light falling in perfect squares across the wooden planks of the train's floor.

He returned to his car when he felt the train brake and slow down. Reynolds had risen too and was stretching and yawning.

"How long are we stopping?" he asked the conductor.

"Maybe 20 minutes," the man said.

"What time is it?" Reynolds asked.

"Just past six in the morning. You can go outside. Get some fresh air."

Diego went for the door and stepped outside, and he turned and saw Reynolds behind him. The sun was rising in the east, and the gray mountains and the hills and valleys slowly came into focus. The dawn's first light faded the last remaining stars, and he stood on the empty platform station watching them vanish little by little. Reynolds leaned up against a support beam and reached into his pocket and rolled a cigarette. Inside the train, people rose, and they watched the silhouettes of arms stretching, hands grabbing at the darkness.

"Would you like one?" Reynolds asked Diego. "Mr. León, is it?"

"Yes," Diego turned now.

"A cigarette? Would you like one?" he asked again.

"That's very kind of you," he said.

Reynolds rolled him one, and Diego stepped forward and took it. Reynolds lit the tip, and the embers turned bright red and glowed and throbbed. The smoke felt warm. Diego imagined the soothing gray swirls whipping around his tongue and in between the slim gaps of his teeth. Reynolds took long puffs and swallowed them and held them in before releasing. An open field lay across from the station, and the new weak light cast a silver hue over the land. There were the crooked shadows of cacti, the outlines of rocks and stones lying on their sides, lonely and far away. They held their cigarettes between their fingers and stood there without saying a word. Diego looked down at his, still lit, the constant thread of smoke curling out from the tip, hovering around his fingers like mist. He took one last puff, held it in without swallowing, and then blew it out.

"Where are you headed?" Reynolds asked. "Me, I'm bound for Veracruz. Taking a boat to New York City before going back home to Chicago."

"I'm going to Mexico City," Diego said.

"Visiting family?" Reynolds asked.

"No," Diego said. "I'm an actor. My teacher got me a job with a theater troupe."

"Oh, that's nice," the man said. "Have you ever traveled to the United States, son?"

"No, I can't say I have."

"Now there's a great place to visit. Yes, sir. The great cities of America. New York. Chicago. Los Angeles to the west. Why, that's one place I'd like to see, like to someday end up. Los Angeles." He whistled and shook his head. Reynolds said what he really wanted to do was write for the pictures. Diego remembered his magazines, packed away beneath his clothing and his mother's pictures, the gold crucifix pressed between the glossy pages. "Writing for the pictures?" Diego asked, confused. "Why, I've seen plenty of moving pictures. There are no words. It's not like the theater."

The movie directors and producers still needed writers, Reynolds said. For the stories. He told Diego about the perpetual sunlight, the warm air that invigorated and rejuvenated the body and the mind. He talked about fruit trees and the ocean, about it being an ideal place to "start over," and to "begin a new life."

"Yes, sir. California," Reynolds said. "Los Angeles and Hollywood. Why, it's like paradise on earth. That's where me and my wife and boy will end up. You bet." He put his cigarette out. "Excuse me," he said, pointing to a small wooden shed a few feet away. "I have to go to the bathroom."

He left, and Diego was alone on the platform. Out there, in the fading darkness, something caught his attention. It scurried back and forth, darting between rocks and dry shrubs. Diego walked to the edge of the platform and tried to get a better look. He saw it again, a flash of silver. Then there was a tail and a long, pointed snout. It was a coyote. Its red eyes stared past him, its nostrils flaring. The creature turned and ran off just before Diego heard the galloping of an approaching horse.

He saw them first, riding across the flat valley, each of them toting rifles. After a while, there came the sounds of gruff voices shouting terse and quick commands. Their dark mares circled the length of the train. They wore sashes over their chests emblazoned with the image of the Virgin of Guadalupe, Queen of the Americas. The horses trotted, swift and steady, while the men continued circling and circling the train. Then came the pop of gunshots, then several shouts and screams, far off, from the very back of the train.

Reynolds came out from behind the shed, fastening his trousers, and grabbed Diego by the arm. "Quick," he whispered. "Hide." He led him back behind the shed, the puddle of dark earth still damp from his urine.

"What are they doing?" Diego asked.

"I don't know."

By now the men, at least fifteen of them, had stopped circling, and they sat atop their horses, lined up along the length of the train.

"Their sashes," Reynolds said. "The image of Guadalupe. You see?"

"I do," Diego said. "They're Cristeros." They were warriors of the church, former priests and clergy and devotees who had decided to fight back against the anti-clerics, against Calles and his atheism.

Another man appeared wearing a pair of riding boots and a large hat. Across his chest was a cross carved of wood, tied to his neck by a thick piece of twine. They had sealed and locked all the train's doors, trapping the people inside. They then watched another man go around with a tank, dousing each car, one by one. The smell of gasoline reached them just as the man shot a bullet, igniting the train cars, releasing heavy plumes of black smoke that blocked out the sun, which was bright and high in the sky by then. The troop galloped off, the sound of neighing horses mixing with the screams of the people inside.

"Good God," Reynolds shouted, and they ran out from behind the shed.

They tried unlatching the doors and breaking the windows, but it was too hot, too dark to see a thing. A group of passengers had managed to shatter the glass, and they pushed and shoved each other out of the way, fighting to squeeze through the opening. The jagged edges cut their clothing and flesh as they leapt out and there was blood everywhere, and Diego saw them engulfed in flames, flailing their arms. Their bodies, from head to toe, burned, and they screamed, running, running, until the fires consumed them and there was nothing left but clumps of charred flesh clinging to bone.

"What do we do?" Diego shouted, coughing.

"I don't know," said Reynolds. "Dear God. I don't know."

They just stood there and watched the train smolder, their backs to a vast cornfield with miles and miles of tall green stalks swaying in place as all those bodies, all those howling faces inside that train, simply fell away.

He fought the urge to turn and look back at the plumes of black smoke, the ash from the charred wooden cars, his clothing and magazines, his cross and his mother's picture, mixing with the remains of all those passengers. He could still hear the wailing, the thumping of fists against the graying glass, the hissing and popping of burning flesh.

"Walk," Reynolds said now, as if sensing Diego's urge to turn around. "Walk with me, son. We'll follow the track. There's bound to be another station around here. Where are you going?"

"I told you."

"Tell me again," said Reynolds. "Just tell me again."

"Mexico," he managed to stammer out. "Mexico City."

"That's right. That's right," Reynolds said, breathing in deep. "Always wanted to go there. Always wanted to go there. Hey," he said, putting a firm hand on Diego's shoulder, "you concentrate on my voice now, you hear? I'll keep talking until we're far away from that, okay?"

"Yes," Diego said.

"Now I'm from Chicago. Why it's just about the best darn city in the entire world. Yes sir, it is. Big baseball town. You like baseball?"

"I don't know."

"You don't know? Why, that's a tale. Tell you what, my friend, I'll give you my address and when you get good and settled there in Mexico City, you send me a letter and we'll make plans and you can come on to Chicago and my wife and I and my boy, we'll take you to see a ball game. Yes. Yes, sir." He was talking fast. "Let's keep walking," Reynolds said. "Steady and away."

He whistled a tune, and the long grass rustled in the wind. But the shouts and screams kept ringing in Diego's ears. "Let's go, son." Reynolds tugged on the sleeve of Diego's jacket when he stopped and tried to look back. "Let's go."

After a few hours, they came into a flat clearing. In the distance, Diego could see a cornfield. To one side of the cornfield there were telegraph poles strung together with cables that sagged. At the very edge of the cornfield was a single paved road, and they followed it. Up ahead, they saw the bodies. Though they saw them clearly, could make out what was hanging there from the poles that lined the road, they walked on, toward them, hoping their eyes were deceiving them. Diego wanted to climb up the poles and pull them down, shroud their bodies and lament for them, for himself, for the sad events that had led his country to this.

Instead, he stood before the long line of wires, and the bodies of those unknown men rocked back and forth and they looked like marionettes, like those he remembered seeing in the marketplaces in Morelia when he first arrived. Their heads drooped down to one side, absurd and comical and frightening in their clumsiness. He didn't want to see but found it difficult to turn away. One of them wore no trousers, his genitals shriveled and sagging between his legs, exposed, and Diego felt shame for this stranger, for his family, for his mother and father and their mothers and fathers. For how could one person do this to another? How could one country, one people, hate itself so much as to turn on itself? To kill and maim itself this way? He tried to find answers in the puzzled and distorted, the misshapen and bloated and cracked faces of those men. But they yielded none, for their eyes were swollen shut, their noses and fingers broken, their ears and tongues ripped out, their voices forever muted.

Saying nothing to each other about the bodies, they walked on, soon arriving at a town. They sat down in a plaza where birds hopped along the trails and paths, collecting seeds and eating worms. Reynolds left to wire his bosses in the United States and when he returned, Diego asked him about the dead men.

"Agraristas," he replied. "One of them was wearing a badge. The kind the federal troops have. Cristeros killed them."

"Of course," Diego said. "Agraristas against Cristeros." Priests and religious zealots fighting against the Agraristas, who were the government-backed troops, who sought to control the power of the Catholic Church. He thought about Javier. Was that who he had become? An Agrarista? Was he capable of murder?

Suddenly, there came shouts and screams in the distance followed by several gunshots. People on the streets scattered in all directions, some running inside shops and buildings to take shelter.

"What's happening?" Diego asked.

Reynolds didn't respond. When two men hurried past, he asked them what was going on.

"Agraristas," one of them said. "They captured a priest they say set a train on fire and ordered a troop to be executed."

"Where are they?" Reynolds asked.

Both men pointed to the church.

"They have the priest there," the first man said. "They're going to kill him."

The reporter ran off toward the church and Diego, not knowing what else to do, followed closely behind. They passed through the narrow streets of that town, past empty barrels and mounds of trash. A handful of weathered shacks, a row of old colonial buildings with moss-covered columns, and a stable were situated around a small courtyard with scraggly trees and a fountain at its center. Beyond a set of large iron gates, he could see a bell tower, a cross, the domed roof of a church with faded plaster. Scattered about the inner courtyard of the church were makeshift tables. Some displayed dried herbs bundled together with twine, bags of seeds and nuts, bolts of fabric, carved trinkets and masks adorned with glass jewels and feathers and strings of long yarn for hair. In the quiet rustle of canvas tarps draped over the tables, in the shifting and brushing of branches and twigs, they heard footsteps, the low chanting of words that sounded like someone was praying. Crouched behind an overturned table was a boy. He wore the clothing of a peasant—white trousers and shirt spun from the fibers of a cactus, leather sandals, and a piece of rope for a belt. The silence was interrupted with a round of gunfire coming from inside the church. The only cover around was next to the shivering boy behind the table, his arms over his head, his eyes shut. When a bullet hit a concrete column a few feet from where Diego and Reynolds stood, they ran over, crouching beside the frightened boy.

"What's happening?" Reynolds asked the boy.

He told them, his voice trembling, that a group of eight men, including a priest, locked themselves up inside when they saw the government troops riding into town.

"They have pistols," the boy said.

"Who?"

"All of them."

The boy said that when the shooting started, everybody around the square ran and hid. He was selling sweets with his two sisters, who left with the rest of the people.

"I was afraid to run," he said. "So I stayed here."

There was more firing around them now; a bullet whizzed past Diego's ear, so fast and high pitched that it left in its wake a ring that disoriented him. Then a second one hit a trunk where some wood carvings were displayed. The figurines and masks flew up into the sky where they remained suspended, like disembodied ghosts, for a brief moment before falling to the ground and shattering. The bullets continued inside the church, speeding past them over and over. Then there was a pause, and everything remained very quiet. The boy quickly turned and ran off across the courtyard just as the firing began anew.

"Let's go," Diego pleaded with Reynolds.

"No," he said.

He should have gone with the boy, Diego thought.

"Look," Reynolds said, pointing up to the church bell tower. "There are three men up there."

Diego turned and gazed upward. The crack of the gun startled a flock of gray doves feasting on the sunflower seeds trampled over when the panicked crowd fled. They flew up into the sky just as the father's body began its descent. The priest seemed not to tumble, but to drift down, and the wide arms of his alb opened up like wings when the wind rushed through them, and his hair stood on its ends, and Diego watched the figure, terrifying and elegant, soaring down and down, and he looked up at the sky and wondered where exactly was the hand of God? Why didn't it break through the film of clouds and reach down to catch him? When the priest hit the ground, his limbs like twisted vines, Diego could see a trail of blood, thin as a thread, coming out from his nose, the bullet hole on the side of his head, bone and tissue caught in the roots of his black hair.

It was his face that Diego fixed his gaze upon, not the mangled body and the broken skull, but the father's expression, how his eyes had remained open, unflinching, at that final hour of his life. The gun he'd held had tumbled down and fallen in a plot of roses, and his other hand had managed to clutch the cross around his neck. Was this faith, Diego thought as he looked upon that serene face, that simple and persistent and knowing gaze? Was this its essence, what they tried to capture in prayers and incantations, in ceremonies and customs? Was this it? This death? This broken body? These fingers holding a splintered cross?

"This is him," Reynolds said after a while. "The one who set our train on fire." He pointed to the dead priest's cross. "I remember that."

A few minutes later, they watched the Agraristas come out from the church, mount their horses, and gallop off.

Diego felt stunned. His knees quivered, and his hands trembled. "I can't . . ." he stammered. "I want to go. I want to leave."

"Very well," Reynolds said now. "But there's a story here. I need to stay and investigate." He looked around the square. "Let's find the train station. Let's get you back to where you were headed."

Diego didn't know what to do. Should he turn around and go back to Morelia or continue on to Mexico City? He couldn't make up his mind. The rail station attendant told him the train to Mexico City had just left.

"What do you have leaving now?" he asked the attendant.

The man removed his hat, the brim small and shiny, and scratched his head. He took a slip of paper and studied it. "I have one departing to Morelia, another to Guadalajara, and another to Guanajuato."

He sighed, and the people behind him in line tapped their feet on the floor and cleared their throats. "What else?" he asked the attendant.

"Well, where do you want to go?" The man put his hat back on and glared at Diego. "Tell me where you want to go, and I'll tell you what I have."

"Anywhere," he insisted. "Anywhere far."

The man picked up the slip of paper and looked again, this time his eyes scanning all the way toward the bottom of the sheet. "Juárez," he said. "The border. Is that far enough?"

The border. From there he could go to the United States. To California. He could escape. He could finally leave this behind. It was up to him to break the tradition, to stop allowing the whims and influences of unseen forces to dictate his life. His past had already been written, but his present and his future were another thing, Diego realized. They were still out there waiting for him. "Very well," he said, reaching into his pocket for his money. "One."

When the train arrived and he handed his ticket to the conductor, the man looked around for Diego's luggage.

"Bag?" he asked.

All his belongings—his clothes, his magazines, and his mother's photograph—had been burned in the train, so he had nothing with him except for his money and his passport. "None," he told the man.

Arriving in Juárez, Diego was told he could not pass into the United States without first going through inspection at the Santa Fe disinfection plant. It was mandated by the United States Department of Health, a woman told him. A large group of passengers had exited the train station on the Juárez side and, not knowing what to do, he decided to follow them.

"The Americans say we're dirty," said a man to Diego as they walked across the bridge, the waters of the Rio Grande spilling over jagged rocks below. The man wore a suit and bright blue spats over his shoes. "That we carry diseases. Now, the Department of Health inspects us before we enter. Tell me, do I look diseased?" He pointed to his suit and tie.

An old man in a straw hat asked, "Is this your first time north?"

"Yes," Diego responded.

The man in the suit chuckled. "Be careful. Some of them hate us. Won't serve you in restaurants. Won't rent rooms or houses out to you."

"No dogs or Mexicans allowed," the old man responded. "That's what the signs will say." He coughed then spit into a rag stained with yellow spots.

"Say you're European," said the first man. "Most of them can't ever tell the difference."

"You're fair-skinned," responded the old man, placing the rag back in his pocket. "Hair's light enough. You'll pass. Look at me." He pointed a crooked finger at his face. "Me? I'm much too dark. Too indio." He chuckled. But Diego didn't want to have to lie about who he was, ever again. Still, what other choice did he have?

The plant was in a brick building on the American side of the bridge. Inside, the men were separated from the women, and they were led into a giant room with tiled floors and warm wooden walls. They lined up along the wall and were told to hold up their passports, which were inspected. They were then told to undress and to leave everything behind. They would then take their clothing to the laundry where they would be washed and disinfected. Naked, the men were taken into a cavernous room with large drums full of white powder. One by one, they were asked to step forward. Guards with masks over their faces scooped the powder out with small trowels and doused their bodies.

"Cover your mouth," shouted a guard to Diego when it was his turn. "Make sure not to breathe any of this in," he said. Another guard came around and ordered Diego to lift his arms, to turn around, to spread his legs. Diego closed his eyes and his mouth, yet the powder still burned his eyes and made him sneeze.

Then they were led down a long, narrow hallway into a room with wooden stalls along either side where inspectors waited. They looked inside his mouth and behind his ears, and they raked his hair with a metal wand while they asked him a series of questions:

How old are you?

Where are you going?

Have you ever had lice?

It was humiliating, and his clothes smelled awful, and the powder dusted his skin, and he coughed and coughed until his eyes watered, until his chest hurt. He sat, catching his breath, and waited, relieved to be through with it, grateful that he was no longer standing in a crowded room full of naked men. Once outside a guard told him where to find the train station.

Arriving now, he was informed that the train to Los Angeles would be arriving the next morning. He sat down, frustrated, tired, his skin dry and itchy, white powder still in his hair and eyelashes. What would he do? He rose and left the station and wandered around the city, down avenues lined with shoe stores, meat markets, and bars. Next to a small church, he came across a movie theater with a blinking marquee and a ticket booth. The movie playing was called *It*. The banner stretched over the theater's entrance featured the black silhouette of a curvy woman and, written in big, bold lettering, Diego read:

Clara Bow has IT. Come see if you've got IT too!

Betty Lou Spencer, played by Bow, is a beautiful and poor, yet spry, shop girl working at "Waltham's: The World's Largest Store." In the opening scene, Betty catches a glimpse of her new boss, Cyrus Waltham Jr., played by a Spanish actor named Antonio Moreno. Betty instantly falls in love with the handsome, sophisticated man. Unbeknownst to her, Cyrus is already romantically linked to blond socialite Adela Von Norman. Through cunning, wit, humor, and a healthy dose of "It," the spunky, poor shop girl manages to win over her wealthy boss and live a happy life. "IT," the film had explained, was "that quality possessed by some which draws all others by its magnetic force. With IT you win all men if you are a woman—all women if you are a man. IT can be a quality of the mind as well as a physical attraction."

Did he have "It," he wondered? Would he find "It" when he arrived in California?

He was forced to spend an uncomfortable night on a cold station bench, so when the train bound for Los Angeles arrived the next day and he boarded, he was relieved to be able to stretch out over his cushioned seat. Soon, he grew drowsy as he stared out the windows. On the north side, the new country passed before him—the wide deserts with their blooming wildflowers, the jagged peaks of the hills and mountains, the rolling sand dunes and the packs of roaming coyotes. Looking south, past a ring of low mountains, beyond a wide field, was Mexico. Everything was passing before him in quick, frantic explosions of light. That world, the one he'd known, was now composed of amorphous figures with no real definition or purpose, uncomplicated and simple. The houses and animals, the very trees and rocks and mountains flattened out, became one-dimensional, as if that whole country was one giant prop, a mere imitation, as if that soil and the people bound to it were made of cardboard, like dolls. He remembered the dead men hanging from the telegraph poles and the passengers on the other train, their hands punching the glass windows or swatting the flames that jumped up and licked their skin away. He imagined dead priests and nuns, the fragments of their bones and tissue seeping out of their skulls and mixing with the dirt and grass and wildflowers of that ancient and pastoral land. The rocking of the train and the sound the wheels made as they brushed over the metal ruts was bliss. It was the sound of erasure, he knew, of things disintegrating and decomposing, of things fading away and returning to the earth and all its elements.

ACT III

SCREENING
Hot Tamales (1941)
Director: Dalton Perry
Cast: Barbara Wells, Chester Hales, and Macy Duncan

This screwball comedy of mistaken identities and wacky hijinks stars Diego León as Gómez. Argentine film actress María Luisa Nava performs the role of both Jane Archer and Flor Fernandez. Features the famous pool scene fight between Jane and Flor.

SCREENING
Sequoyah's Talking Leaves (1947)
Director: Dalton Perry
Cast: Marie Howland, Morris Anderson, Lester Frank.

This 1947 biopic follows the life of Sequoyah, the sliver smith credited with inventing the Cherokee alphabet. Diego León is Sequoyah.

SCREENING
Double-Cross (1951)
Director: Nestor Gaynes
Cast: Camille La Fleur, Vic Vale, Glenda St. Gerard, and Tod Spencer

When Private Detective Sam Castle (Diego León) investigates the mystery surrounding the murder of an old college acquaintance, he encounters a series of strange clues, an elusive veiled woman, and his friend's involvement with German spies and the French Foreign Legion.

1

Los Angeles, California
March 1927

DIEGO FELT EMPTY on the day the train pulled into the station alongside a simple building made of wood and plaster in downtown Los Angeles. He had made it safely, his feet touching the fertile soil of the great wide West. That new city looked out across the ocean, hanging there like a trembling raindrop at the tip of a leaf, its face staring out to the edge of the world. The past, Mexico, the life he would have lived had Diego stayed—it all felt worlds away now. Was this what his father experienced when he left San Antonio for Morelia? Empty? Ready for something new to come and fill him up? Diego took a deep breath as he followed the rest of the passengers through the glass doors that led to the street.

There was all manner of commotion around the train station. Boys held newspapers up in the air, their voices shouting over the honks and roars of cars. People shoved past him, nearly knocking Diego down. There were sailors in black-and-white uniforms, street preachers shouting out from paper bullhorns, and prostitutes soliciting men on the corners across the street. Everywhere there was the stench of automobile exhaust and oil and dust. It was a big city with grids of wide avenues flanked with concrete buildings rising many stories high, expansive parks where pedestrians strolled under shaded walkways and paths, a ring of low hills in the distance dotted with houses perched on their steep cliffs. Far off, past the city grid, where the streets and avenues ended, was the ocean, the salt-scented air, the end of the earth.

"Just arrived?" a heavy man with big hands shouted at a girl in a pink dress and a cloche hat. "Need a place to stay?"

The girl said something then darted off, passing through a crowd where other men shouted at her.

"Looking to make it in pictures, honey?" one screamed.

"Sign up here for free screen tests!" cried another. "Free screen tests!"

"Clean beds and hot meals at the Rancho Hotel," shouted a skinny man in a green vest. "Close to all the studios."

Each girl that left the station was accosted, told about immediate screen tests and free rides to the homes of movie directors and producers. They all looked alike, all of them thin and dressed in plain skirts and blouses, wearing cheap furs dyed to look expensive, their hair neatly coiffed or marcelled, a quick and panicked feel to their steps.

"Clean rooms at the Ruby Rose. Close to MGM, Paramount, Pioneer, Frontier. Daily, weekly, and monthly rates at the Ruby Rose."

He remembered his school English lessons and the practicing he would do with Carolina during their rehearsals. "Excuse me?" Diego spoke slowly, tapping the man on the shoulder. "You have rooms?" he asked.

"Do *we* got *rooms*?" The man turned around. "Only the best and most comfortable rooms in all the city."

"I need one," Diego said. "I haven't got a lot of money."

"Don't you worry about that, son." He led him to a truck with wooden sideboards and a tattered front seat. "Get in," he said. "I'll take you there."

They drove down Broadway Avenue, lined with pawnshops and penny arcades, theaters and diners. There was noise, all manner of noise, and there were people everywhere. They passed a section where trucks with massive tires flattened out the land and hauled piles of dirt, and men in hardhats and overalls climbed like ants around and atop the great square base of a mammoth structure and up toward its metal skeleton. That would be the city hall, the driver explained. He eyed Diego curiously.

"Say," he said. "You foreign?"

"Excuse me?"

"I noticed your accent. You ain't Mexican, are you? Because if you are, the Ruby Rose won't rent to you."

He recalled the conversation he had with the men when they were on their way to the disinfection plant. He would have to lie again. "No," Diego said, remembering the lies his grandparents forced him to rehearse and memorize. "I'm French. I was born near Nice. My father was from—"

"I don't need your life story, kid," he said, interjecting. "As long as you ain't Mexican, it'll be fine."

Diego stared out the car window. He found, as they drove down the street, the sun shining through the cracks between buildings, a sense of newness, of opportunity, of rejuvenation that was palpable, as if one could simply reach out and grab this and hold it for some time. The driver, who introduced himself as Mel, pointed things out. The palm trees. The San Gabriel Mountains, and, he said, "It's a sight when they're covered in snow while, down here in the city, it's sunny and 76 degrees." He pointed out the citrus groves and oil derricks along Wilshire Boulevard, the steel pumps bobbing their heads up and down like a herd of magnificent beasts. "There was the beach," Mel said. The intricate and scenic highways threading throughout the Southland, perfect for long Sunday drives. There were the Big Red electric cars that would take you to the farmlands of San Fernando, the walnut groves in La Puente, the mission in San Gabriel. "There's a lot to do," Mel said. "You'll have fun. There's everything," he told him, "right here in Los Angeles. You won't ever want to leave." He told him that the majority of the tenants at the Ruby Rose were actors and actresses. "Hell," he said, chuckling. "There were even a few circus sideshow performers."

"Performers?" Diego asked.

"Sideshow freaks," he said. "You know?"

They worked around the studios, taking bit parts in films here and there whenever someone with special talents was needed, he told him. "So don't expect a warm welcome, sonny," Mel said. "That lot doesn't take kindly to outsiders."

He said they were a suspicious group, very guarded, not likely to open up much unless they got to know you. Two of the units were currently occupied with circus folks. There was Aldo the Strongman and his wife, Mary, the tattooed lady, and their daughter, Anabelle. The other unit was occupied by Kristof, the contortionist.

"Are you an actor too?" Diego asked.

"Me? Nah," he said. "I get a cut of the first month of rent for each person I bring in. It ain't much, but every little bit helps, you know?"

The boardinghouse was owned and operated by two sisters named Ruby and Rose. "Identical twins," Mel told Diego as they parked and got out of the car. "They were really big in the vaudeville circuit. 'The Dancing Deere Sisters' is what they was called."

They came out to Hollywood, determined to make it in films and instead ended up buying and running the boardinghouse. Quarreled over what to name the place and settled on the Ruby Rose. "'Course," Mel said, "Ruby's name came first on account of she was three minutes older than Rose."

Inside, the place was dark and shabby with imposing wood furniture, smudged plaster walls, and thick faded drapes. A thin old woman in a sequined outfit stood behind a large desk reading a newspaper.

"Hiya, Mel" she said, looking up. "How's tricks?"

Mel removed his hat and shook his head. "Hi. Ruby?"

"Rose," she snapped back, rolling up her newspaper and looking up at them. Her face was gaunt and tinged unnaturally yellow. Her eyelids were dusted bright white, her lips painted a vibrant red. She wore her hair pulled back in short pigtails. "Well, hello," Rose said, regarding Diego.

"Hello." He reached his hand out, and they shook.

"Friend here's looking for a room," said Mel.

"You're in luck," she said. "I got some empties." She leaned in and beckoned Diego to come closer. He stepped forward and she lowered her voice. "One next to me's free, handsome." She chuckled and slapped her knee. Rose wore thick stockings and shiny black tap shoes that clicked as she moved about.

"Rose," shouted a voice. "Quit harassing the clients." Ruby stepped out from behind a thin curtain draped across a doorway. She wore the same sequined outfit as her sister, the same color of makeup, and her hair in the same style. They looked so much alike it was unsettling and, as he watched them mill about, bickering with one another, the sight of the two of them made Diego uneasy.

"You okay?" the first twin asked.

"Yes," he said, hesitating before answering. "Just tired. Thank you. Rose?"

Rose jabbed her elbow into Mel's side. "Kid's here but fifteen minutes and he can tell who's who. You known us for fifteen years and *still* can't tell the difference."

"We'll get you settled," Ruby said, reaching for a key. "You just hang on."

Mel put his cap back on. "Good luck, kid." He turned and left.

"Where's your luggage, handsome?" asked Rose.

"Don't have any," Diego said.

"Take him to his room," said Ruby to her sister.

"Gladly." Rose grabbed him by the arm. "We're going to take these stairs," she said, her voice low and gentle. He followed her, the faint sound of her tapping leading the way.

A man in a dark jacket passed them as they climbed up. "Morning," he said, tipping his hat. "I'll have that money for you by the end of next week," he said to Rose.

"Fine by me," she answered. "But you gotta tell Ruby. She's in a foul mood today."

"Today?" He laughed. "Every day."

By the time they reached the top step, Rose's breathing was heavy and ragged. She was panting excessively, her yellow face now flushed.

"Are you okay?" Diego asked, gripping her wrist.

"I get my exercise this way," she said. "Just give me a moment, honey." After a few minutes, Ruby took a deep breath, stood, and squeezed Diego's arm. "Here we go, handsome."

She let go now, and he followed closely behind. They continued down a well-lit carpeted hallway whose walls were stained and dirty. At the very end, resting on top of a table was a telephone.

"That's our telephone," said Ruby. "Yes, sir. A brand-new desk set *telephone*. There's one on all our floors."

The doors to each unit were the same size, extending all the way from one end of the hall to the other so it looked like they were standing inside the mouth of some giant beast, rowed end to end with large brown teeth. Rose stopped at one door numbered 202.

There was a closet and a wooden armoire with drawers and a shelf inside. It was a drab room, drafty and uninviting. It was like living inside a sealed coffin, Diego thought. He shivered. The bed's mattress bounced, the metal coils groaning, when he reached down to press on it. The bathroom sink dripped a steady drop into the rusted drain, and the tiles were dirty, the grout cracked and flaking off. Diego lit a cigarette and sat in a lumpy upholstered chair pushed up against the wall.

"The Ruby Rose is a respectable establishment," Rose said. She placed the room key on the shelf inside the armoire. "No monkey business. You hear?"

"Yes," he said.

"Unless you and me are involved," Rose said, winking. She then turned and left, swaying her bony hips from side to side. She glanced back over her shoulder and batted her eyelashes. She blew a kiss at him then closed the door.

He put his cigarette out and sat there, his limbs heavy, his eyes unable to stay open. Diego considered the wallpaper, its scrolled pattern faded and flaking off, the mismatched furniture, the coarse coverlet and pillows. He took a deep breath, rose, and went into the bathroom. The handle was hard to turn, but the tub filled quickly with hot water once he managed to get it. He undid his tie and unbuttoned his shirt and sat on the bed watching steam float out and into the room.

He couldn't sleep and the next day, bright and early, Diego ventured out and ended up on Hollywood Boulevard. There was a great clamor as people walked along the sidewalks and the shops opened up their gates. Out of sheer obligation, he sent his grandparents a wire, letting them know that he was fine, that he was in Los Angeles. He gave them the address of the Ruby Rose and told them not to worry, to tell Paloma that he just needed some time away, that he would return and they would be married. Just in case, he told himself. In case things here don't work out.

He smelled coffee and bacon and followed the scent to a diner called Joe's. A sign that read, *Orientals and Mexicans Must Use Back Entrance* was posted near the front door. In all his talk about it being like paradise here, Reynolds never mentioned that Americans were just as hateful of Mexicans as his grandparents were of peasants. He took a deep breath and entered. A waitress in a white outfit and handkerchief folded neatly in her pocket seated him at the counter and took his order.

"Coffee," he told her.

"Just coffee?"

"Yes."

"You got it, doll."

A man about his age sat at the stool next to Diego, reading a newspaper and sipping coffee. When Diego reached into his pocket and lit a cigarette, the guy looked up.

"Got an extra?" His voice was high-pitched and sounded more like a squeal.

"Yes," he said. Diego gave him one, and the man lit it and tapped the edge against the rim of an ashtray.

When the man reached out to take it, he said, "Say. I know you."

"Oh?" Diego was surprised. "I'm sure you're confused. See, I just—"

"The Ruby Rose," he said. "Yesterday afternoon. On the stairs."

He remembered now. "Yes. Of course."

"Charlie," he said, extending his hand. "Charlie Applebaum."

"Diego." He took it and shook.

"Diego?" Charlie tapped his finger on the counter. "That Italian?"

"No."

"Spanish?" Charlie asked.

"Well, I'm French. My father was born—"

"I knew it," Charlie interjected. "You look Latin. That's all the rage at the studios." He laughed. "Too bad for me; my parents are Jews."

"Any luck today, Charlie?" the waitress asked, setting Diego's coffee in front of him.

Charlie puffed on his cigarette and shook his head. "No way. I tell ya, Jean, maybe I should just call it quits and move back home. Seems every day there are trains full of people like me pouring into Los Angeles looking to be picture stars."

"Don't give up," Jean said. "Ain't that right, doll?" She looked at Diego.

"Yes," he said. "You should absolutely not give up your dream."

"Thanks," Charlie said. He gathered his coat and hat and left. He forgot his paper, so Diego grabbed it, and walked out after him.

"Charlie," he said, tapping his shoulder.

"Yeah?" He turned around. He was short and his blond hair, the color of dry weeds, was thinning some. Charlie's eyes were wide, unblinking, and his stare was that of a person who had just been startled.

"Your paper," Diego said. "You left it inside." He recognized it: *Cast Call*. Somehow, a few copies had managed to make their way to newsstands around Morelia. He had brought an old issue with him, but it had burned in the fire.

"I don't need it," Charlie said, sighing, shaking his head. "Just throw it away, will ya?"

"Excuse me," Diego said just before he turned away, "you're an actor, right?"

He chuckled. "Why, sure."

"Been in anything I've seen?"

He then rattled off a list of movies Diego had never heard of. "But I'm still looking for that big break, you know?" Charlie pointed to the newspaper. "That would explain the *Cast Call*."

"Sure," Diego said.

"You're one too, ain't ya?" Charlie asked.

"Of course."

He laughed. "I knew it. I could tell. Well, good luck with the ads. There wasn't anything in there for me, but there might be something for someone like you." He stopped and stroked his chin. "You got a look," he said. "Very interesting."

"Thanks," Diego said.

"Anytime," he said, saluting as the light turned. He joined the crowd, and the mass of people crossed over to the raised concrete platform in the middle of the street where they waited for the trolley.

His money wasn't going to last forever, so Diego wouldn't be able to afford to buy new issues of *Cast Call*. Fortunately, he discovered a newsstand near the boardinghouse that was managed by an old man with a patch covering his left eye. He moved slowly, chatting with the men in suits who stopped by for the paper or a magazine, and Diego got good at quickly shoving copies of *Cast Call* down his trousers and strolling off without his noticing. He had spent two weeks thumbing through page after page of the paper, reading the calls for auditions, the calls for extras. The roles in question were usually billed "walk on part" or "people for a crowd scene," and they advertised very low pay.

By that time, all he had left was $30. The room was five dollars a week, so what remained would have to be stretched. He didn't buy food but instead picked oranges and grapefruits from trees whose branches hung over the edges of the sidewalks. He stole apples and bananas from fruit vendors on busy Sunday mornings as he wandered through the street stalls. At a drugstore, while the soda jerk was busy making orange phosphates and mixing tonics, Diego filled his pockets with candy mints and jelly drops from the large glass jars lining the counters. He picked an old woman's purse while she waited for the trolley at a stop, ran off with a bag of tobacco and papers from a vagrant stumbling out of a pool hall. He waited in the long lines at the soup kitchens, eating runny clam chowder out of tin cups in the large and drafty cafeterias with hundreds of men and women in frayed and tattered clothing, their faces smudged with dirt, their children skinny, their legs so thin he wondered how they were capable of sustaining their little bodies. This wasn't what he had imagined, but at least he was living his own life, not one dictated to him by someone else.

There were nights when the hunger was too much, too overpowering, and he would dress, walk up and down Hollywood Boulevard toward the restaurants where men in suits and women with fancy dresses and complexions smooth as porcelain dined. He watched them through the glass windows savoring their meals, sipping from large goblets. He caught the faint smell of food, and this made him salivate, made his head spin. He would have to force himself not to wander behind the alleys of the restaurants, not to pick through the large barrels of trash for scraps of food as he had watched others do. He had seen two men fighting over a bag of moldy bread, each of them shouting that they had a wife, kids, and that there was no work, nothing to eat. One of them pulled a knife out from his pocket, threatening the other, who tossed the bag on the floor and ran off, sobbing.

He bit his lip so hard it bled, and he no longer felt hungry. He took slow steps toward the large theater houses along the boulevard. In that daze brought on by hunger and fatigue and confusion, he looked up, saw his name there in large black letters, saw his picture on the lobby card sketches that faced the street. The hunger, he told himself, was part of the sacrifice. He walked with new vigor down Hollywood Boulevard, passing the diners and pool halls, the dress shops and shoe stores, swinging his arms, his stride long and assured. He straightened his hat, pushed his shoulders back, and pointed his chin down. He would see things differently the next day.

Arriving back at the Ruby Rose, he fumbled through the dark sitting room and collapsed on the bed, sweating, trembling, weak and defeated. It was easy to doubt, easy to toy with the idea of returning to Mexico. But how would he afford it? He was stranded here for now, but it was fine, he told himself. Besides, there was no way he was giving up. Not yet. He was thirsty for something cool, not the tepid water from the bathroom. He bit into a warm apple, felt the pulp run down to his chin, felt his stomach clench and then let go. It was his last, and the skin had already started to brown, just like the bananas. He finished the apple then sucked on the core and chewed on the seeds. There were three oranges left, nothing more. It wouldn't be enough. He closed his eyes and gripped his stomach, hoping for the sleep to come. Only this would relieve him. Only this.

Almost a month had passed. Diego made it through the days and nights, fending off the hunger, taking here and there, and reading his stolen copies of trade magazines, hoping something, anything, might catch his eye. An article in *Screenshots* talked about headshots, and Diego used what little money he had left to get some photos taken, which he carried around with him in a paper envelope. He was careful not to soil his clothing, draped his only shirt and pair of trousers on the chair every night and smoothed them with his hands each morning before putting them back on. He felt worn away from not eating right. His skin went pale, his vision blurred and grew fuzzy. He found a razor blade one afternoon while rummaging through a pile of trash behind a barbershop and had been using this to shave, but the blade was dulling and scratching and cutting him up. On the bathroom counter there were the peeled skins of oranges curling like large fingernails. At the sight of them, Diego's stomach turned and knotted. Their taste was no longer sweet but acrid, foul, deadening the sensation in his mouth. He had to save his money. But he just couldn't help it. He suddenly felt desperate for company, for something warm to put in his stomach. Diego searched through his pockets and found enough for a cup of coffee. He splashed cold water on his face, dressed quickly, and walked to Joe's.

He savored the coffee, taking small sips, closing his eyes each time he brought the cup to his nose. Jean laughed, said to a couple sitting near him at the counter, "Look at this guy. Like he's never seen coffee before."

"Maybe he's auditioning for a part," said the lady to the man.

"Don't be an idiot," the man told her.

"Well," she said, grabbing her coat, "I refuse to go back to Minnesota until I've seen at least one star."

"Oh, Helen," said the man, rising from his stool. He reached into his pocket and set some money down.

Jean was in the kitchen, arguing with the cook about a botched order. Diego could see the cook's red face, his fat fingers pointing accusingly at her. The other diners sat around either reading or talking. Nobody was looking. Diego reached across the counter, scooped up the money, and shoved it in his pocket.

"Well, how about that?" Jean said when she came back out, her hands her hips, shaking her head.

A man in a pair of dirty coveralls and a hat placed crookedly on his head looked up from his newspaper. "How about what?"

"Those two stiffed me," said Jean when she picked up the plates and cups and saucers the couple had left behind. "Damn tourists. City's getting overrun with their likes, flocking in to gawk at the stars. They get all the attention, and we get stiffed. Damn them all."

"Send the bill to DeMille," shouted a diner and laughed.

"Aw, horse feathers," said Jean. "Another cup?" she asked Diego.

"Why sure," he said, reaching into his pocket. He counted the money, looked over to a pastry case at the edge of the counter. Glazed donuts filled with cream and jam, slices of apple pie and chocolate cake on glass shelves twirled around inside. "And a donut. Cream filled," he said.

Jean brought it to him and poured Diego another cup of coffee. "You, I like," she said, setting the pot down. "You, I can tell, would never stiff a person. You got a heart. A big heart, son. Keep it that way."

He had been sitting there all morning, flirting with Jean, telling her just how much he liked her new hairdo, cracking jokes, making her laugh.

"42?" he asked, astonished, when she admitted her age. "I would have guessed 30."

"Oh, stop," she said, removing her thick bifocals and cleaning the lenses with the edge of her apron. "You're kind."

A diner paying his ticket looked at Diego and rolled his eyes.

"Get lost," he said to the man, remembering the expression when someone else used it that morning.

"Dirty foreign punk," the man muttered and stormed off.

She poured him cup after cup of coffee as long as he kept the compliments coming, as long as he engaged her in conversation. "You really got a way of making a girl feel special," Jean said to him. All the booths, their blue vinyl glossy and bright, were empty, their speckled Formica tops clean. Each salt and pepper shaker, each sugar jar and napkin dispenser, was full. It was just before noon, and Jean told him it always quieted down right around that time.

"Everyone's at work," she said.

Jean walked around the counter and took a seat on the stool beside Diego. She sighed loudly when she sat. He saw her pale legs, a series of thick green and blue veins threading like spiderwebs just beneath her skin. "Oh, Lord. I'm tired."

He sipped his coffee. "I bet."

She rubbed her temples then stopped and regarded him. "Child," she said. "You look terrible."

"What are you talking about?"

She reached a hand out, the skin around her fingernails rough and dry. Jean touched his forehead, his cheeks. "You're pale. Thin. You been eating all right?"

"Why sure." He chuckled. "I have."

"Hum," she said. "I raised eight children, all of them ungrateful savages, but I raised them. I know the look of hunger in a face." Jean rose, shouted to the cook, "Hey, Fred. Get your hide off that stool and make me a plate of eggs and bacon, will you?"

Fred muttered something, and soon Diego heard the sound of eggs frying, caught the familiar scent of bacon, of toast. The plate was big, the eggs fluffy and yellow, the bacon thick and salty. He devoured it, eating so fast he nearly choked a few times.

"Easy there," Jean said. "Easy." She stood behind the counter again, her arms crossed, a sweater draped over her shoulders. "Where'd you come from?" she asked.

He didn't want her to know. He continued eating, ignoring her question.

"Fine. You don't have to tell me." She reached for the pot of hot coffee and poured him more. "You got any money?"

"Some."

"A job?"

He shook his head.

She sighed. "You come empty-handed, right?"

"Yes," he said, finished up the last of the eggs.

"You expecting to live off of charity?"

"No," he said. "Certainly not."

She was quiet for a long time. "I might be able to help you."

"How so?"

Joe, the owner, had been thinking about hiring someone to come in every day to mop and clean up the place. It wouldn't be a lot, Jean said. But it would be something. "What do you say?" she asked. "I think it'd be perfect for someone like you. A lot of people would kill for anything these days. But I like you. I'm gonna give you the first crack at it."

His situation was bad, and it would only get worse if he ran out of money. It was this or he would have to wire his grandfather, ask him for money for a ticket back. *No*, he told himself. *Not that. Not yet.*

"Sure," he said to Jean. "Fine."

2

April–October 1927

HE WAS PAID IN TIPS. Measly tips. Chump change. If he was lucky, a crumpled dollar bill. Whatever Jean saw fit to give him. For this, he had to sweep and mop. He had to pour coffee and get shouted at by the diners. He was cursed at, ridiculed, never acknowledged, never looked in the eye. He cleaned up spilled milk and water. He gathered dirty dishes and washed them in the large sink in the back kitchen, the hot water scalding his skin, his face moist from the steam. The cooks made fun of him, and there were days when Jean came to work in a foul mood and hardly spoke to Diego, never called him sweetie or honey or doll the way she did to the diners, the way she used to with him. Over one month with the job, and Diego was starting to feel it affect him. Though he was grateful for Jean, for the opportunity to make some money, for her feeding him when he complained about being hungry, he was always tired now, frustrated, and the pay was very little.

"Could be worse," Jean said on one of her good days, laughing, as she carried out plates of eggs and pancakes, and ham and cheese sandwiches. "Never forget that. Could be a hell of a lot worse, kid."

Diego sighed, took his broom handle, and continued sweeping. "I guess you're right."

"It ain't that bad, angel," Jean said, pushing the swivel door open with her hip. "Trust Jean."

Rose flirted with Diego whenever she saw him. Once, when he bent down to pick up a handkerchief she had dropped, she pinched his behind. Rose was always charming and warm to him and most of the other clients. Ruby, however, was usually in a bad mood. Where Rose greeted him with a smile and a compliment, Ruby was reticent. She never seemed to smile. The afternoon he received the telegram, Ruby greeted him without looking up to Diego.

"Good afternoon, Ruby," he said.

"Afternoon." She sat on a wooden stool behind the front desk, smoking a cigarette and jotting down figures in a leather-bound book. She reached for the slots behind her, found 202, and plucked a yellow telegram envelope out. "This came for you." She slid it across the desk to him.

He took it, then regarded her. He watched as she added more numbers to a long column, a lit cigarette dangling from her lips.

"Are you all right?" he asked

She shrugged her shoulders. "I'm fine." She looked exhausted.

Back in his room, he removed his apron, smeared with grease, and threw it on the floor. He knew the telegram could only be from his grandparents. He took a deep breath, opened it, and read:

YOUR GRANDFATHER IS SICK WITH WORRY. ALL THIS HAS BEEN A STRAIN ON HIS HEART. HE'S SLOWING DOWN AT WORK. PALOMA IS DEVASTATED. WHEN ARE YOU RETURNING?

YOUR GRANDMOTHER

That night he tossed and turned in his bed, unable to sleep, his grandmother's words seared into the backs of his eyelids. He tried to push the guilt aside as he thought about his grandfather, who, despite everything, had given Diego so much. How could he return now, though? He didn't want them to know he had little money; they would likely offer to wire him some or to pay for his ticket back. *No, they couldn't find out.* He rose early the next morning and went down to the Western Union office on Hollywood Boulevard. He wrote:

GRANDMOTHER

SORRY TO HEAR ABOUT GRANDFATHER. WILL RETURN AS SOON AS I CAN.

DIEGO

In Hollywood, average people were transformed into movie stars overnight. They were discovered on trains pulling in from Omaha, Tulsa, Billings. They were discovered painting houses, playing tennis, sunning on the beach, pumping gas, on walks, sitting on bus benches, at intersections, and even waiting tables. He wondered about this as he watched the men in suits and ties parade in and out of the diner. Were there directors and producers among them? Would he be discovered there? He imagined being interviewed, telling the reporter that yes, he had indeed been found at Joe's, mopping floors, washing dirty dishes, running around with a coffeepot, filling cups, working for a few tips when there he was, the director who saw "star quality" in him and discovered Diego León. Can you imagine it?

He was nice to any man in a tie, just in case. Diego poured the coffee slowly, engaged them in idle chitchat. How about the weather, huh? How's the family? You should try the special today. He made sure to smile a lot, to look them in the eye when he spoke, to always be kind and courteous no matter how rude they were.

"What's gotten into you?" Jean said to Diego one day, a hand on her hip. "You stand around talking to everyone like you're the mayor or something."

He shrugged his shoulders. "I just feel like talking. That's all."

"Well, take the molasses out of your ass and get going," she said, snapping her fingers. "Pronto!" She pointed with a dripping rag across the diner to a table. "Clean up table eight before the lunch crowd comes."

He loaded the tray and scooped up the remainder of the tip she had left for him.

He saved it all. Little by little. After paying rent and buying a few necessities, there wasn't much left. *Maybe coming was a mistake,* he thought. If he went back, would they forgive him? Would they take him in again? And what about Paloma?

"You look like you lost a friend," Charlie told him that morning. He sat at the counter sipping black coffee. It was still too early, so the diner was empty. It was one of those rare days in the city when the sky was gray and overcast. Outside, a thin fog clung to the trolley car wires and veiled the trees and grass.

Diego sighed and leaned on the counter, his elbows resting on the Formica. "I shouldn't have come. I was dumb to think I could break into films. A few months ago I arrived, and I'm still here, still just mopping floors. Boy, was I stupid."

Charlie took a sip of his coffee and shook his head. "Not stupid. A bit naïve, maybe. Like all of us. But not stupid."

"What do you mean?" Diego asked. He removed his elbows from the counter, straightened his back, and folded his arms.

"Well, where most go wrong isn't in coming here. It's in not educating themselves about the way the show's run." He pointed to his temple. "It's all about having the smarts. About knowing what to do once you're here. How to see and be seen." The first thing Charlie said he had to do was to go down and register with Central Casting.

"Come again?" Diego asked.

"Register," Charlie said.

"Register?"

"Yeah," he said, taking a sip of coffee. "That's where you gotta start."

All the big studios hired extras through Central Casting, Charlie said.

"Go on," Diego urged. How could he have not known this before? In all his reading, Diego had never heard anything about Central Casting. How could he have missed it?

He said, "Each studio hires through the office. You walk in there, and they have you fill out forms, have you tell them your height, your weight, just all the basic stuff. You give them a photo, and they give you a number to call if you wanna check in and see if there's anything." He talked about a large switchboard with lights that blinked off and on, manned by operators whose only job it was to answer. " 'Try again,'" he explained. "That's what they say. Over and over. 'Try again.' 'Try again.'"

"And what if you get something?"

"Jackpot!" Charlie shouted. "Operator tells you to report to a certain studio stage at a certain time."

"What if there's nothing?" Diego asked.

"Then it's back to the same old thing," Charlie said, pointing to Diego's mop. "But every now and again you'll get lucky. Get called out of the blue if you're what a casting director needs and such. They'll tell you where to be and you go."

It's the only way to do it, Charlie explained. You register with Central Casting. Then you call, you hope and pray. If your number doesn't come, you try again the next day, or the next, or the next. In the meantime, Charlie said, you read *Cast Call*. You look for open calls for auditions. You try out for everything no matter how serious or outlandish, how vague or how specific. You call, you hope, you audition, he said. Over and over.

"Wow," Diego said. "You sure know a thing or two about this game."

"I do," he said. "Did my time. Hoped to make it into films, but at this point I don't think it's going to happen. I'm still looking, though. For a chance to work somehow in the business." Charlie looked at Diego. "You look a bit bewildered, kid. Why don't I give you a hand?"

"How?" Diego asked.

"Tell you what," he said. "I'll take you down to the Central Casting office. It's a zoo, but I think I can get you through the front door. The gals down there know me very well."

"You'd really do that for me?" Diego asked.

"Why sure. Afterward, I can take you to Frontier Pictures. I can get us through the front gate on account of I worked there designing props. I can show you how the operation works. All that. What do you say, pal?"

"That would be swell," Diego told him

They shook hands just as the sun was breaking through the fog outside.

The next morning, he and Charlie took a taxi up Vermont, past Santa Monica, Fountain, and Sunset, where they were dropped off because Charlie said he felt like walking the rest of the way. On Hollywood Boulevard, they waited on the trolley platform for the next train. Charlie was an odd fellow, Diego thought, the kind of guy who went through life as though absolutely nothing bothered him or spoiled his mood. He seemed to possess the mind and sensibilities of a child, struck and awed by the simplest things, chipper all the time. Still, he didn't mind Charlie. It was nice to have a friend.

On the way, Charlie talked endlessly about his first year in the city. He'd been a sick boy, and an isolated dairy farm in Wisconsin wasn't exactly the best place for an introverted, awkward child prone to illnesses and bouts of nervous attacks. After high school, he completed college with a degree in art and painting. His parents wanted Charlie to seek out new adventures, and the boy was eager to get out and see the world. The mysterious illnesses continued to plague him, and his physician, along with his mother and father, urged Charlie to consider moving to California, just for a little while.

"'Course I was thrilled," Charlie said, over the ding of the trolley car and the honks of car horns and trucks as they traveled west on Hollywood Boulevard. "New situations, new people, that gets me excited, makes me feel alive."

He told Diego that he had lived at the Ruby Rose for several years now. Many people had come and gone, he told him, so it was hard to keep track of who was who and it was hard establishing lasting friendships. But the place, he said, was swell, real swell. Charlie kept on talking—there wasn't even an opportunity for Diego to interject, so he just sat back and listened. He told Diego how one of his professors in Wisconsin had a friend who painted sets for movies out here in Hollywood, how he was put in touch with this man named Heiny, and ain't that a kicker of a name? "I bet his wife's name is Fanny," Charlie said, slapping his knee. He spent time with this Heiny fellow, painting sets in a small back office, away from all the hustle and bustle of the studios. He was let go when the studio had some financial troubles.

"So that's when I decided to become an actor," he said. "But, aside from a few gigs, I haven't made much progress in all this time. I take jobs here and there, survive by doing a little bit of everything." When the trolley reached their stop, Charlie said to him, "Here we are. Central Casting."

The Central Casting offices were in a large building on the corner of Hollywood Boulevard and Western Avenue. Inside the crammed lobby, they found a long line of people standing along the walls. A woman in a suit went around jotting names down on a piece of paper.

"Hiya, Birdie," Charlie said.

"Hi, Charlie." The woman stopped, looked up, and regarded Diego. "What's new?"

"Aw, not a whole lot." Charlie put his hand on Diego's shoulder. "My friend here wants to register. I know it's first come, first serve and all but—"

"Sure," Birdie said, waving her hand. "Let's sneak you on in."

"Hello, Birdie." Diego removed his hat and reached his hand out. He knew he had to get on her good side. When she took his hand, he leaned in and kissed hers.

"Oh my," Birdie said. "But you are a charmer, ain't ya?"

"Hey, wait a minute," said an overweight lady holding a small dog on a leash. "Me and Adore been waiting here all morning. You can't just . . ."

Birdie ignored her, though. She led them behind a counter, through a set of double doors, and into a vast room with many windows. Diego saw row after row of desks. At each one sat a secretary, a typewriter before her.

"Tell them Birdie sent you," she said.

"Thanks," Charlie told her. He looked at Diego. "First chair beside a desk you see empty, go to it."

A woman wearing horn-rimmed glasses fastened around her neck with a silver chain and a plain white blouse sat behind her desk pecking at the keys of a typewriter.

"Name?" she asked.

He gave it to her.

She filled out the information on the index cards, the typewriter's keys clicking and snapping as she hit them. "Very well," she said. "Address?"

He gave her his new address.

"Height?"

Six foot one inch."

"Weight?"

"170 pounds," he responded. "Hair color?"

"Brown," he responded.

She looked up, squinted behind the thick lenses of her glasses.

"*Light* brown's more like it."

"Very well," he replied. "Light brown it is."

"Eyes?"

"Brown," he responded.

"Experience acting?"

He hesitated, thought about making something up, but decided against it. "None."

She shook her head. "If I put that down you might as well forget about ever getting called in." She glanced quickly over her shoulder. "I'll just put here that you've done some theater work." She removed her glasses and tapped her fingernail against the desk's wooden surface. After a while she lifted her hands, fingers hovering over the typewriter's keys, and filled the rest out. "There!" she said, an air of relief in her voice. "Hopefully that'll get you something." She removed the typed card and had him look it over.

"Thank you," he told her.

"There's no guarantee, of course," she said. "But at least this way you'll look more attractive to the studios. Word of advice, kid?" She put her glasses back on.

"Sure. Yes."

"Don't be so honest. In this town, people get rich by fibbing and go nowhere fast when they tell the truth."

"I'll remember that."

She took the application containing his information and his picture and added it to a stack next to her phone, then, on a slip of paper, wrote a number down. "Call this number whenever you want to check and see if there's work."

"Very well," he said. He took the slip and placed it in his pocket.

Beyond a set of wooden doors there was a hallway, and through a set of windows he saw a long table where several women worked a giant console. This was the switchboard Charlie had talked about.

Lights blinked off and on, and each operator wore a headset covering only the left ear. A microphone speaker extended out from the side and wrapped around, coming to rest a few inches away from their mouths. A thick black coil reached out from the headset. This had a plug at its end, and the operators jabbed this into the various holes of the console when a light blinked on. They murmured on and on, incessantly, "Try again," or "Not today." It was monotonous and repetitive, like a chant, and he stepped away from the glass. All those lights were people, he knew, just like him, desperate for work, hungry for a job, with aspirations and hopes. What would set him apart from all of them?

Gates marked the entrance to Frontier Pictures. From a little booth, a guard watched the comings and goings of everyone who entered or exited.

"Good morning, Sam," Charlie shouted as they approached.

The guard smiled and held his hand up. He nodded at Diego.

"Friend of mine here's new to the film business," Charlie said. "Thought I might show him around."

The guard chuckled. "Have fun."

"Thanks, Sam," Charlie shouted. "I'll see you on the way out."

"Not if I'm dead you won't," he responded and laughed so hard at his own joke that it made him cough and cough.

Charlie led him through the studio lots, weaving between tall soundstages and hand-painted backdrops of a sky, the Grand Canyon, an armada of Spanish galleons sailing across the ocean. There was all manner of activity around the huge lot. Men in overalls and heavy boots lugged equipment back and forth between the gaping mouths of the enormous soundstages, their numbers painted thick and black on the sides and doors. There were floodlights and cameras, coils and heavy metal cases with snaps and buckles. Still others moved stage props—foam chunks of blue ice, cacti, fake boulders and palm trees and birds of paradise. They looked so lifelike, so utterly real, that Diego was amazed.

"Those must be for some film set in the South Pacific," Charlie said. "Big-budget number. Frontier's putting a lot of money behind that one. I heard Levitt's looking over that one himself."

"R. J. Levitt, you mean?" he asked.

"The very one."

Diego had read all about R. J. Levitt in the trade magazines. Levitt had made his fortune selling photo cameras around the turn of the century. He was so successful that he moved out west to stake his claim in California. He bought a plot of land—nothing back then, just several acres on Gower—hired himself a fleet of horses and some two-bit stage actors and former vaudevillians, and started filming them riding around the Hollywood Hills, pretending to shoot at Indians and bandits. The silent films were short at first, with no real script or direction, but they eventually grew into larger and larger productions featuring lavish costumes and exotic location shoots, hundreds of extras, and action and adventure. Soon they started playing in the theaters that were springing up around the country. Before anybody knew it, Levitt was at the forefront of the filmmaking revolution that was about to take over the world. His quiet project grew exponentially until he had a troupe of several hundred actors, cameramen, wardrobe, and costume crews. Elaborate sets were built—ancient Egypt, Rome, China—each more spectacular than the previous. The productions became more and more sophisticated and impressive, and people loved it. R. J. Levitt came to define the filmmaking industry and was its first success story. He was said to be ruthless, brutal, crushing any opponents or foe, but Diego admired him anyway. He had the power to make or break a career; if you betrayed him, it was the end. Diego read once in a celebrity magazine that an actor had a falling-out with Levitt over a contract dispute. As a result, the actor's ties to Levitt and Frontier were severed, and Levitt went as far as to have stories fed to the press about this actor's extramarital affairs. But Diego also heard there was a soft spot underneath the tough veneer. Levitt had a brother who died of influenza, and he cared for his invalid mother after their father abandoned the family, leaving them in abject poverty.

"Have you met him?" Diego asked Charlie. They now stood in a great central square surrounded by buildings and a water tower perched on wooden stilts.

"Who?"

"Levitt."

He laughed. "Oh, no. Mimi Mills. Lester Frank. Those big-time Frontier actors are the ones who've met him. Do I look like Mimi Mills?" Charlie pointed to an imposing twelve-story building. It was a dreary and cold structure the color of smoke. "See that?" He pointed to the very top, to a set of windows gleaming bright and white in the morning sun. "That's where R. J. works. From there he looks down on all of us. We must be like ants to him, scurrying here and there, carrying loads of stuff on our backs."

Behind the soundstages, mammoth scaffolds and the facades of churches and buildings rose so that the whole sky was a jumbled mixture of architecture spanning thousands of years of human history. Egyptian pyramids, Greek temples, Sumerian ziggurats, Buddhist shrines, office buildings, and grass huts smashed and collided into one another. It was timeless there, no real past, no real future.

After a while, Charlie said, "Well, let's move on."

But Diego wanted to stay there, in that magnificent studio lot where French cancan dancers walked alongside nurses, where police officers mingled with criminals, where barons in fancy top hats and tuxedos shared cigarettes with homeless men in rags. It was all absurd and funny and dizzying. And yet he felt at home there, among the costumes and extravagance, among the chaos and commotion. This was where he wanted to be, where he *needed* to be.

At Joe's, Charlie sat next to him, a toothpick in his mouth, scanning the ads for audition calls. When he came across one he liked, he whistled and said, "Yes, indeed." Meanwhile, Jean was arguing with a customer who was accusing her of overcharging him. The man wore a coat, the elbows worn, and trousers too short for him.

"That's not what the menu says," he said to Jean, who stood near the front door, one hand on her hip. "Rat finks is what you guys are."

"Harry, go or I'm calling the police," Jean said.

"Aw," said the man. "Keep the lousy nickel. You'll never see good old Harry in this establishment again."

"Then adiós," said Jean.

"Adiós indeed," said Harry, then stormed out.

Diego couldn't remember the last time he'd heard anyone speak in Spanish. The word sounded so far away to him, so unrecognizable, that he felt as if he could no longer pronounce any of it if he had to.

"Adiós," he said in a low voice.

"Yeah," Jean said, coming around the counter. "Can you believe that guy?"

It wasn't his time to leave, he thought, wasn't his time to say adiós to all of this and board a train back for Mexico. He had to give it time. And he had a friend to help him now. He looked over at Charlie, his eyes squinting over the small print of the ads, circling things with a pencil.

"Nothing for the likes of you, buddy," he said, putting the ads down. "I'm sorry to tell you."

Diego picked it up and looked for himself, just to be sure. There were ads calling for "leggy beauties with dancing experience," "children six to eight months of age for a baby food advertisement," and "blond-haired gents with broad physiques and acting experience who aren't afraid of danger."

Diego tossed the magazine aside.

"Cheer up, pal," Charlie said. "Your ship's bound to come in. One way or another."

3

DIEGO HAD SPENT MONTHS this way. He worked at the diner and called the Central Casting office each day. Clearly it wasn't working, so as 1928 began, Diego decided to add a tactic to his strategy. He would go on open calls whenever he had free time.

One day, before taking the trolley, he stopped by the Western Union office on Sunset and wired his grandparents a message:

WORKING NOW. MAKING MONEY. WILL RETURN SOON. I PROMISE.

DIEGO

His first year in Los Angeles was quickly coming to a close, and he still wasn't sure what he would do. There wasn't enough money for a return ticket, though, so Diego figured the best thing for now was to remain, to continue along just as he had. He caught the trolley a few blocks away and watched it inch down the street, gliding over the metal rails that shone in the strong morning sun. Several stops later, he exited.

The open call was being conducted in a small office above a shoe store, and after walking a few blocks down the boulevard, darting past honking cars and lumbering buses, he found the place and climbed a set of dark and narrow steps up to a door and entered. The room was crowded with men and women, some pacing back and forth, others sitting down in one of many chairs pushed up against the wall, reading the newspaper or glancing around impatiently. Diego was uneasy, but he tried his best to hide it—he knew it was important to exude confidence.

"You there," said a short lady wearing too much perfume and rouge. "You." She had on a polka-dotted blouse with a plunging neckline and billowing sleeves. "Are you here to audition?"

"Yes."

"What part?" the lady said.

"Waiter," he told her.

"Okay then," said the lady. "Take a seat with that crowd over there." She clapped her hands loudly then pointed to a handful of men clustered in one corner of the stuffy room. Soon, a skinny man with a sallow complexion and a scarf tied around his neck came out from behind a set of curtains.

"Very well," he said. "Gentlemen, gentlemen. We will march you in shoulder to shoulder so that the casting director can take a look at you." He lined them up and led them through the curtains and into a large room with mirrored walls and hardwood floors that gleamed and creaked as they walked across. "Shoulder to shoulder," the thin man shouted, and they lined up against the wall. The casting director stood behind a large table, writing something down. The thin man walked over to him and whispered in his ear.

"Let's get going then," the man said as he rose. He scrutinized each of them, sometimes muttering to himself, other times shouting loudly. "This one here," he said, turning to the thin man who walked a few paces behind him. "He's much too portly."

"Yes," said the thin man. "Portly."

The casting director made his way down slowly, stopping from time to time to sigh and shake his head. "These are all wrong," he said. "They look much too naïve, much too . . . too startled."

He continued nonetheless, moving down the line, slowly, until he came to Diego. "Too tall," he said.

"Too tall," repeated the thin man.

"These are all wrong," said the director again. "All terribly wrong."

"But there's gotta be one, two—"

"Very well," said the director. "We'll test 12. The first 12."

"Twelve?" the thin man asked.

"Twelve!" the casting director shouted. He walked over to the end of the line and counted, "One, two, three, four, five, six, seven, eight, nine, ten, 11, 12."

"Yes, well then," said the thin man. "The rest of you are all free to go." He waved his arms.

The assistant had stopped at Diego. He was number thirteen. He had been that close. Number thirteen.

At the next open call, the spots had already been filled by the time he arrived. At another, he was required to dance for a big number set in a fancy ballroom. Diego knew this was his opportunity—he knew he was a great dancer. He was nervous though and tripped a few times before the head of casting stopped the music and said, "Sorry, kid. It's not working."

"Let me give it another shot," Diego pleaded. "I need a partner," he said, lying, stalling. "I dance better with a partner."

The director sighed. "Lucille?" he said to a woman. "What do you think of this one here?"

Lucille walked over. She put her hands on her hip, leaned in so close that Diego caught the faint scent of coffee on her breath.

The director scratched his head. "Could you be his dance partner? I'm not asking you to kiss him."

"Sure," she said, removing her sweater and placing her forms down on the table. "I'd love to dance."

Diego rolled up the sleeves of his dress shirt, took Lucille, and led her in a waltz, humming in her ear. If he charmed her enough, maybe there was a chance. She giggled, threw her head back, and closed her eyes. He felt the wind rushing through his hair, felt it whistling in his ears, as he moved elegantly across the floor. This, he thought, would surely convince them. When the music stopped, he let go of Lucille, who fixed her hair, and said, "Oh my goodness. What a divine dancer you are."

"Why, thank you," Diego said, smiling.

"But you're still wrong for the part," the casting director said.

"What do you mean?" he asked.

"Just what the man said," Lucille told him.

"But why? Surely I meet your requirements," he said, not fully knowing what they were.

The director sighed, folded his arms. "Just look at you." He stepped forward, grabbed Diego gently by the shoulders, and walked him over to the mirrored wall. He stared at his reflection— his hair, his olive skin, his dark eyes. Diego stood straight, pushed his shoulders back, and took a deep breath.

"What's wrong with me?" he asked. "I tell you, what's wrong?"

"Son," the man finally said, letting go of his shoulder. "You're much too ethnic looking. This part is for an American soldier. American," he repeated. "Not Italian or Gypsy." He scratched his head again. "I'm sorry, kid. You're great. Handsome in that exotic way. A wonderful dancer. But you're not what we're looking for. Not right now. You don't have it. Not for us."

It was the same thing at the next open audition. And the next one. He was exhausted, angry, and impatient. He remained quiet on the trolley ride back, fiddling with the loose change in the pockets of his trousers, the last of the money he had. A man in a suit and black spats covering his shoes looked at him a few times and rolled his eyes. After a while, he rose and took a spot toward the rear of the car.

Diego tried to get his mind off things. He focused on the moving trolley, the clumsy jolting forward as they inched up Santa Monica. At the next stop, Diego rose and got off. Out on the sidewalk, he lit a cigarette and sat down on a stone bench. While he smoked, he watched an ice vendor haul heavy dripping blocks back and forth, between his truck and a cluster of small bungalows farther down the street. A woman in curlers and a housecoat steadied a baby on her hip and chatted loudly with him as he worked. He could just turn around and forget about it, he thought. Go back to Mexico and stay there. This time for good. He felt broken, defeated, foolish.

Across the street there was a small church with a cross that was made of lightbulbs that blinked over the front door. He thought about going in, praying to God to give him a sign, to help him figure out what he should do. Then, little by little, people began filing in. He watched them now, the faithful, the believers. He felt envious. At least they belonged to something. But there was nothing, no place for him.

4

October 1928

IT WAS THE TIME when the monarch butterflies, which migrate down from Canada and the United States, returned to Mexico to spend the winters under the lush and temperate canopies of tall trees in the hills and valleys of Michoacán. It was also the time of the year when the dead returned to the earth from the afterlife. The city of Morelia would no doubt be making preparations for the Day of the Dead festivals, Diego thought. The bakers would be making pan de muerto, tracing into the loaves of warm bread designs meant to resemble crosses or doves or human bones. Vendors would set up makeshift stands along the streets to sell sugar skulls, their faces and foreheads decorated with brightly colored intricate scrolls. Campesinos would come from the hills, carrying bundles of red and yellow marigolds that they called *cempazúchil* on their backs. Elva once told him the P'urhépecha referred to them as the "flowers of the dead" because their color helped guide the spirits of the deceased back to the altars their families erected for them, adorned with food and alcohol and candles. It was Elva who taught him not to fear death, not to fear the spirits that returned each year.

It seemed only fitting that the news reached him then, during that time of migration and return, that time when the air is heavy with spirits and echoes. He was in the courtyard of the Ruby Rose, sketching clouds in the sky with a thick charcoal pencil—remembering their name in P'urhépecha, *janikua*—when a Western Union messenger approached and handed Diego the telegram.

It was from his grandmother. He signed for it, and the messenger bid him good day before turning to leave. No doubt it would be another plea for him to return. But, no it wasn't. His father, she wrote, was dead. Her message was brief. He glanced at it, catching only a few words and phrases as he felt the blood rush to his face. An old woman had appeared at the door with a man who identified himself as Luis Vara. Gabriel León, she wrote, his father, was dead. He had shot himself with a gun.

The "old woman." Had it been Elva? Was she still alive? He whispered her name a few times as he held the telegram. Elva, he said. Elva. *Tsánda. Janikua. Anhatapu.* He conjured up an image of her, a scent, or a sound, something to remind him of her, of her presence in his life. He tried remembering his father's face, but all he remembered was his scar, the one he came with after fleeing the revolution. Diego rose now, and the notepad and pencil fell from his lap and onto the floor of the courtyard. He had to go. He had to find a church.

Ruby, who was manning the front desk, told him to go to Saint Luke's. "You all right, son?"

"Yes," he responded. "Thank you, Ruby."

The walk to the church felt long, his footsteps heavy, agonizing. He tried imagining his father's last hour, the look of terror he must have worn on his face in that final moment, the sharp metal point of the gun pressed to his head. What must have gone through his mind? Why did he end his life? Maybe it was a lie, a ploy by his grandparents to get him to return. Had the old woman indeed been Elva? But she didn't know where his grandparents lived in Morelia. Maybe Luis Vara did, after all he was his father's close friend.

By the time he reached Saint Luke's, he felt exhausted, confused. He sat in one of the pews near the front. This church was different from the churches in Mexico. There were no lit candles, and the statues stood in alcoves and niches carved into the concrete walls, not high up on pedestals. It was completely empty. He was startled by the sound of fluttering wings. High up in the rafters and trusses of the church were two pigeons that had drifted inside through the open doors. They hopped around, their short necks bobbing forward and backward, their claws bright pink. He sat back in the pew, the polished hardwood smooth against the fabric of his trousers. The pigeons had settled now, and the faint sound of cooing drifted down from the rafters, the harmony mixing with the gong of the church bells and the rush of cars farther in the distance. He closed his eyes, breathing in and out, and imagined himself back there, in Mexico.

What he understood was that he was now alone. Diego could feel it. He needed no further proof. He knew that he was the last of the Leóns, the last of his kind.

Early morning, he dressed for work. His grandmother's telegram lay on the table near the window, the edges frayed and tattered. His stomach turned upon seeing it. He grabbed his coat and hat and left for Joe's. Downstairs, he stopped at the front desk and put his cigarette out in an ashtray. A few feet away, sitting atop the counter was a new Bakelite telephone. One of the twins came out from behind the curtained door. He knew it was Rose when, upon seeing Diego there, she smiled, her bright white teeth shining full in the light.

"My sister says you seemed rattled the other day," she said, reaching out to take his hand. "You all right, honey?"

"I'm fine." He sighed. "How are you?"

She squeezed his hand and petted his palm. "I'm all right," she said, taking a deep breath. She covered her mouth with a handkerchief and coughed. "Damned cold."

"It's not serious?" he asked, lighting another cigarette. He offered her one, and she nearly snatched it from his hand. Diego lit it for her and reached for the ashtray.

She wore a pair of long silk gloves that were bright orange and waved her hand. "A pesky old cough. And I get a little winded climbing up and down those blasted stairs. 'Course, Ruby worries. Just like our ma, she is."

"That's nice of her," Diego said.

"She's a real doll," said Rose. "I know she spends all her time going about this place like a real sourpuss. But it's all an act."

"Still," Diego told her. "I want you taking good care of yourself."

"Oh, you," she said. "Look at me. I'm blushing. Like a little girl." Rose finished her cigarette and walked into the back just as a teakettle whistled. "Doctor gave me an herbal infusion. Told me to drink it each morning. 'Course, it's better with a little brandy." The phone began to ring, and she shouted at Diego to answer it.

Diego placed his cigarette in the ashtray and picked up the telephone. "Yes?"

"Central Casting calling for a Mister Charlie Applebaum," said a lady's voice.

"Yes?" he repeated.

"Mister Applebaum, please."

"Yes?" he said again.

"Charlie Applebaum?" There was a pause.

He remained quiet.

"You there? Charlie Applebaum?" asked the lady again.

He took a deep breath, concentrating on the sound of Charlie's voice. "Yes. It's me. Charlie. How ya doing, doll?" Diego began to perspire. He took another deep breath. Rose was still in the back. He could hear her whistling, shuffling about as she prepared her tea.

"Report to Frontier Pictures," said the lady.

"Swell," he said. "That's just swell."

"Studio 12."

"Swell," he repeated.

"Today at 11 a.m. They need a Jew. Can you make it?"

He reached for a slip of paper and a wooden pencil and marked the information down. "Great," he said. "I'll be there." He hung up without saying good-bye. Diego placed the phone back down, the slip of paper clenched in his fist. Rose came out holding two hot cups of tea in each hand.

"Anything important?" she asked.

"Sorry, doll, but I have to run." He took his pocket watch out and glanced at the time. 10:15. He could make it.

"What a pity," said Rose. "I have brandy."

The lady at Studio 12 held a stack of wrinkled forms in her hand, scratched her scalp with the tip of a pencil, and arched her thin eyebrow.

"*You* are *not* Charlie Applebaum."

Diego cleared his throat, and fiddled with the buttons of his jacket. Inside, Studio 12 was a mammoth structure so vast and high that he felt infinitesimally small. The tall ceiling was filled with lights and scaffolds that crisscrossed along the length and sides of the massive building. Cameras were positioned, men in overalls used ropes and pulleys to heave a massive stone wall upright. The set was a village square with a fountain in the middle of a courtyard. The fake buildings had heavy wooden doors and windows with brightly colored shutters. There were artificial shrubs and trees, and large fans with metal crescent-shaped blades created a breeze that ruffled the branches and stirred the fake weeds breaking through the cobblestone steps. Women in plain yellow dresses with aprons tied around their waists and men in suspenders and wool caps stood near wooden carts filled with foam loaves of bread or bouquets of artificial flowers.

"'Course I am," Diego said. He continued fiddling with the buttons on his jacket. His hands trembled.

"You're not. I know Charlie Applebaum, and you ain't him, doll," the lady said, her hands on her hips. "You better get outta here before I—"

"Trudy!" a man with a loud voice interjected, startling the woman. He walked over. "Please tell me this is our Jew!"

"But, sir—" Trudy started to say when the large man interrupted her again.

"Thank God you're here," he said to Diego. "What took you so long? We've been waiting all morning. We need a Jew." He turned to Trudy. "I suggest you get him to the costume trailer immediately, Trudy. Time is money. Time is money." He clapped his hands loudly, the sound echoing throughout the entire studio.

"You heard the man," Trudy said, pointing toward a small trailer at the far end of the studio.

Diego stood there, looking at her, confused.

"Go on," she said. "Oh, for the love of God. Just go. Don't cost me any added delays. The last thing I need more of today is that incorrigible man yelling at me."

The inside of the trailer was cramped. Dresses and suits hung from large racks along the wall. A wide table dominated much of the space, and thick bolts of fabric and swatches lined the floor. It was stuffy, and an electric fan whirred incessantly in a corner. A little impish man with messy hair walked around the room with a measuring tape draped over his shoulder and a pincushion wrapped around his wrist by an elastic cord.

"You!" he exclaimed. "Jewish rabbi, am I correct?"

"Yes," said Diego.

"Very good. *Very* good." The man looked around, rummaging through piles and piles of clothing and fabric. "Here we are," said the man, pulling out a wrinkled black cassock with gold clasp buttons, an embroidered tallith with tied and knotted fringes, and a gold yarmulke. He looked at the costume then at Diego.

"Is everything all right, sir?"

"Cecil," said the man.

"Come again?"

"Cecil," said the man. "Please call me Cecil." Cecil's face wore an expression of concern. He sighed then shook his head. "Oh dear. They've done it again."

"Done what?" Diego asked.

"Central Casting. Botched measurements." He shook his head. "We'll do what we can, I suppose." Cecil shoved the costume at Diego and pushed him into a tiny dressing room with mirrors on all sides.

The cassock was much too short, and when he stepped out, Cecil rolled his eyes. "I was afraid of this. I'm going to have to lengthen it."

Trudy burst into the dressing room and shouted, "Cecil, no time! Get the beard on him."

"Very well," Cecil said. He sat him down in a canvas chair and smeared adhesive over his cheeks and across his chin. He placed the beard on carefully, and it itched and the adhesive smelled bad. He tried not to grimace when Cecil asked if it felt fine. He wasn't about to let minor discomforts get in the way of this, his first ever part.

Cecil stepped back and said, "You're all done, tiger."

"Let's go, *Applebaum*," said Trudy. She led him to the door.

The director told him to stand near the entrance to the synagogue. Once he was there, on the set, Diego couldn't see because so many lights were pointed in his direction, each bright and intrusive. The people standing behind the cameras and coils and wires were just shadows, faceless, disembodied mouths that screamed out orders. In the cacophony, he listened only for the director's voice, for his was the loudest, shouting into a bullhorn. More lights, he demanded. Less sun. More wind. No, that's too much. Just as he was about to shout action, the director rose from his chair, gasped, and took his bullhorn.

"Oh, for the love of God!" he shouted, "Torah. We can't have a rabbi without a Torah. Fiona," he screamed, "Gary, Trudy! Someone, get out here now and get this rabbi a Torah!"

A figure appeared and handed him a book. "How's that beard?" asked a beautiful young woman. As she approached, he could see that she had bright blond hair and green eyes. "I normally do prosthetics and wigs and hair but I had my hands tied with other things, and Cecil was kind enough to help. It's not too uncomfortable, is it?" She combed it with a soft brush.

"It itches terribly, to be honest," he said.

"You'll have to grin and bear it, toots. We're about to roll." She handed him his Torah then smiled, turned and walked away.

"Thank you, miss," he said.

"Fiona," she responded.

"Fiona," he repeated.

The technicians heaved the cameras back and forth. There were shouts and voices everywhere, and all the other actors and actresses were getting back into position, standing behind the carts, or sitting on benches pretending to sleep, or walking by with bags full of fake parcels wrapped in brown butcher paper.

They had to shoot the scene again and again. He lost count of how many times the director ordered it redone from multiple angles, because Diego's expression wasn't quite convincing or because there was a shadow on his face from the lights. When it was all finished seven hours later, he was exhausted from standing, the beard itched more than ever, and the cheap fabric of the cassock was making him perspire. They had worked straight through lunch, and he was faint and thirsty from being under the hot lights, but he was also excited. He had completed his first performance, and he felt triumphant. Walking off set, he spotted Fiona and thanked her.

She gave him a curious look. "For what?"

"It was my first time on set," he said. "I felt better knowing there was a kind soul out there on my side."

She set her makeup bottles and jars down and walked over to him and put her hand on his shoulder. "You were fine."

"Honest?"

"Honest," she said. "Sit." Fiona leaned in and began pulling the fake beard off, inch by inch. When she had completely removed it, she took a jar of cream, scooped some out, rubbed it between her palms and fingers and massaged this into his skin. It smelled of peppermint and tingled as it dried. "You're a swell guy," she said, looking at him. "And a real looker, too."

"Thanks," he said.

Fiona gathered her things up. "It's nice. Finding another human being in this business. Someone who isn't full of himself or damaged somehow."

He smiled.

"Well, I thought that, for your very first job, you did splendidly," Fiona said.

He followed her out. The sun was still shining, but the domed roofs of the large soundstages shielded them. They walked along, Diego's legs stiff from standing.

"You ever been to the Pig 'n Whistle?" she asked.

"No," he said.

"Good. Because you're taking me there. This weekend."

"Sounds great," he said. It could help to have an ally like her at Frontier, he thought.

She jotted her address down and told him she would be ready by five that Saturday. She then looked at him, and said, "Oh, geez, you better go to the wardrobe trailer and change."

Diego went into the trailer, removed the costume, and handed it to Cecil. The set was empty and still now; the floodlights were turned off, the fan blades no longer rotating, the cameras tucked to one side and covered by large canvas tarps. Diego stopped, lit a cigarette, and stood there looking at the spot where he'd spent a good portion of the day. He was proud of himself, proud of the fine work he'd done. He thought about Charlie, his friend. What had Diego done? But it was just a part, he thought. One small, irrelevant part. Nothing would come of it anyway, he thought. No harm was done.

5

November 1928

HIS PAYMENT WAS ENOUGH to cover the rent, plus a little extra, so he used some of his earnings to purchase a pair of plus four trousers, argyle socks, a new shirt, and a tweed checkered flat cap to wear on his date with Fiona. That night he bathed and dressed and adjusted his tie in the mirror. He placed the flat cap on his head, turned, and walked out the door, whistling all the way down the steps.

"Say," Rose said, seeing Diego as he entered the lobby. "Don't you look spiffy. You taking me out for a night on the town?"

Diego shrugged his shoulders. "I'm afraid I can't."

"Two-timing on me?" Rose asked. "What's her name?"

"Fiona."

"Fiona, huh? Bring her here. I'll scratch her eyes out. Good-for-nothing hussy." He laughed as she continued twirling, swaying her hips back and forth.

"You'll always be my one and only, Rose." Diego kissed her softly on the cheek; her thin skin smelled of lemon. "Always you, Rose."

She laughed. "Liar. But I'll take a lie like that over any old truth."

Ruby came out from the back room with a pile of receipts in her hand. She shook her head and scratched her forehead. Her hair was a mess, and there were large bags under her eyes.

"Rose, honey," she said, her voice exhausted, "stop fooling around now. We got a ton to do."

"Is everything okay?" Diego asked.

"No," she said. "No it ain't. But thanks for asking."

"The first of the month," Rose whispered. "Always gets her tense. Goes around collecting rent—"

"I paid." Diego interrupted. "Early. Placed my check in your box there."

"I know," Ruby said, handing him a receipt. "But it looks like we'll be having a couple of evictions." She thumbed through a ledger and shook her head.

Rose whistled and snapped her fingers. "They'll be out by tonight."

"Rose," said Ruby, slamming her hands on the desk. "Get the locks."

Just then Charlie came shuffling down the stairs, a suitcase in his hand. His coat was wrinkled and dusty, and his trousers were dotted with several black stains. "I'm going, ladies. I'm going." He placed his suitcase down.

"Charlie," said Ruby. "I'm real sorry. But I ain't running on charity alone."

"It's fine. I understand," he said. "You been good to me. Real patient."

Rose walked over to Charlie and kissed him on the cheek. "What'll you do now, honey?"

Charlie shrugged his shoulders. "Don't know. Maybe go back home." He took a deep breath, picked up his bag and moved toward the front door.

"I'm real sorry, Charlie," Diego said, reaching out to shake his hand.

He only looked at him, staring intently into Diego's eyes. "Of course you are. Of course you're sorry, pal. I am too."

Charlie walked out without taking Diego's hand.

He tried forgetting about Charlie and the eviction. It wasn't his fault, he told himself, as he walked down the street in his new glad rags, whistling to himself. He tipped his hat to a woman walking a poodle and two young girls in coats with matted fur collars. Something was different about the people he passed on his way to the trolley platform. They were all looking *at* him, Diego realized, not through him. They were all *noticing* him. Getting the part had put a bounce in his step. He walked, his shoulders back and his head up. He was chipper as he continued on to Fiona's building. Fiona was an exquisite sight in a shimmering green dress that accentuated the curves of her body.

"You look marvelous," she said, taking his arm.

"Thank you," he said. "You do, too. Let's go then. Shall we?"

She wore a wrap around her shoulders, which she had sprayed with a lilac perfume, so every time she adjusted it, he caught the scent. They walked down Hollywood Boulevard, toward the dazzling and flashing lights of the new Grauman's Chinese Theatre with its searchlights shooting bright blue beams into the hazy night sky.

"Grauman's Chinese Theatre's nice," said Fiona, "but I prefer the Egyptian Theatre."

"And why's that?" he asked.

"It's old," she said. "Anything old—structures, cars, people— have an inherent quality that I admire. A sageness."

They walked past the Chinese Theatre and strolled around inside the main courtyard of the Egyptian Theatre, immediately off the street. Inside, there were wide and impressive columns, intricate murals with hieroglyphics, and large gilded vases with lush plants. Near the main portico, toward the back of the courtyard, there stood a statue, about 12 feet high, of an Egyptian deity. The figure wore a gown and held a flail in the crook of its arm. Though the body was that of a human's, the figure's head was that of a dog's.

"What an odd fellow," Fiona said. "I don't know anything about Egyptian culture."

"That's Anubis," Diego said, approaching the figure, staring long and hard at its snout and pointed ears.

"Why, who's that?" Fiona asked.

"The Egyptians believed he was the guardian of the underworld. The god of death and rebirths."

"Well, that's something else," said Fiona. "How do you know so much?"

He laughed. "I was a good student."

Through a side entrance off the main courtyard of the Egyptian Theatre was the Pig 'n Whistle restaurant, whose logo featured a dancing pig playing a small flute. Inside, they walked past a man holding an organ. The main dining room was lined with booths that were cozy and private, everything done in ornate dark woods, polished smooth and gleaming. There were stained glass windows, and the chairs were hand-carved. There was an exciting rush in the air, and the atmosphere was festive and lively with children running around the tables and the organ grinder piping out lighthearted tunes.

Fiona and Diego had a delicious meal, talking all through it, gossiping about the actors and actresses around the studio, filling each other in on what they'd read in the trade magazines, and speculating about the next big Frontier movie.

"A thing that never ceases to amaze me about Hollywood," Fiona said as she sipped her after-dinner coffee, "is that we can be in ancient Egypt one minute then tumble into this whimsical restaurant with organ grinders and dancing pigs the next."

"It's disorienting," he said, wiping his mouth.

"You don't like it?"

"It takes some getting used to is all." He sat back in his chair. "But I like it. You know what else I like?"

"What's that?"

"Being with you tonight," Diego said.

"I'd be crushed if you hadn't. Why would you not want to join me for a night on the town? What other things have you got going on, dare I ask?" She placed her elbows on the table, cupped her chin in her hands, and leaned in closer. Her shoulders were bare and dotted with moles and freckles.

"Oh, nothing," he said. "It's just that, well, I'm still not very good at going out, being sociable. Since I came here, my evenings mainly have involved sitting alone in my apartment with a good book and a pack of cigarettes." He thought about Charlie and Javier back in Mexico. The friends he had lost.

"That's a real shame if you ask me."

"So," he asked, wanting nothing more than to change the subject. "I haven't asked what brought you here. To the great and wild and possible West."

"My mother." She removed her elbows from the table and sat back in her chair. "She started getting awful pains in her joints. Her doctor said it was her bones. It would get really bad during the winter. You haven't felt cold until you've spent a winter in Montana, let me tell you. Warm weather and sunshine was the solution, her doctor told us. So we packed up. Me and my folks and my two sisters. After I finished up high school I sort of fell into the show business thing. My friend Georgie got me in. I was doing real low-level stuff at first, mainly working in costuming, sorting out the inventory, repairing damaged corsets and outfits, stuff like that. I had always liked doing makeup, used to practice on my sisters when we were younger. I started helping the assistants, learning the tricks, and before I knew it, I was being asked to do it more and more. I've been at it for several years now. I like it enough, I guess. Though Hollywood's a tough place if you're a young girl like me." She gave him a long and pleasing look and asked, "What about you?"

"It's a boring story."

"That's all right. Let's have it."

He told her only bits and pieces, the important parts. How he left Mexico after having lived with his grandparents. How life here had been a series of challenges so far, how he's been riddled with doubt and guilt about having left his grandparents alone, about whether there was even such a future for a person like him in films. "I think there is," she said. "We can do whatever we set our minds to do. I think my future's bright, and so is yours. We are the makers of our own destinies. It was a very courageous thing you did, coming here like that, with nothing. You should be very proud."

When they raised their glasses of water and toasted, Diego felt at home for the very first time.

ACT IV

SCREENING
Attack! (1955)
Director: Roberto Osmond
Cast: C. Bob West, Florence Freed, and Chip Bennett

After being exposed to radiation from a series of bomb tests at nearby Del Oro nuclear facility, a giant cockroach terrorizes the border town of Moon Junction. The danger escalates when it is discovered that the roach is pregnant and about to give birth to thousands of large babies. Diego León plays Dr. Frank Ramirez.

SCREENING
The Adventures of Aeneas (1961)
Director: Saul M. Templeton
Cast: Gordon Gray, Marco dos Santo, Constance Hartley, and Eva Marino

Based on the poem by Virgil, this three-hour long saga recounts the epic journey of Aeneas after having escaped the sacking of Troy with his father and his son. Diego León is Latinus in this international all-star cast.

SCREENING
Destination: Diamondhead (1969)
Director: Craig Carlisle
Cast: Jack Kelly, Amanda Everett, and Lou Chen

When a syndicate identifying itself as ORCHID, an influential group of Polynesian purists, takes credit for the assassination of the governor of Hawaii, agent Miles West of ORACLE (the Organization Against Crimes, Larceny, and Evil) must investigate and thwart ORCHID'S evil plans. Features Diego León as Kaupe.

1

October 1929–December 1930

BLACK THURSDAY. HE WAS remembering his father that 24th day in October of 1929. It was early morning, and he was at Joe's, standing in the kitchen washing piles of dirty dishes, and thinking of his father, him dying alone, forgotten, penniless, when the first reports came in over the small radio the cooks kept on the shelf above the grill.

"It's the end of days," Jean said, reaching over to turn the volume up. They were alone in the diner. It was completely empty, and there was no one on the street at that hour.

"Come again?" Diego asked, his hands submerged in hot water.

"The stock market," Jean said, clenching her fists, "just crashed. A whole lot of people are in a whole heap of trouble. And things are about to get ugly."

The initial news was bad and, in the days that followed, things only worsened. Newspapers around the country reported that businessmen and financiers were leaping out of office windows because the money was now all gone. Factories went bust. Banks foreclosed on farms. Pantries across America went empty. The people of the great nation were suddenly out of work, destitute, vulnerable, confused, dying of hunger.

Diego had abandoned one ruined country for another. The winter of 1930, the bread and soup lines grew longer and longer day after day. More people were out of work, more men with startled looks on their faces could be seen darting across the street, the sidewalks, wandering through the parks and alleyways of the city searching for work or, worse, scavenging through trash cans for pieces of moldy bread or bruised fruits and vegetables. "You should be thanking your lucky stars you at least got this," Jean said one day.

"Yeah, yeah," he responded.

"What?" she said, her hands on her hips. "You expecting to make it in pictures? Like all those other ones who are coming now by the hundreds since this crash?"

"I will," he said. "Soon."

"Then why don't you just leave?"

She was right. Why didn't he? The job paid very little anyway. He untied his apron, balled it up, and tossed it on the ground. "I'm quitting, Jean."

"Hey," she said, bending down to pick up the apron. "I was only teasing."

"I know," he said. "Still. I'm wasting my time here."

She shook her head and smiled. "Yeah. You're right." Jean walked over, gave him a hug and a kiss on the cheek. "Good luck, kid. I'm gonna miss you."

At least he had a contract now after building for himself a solid reputation as a dependable extra, thanks to his experience playing the part that should have gone to Charlie. Fiona, who had an in with many of the lesser-known directors at Frontier, began to spread the word throughout the studio about him, the tall Latin actor with versatility who was dependable. And though the parts weren't anything major—a face in a crowd scene, a dancer at a costume party, a bank robber—the work kept him hopeful that he might, just might, make it. At least he was in the movies now, he reminded himself. By 1929, Diego was a contracted player for Frontier Pictures, the oldest movie studio in Hollywood. Yes, the hours were endless, tedious, the money only enough to keep him going, but it was what he'd come to do. He thought about this now as he left Joe's after quitting, passing the men on the corners begging for spare change, the bread lines, the people combing the back alleys of restaurants and grocery stores or selling apples from wooden push-carts. Everywhere he turned, it was as though the whole country was on the verge of collapsing in on itself. But he had work. He had a signed piece of paper from the studio. He had Fiona, whom he'd been spending more time with. He had his *own* life.

The studios, like all other enterprises, had started to cut back. Fewer big epics. Rein in spending. Reduce, reduce, reduce. Diego read in the trade circulars and news columns how the studios were cutting their losses, firing people, eliminating entire departments. He was nervous a lot, worried he would be told he was being canned and that would be it. The end of his film career. Finished just as it was starting.

"If there's one thing a studio needs," Fiona told him, "is people like you and me. Extras and makeup and costume folks. We're safe. We don't cost much. It's the bigwigs who should be quaking in their boots, if you ask me."

"You're right," he said, taking a deep breath. "I'll do my job and feel secure."

"That's the spirit."

The "talkies" appeared at the Frontier lot gradually, in the form of large microphones, sound coils, and bizarre-looking contraptions. Over time, the wooden consoles that the "sound technicians," as they were called, wheeled from studio to studio appeared more and more frequently. The trade magazines wrote about sound, about the death of films and the picture industry.

"I thought you said we'd be safe," he asked Fiona one day as they watched two crewmembers attach a wired microphone to an actor's lapel while on a shoot. The picture was about a nun in a convent in Brazil, and the actor was dressed as an affluent businessman. "These talking pictures are going to ruin our careers."

"Or make them," she said. "A lot of the silent film stars are being canned. That means more chances for us."

So he followed it all, reading everything he could about this in-novation. The first attempts were on wax discs, but it was hard to synchronize the sounds with the moving pictures because it had something to do, they said, with the speed at which sound traveled. Once in a while the sound engineers would get it right, would be patient enough to match the sound of the voice with the image of the singer moving his mouth on the screen. These moments, few and brief, were enough to get people curious, were hailed as landmarks, triumphs in the evolution of moving pictures. The discs took too much time, though, they soon realized, and another way to introduce sound to films was needed, and that, they concluded, would be sound *on* film. So there was, in 1926, *Don Juan*, which starred John Barrymore and featured synchronized songs and sound effects. A year later, there was *The Jazz Singer*, Al Jolson singing to his mother at the end of the film. That same year there came *Fifi*, in which Marguerite La Salle recited a whole speech in French. There was the roar of exploding cannons during the famous battle scene in *A Darkened Heart,* less than a year later. Movie theaters were slowly being fitted with speakers and microphones to pipe in sound, and audiences got to hear their favorite stars speak, deliver their lines, sing like angels. As a result, anyone with a thick accent, with a speech impediment or a low and unappealing voice was finding themselves out of a job. Diego could sing, but what of his accent? Would it destroy his career?

Diego watched how, almost overnight, many of the studios underwent the change, crammed their lots and stages with sound, fired their silent film stars to make way for the new generation. Except for studios such as Frontier. It had done little to change with the growing trend. It was known that R. J. Levitt was wary of such a new invention, that he was skeptical, suspicious. Coasting more on its reputation as the first film studio in Hollywood, Frontier was still hobbling along with Levitt at the helm—stubborn, tough as nails, unflinching. He had become the underdog, the dark horse in an industry he had helped define and establish.

The tensions playing out at Frontier between Levitt and his partner, William Cage, over the talkies were gold for the columnists covering all that was worth knowing in Hollywood. Everyone knew that the shrewd old businessman mistrusted the new technology. But his young partner, the production manager of Frontier, saw it differently. Cage understood what was happening, understood that, if they were to be successful and compete with the other studios, then they would have to follow suit and convert to sound. The rumored clashes between the two—the old lion and the young—left everyone curious to see what would happen.

Fascinated by these developments, Diego began reading the trade columns and articles with a passion that Fiona called "admirable yet unusual."

"If I want to succeed in this business," he said, "I must be well informed."

They were sitting in his room. Past issues of *Snapshots* and *Cast Call* were strewn across his bed. She flipped though one and stopped at a feature article on William Cage. "Is Cage the real brains behind Frontier?" a line in the article read.

"Let me see that," Diego said, snatching it from Fiona.

"Hey," she protested. "I thought you read these already. Give a girl a chance."

"I just picked it up this morning," he said. His eyes fell on a photograph of Cage. He wore a suit and a tie, and his hair was combed neatly and parted down the middle. He had bright green eyes and a slight grin. He studied the picture closely. "Have you ever met him?" he asked Fiona.

"Once," she said.

"What's he like?"

"Real swell. He's tall. Good-looking. Commanding and confident. Really makes a girl's knees go shaky."

"So you're attracted to him?" he asked.

She laughed. "Well. He's a looker. But there are rumors. They say he's funny."

"Funny?"

"Yeah. *Funny.*" She raised her eyebrow. "They say he prefers the company of men."

"I see," Diego said, studying the picture.

"Enough of that," Fiona said, taking the magazine from him and tossing it on the floor. She wrapped her arms around his neck. "Kiss me, angel."

As Fiona pressed her lips against his own, he couldn't stop thinking of William Cage. *He was funny*, Diego repeated to himself. *Funny. Funny.*

He envied the bigger stars, the ones with clout and success and glamour, the ones keeping the studio afloat. He didn't want to be stuck working on such films—poorly written and acted and produced— nor always be needed to fill ethnic roles—an Indian brave, a Gypsy, a Chinaman, an Arab in the Sahara.

"Is that all I'll ever be?" he asked Fiona one Saturday morning. "Is this all I'll ever be? Some schlub? An ethnic actor?" He sighed and she gripped his arm.

"You're a contracted star," Fiona reminded him. "You landed one after being here only a short time. You're lucky! What more do you want?"

"I suppose you're right."

Still, he thought, *to star in a picture. To receive top billing.* And though Fiona liked reminding him to be patient, Diego was having a hard time with the waiting, all the sacrificing. How long would it be? If he was to return to Mexico, he would not do so as a failure or, worse, someone who had gotten so close to success yet never achieved it. He had been reading the trade columns, following any advice to the letter when there was anything written about making it. He frequented places—cafés, parks, hotel swimming pools where stars and directors went on weekends to relax—where others had been discovered. What little money he had, after rent and necessities, went to buying more clothing. "If you want to get the part," one magazine told, "you have to dress the part. You must surround yourself with like-minded individuals whose goals are your own." He had done so by striking up conversations with the leads on productions he was assigned to, asking them questions when he could, gleaning as much as he could from them. Since he quit working at Joe's four months ago, he stopped going there altogether. That Saturday morning, however, Fiona was hungry and suggested they stop there.

"The magazines say you should frequent establishments where people in the industry go," he explained.

"You used to be real keen on the place," she said as they strolled down Hollywood Boulevard toward the diner.

"It's full of a bunch of know-nothings and nobodies," he said. "Why, if we want this racket to consider us serious stars, we gotta go to the places where they go like the Brown Derby or Romanoff's. Not some crummy diner with busted lights and bad food in a seedy part of town."

"The Brown Derby? Romanoff's?" Fiona adjusted her cloche, closed her eyes, and laughed a little laugh. "Why, we can't ever afford such places. Not on our salaries."

"And we never will as long as we continue coming to this hole in the wall, I'll tell you that." They stood in front of Joe's, and Diego peered inside. Through the glass, past the blurred reflection, he saw Charlie sitting at the counter, near the front door, his back slightly turned. Diego stopped, hesitating as Fiona stood there with the door opened.

"Why are you all twisty?" Fiona asked. "Come on, now. The smell of bacon's making me hungry." She tugged on his arm.

"Let's go somewhere else. Please, Fi."

"No," protested Fiona. "We're here now. Just a quick bite. And we can still catch the Big Red to Santa Monica." She pointed to the trolley stop. "You promised you'd take me today. I want to ride the carousel and listen to the calliope play. That sound makes me happy."

Diego sighed. So what, he thought? So what if Charlie sees him? What was he going to do anyway?

"Fine. Let's skedaddle." He grabbed Fiona by the arm and they rushed in, past the counter, toward a booth at the very back of the restaurant.

"Why the rush?" Fiona asked. "Boy, you're sure acting funny. What's with you?"

"Nothing," he said. "Nothing at all."

It wasn't Jean who served them. It was an older lady with thinning hair and a hunched back. She must be new, Diego thought. Stitched to the lapel of her uniform was the name Zadie. He wondered what happened to Jean. He still felt bad over the way he quit. She had done so much to help him. "Where's Jean?" he asked Zadie.

The woman looked at him and said, "Who? What now?"

"Jean."

"Don't know a Eugene, mister. Just me. Now, what'll it be for you and the little lady?"

Diego ordered a cup of coffee and a donut. Fiona ordered a bowl of oatmeal with raisins and a glass of warm milk.

"Is that all you're eating?" Fiona asked when Zadie returned with their food. "A plain donut and a cup of coffee?"

"Yeah," he said. "Why?"

"You need something heartier."

In between bites of his donut and sips of his coffee, he took quick glances toward Charlie. He sat at the counter, eating cold cereal and reading the paper. Surprisingly, he looked rather nice. He wore a new suit and shoes that were polished and glossy. His hair was combed back, and a handkerchief poked out from his front jacket pocket. Diego was quite shocked. No longer frumpy and disheveled, Charlie seemed composed and at ease. He joked with the waitress, and his smile was warm and genuine.

"You know that fella?" asked Fiona, putting her bonnet back on as they gathered their things to go.

"Who?"

"That guy there. The one in the blue suit. You've been staring at him since we walked in."

"No," Diego said. "I don't."

Charlie gathered his things, rose from his chair, and headed for the door. Diego stalled, giving him enough time to walk out before they did.

"Let's get going now," said Fiona. "It'll get hot once the sun's out."

"Sure, sure," he said. He rose and, as they went for the door, he noticed Charlie left something on the counter. It was a pair of goldrimmed glasses. Diego stopped, took them, and looked over at the waitress who was wiping down a table.

"Say," he said. "The man sitting here left his glasses."

"What?" She came closer. She held a wet rag.

"The man sitting here left these glasses."

"Oh? Imagine that." She looked around. "It's Charlie. Give them here. I'll hold on until he comes back in."

Diego held the glasses, let his fingers run over the thick lenses. He felt the wire rims, imagined Charlie wearing them as he read. In a room. A drab place. Charlie. They left and waited on the trolley landing. As the car approached, Fiona turned to him and said, "Are you all right, dear?"

He smiled. "Yes. I'm fine. Perfectly fine." Diego gave her a peck on the cheek, and they boarded the trolley.

That night, after a modest dinner at a restaurant popular with some movie directors, they ran into Fiona's friend Georgie. Georgie worked as a seamstress in the costume department at Frontier and had gotten Fiona in at the studio years before. Georgie was a buxom girl with full and swollen lips painted a soft plum color. She wore an elegant black dress with a deep plunge neckline and a sheer wrap that she gripped with gloved hands. Her boyfriend, Nick, shook Diego's hand rather forcefully. His face was bright red; he appeared to be inebriated. Nick was the son of an influential Los Angeles attorney named Simon Wexler, Fiona told him, who had become popular for representing many of the powerful movie moguls in Hollywood. Nick was rich, well connected, and known for his wild antics and behavior. He called Diego "partner."

"Where you two kids headed?" Georgie asked, leaning into Nick outside the restaurant.

"Who knows," said Fiona. "Night's still young."

"Come with us," Nick said, reaching out and placing his arm around Diego's shoulder. "We got ourselves an *interesting* night in store."

"A real gas," said Georgie. She lowered her voice. "We're going to the Babylon."

"What's the Babylon?" asked Fiona.

"A restaurant run by an old queer," said Nick. "After 10 o'clock they put on a swell cabaret show. Men in women's clothing. A real sight."

"Maybe we should get—" Fiona started to say when Diego interrupted.

"Is there booze?" Diego asked. He couldn't remember the last time he had tasted alcohol.

"You bet," said Nick. "You bet, my friend."

Diego looked at Fiona. "Oh, let's have a go at it."

"Sure," she said. "Why not?"

"Trust me," Georgie said to Fiona. "The Babylon's like nothing you've ever experienced. Hollywood's best-kept secret."

The Babylon was down a quiet and narrow street lined on either side with storefronts and restaurants that were closed for the evening, their windows and doors darkened. Men stood on street corners, smoking cigarettes under the dull, yellowing light of a street lamp. They watched as the cab drove past.

"Are you sure you know where you're going, Nicky?" asked Georgie.

"There!" he exclaimed, pointing to a dark building at the end of the block. It was an unassuming, rather drab place with a torn red awning and burned-out lights.

"This is it?" whispered Georgie as they stumbled out of the cab. "Looks rather questionable."

"Oh, this is it, baby," Nick said.

Inside, people sat around small tables along the outer perimeter of a narrow dance floor with a large chandelier hanging high above from the ceiling. It was crowded, and patrons milled about, chatting and smoking cigarettes and dancing. He noticed a few women dressed in suits and ties, thin mustaches drawn in pencil above their lips. They stood at the bar, holding hands and kissing the women accompanying them. A handful of other couples, all men, danced with one another. Everything was dimly lit, the air thick with smoke.

They took a table near the front, right by the dance floor. Nick stood, peering out, whistled, and got the attention of a little black man who weaved through the crowd and darted over, holding a round tray. "Ah," he said, smiling. "Mister Nick. How are you?"

"Good, Jo Jo. Thank you for asking." Nick lit a cigarette.

"Now," Jo Jo said, "let me get you and your friends some drinks before the show starts. Promises to be a real swing."

Fiona and Georgie ordered vodka and soda, Diego a whiskey on the rocks with a splash of water, and Nick rum with milk. After Jo Jo returned with their drinks, they sat there watching the people. By the time they finished their second round, Diego asked Fiona to dance with him.

"Why, it's about time," she said. "I'd love to."

The song was something soft, and they stood, swaying among

the other dancers. "This is a little strange," she said, glancing about.

"What is?" he asked.

"Us. The only boy and girl dancing." She giggled.

"Do you like it?"

"I do." She was quiet for a while and hummed along with the song. "I like you."

"I like you, too," he said, kissing her.

"I still can't get over what a good dancer you are," Fiona said and placed her head on his shoulder.

"Practice, practice, practice. As a boy I thought of nothing but singing and dancing."

"I bet you were adorable."

When they made their way back to the table, Nick and Georgie were nowhere to be found. Diego looked around and said, "There," to Fiona when he spotted them. In a dark corner, at a booth tucked in the very back of the room, near a service entrance, Nick and Georgie stood talking with two men whose faces Diego could not make out. He led Fiona through the crowd, and when Nick saw them approach, he smiled and patted Diego on the back.

"These are my friends," Nick said, and both men nodded.

Diego reached over and shook their hands. "How do you do?" It wasn't until he pulled his arm back that he realized that one of the men bore a striking resemblance to none other than William Cage.

He rose now. "Where are my manners?" the man asked. "Bill," he said, shaking their hands. He pointed to his partner. "This is my friend, Stephen."

"Pleasure," said Stephen, his tone indifferent. He shook their hands and placed his elbows on the table.

"Come. Join us," said Bill.

"We should really—" Stephen began just as Fiona and Georgie squeezed in, sitting on either side of him. Nick followed, leaving Diego and Bill to occupy the opposite ends of the table. While they all chatted idly about the weather, politics, and the crowd on the dance floor, Stephen stirred the ice in his drink and sighed repeatedly.

"I can call you a cab," Bill shouted to him.

"It's quite all right," he said. "I wouldn't dream of leaving you here alone."

Bill ordered a round of drinks, and then another. By the time the table was on its fourth round, it was well past one in the morning.

The club was even more crowded by now, and a female impersonator named Starla stood on a small stage at the end of the dance floor, performing a song that made everyone cheer. Starla wore a green dress and a bright red wig and strutted around, singing and flirting playfully with the crowd. The place was really swinging, and Diego was feeling rather drunk. Bill kept smiling at him from across the table.

"Do you dance?" asked Bill, leaning in.

"Does he dance?" shouted Fiona, giggling. "Like an angel."

"Heavenly," said Nick, sipping his cocktail. He and Georgie kissed while Fiona talked to Stephen about the latest picture she was working on, about a Southern belle who tries saving a runaway black slave named Mokata, and, geez, you wouldn't believe just how awkward and cumbersome those hoop dresses they wore back then were. Stephen was obviously bored, but Bill ignored him. The angrier Stephen appeared to be, the more Bill seemed to flirt with Diego, smiling and nodding, leaning in and whispering in his ear from across the table.

"I think your friend wants to go home," Diego told Bill.

"I'm not ready yet," Bill said, finishing his cocktail. "I want to dance."

"Then dance," Nick shouted and Georgie squealed then Fiona did too.

Bill rose, cleared his throat, and said to Diego, "May I?" He reached his hand out.

Fiona was laughing at something Georgie was saying then stopped, her expression crestfallen, as she watched Diego rise and take Bill's hand. "Come again?" she asked.

"Just one dance," he said to her as Bill led him through the crowd of bodies pressed together, the beautiful young men parting to let them pass.

Bill was drunk and stumbled as they began to dance. Strands of his blond hair fell forward, covering his eyes, and Diego reached out to brush them aside.

"I'm gone," he said, leaning in and whispering in Diego's ear. "Quite drunk indeed."

"I can tell." He held him tight, arms wrapped around his waist. "Don't you worry, Mister Cage. I got you. I got you."

He laughed. "You know me?" he slurred. "Who I am?"

"Of course. I've seen your picture in the magazines. I work for you, sir."

"Everyone does. In one form or another. Works for me."

"I'm an actor," Diego said.

Bill tickled the tip of his nose. "And a gorgeous one at that."

Back at the table, Nick and Georgie had vanished, and Fiona sat with Stephen, both of them watching Bill and Diego intently, angry and troubled looks on their faces.

"Your friend's mad," Diego said.

Bill laughed and strands of his hair tumbled forward again. "Your girl's none too happy with you either, my boy. What a pair we make." Bill looked into Diego's face; his green eyes were bright and so beautiful and warm and alive that it terrified him. They danced through the rest of the song and the beginning of the next before Bill spoke again.

"Am I your type?" he asked, stroking Diego's cheek.

"I'm rather new at this. I don't think I have a type."

"I do," he said. "And you're it." And with these words, he leaned in and kissed him on the lips. It felt as though they were like that for an eternity, but it was only a few seconds, when he suddenly heard shouts and felt someone grab him by the lapels of his shirt and shove him to the ground. Diego fell back, crashing into Starla, who had finished his routine some time ago, and was now dancing with a woman in a man's tuxedo. Starla's red wig flew off as he was knocked over by the blow of Diego's body. There was a sound like glass breaking and a scream and curses.

"Starla!" shouted someone.

"You son of a bitch!" the queen yelled, rolling on the ground.

Stephen turned around now and attacked Bill. "You filthy bastard," he shouted. "I loved you. I loved you."

The doorman and a waiter rushed through the crowd and tackled Stephen as the rest of the people on the dance floor separated to watch the spectacle.

"Let's take you outside, sonny," said the doorman. "You're boozed. Fresh air'll do you good."

Bill rose now, his lip cracked and bleeding. Diego turned and helped the queen get up. He adjusted his green dress as Diego reached down and grabbed his wig.

"He came after me," said Diego, handing him his wig, which

was now a nest of tangled red hair with broken shards of glass that glinted as Starla placed it back on. "I'm sorry."

"No worries," said Starla. "I saw the whole thing. That little twerp came after you and your honey there. I saw the whole thing." Starla adjusted himself and the woman in the black tuxedo asked if everything was fine. "I am, baby. Thanks to this gracious gentleman here."

Bill reached for a handkerchief in his pocket and used it to staunch his bleeding lip. "Sorry," he said, as they made their way back. "Looks like Stephen's not the only one who's had a bit too much."

Fiona was asleep at the table, her head resting between halfempty cocktail glasses. Diego couldn't tell how long she'd been out. Nick and Georgie were nowhere to be found.

"I better go find Stephen," Bill said, still holding the handkerchief up to his lip. He winced when he removed it. "It's bad, ain't it?"

Diego leaned in to examine the cut. He took a piece of ice out of one of the glasses and rubbed it over the abrasion. "You'll survive," he said. "Though I recommend immediate attention and care."

Bill took the piece of ice from him and wrapped it in the handkerchief then pressed it to his lip again. "Are you offering your services?"

"Perhaps."

"You act. You dance. You dress wounds. You're full of surprises." Diego smiled. "I am."

Before he turned to leave, Diego grabbed him by the wrist, removed the handkerchief, and leaned in to kiss him. He felt the coldness from the ice cube and tasted the faint tang of Bill's blood. Then, just like that, William Cage walked through the crowd and out of the club. Would Diego ever see him again? Did he even want to? What had come over him? Back at the table, Fiona was still passed out. Nick and Georgie came out of the men's bathroom a few minutes later, while Diego was trying to revive Fiona. Georgie's lipstick was smeared, and Nick's shirt was unbuttoned.

"We miss any of the show?" he asked.

Georgie giggled and wrapped her arms around his neck.

Luckily, Fiona didn't remember much of what happened that night. Everything after the moment when they joined Bill and his friend was a blur, she said.

"What a nice guy, that Bill Cage," she said. "Treating us like honest to goodness celebrities. Then I go and get sauced and black out. What an embarrassment."

"He didn't seem to mind, darling," Diego told her. "We all had a real swell time."

"That's a relief," Fiona said.

"I'm sure he doesn't even remember any of it."

Diego, meanwhile, couldn't get Bill Cage out of his mind. At night, he lay in bed, smoking cigarette after cigarette, imagining him, trying to recall the sensation of his lips pressed against Diego's own. He remembered the taste of his blood, the cool sensation from the ice when he rubbed and kissed Bill's cut. In the days that followed, when he was in between takes or running from set to set, he had taken to sitting on the benches outside the Frontier executive office building, hoping to catch a glimpse of him. Several times— one day dressed as an Indian brave, the next a bank robber, the next an Italian gondolier—he watched Bill come and go, his pearl blue Cadillac with its white-walled tires and shiny chrome bumpers speeding off or arriving. Bill in a suit and tie and hat, a stern look on his face as he stood at the curb waiting for the valet to pull his car around, never noticed Diego, disguised as he was. It was those moments, just a few, when Bill was alone—uninterrupted, with no frazzled secretary trailing behind him, no studio executives with nervous and panicked looks on their faces—that Diego relished the most. Diego sensed Bill's loneliness, his isolation, and he told himself that they were similar in that way, both of them in need of one another.

A week after the incident at the Babylon, he and Fiona went to the park with a basket packed with sandwiches and sliced fruit. Fiona wanted to spend a lazy afternoon under a big tree watching the clouds roll by, she insisted.

"But there aren't any," he said when they arrived. Diego spread a blanket out on the grass, removed his cap, and looked up toward the sky. "It's clear blue, Fi."

"Oh, well." She removed her bonnet and sat down on the blanket. Fiona shook her head as she watched Diego remove the latest issue of *Photoplay* from a small leather satchel he had recently purchased from a shop next to the Western Union office where he went to wire his grandparents. His grandmother's last telegram to him had read: *When are you coming back?* He didn't have the courage to respond yet—he didn't know what he would say.

"Boy," Fiona said, "you and those magazines."

"Whatever do you mean?" he asked, trying to push Mexico and his grandparents out of his thoughts.

Fiona laughed. "It's become something of an obsession."

"Passion," he said, rolling down on the blanket and staring up at the thick branches of the oak they lay under. "I want stardom more than anything. I'm passionate."

"Is there a difference between passion and obsession?" she asked, breaking off pieces of bread and throwing them on the concrete path a few feet away for the birds to pick at. "It's all you read."

"Why read anything else? Why read the newspapers? They're full of bad news these days. Joblessness. Poverty. People going hungry."

"That's life," said Fiona.

"It doesn't have to be. It isn't," he said. Diego propped himself up on his elbows, felt the soft earth beneath him break and give. "Not for us."

"It can blind you," she said. Her tone was serious now. "The business. The fame. People die for it." Fiona pointed across the wide green park toward the Hollywoodland sign in the distant hills.

"It won't blind me. Won't kill me. I believe in this. In myself. It's all I have left. I will not live for nothing. I want to be famous. Remembered. Loved. Not unknown and disrespected, like my father or mother. I will do whatever it takes to achieve this."

"No matter the cost?" she asked.

"No matter the cost," he said.

"Very well," she told him. "Then, if you're serious, there are a few things you should know." Fiona stood now and spoke to him, pointing a finger accusingly. "If I say this to you it's because I want to help."

"Very well. Tell me."

"The truth," she said.

"The truth," he repeated.

"Your acting stinks." She paused here. "There. I said it."

Diego rose now and crossed his arms. He scowled at her. "I'll have you know that I studied with a very prominent performer when I was a boy. What do you know about acting? You're just a makeup girl."

"I know a thing or two," Fiona said. "When you've spent enough time on the set as I have, you pick up some know-how."

"Ah, baloney!"

"Don't be sore. I'm only trying to help you out. If you're as determined as you say, then I'd like to lend my services."

"Why?" He uncrossed his arms and sat back down, slouching his shoulders.

"Because I care about you. Because I want you to succeed."

"Honestly?" he asked.

She nodded.

"But how can *you* help me?"

Fiona placed the palm of her hand against his lower back. "First, you'll have to learn posture. Now sit properly," she said.

He remembered his grandfather, how obsessed with etiquette the old man had been. Diego sat straight up, smiled a congenial smile, and said, "How's this?"

"Very good," Fiona said. "That's a start."

Over the next few weeks, Fiona had him practice walking around with a book balanced on his head, urging him to focus, to concentrate.

"Head up," she clapped. "Shoulders back. Eyes forward. If you want to be a leading man, you need to move like one."

He dedicated an hour a day to climbing up and down the four flights of stairs at the Ruby Rose. He gave himself a full eight hours of sleep each night, began eating more greens and vegetables, and took daily vitamins with minerals that Fiona said helped with his concentration and focus. She told him it was important to take care of his skin, so she made him use face masks that hardened into clay over his nose and cheeks and mouth. He was to exercise three times a day with weights and dumbbells and go on runs.

"I have to do all the exercising and running and eating right, and you get to just sit there enjoying the sun," he said to Fiona one day at the beach. Diego had stopped his run to rest and towel his face off. Fiona was under a striped umbrella, reading a romance novel. She wore a whistle around her neck that she would use from time to time on Diego.

"I'm not the one wanting to be a picture star," Fiona said, looking up from her book.

"Oh, baloney." When he finished wiping his face with his towel, he tossed it on the sand and collapsed next to her. "I feel like a fool. Running around in circles. Walking with a book on my head. Just look at me," he said. Diego wore athletic shorts, a white undershirt, and a pair of sneakers. "A person shouldn't be allowed out of the house with such little on."

Fiona rolled her eyes and shook her head.

"Stop that," he said, picking up a handful of sand and tossing it at her feet.

"Oh, now you've done it." Fiona removed her shoes and socks and shook the sand away. "I don't know why I bother."

"Because you love me," he said.

Fiona's smile faded. She looked at him with a serious face. "Perhaps. But I also happen to think you're very talented. And rather dashing. But you need to still learn a thing or two about acting."

"Then teach me what you know."

"Very well." She put her shoes and socks back on and stood. She placed her hands on her hips. "I heard a director once tell Margaret Dillon—"

"*The* Margaret Dillon," Diego interjected. "Star of—"

"Well, she wasn't quite there yet," Fiona said. "This was in the early days of her career. I had just started at Frontier. Anyway, he says to always be aware of your body. Hands, feet, eyes, everything. Always remain in control of it, of its limits and capabilities."

She said he needed to use everything—shoulders and hair, mouth and nose—to convey feeling. "There's a difference between picking something up"—and she bent down and plucked a small shell rather gingerly from the sand—"and *lifting* something up."

"Okay," he said.

"Lifting it and treating it as though it is the single most important, most cherished thing in the world."

She set the shell back down, took a deep breath, and then did the most extraordinary thing. Her movements were different the second time, not casual and glib, but they were artful and fluid, as though they'd been choreographed. Fiona started first by tucking back a fragile curl of hair behind her ear, letting her hand linger on her neck. Then, with so much care and attention, she reached out, picked the shell back up and, cradling it in her hands, brought it close to her face, which wore a look of soft concern, her eyes sorrowful, as if she were about to burst into tears. The gesture was heartwrenching but also very lovely, for she had made him believe that that seashell was no longer simply an insignificant object but something rare and cherished.

When she broke character, he applauded. "Fi," he said. "I didn't know you had it in you!"

She bowed. "But don't overdo it," she told him. "Don't overact, don't overemphasize. Otherwise all meaning gets lost, and the danger is that it comes out looking absurd and comical."

"How do you know all of this?"

She shrugged her shoulders. "Watching people. The strangest things are revealed when you're just a spectator in all of this. People forget you're there. Until you blow the whistle on them. Speaking of—" Here, she grabbed hers and blew. "Up. One more lap then we can go home."

Diego sighed and rose.

"Catch me if you can," she shouted, running off fast, her small feet kicking up grains of sand.

Diego ran, almost certain that he would never catch her.

2

March 1931

STUDIO 8 HAD BEEN CONVERTED into a lavish Roman temple honoring Bacchus. The round pool lay in the middle of the set, the water bright blue and shimmering. Wide imitation marble columns supported large and elegant arches stretching around the pool. Fake plaster statues of Roman gods—Jupiter, Mars, Saturn—were perched on pedestals standing more than 10 feet high. The walls were covered in decorative mosaic tiles of bright crimson, deep blue, and pastel green and lit by torches and sconces that gave off a dim glow.

The film told the story of Bacchus, the god of wine, debauchery, and excess, who falls in love with a mortal girl. Diego and a number of other young men had been cast as Roman subjects whose job it was to entertain the god, while he sat atop a gold throne, eating grapes, surrounded by a group of beautiful maidens. Diego and other young men all wore the same costume—a black wig with a crown of artificial laurel leaves painted gold, and a skimpy loincloth—and they huddled together around the small pool, dipping their feet in the water. The director was milling around, shouting something to technicians high above on the scaffolds, positioning the actor playing Bacchus. Diego glanced around, the light low, the faces of the others obscured by shadows.

"I hope the water isn't too cold," said someone.

Diego said, "Yes. I hope not either." His face was only dimly lit, and Diego squinted, tried making the features out. "Javier?" he asked, his heart pounding. "Is that you, hermano?"

But the young man didn't hear him. There was too much shouting, and the director was barking out orders. Then the lights faded even more and the cameras started up. The group of men migrated toward the pool.

"I guess there's no other way than to just plunge right in," the young man said and he gripped Diego's arm and pulled him in. Once in the water, Diego looked around, watching the others surrounding the perimeter of the pool step inside, one after the other. The director yelled action and shouted commands, and there was music, and the maidens at the foot of Bacchus's throne danced, while the god ate grapes and drank from a large silver goblet. The director barked out orders through his bullhorn, as the camera turned from one end of the set to the other, and Diego stretched his neck, trying to find the figure he thought was Javier.

When the director called it a wrap, they emerged out of the water, dripping, the thin fabric of their loincloths clinging to their skin. The group joined the dancing maidens, the actor playing Bacchus, the musicians, and the lighting technicians as the group made its way toward the giant studio door in one large and imposing herd. Diego followed, not fully knowing where they were headed, his eyes fixed on the one he thought was Javier.

"Javier?" he shouted. "It's me. Diego."

He was striking like that, his hair a dark mane, skin glistening and almost iridescent in the light. He turned now, just as Diego reached for him, and walked out the studio doors. Someone had left a towel draped over a chair, and Diego reached out and grabbed this. By the time he was able to tie it around his waist, he looked around for them, but they were gone. Outside, the swimmers had left wet footprints on the asphalt, and he followed these. In spots where there was no shade, though, the footprints were already evaporating, continuing again on the other side of the path shadowed by the soundstages. He ran across the drawbridge of a castle surrounded by a fake moat, turned left and collided with a procession of men in marching band attire, toting trumpets and horns and xylophones.

"Watch it," yelled one of them. "You nearly knocked me down."

"Sorry," Diego said. "I apologize." He ran along, down the wide driveways and through the back lots, looking for him. It was him, wasn't it? But it couldn't be.

On he ran, past a jungle, past a western town, through a narrow alleyway in New York City, until the wet prints ended just outside the doors to the Frontier Pictures diner. The place was crowded with people at every table dressed in costumes and outfits, smoking cigarettes and sipping cups of hot black coffee. He looked around the room but couldn't find any of the other swimmers. They had all simply vanished without a trace.

Maybe the vision of Javier was a sign. An omen. Maybe the spirits of his parents were calling him back home now that he was nearly certain he could make a good life for himself in Los Angeles. But, it was looking more and more as though the United States government might make that decision for him.

As the Depression continued into 1931 and gradually worsened, as people around the country struggled to feed their families, as jobs became more and more scarce, the good people of America looked for someone, something, to blame. The newspapers around Los Angeles reported on the "scourge of Mexicans" living in tightly packed dwellings around some of the more disagreeable areas of the city. Shacks, the reporters observed, with no electricity, no running water, where crime was rampant and so was disease—typhoid, tuberculosis, cholera. They were called animals by the press, uneducated, dirty scoundrels. The Los Angeles police department conducted mass deportations—rounding up as many as they could catch and hauling them away, back to the border, back to a country many of their children had never known—emptying out whole city blocks, whole neighborhoods. They were to blame for the economic catastrophes taking place so far away. They were to blame for taking jobs away from needy Americans. They were to blame for spreading diseases, for crimes and robberies and murders, for soiling the fabric of a great nation, indivisible, with liberty and justice for all.

Diego's hands shook as he read the reports of thousands of Mexicans, "strains on the economy," the paper said, being forced against their will to return. Women, children, men, teenagers, people who had escaped the revolution—the very one that had caused his father to lose himself, to return to the rancho a changed person, forever withdrawn and sullen—had no other choice but to go back. What if they came for him? He imagined it: a loud knock on the door late in the middle of the night. Two police detectives in sharp suits and fedora hats wielding steel guns and shiny badges.

"Come with us," they would say.

"Where?" he would ask.

"Mexico. You're being repatriated."

That's what the papers called it. "Repatriation." It sounded so nice, so benevolent, Diego thought. He would be "repatriated," reunited with his grandparents who had been waiting for his return for several years now. Every month, he sent messages, urging them to hold on, that he was working, that he was fine, that he would return soon, very soon. His grandmother, in turn, would reply each time she received his wires: "Your grandfather is drinking more and more each day"; "Please return. We need you."

Caught between there and here. Between two lives, two cultures, two identities. He was frightened all the time now and carried with him a strong feeling of anxiety that he couldn't shake away no matter how hard he tried. It was only a matter of time, he believed, before he would be forced to return there, penniless, empty, shamed, with nothing at all to show for his sacrifices. His father had returned to San Antonio de la Fe with his mother, the beautiful and refined city girl, the daughter of a wealthy business owner. But what would Diego return with? Only disappointment. He would die a failure. The passport sat on the bed, the ink from the stamp smudged, the words and numbers slightly faded, but he could see that the visa had expired some time ago now. The only person he had confided in was Fiona. Only she knew his true beginning. To everyone else, he was the young Portuguese or Spanish man. He was whatever they wanted him to be.

A few days later, when he and Fiona were out walking around and window-shopping, Diego was uneasy. He felt as though people were staring at him as they meandered down the street. "Mexican!" he imagined a pedestrian shouting. "Arrest him!"

"What's with you?" Fiona asked, sensing he was tense.

"Nothing," he said. "Everything's fine, my dear."

They stopped at an intersection and waited for the light to turn. Fiona touched his forehead. "I think you got too much sun today." She glanced about and pointed across the street. "We're going into that drugstore to get you something to drink."

Inside, the electric fans whirred, and the air felt cool and moist. They took a seat at the very end of the counter, and Fiona removed her hat and Diego's and asked the soda jerk behind the counter—a freckle-faced young man with bright red hair and thick eyeglasses—to tilt the fan in their direction.

"Sure, miss," he said. The soda jerk walked, clumsy and uncoordinated, to the fan, and fiddled with it a few times before getting it right.

Fiona loosened Diego's tie for him. "He'll take a Dr. Pepper," she said to the jerk. "I'll have a cherry phosphate, please. Can you make it quick? He's ill here."

"Yes, ma'am," he said, pushing the glasses up the bridge of his bony nose. "Coming right up."

"Fi," Diego said, as she struggled with the knot of his tie. "I'm fine. Really, darling."

"Hush now," she said. "You feel warm to me. We'll sit here for a bit and cool off then head home."

The soda jerk rushed over with their drinks, and while they drank, Diego looked around the drugstore. It was empty except for a handful of diners scattered here and there throughout the place. When they were nearly done with their drinks, and Diego was swishing around the bits of ice in his glass while Fiona was talking about how important it was for him to take care of himself, and that she felt real bad because maybe she was making him exercise too much, the two brown men walked in. They wore baggy trousers and shirts with wide lapels, and their black hair was long and combed back, held in place by generous amounts of hair grease that perfumed the air as they passed. They took a seat at a booth near the back, next to a service exit. Several of the other patrons eyed them, and an old lady in a frilly white hat and gloves took the child she was with by the hand, stood, and stormed out, dragging the little girl with her.

The jerk stood behind the counter, arms crossed, glaring at the two of them. "Can you believe those people?" he said to Diego and Fiona. "The city's overrun with their kind. Filthy greasers."

Fiona took a few sips of her cherry phosphate, grabbed her things, and said to Diego, "Let's go."

He stood there, though, unmoving. "I'm still not well," he said. He pointed to his glass. "Besides, I'm drinking this."

She sat back down in a huff. "*What's* with you?"

The soda jerk continued to glare at the two greasers. A few times, he went around waiting on the other customers, serving sodas and malteds he carried on a silver tray. Each time, he walked by the greasers' table, ignoring them altogether. Finally, after a few minutes, one of them rose, walked over to the counter and leaned in, between Diego and Fiona.

"Hey!" he shouted. "Service."

"Come on," Fiona urged Diego. "Let's go. Really now."

But Diego didn't budge.

"Service!" the man shouted again, this time pounding his fist against the counter.

The soda jerk stood behind the counter, unmoving. "Get out of here before I call the police," he said. "We don't serve Mexicans." He took a few steps back and grabbed a nearby telephone. "Do it now, or you'll be sorry."

Instead, he reached across, grabbed a jar of peppermint sticks, and flung them at the shelves behind the counter. The glass shattered, and the red and green peppermint sticks lay strewn across the floor among shards of broken bottles. Then the other one stood up from the table and made his way to the door. He took in the whole drugstore—its bleached walls, the checkered black-and-white floor, the bright vinyl booths that were smooth and spotless. His eyes were narrow slits, the pupils black as obsidian. He had high and defined cheekbones, a wide and low forehead, and a set of thick, hearty eyebrows. His skin was dark, darker than anything Diego had seen in some time. Diego sat completely still as Fiona clung to his arm, terrified. He gripped the door's knob, his arm taut and lean. His large Adam's apple quivered and rolled up and down the length of his neck as he spoke, his eyes resting squarely on Diego, his gaze bitter and unflinching.

"Güachate, guerinche," he said then turned around and he and his friend ran off down the street.

"What was that?" the soda jerk asked, his voice shaky, startled. "What did he say to you? Was that Spanish?"

"No," Diego said, finishing his soda now. He rose and placed his hat back on. "I don't know what language he was speaking."

"You know him?" the soda jerk asked. "Are you one of them?"

The other patrons sat there, frozen, eyes unblinking. Two teen-aged girls huddled together. A woman in a red velvet coat clutched her purse and wept. The soda jerk's face was bright and flushed, the freckles there now nearly vanished, concealed by his skin's redness.

"No," he said. "I'm not. I'm *not* one of them." Diego stood, grabbed his hat, and took Fiona by the hand. "Let's go," he hissed, and they walked out the front door.

He would work today on a film set in "dark Africa," he was told, where he'd play a native savage. He was wearing his costume—a short loincloth, no shoes, a necklace made of bones and shells and feathers—when he sat down in the makeup chair. Fiona had been there since six in the morning, setting out her greasepaints and brushes and creams at a nearby station. When she saw Diego, she walked over and began smearing black paint all over his arms and face.

"Did you hear about Sancho?" she asked.

"Sancho? What do you mean?"

"He and a huge bunch of the others living in the same neigh-borhood were rounded up last night and sent back to Mexico. Can you believe it?"

"Who told you that?"

"One of the other extras who lives around there saw it happen and ran off before they could catch him." Fiona continued applying the black face paint until it completely covered Diego. He stared at his reflection, the grease hardening over his skin. It was only a matter of time before they came for him, he thought.

Sancho Gutiérrez was one of the few Frontier extras that Diego knew by name. As two of the only ethnic-looking bit players around the studio, Diego and Sancho were often assigned to the same pic-tures and scenes. One week they were Alaskan Inuits, the next Indi-an chiefs and braves, the next Chinese boatmen. In his mid-forties, Sancho was overweight and always jovial, his hair already graying around the back and sides of his head. Diego had heard him tell one of the other extras, a girl, that he was from the state of Jalisco.

"*Ja-lis-co*," he repeated, stressing each syllable when the girl couldn't pronounce it.

When Sancho spoke English, he did so with a heavy accent, and some of the cameramen and set builders loved teasing him about this. Sancho would laugh with them, but when he stepped away, the men would shake their heads and call him "stupid beaner" and "dirty Meskin." In those moments, Diego was glad not to have been honest about who he was.

He only spoke with Sancho briefly, while they sat in the makeup chairs or waited in between takes. Sancho had a daughter named Evangelina, a wife named Carmen, and a younger brother back in Jalisco who he hoped to convince to move to California.

"I took my family out of there just after the revolution started," he told Diego one afternoon. "It was hopeless. My brother wants to stay. Work the land that belonged to our father, but I say to him, 'What is left there? Just a barren piece of earth. Leave it and come here where there's plenty of work.'"

Diego wanted to tell him that he knew very well what Sancho's brother was going through, that he knew about family obligations and responsibilities, that he understood the loyalty that kept him shackled to that volatile land—he had only felt it too late, himself. Instead he remained quiet.

"Do you ever want to go back there?" Diego finally said to him.

Sancho chuckled and shook his head. "No. Never. My daughter, she was born here. She's an American now. This is her home. I want her to grow up in America. Marry. Raise a family. In Mexico, that would not be possible. Mexico's not a place for people like me." Here he stopped and pointed at Diego. "People like us."

"Like us?" he asked.

"Yes." Sancho stood and started making his way back inside the soundstage. "Us. People not part of the elite."

"No. My grandfather was rich. He owned—" Diego started to say, but Sancho was already inside and unable to hear him.

He thought about Sancho as Fiona finished applying his makeup. An assistant to the director came over to him and clapped her hands loudly. "Don't you look amazing, darling," she told Diego and the other extras who stood in line, waiting for further instructions. "Like real African *savages*."

The set had been designed to resemble the Serengeti. There was tall grass, a foam tree and rocks, and a shallow pool of water where they were to gather and dance as another member of the tribe beat a ceremonial drum. The painted backdrop featured herds of wildebeests and a flat plain dotted with more trees.

The director was in a good mood, and he surveyed the set and shook the hand of each of the tribesmen. "Excellent, gentlemen," he said as they took their places. "It's time!"

The director yelled "action" and the drumbeats sounded, and he and the others danced around, flailing their limbs and shuffling their feet. He fed off the rhythm, and that energy that flowed through everything and through him. Diego was a part of it, and he felt that this giant machine had now taken him in and claimed him as one of its own. As he danced with the other men, he remembered the first time he performed with the other boys when he lived in San Antonio. He remembered the sound of Gonzalo's flute, and he heard Elva's claps again. He felt a camaraderie, a kinship that was ancient and sacred, and he told himself that this was where he belonged. This was his tribe. This was his land. These were his people.

Diego was still wiping away traces of black body paint from his arms while he stood near the studio's front gate waiting for Fiona. He was growing hungry and irritable. Why was she taking so long? He smoked and paced as he waited. He realized he hadn't thought about William Cage for days when he saw him suddenly emerge from the revolving glass doors of the executive building across the street. A jacket and fedora were cradled in his arm and he held a leather briefcase. He fumbled through his pockets for his keys, which he handed to a sweaty-faced valet who darted off to fetch the car. Diego took several deep breaths as he approached. He tapped him on the shoulder and Cage swung around, an unlit cigarette in his mouth. When Cage saw Diego, the briefcase fell from his hand and hit the floor with a soft thump.

"You startled me!" he said, bending down to grab it.

"I'm sorry," Diego said. "Please forgive me, Mister Cage."

"It's quite all right." He searched through his pockets for something to light his cigarette with. "Do I know you?"

Diego reached into his own jacket and found a box of matches, struck one, and lit the cigarette for him. "We met once."

"Oh?" He furrowed his eyebrows. "Did we?"

"Yes," Diego said, pointing to Cage's lip. He was disappointed that Bill hadn't remembered him. The cut had left a scar that was faint, but he could still see it. It gave his otherwise flawless face an air of imperfection that Diego found endearing, dangerous, and very enticing.

Cage's frown softened now. "Yes," he said. "I remember now. I remember." Cage frowned again. "But what are you doing here? You're not some reporter, are you? Looking to bribe me? I'll have you know that many people in the business frequent those types of places. They're bohemian. There's nothing indecent—"

"I work for Frontier. As an extra," Diego interjected. "I mentioned it that night, but you were rather drunk."

Cage puffed on his cigarette. "I see. So, you're not a reporter?" Here he leaned in.

"No," Diego said, smiling. "Your secret's safe with me."

Cage winked at him. "Good. A good man, you are." The valet came speeding around the corner with his car. "Well, I'm off then," he said, flinging his coat, hat, and briefcase in the car and getting in. He was about to close the door when Diego grabbed it and held it. "Excuse me," Cage said as he tried shutting it.

Diego held on.

"What are you doing?" he grunted, giving up, out of breath.

"I need you," Diego said to him.

"I hear that from a great deal of men," he said. "Make an appointment with Marjorie and she'll—"

"No," he insisted. "This can't wait."

William Cage let go of the door handle, smiled up at Diego, and said, "You know? You're awfully cute when you're determined."

Diego stood straight up, broad-shouldered, head held high. Just like his grandfather, just like Fiona would always urge him to do. He took a deep breath and cleared his throat before he spoke: "Look, sir, I'm not here to flirt or play games with you. I am here to ask you for help. For the past few years, I've worked diligently and loyally for you and this studio, which I admire greatly. I'm proud of my work and proud of what I do, and you can ask any of the directors in your employ; they will attest to my dedication and drive. I only ask that you consider—"

"Shut up," Cage said.

"Excuse me?"

"Shut up and have dinner with me. Tonight. My house." He closed the car door and started the engine. He rolled the window down. "I'll send a car for you at six."

"But you don't know where I—" he started to say, but Cage drove off.

He didn't wait for Fiona. He ran all the way back to the Ruby Rose. That afternoon, Diego lay down in his bed, his shirt off, smoking, staring up at the chipped ceiling, the pipes in the walls groaning and hissing. He checked his pocket watch over and over. Two hours before the car would arrive, he bathed, shaved, and put on his good blue suit. He mixed himself a tonic to settle his stomach, sat in the chair by the window, and thumbed through a copy of the month's issue of *Reel News*, finally stopping at a black-and-white photograph of actor Samuel Sloan. In the photo, he wore a plaid tam-o'-shanter hat with an exceedingly large pom-pom on the top, checkered plus fours, and sheer stockings. In his hand he held a golf club. Accompanying the photo was a short write-up about Sloan's most recent picture for Frontier, a comedy titled *Mister Ne'er Do Well*. Once while they milled about on the set between takes, one of the other extras, a skinny kid with buckteeth and clumsy feet, had told Diego that he'd heard Samuel Sloan was actually a Jew.

"Passes himself off as wholesome all-American. Corn fed," the extra said. "But he's a Jew. Went from Weisman to Sloan, and like that," he said, snapping his fingers, "he starts getting parts and becomes a Frontier darling."

People did it all the time, Diego knew. They changed or hid their identities to get what they wanted. It wasn't anything shocking or unheard of. He had chuckled at the extra's naïveté. He put the magazine down, took his watch out, and looked again at the time. Restless, he lit another cigarette, rolled the magazine up, and sat back in the chair. There came a knock on the door, and he rose and opened it. A man in a black jacket and chauffeur's cap stood in the entryway.

"Car for you, sir?" the man said.

The neon lights made trails of bright streaks as they drove west on Sunset Boulevard. Soon, they pulled into a large circular drive-way lined with tall Italian cypress trees that swayed in the breeze. The house sat on a large plot of land known as Bel Air—past West Hollywood and Beverly Hills—in the folds of the rolling green hills in the western part of the city. It was a Spanish-style structure with an arched portico, a tiled roof, and wrought iron fixtures. The chauffeur stopped the car, swung open the door, and climbed out.

Inside, the floors in the vestibule and living room and dining hall were laid in brightly colored mosaic tiles and the winding stair-case banister and handrail were made of a black iron that was rather imposing.

A butler in a black suit and bow tie led him to a sitting room and pointed to a bar near a large window. "Would you care for a drink, sir?" the man asked.

"Whiskey." He sat, lit a cigarette, and tried to relax. "With ice."

"Yes, sir," said the butler. "Beautiful day out." He plucked ice cubes out of a bucket with his gloved hands and poured the whiskey from a glass bottle.

"Indeed," he responded, absentmindedly.

The butler handed him the glass. His face was gaunt and his skin very pale. His eyes were watery and red. "Mister Cage will be with you shortly. My name is Lawrence, if you need anything in the meantime."

Diego was starting to get impatient when Cage finally walked in. He wore tan trousers, black loafers without socks, and a silk smok-ing jacket with nothing else underneath. His bare chest appeared through the jacket's smooth shawl collar.

"Welcome," Cage said. He reached out, took Diego's hand, shook it, then leaned in and gave him a soft kiss on the cheek.

"Thank you."

They had more drinks and sat in the living room. By the time Lawrence came in again and announced that dinner would be served shortly, they were both quite drunk. Cage sat near him. He reached out and placed his hand on Diego's knee. Then he rose and led Diego through a pair of French doors and into the next room. They ate in the large dining room, which was grander than any room Diego had seen. A large chandelier hung from the tall ceiling. Long curtains covered the windows, and there were candles lit and fresh flowers in glass vases.

"So," Bill said as they ate. "Do you enjoy working at the studio?"

"I do."

"Why?"

Diego smiled. "I've always wanted to perform. It gives me the greatest thrill in the world."

"What roles have you taken?" Bill lit them both a cigarette.

"Everything," Diego said. "A bank robber, a policeman, a pirate, a French peasant."

"Sounds a bit menial," Bill said, laughing.

Diego took a puff of his cigarette, shrugged his shoulders, and said, "It's steady work. Not exactly what I would like to be doing forever, but it's good for now."

Lawrence and a plump maid in white nylon stockings cleared the dishes, and the two remained there, drinking more wine, then whiskey, smoking cigarettes as the gramophone in the adjacent room played on and on. It was getting late, and Bill started stumbling about, changing the records and singing along. When Lawrence walked in and asked if there was anything else, sir, Bill waved him along.

"No, no," Bill slurred. "You can both retire."

"Very well," said Lawrence, who turned and left.

"Are we alone?" Diego asked.

"Yes," said Bill, who led him to the living room. They sat close to one another on a couch with velvet pillows and oversized arms. "Finally," he said. "At last."

Their knees touched. Diego looked into William Cage's eyes. He placed his hand on Cage's leg. "Thanks for having me over."

Bill smiled, his hair tousled, untamed, crazy. "My pleasure." He leaned in and whispered, "You're a very handsome young man."

"I'm glad you think so." He kept his hand on Bill's leg when he leaned in and kissed him on the lips.

Bill then rose, cleared his throat, and said, "I need some air." He reached his hand out. "Come with me," he said. "Come on, come on."

He led them to the backyard where, beyond an expansive green lawn, the pool sat, lined on either side with stone pots. Bill stood at the end of the pool, taking deep breaths, swaying on the balls of his feet. He removed a loafer, and when he went to dip his toe in the water, collapsed and fell in, splashing about, arms flailing uncontrollably.

Diego laughed. "You're drunk."

"You're adorable," Bill said. "Come. Jump in."

"Like this? I'm fully dressed."

"Then undress."

"Here? Now?"

"You're not ashamed, are you?"

"Why, no," Diego said.

"Because you shouldn't be," Bill said. "You have a wonderful body."

He undressed slowly, removing one piece of clothing at a time and tossing them in a pile near one of the large pots. The water was warm when he jumped in, and he watched as Bill flung his soaked smoking jacket and trousers out of the water until the only thing left were his underpants, which he kept on. They swam for a while, splashing one another before slowly crawling out.

"There," Bill said, draping a towel over Diego's shoulders and drying him off. "Better?"

"Yes." Diego turned, faced him, and they kissed. He pointed to the cabana behind the pool. "Got anything to drink in there?"

"I believe I do." He opened the door and switched the lights on. "Be my guest," he said, bowing slightly.

The cabana was small but tidy and well kept. There was a lounge area with two seats and a couch, a kitchenette, and a bedroom and bathroom. Enough for someone to live comfortably back there, Bill said, as he reached inside a closet and grabbed two robes.

"Put this on," he said. They changed, and Diego sat on the ground, which was covered by a large mohair area rug.

Bill walked to a cabinet and pulled out bottles of whiskey and scotch, seltzer water, and a container of ice from the icebox. He poured two strong drinks, handed Diego one, and sat on the floor next to him. From there, he could see through the double doors to the pool, the water aquamarine, shimmering ghostly, as the moonlight bounced off the surface. He took a sip of his drink and relaxed.

They lit cigarettes, and soon the air was thick with smoke, the scent of tobacco perfuming everything—their robes, the furniture, the rug.

Bill talked on and on. He told of how he was born in Massachusetts. He'd been a banker, he explained, a financier. He met R. J. Levitt on a business trip out to California many years back, when the movie industry was just beginning. R. J. had a dream, a vision about starting what he hoped would become one of the biggest and most influential movie studios in Hollywood. So Bill agreed to help him fund his business, and the two founded Frontier Pictures with R. J. as president and Bill as head of production and finance.

"What does that mean?" Diego asked. "What do you do?"

"Supervise mainly," he said.

"Supervise what?"

"Everything!" Contracts. Budgets. Actors and actresses. Stagehands. Directors. Assistant directors. Set designers. Carpenters. Painters. Casting, which he said oversaw the hundreds and hundreds of extras. Accountants. Scripts. Wardrobe and costume designers. Makeup and hairstylists. The publicity department and advertising. "With all that you do, it sounds like R. J. Levitt doesn't have to lift a finger," Diego said.

Bill laughed, and his Adam's apple rolled up and down over his throat when he threw his head back. He stroked Diego's cheek. He touched his hair and his arms, his fingers and palms. "You're something else," Bill leaned in and whispered in his ear. "Do you like working for me?"

"Sometimes I do," Diego said. He reached out, took his glass of whiskey, drank some, and handed it back. "The things I do aren't exactly the best, but they're fine. Steady. What I really need is a chance," Diego whispered. He untied Bill's robe and reached between his legs.

"A chance?" Bill asked, moaning softly.

Diego kissed his cheek, felt Bill's hardness. "A chance. I want people to know my name. I want to be recognized. I'm tired of always being in the background. A face in the crowd."

"I can see," Bill said, panting now, closing his eyes. "I can maybe ask . . ."

Diego crouched and took him inside his own mouth. Bill moaned—soft, gentle—and breathed in and out, faster and faster, his thighs clenching, hips thrusting up just before the release. Diego reached for the glass of whiskey and took a gulp. He let the liquor mix with Bill's seed before swallowing everything down, his eyes watering. He stood now, and Bill lay there, still moaning, muttering something until, slowly, his breathing grew heavier and deeper. Diego knew he had fallen fast asleep.

He gathered his things and walked out of the cabana and up to the house. Inside, he wandered from room to room. Upstairs, he walked down the long main corridor. In one room, he saw that a light was on. He pushed the door open and entered and found Bill's office. There was a large claw-footed wooden desk, a leather swivel chair with brass studs along the seat cushion and back, and a globe beside a stack of papers and documents. He walked toward a credenza crowded with photographs: Bill in a hunting jacket and hat holding a rifle; Bill and R. J. in tuxedos with a group of men and women in suits and ball gowns; Bill and an older man standing in front of a palm tree. He picked this one up, regarded it, let his finger run over the smooth glass, the heavy silver frame. He studied the image carefully, slowly, noting how close the old man held Bill, how tight around his shoulders his grip was, the genuine warmth of his smile. It was William Cage's father, Diego could tell. The old man wore a look of pride on his face. Here was his son. Handsome. Successful. Known the world over.

Diego set the picture back down and went into the library to call a taxi. He waited at the curb until he saw the yellow headlights appear in the distance.

3

April 1931

STRICTLY BUSINESS. THAT'S WHAT Bill's message had said when he contacted him again. It was business. A discussion. Bill said he had some ideas.

The car came once more, and so did the same driver, in his white gloves and little cap. They drove into the sun, which was a rust orange ring hovering just above the gray-green ocean, until the chauffeur pulled up to a small building with white plaster walls and dark windows perched on a cliff. Below, boats bobbed up and down as they skimmed across the choppy waters of the Pacific. He came around and opened the door.

"Mister Cage will see you home," the driver told him and left.

It was dark inside, and the air smelled of brine and cigarette smoke. He was led by the maître d', past a maze of tables where diners ate and drank in the shadowed darkness of the restaurant, to the very back of the restaurant. Bill sat in a large booth, a glass of wine and a lit cigarette before him. He was talking on a telephone that was connected to a nearby wall. The waiters that walked into and out of the kitchen made sure to step lightly over the coil stretched out across the carpeted floor each time they passed. Bill smiled at Diego and beckoned him to sit as he finished up his conversation. He placed the phone down and he poured Diego a glass of wine.

"A very dry, very crisp chardonnay," Bill said, stabbing his cigarette into the ashtray. "Goes perfect with seafood."

"Thank you," Diego said. He could hardly see the glass because it was so dark. He groped the air, inching his hand across the table. "There's not much light in here."

"I like it," Bill said. "The darkness. No prying eyes."

Diego agreed.

"I've been thinking a lot about you ever since our night together," Bill said, lighting a cigarette for Diego, then another for himself.

"Oh?" Diego took it, and their fingers touched. "I have, too."

"You're very bold, very brash. I like that in someone. You're a confident person. What compelled you?"

"I want to succeed," he said. "I want to be recognized, admired."

"Why?" Bill asked, stabbing his cigarette into the ashtray and lighting another.

"Because I love acting, this industry. When I perform, I can become anyone other than myself. It makes me feel like I belong to something more. I want to be a leading man. More than anything."

"Anything?"

"Anything." Diego looked him straight in the eye, his gaze unflinching. "Can you help me? Will you help me?"

Bill sat back in the booth. He loosened his tie and ran his fingers through his hair. He was quiet for some time before he spoke again. He said he had asked around, and people told him that Diego was good, a dependable worker, loyal, punctual, that he never complained. Still, he admitted, he was hesitant about his abilities.

"What do you mean?" Diego lit another cigarette.

"You're good-looking," Bill said, crossing his legs under the table. He was very stern when he spoke, matter-of-fact, businesslike. "But look," he said. "I must level with you."

"Fine. Go ahead. Level with me."

He was about to begin when their stuffed crab arrived. "It's very good," Bill said, picking up his fork and knife. "You should have some before it gets cold."

Diego studied the dish—the creature's hard outer shell, small rings of green scallions chopped and sprinkled throughout, cloves of garlic swimming in the buttery sauce—and pushed it aside. "I would rather you say what you were about to say." He took another gulp of wine and puffed on his cigarette.

Bill placed his fork and knife down and sighed. "I've asked around about you," he said. "I hear your acting needs some finessing. Some depth."

"But every director I've worked with—"

"The people you've been working with are not the studio's best and brightest. You've been relegated to the low-budget productions. What I'm saying is that you are forgettable. That the majority of the people out in the world don't even know someone like you— countless others like you—exist." Bill sat back and folded his arms, then continued. "I'm not trying to discourage you. I want to help you realize just how harsh, just how competitive and scrutinizing the business could be. It's more than just working hard, more than just staying on your mark or taking direction well. It's the full package."

"What do you mean, by the full package?" Diego asked.

"Looks," Bill said. "Personality. Charisma. Charm. Resilience. Intelligence."

"And talent?" Diego asked.

Bill shrugged his shoulders. "Sometimes a little of that, too. If one is lucky. Like I said, it's the full package."

"What are you saying?"

"We make stars by assessing what they have and what they lack."

"So, what do I lack? What can I do to have the full package?" Diego took a bite of the crab.

Bill cleared his throat and leaned in. "You have the looks, though they need some work. An element of danger, of mystery perhaps. Your talent's raw, all over the place."

Diego took another bite of the crab and sipped his wine.

"May I be frank?" Bill said.

"I thought that was what you were doing," he said, laughing.

"Why should I and my company invest in someone like you?" Bill explained that each of the major studios had a Latin actor under contract. MGM had Ramón Novarro. Empire Pictures had Orlando Mendoza. Frontier, he said, had no one. "I was thinking that maybe you could be it," Bill said. "But I'm not entirely sure."

Diego asked, "Why aren't you sure?"

"What makes you so different from those others? What makes you unique?"

"I'm talented. I'm hardworking. I won't let you down."

Bill rolled his eyes. "Spare me the pat responses. Do you know how many times I've heard that before?" He raised his voice above the hum of conversations, the din of dishes and glasses and silverware around them. Suddenly the darkness was quiet, everything still, only the roar of the ocean outside penetrating the silence. "Go on," he said. "I haven't got time for rank amateurs. Go home. Go back to wherever it was you came from." He picked up the telephone and began to dial.

Diego felt his face flush, felt all eyes piercing through the darkness, watching him. "No," he said, his voice low and weak. "I won't go. I won't go back."

"Murray 9-4545," Bill said into the telephone. "Yes, operator. Marjorie Curtis."

"I said I won't go," Diego said again.

"Marjorie," Bill said. "I need you to set up a meeting with the Teamsters. We need to go over the outlines of this new contract of theirs—"

"Don't ignore me, sir," he shouted.

"—to avoid another strike. Now you tell R. J. that I need him there to—"

Diego reached over, snapped the phone from his hand and slammed it against the table. "Listen to me," he said. He leaned in close, very close, his face only a few inches away from Bill's own. "I won't go away. I simply won't. Not until you help me." His hands trembled. His skin grew hot. He breathed heavily and profound and the look Bill wore as he gazed into Diego's eyes was one of excitement and fear, attraction and revulsion all at the same time.

He picked the telephone up. "Marjorie," he said. "I'll call you back." He placed it down and smiled at Diego. "Very well," he said. "Very well, my friend." He took Diego's hand and kissed it. "I was merely looking to see how much this means to you, how passionate you are. Now I know."

When they finished their meal, and Diego followed him out, they drove off in his car, speeding around the sharp curves and jagged cliffs. Below, he caught glimpses of the sea, the water dark, churning and churning. Bill placed his arm around Diego, and he understood what he would have to do now, all he would have to sacrifice, those things Carolina had talked about so many years before, to become what he wanted.

He ran into Fiona at the studio diner. She sat with a group of make-up girls who were drinking coffee and chattering in loud and shrill voices.

"Hey, Fi," said one, pointing to Diego as soon as he walked in. "Ain't that bellboy over there your guy?" he heard her ask.

He wore a maroon jacket with gold stripes and matching trousers, white gloves, and a cap. He was working on a film in which he played a bellboy working at a hotel. He was supposed to walk in on the two leads—characters Polly Page and Gordie Green who were being played by Hilda Avery and Lester Frank—in the middle of a kiss and embrace and nervously utter the words, "Pardon me. I was looking for the woman traveling with the schnauzer," prompting Gordie to shake his fist and shout, "I'll give you schnauzer, you good for nothing . . ." as he chased the bellboy down the hall in the picture's closing scene. At the last minute the director had decided to postpone filming of that particular moment and reshoot another that took place earlier in the picture, involving a zoo, an escaped mother gorilla, and Gordie. Diego had been instructed to kill some time and return in a few hours.

Fiona walked over to where he sat and gave him a peck on the cheek. "Where've you been?" she asked. "I've been trying your number. Leaving messages with that old gal who calls me sugar. You ain't two-timing me, are you?"

"No," he said, pretending to be frustrated. "Of course not. They've been running me from one end of this place to another the past few days."

She drummed her lacquered nails on the clear countertop. "You haven't been around much is all. Guess I'm just being silly."

"Look," he said. "I need to get back to the set. What say me and you go out later tonight, huh?"

"Promise?" she said.

"Promise."

He was ready when she came to the Ruby Rose that evening, dressed in a new suit and shoes. He kissed and thanked her as they walked down the street. "Thanks for all your help, dear."

"Help with what?"

"The advice. The exercising. The whole thing." He remembered his conversation with Cage a few nights before, his opinion regarding his talents, his acting. Though he knew that he still had much to learn, and much to improve on, he was grateful to Fiona for all her help, her companionship, her care.

"It was nothing. Honest."

Fiona said, as they boarded the trolley bus, holding on to the seat rail in front of her with her gloved hands, "Truth is I kinda like helping."

"Really?" he asked, looking away and smiling.

"Really," she said.

As the trolley wound its way up Santa Monica, the sun was starting to set in the west, and everything was golden, radiating. He pulled the window shade down, turned, and gently kissed Fiona's cheek.

"I feel like I'd be lost without you, dear," he said.

She reached out and squeezed his hand, and he tried not to think about Cage, their night together. And the lie had come easy to him. So simple. So effortlessly. Like breathing or walking or blinking, any number of things the body does in response to a shift in light, temperature, or functions necessary for survival. He didn't know whether to be proud of himself or ashamed of what he had done.

They were out all night, going from one dance club to the next. At the Rio, they ran into another Frontier extra, a handsome young man named Alfred who had once offered Diego a chance to make more money on the side when he complained about being broke. They were both working on a film. They were Spartan soldiers. They had already been fitted with their crimson tunics and bronze cuirasses, which covered their torsos. The costume supervisor had led them to a wooden table upon which sat leg greaves, the armor that would be placed over their exposed shins, fastened with clasps the costume supervisor said needed to be hidden because they were not "historically accurate." They stood before long, rectangular mirrors fussing with the heavy woolen cloaks, called himations, the costume supervisor stated, when Alfred said hello to Diego.

"Here," he had said. "Let me help with that." Alfred's fingers stroked Diego's shoulders and jaw as he helped him adjust his cloak.

After the shoot, in which they had endured hours upon hours of marching under the blazing sun, sweating in their wool capes and metal armor, Diego muttered something to Alfred about the bad pay.

"I entertain men," he said as they walked back to the soundstage. "I make money by going out with them. They're very nice fellows. Quite rich and eccentric. You should think about doing it. I can introduce you to some of my clients. You're very handsome and have a wonderful physique. You'd be very popular."

"Thank you," Diego had said. "But I'll make do."

After Diego had changed and left the soundstage, he heard a whistle, turned, and saw Alfred running after him. He held a slip of paper, handed this to Diego, and ran off. *In case you change your mind*, it read. Below that, he had written a telephone number.

Diego introduced Fiona to Alfred now. He smiled, took Fiona's hand, and kissed it. "Charmed," Alfred said. He wore a black tuxedo and a red silk scarf draped over his shoulders.

"What sort of trouble are you getting into tonight, Alfred?" Diego asked.

Alfred pointed to an older overweight man dancing with a tall, blond woman who he told them was a French socialite named Veronique. The poor idiot, Alfred said as the three watched the couple dancing clumsily.

"The fat man's a wealthy financier who's funding her little endeavor in the hopes she'll marry him once she's famous," Alfred explained.

"But?" Fiona asked.

"She's never going to make it," Alfred said, laughing. "You should hear her singing voice. Just horrible. And that accent."

"Well, at least she's tall, pretty," Fiona said. "She may—"

"Beauty's one thing. Talent's another," Diego said.

"Touché," said Alfred.

"And you?" Fiona asked. "Where do you fit in?"

Diego and Alfred exchanged knowing glances. Alfred lit himself a cigarette then handed one to Diego. "Honey," he said, puffing a long thread of smoke out. "I'm just along for the ride."

The air was fragrant as they walked back to Fiona's apartment; the night-blooming jasmines and gardenias perfumed the cool evening. They strolled under the thick branches of trees, crushing purple jacaranda petals along the way.

"All the girls on my floor have been teasing me," Fiona admitted, once they reached the front stoop of the apartment. The ice vendor had forgotten one of the racks they used to haul chunks of ice from their trucks across the sidewalks and up into the buildings or homes. Fiona kicked the wooden slats with the tip of her shoe.

"Teasing you?" he asked. "Why?"

"It's nothing. Just silly girl talk. That's all."

"Tell me," he urged.

"Mary's boyfriend just got back from the service," Fiona said. "And they plan on getting married in a few months. And Georgie says she found a receipt for an engagement ring in the pockets of Nick's trousers."

Diego cleared his throat, shuffled uncomfortably. "What's that all about, now?"

"They tease me something, I'll say. 'When's he proposing? Where's the ring?' they'll ask." She shrugged her shoulders. "I don't know what to say."

"Well," he said. "See, that's, that's . . ."

"Just look how twisty you get whenever our talks get serious."

"What do you mean?" He laughed, trying to sound lighthearted. "Why, we're fine. We're just fine, doll." He reached out and embraced her when he saw that she was starting to cry.

"I'm getting old," she said, in between sobs. "That's what my mother keeps saying. Almost 25. And who'll want an old hag like me once I'm nearing 30?"

"Nonsense," he urged. "Nonsense. There's plenty of time. Why, we got our careers, remember?"

"I haven't got a career. Makeup. I got crummy makeup. Putting cream and goop and glue on the faces of a bunch of second and third-rate actors. That's all I'm surrounded by. Nothing but a bunch of untalented louts." She took her hat off and flung it across the lawn.

He didn't need this. Not now, he thought as he turned to retrieve her hat. "Fi," he said, placing it back on her head crookedly. Moist blades of grass clung to the fabric, and he plucked them away, trying to calm her down. "Get ahold of yourself. Stop being hysterical. Why, you're acting like a child."

She looked at him, shivering in the warm night, her bare shoulders jerking up and down. "You love me, don't you?"

"I do," he said. And he did, he really did, but not in the same way.

"And, if this whole acting thing don't work out, promise me that you'll give it up. That you'll do something else? That we'll be together. Because, honestly," she said, "that's all I've ever wanted for the past two years, from the moment I met you. For us to be together."

"But my contract is for seven years," he said. "There's no telling what will—"

"Yeah," she said. "That's just it. There's no telling. A contract don't mean diddly." She calmed down some then asked, "Do you love me or don't you?"

Just words, he repeated to himself, again and again. *They don't mean a thing. Just words. Say them. Say them.* "Yes, Fi," he assured her. "I do."

She didn't want to be alone, so he took her back to his apartment, and they stayed up late listening to music, smoking cigarettes, and drinking milk with rum. They made love, but all the while he was thinking about Cage, the power of his naked body, the things they had done that night after their second dinner, Diego on his back, on his knees, Bill's mouth on the nape of his neck, across his chest, between his legs. *Bill, Bill*, he told himself, remembering how he'd pushed himself inside of Diego, how the power of his heavy body felt towering over his own, how weak and needed he made Diego feel as he penetrated him, and Diego had cried from the pain of this and so much more and Bill had held him tight, had rocked him in his arms, had soothed him to sleep.

4

January 1932

THEY CELEBRATED THE NEW Year with a shower of champagne and, that evening, Georgie and Nick announced their engagement. Fiona would be Georgie's maid of honor and, though they hardly knew one another, Nick asked Diego to be his best man when the four of them were out at the ballroom in the Biltmore Hotel. As midnight approached and the crowd became increasingly lively and energetic, Nick tapped his wineglass and cleared his throat and Diego, Fiona, and Georgie turned to him.

"I know we haven't known each other very long," Nick said to Diego as the girls looked on. "But, well, I don't have very many friends and, well, you're the only real guy I know." Nick's face was bright red.

Diego felt sorry for him, truly sorry for Nick, and this was why he gave in and told him he would. "Sure," he said. "Sure. Why not?"

Georgie clapped.

Fiona squealed. "It'll be such fun!"

A date was set: Valentine's Day of the following month. A Sunday. The wedding was to take place at the United Methodist Church on Highland and Franklin, and the reception would be at the home of Nick's mother and father in Bel Air. In the weeks leading up to the wedding, Fiona was busy helping prepare for the event. He was grateful for the distractions; it kept Fiona preoccupied and always pressed for time. They hardly saw one another and this freed him up to continue his affair with Bill without having to sneak around or lie to her like he had been doing for the past few months. But still, he couldn't help but feel that she was beginning to suspect. He tried hard not to seem distracted, to feign attraction to her even though, during their times together, he only longed to be with him.

"It's like you're far away these days," she said one night while they lay in his bed together. Lately, he had been having difficulties being intimate with her and, though he tried chalking his inability to perform to fatigue, she was starting to sense that it was something more. That evening, after several attempts, Diego had managed, by concentrating on Bill and their lovemaking, by imagining her as him, to perform, much to Fiona's delight. Still, once they had finished, she remained troubled.

"Why do I get the feeling that you're just going through the motions?" she asked.

"What are you talking about?" he said.

"I'm talking about us," she said. Fiona stood now. She placed her stockings and skirt back on. She adjusted and smoothed out the ruffles on her blouse. In front of the mirror, he watched her straighten her hair and touch up her face. "You've been less than passionate lately. Things aren't going as smoothly as they used to. And it makes a girl feel undesirable, unattractive."

"I'm just tired," he said, collapsing on his bed, staring up at the faded ceiling, tracing the black veins running across the cracked plaster walls. "I'm tired and very overwhelmed." But he could tell she wasn't buying this.

Abruptly, she grabbed her handbag and reached for the door. "I have to go," she said. "I'm meeting Georgie for a fitting."

"Wait," he told her. "I'll dress and go with you. Then, afterward, we can go to dinner. I'll buy."

"No." Her tone was sharp. "I'll just see you. Tomorrow. At the rehearsal." She walked out of the room and closed the door.

He didn't want to move. He sat there and smoked cigarettes all morning, then bathed and dressed and decided he would call Bill and try to see him that evening.

In the trolley to Bel Air, he ran his hand across the green mohair seat back and tried relaxing, but it didn't help. What would he do about Fiona? He didn't know if it was love he was beginning to feel, or if Bill saw him as nothing more than a fling. What Diego did know was that the man excited him. It was his power, his influence, the control he exerted, his charm and sophistication, the way he doted on Diego, how he looked at him. It was partly Bill himself, and partly what he could do for Diego's career. Bill took him places because, he said, it was necessary for his success.

"Building excitement," he said. "Until we assign a press agent to you. Until we find the right vehicle to launch you, you need to be seen."

"Aren't you afraid?" he asked. "That people seeing us together will rouse suspicion? About your tendencies?"

He chuckled. "I've the best reason. You're my protégé. Besides, everyone in Hollywood knows about me, about countless others in this business. They just don't talk about it in public."

There were secrets that weren't, Diego soon realized, scandals that were orchestrated, and others that were allowed to continue without intervention. But when these things were exposed, the parties involved were usually quick to distance themselves, to claim ignorance. Nothing was ever as it seemed. Bill's secret was anything but, and Diego was more than happy to go along with the charade. He was "the handsome young man with Mister Cage," or "the new young foreign actor William Cage discovered." And when they were out together, dining at a restaurant, at polo tournaments, or at the racetracks in Santa Anita, and Bill introduced Diego to people he knew—christening him Frontier's "next bright star," its "newest talent," its "most exciting discovery"—they regarded him differently, they noticed him, they remembered his name when he ran into them at cocktail parties, dance clubs, and around the studio.

He didn't want to think about Fiona. He felt his attraction for her weakening just as hers toward him seemed to strengthen. Lately, all she talked about was Georgie's wedding, the beautiful dress, and Nick's plans for them once they were wed.

"They'll honeymoon in Venice," she'd told him one night when they were out, her voice tinged with romance, with passion. "A villa with a balcony in the countryside. They'll be moving to New Haven. Nick will go to school. Yale. Study law. Afterward, he'll take a job in a firm run by his father's close friend in Manhattan. They'll buy a house in the suburbs, and Nick will take the train into the city. They'll have children and raise their family."

It was all planned out, she had said, waving her hand across the table where they sat sipping coffee. Their entire life. Right down to the number of children they would have. The kind of car they would drive. The age at which Nick would retire. The countries they would visit as they traveled the world. He would take up golf. She would become a pillar of the community, host bake sales and afternoon tea parties.

"Doesn't that sound nice?" she asked. "Don't you want that too someday? I know I do. I crave security. There's only so much make-up I can put on before I lose it."

He said nothing. He lit a cigarette and watched the smoke. He thought about his grandparents again, about Paloma. "Everyone has always had plans for me, for my life," he said. He stabbed his cigarette into the ashtray and ground it in with force. "But nobody ever asks what I want. What I see."

"But I just did, sweetheart," Fiona said, pleading with her hands. "I just did."

"I want to act," he said. "I want to be a star. It's what I've always craved. I love acting, performing, more than anything in the world."

"But what if it never happens? You've got to have another plan. Something lined up in case."

"It'll happen," he said. "I'll make it happen."

He repeated those words now as the trolley made its way down the boulevard. People exited the car and others boarded. The men wore cheap suits and ties, the women wore plain dresses and outdated hats. It was unseasonably hot that February day. Nobody sweated, and each time Diego breathed it pained his chest, and he imagined that dirty and parched air sticking to the linings of his lungs like cactus thorns. He swallowed several times, but this only made him cough, made his eyes water. Diego stared out the window, at the dust-coated palm trees that lined the street, the brittle fronds blowing in the warm air like the dry fingers of old people.

A father and his daughter boarded the train next. They sat in the bench across from him. The girl wore a bonnet and a tan jacket, and black Mary Jane shoes with white socks. She was eating an ice cream cone. The father nodded at Diego and tipped his hat.

"Good evening," he said.

"Evening," Diego responded, tipping his own hat.

"Grace," he said to his daughter. "Be careful not to get any of that on your dress."

The ice cream was melting and white swirls dripped down along the side of the cone. She licked it faster and faster. Her pink tongue moved with a precision, with a greed that was uncomfortable. Grace ate and watched Diego, her bright blue eyes big and glassy and unblinking. He was relieved when they rose and prepared to exit the next stop.

"Say 'bye,' Gracie Mae," the father said to his daughter as he pointed to Diego.

She raised her hand and waved. The ice cream dripped down, leaving small white puddles on the floor of the trolley. He tried not to step on them as he exited the train once it reached his stop, but the car bucked forward, and the sole of his shoe came to rest over one of the drops. As he made his way down the sidewalk, the ice cream hardened and created an annoying sticking sound with each step that he took. The sound grew louder and louder, more aggravating, as he went along.

That night he learned that, since Bill was a good friend of Nick's father, he would be at the wedding and the reception.

"Simon Wexler's gotten me out of some pretty sticky situations," Bill told him as they lay in front of the fireplace, his arms wrapped tightly around Diego's shoulders. "We go way back. I'm happy for Nicky. I was beginning to think the guy would never settle down."

Diego said, "Do you ever think about that? Settling down?"

Bill was quiet for a long while. "Yes," he said. "But as long as I could set up the rules. As long as I could keep my affairs from my wife and family."

"Family?" Diego asked. "You think about family?"

Bill chuckled. "Of course I do. Don't you?"

He didn't answer.

Bill squeezed his shoulders. "I bet you're going to look absolutely dashing in your tuxedo." He kissed Diego on the cheek and mouth and whispered, "It'll take all my will not to rip your clothes off and have you right there. In front of all those people."

They made love that night, and as Bill slept, Diego lay awake thinking about the question of family. About marriage. About the future and Fiona. The upcoming wedding made him nervous. He closed his eyes and tried to sleep, but it never came.

The Hollywood United Methodist Church had been completed just two years earlier in 1930. Its smooth stone facade gleamed new and pristine that day as Diego sped up Highland Avenue. A row of cars lined the front of the curb when he pulled around with Nick in the red roadster Simon had purchased for his son as a wedding gift. As was dictated by Fiona, Diego's duty was to take Nick out for one last night on the town as a single man before he was to exchange vows with Georgie. He had taken Nick to several nightclubs around the city, just the two of them, the previous evening, but the party was cut short when Nick overindulged and passed out by 11 o'clock. Diego, for one, had been relieved. He wasn't looking forward to a night out with just Nick. They had very little in common, and their conversations usually consisted of breezy talks about the horse races or football games. Nick was severely hungover and groaned in the passenger seat.

"Where did you learn how to drive?" he asked as he stumbled out of the car.

Diego ran around and straightened Nick's bow tie and fixed his hair. "Never mind that, Nick," he said. "Pull yourself together. You're about to get married."

An old man in a ridiculously large top hat and monocle strolled over. With a shaky hand, he reached into his suit pocket and pulled out a metal flask. "Hair of the dog that bit ya, Nicky."

Nick took it and drank. "Thank you, Mister Riley." He handed it back.

"No, son," said Mister Riley. "You keep it. I've a feeling you'll be needing more of that." He winked and climbed the steps and into the church.

Nick finished the rest of the booze and tossed the flask inside the roadster. "Let's go then," he said. "Let's get me married."

The wedding ceremony was slow to start. The attendees, all mainly family members and friends of Nick, sat with patient but annoyed looks on their faces as the minister and the organ player fussed about doing who knew what. The alcohol had relaxed Nick and he smiled repeatedly and patted Diego on the back.

"Before long it'll be you and Fi up here, old buddy," he said to him.

Diego nodded just as the wedding march began and the last few guests trickled in. He saw Cage walking down the aisle with a tall and very striking woman.

"Bill's latest discovery," Nick whispered in Diego's ear. "What I wouldn't give to be that guy. A different girl on his arm each time."

Now the wedding procession began. Fiona made her way down the aisle with small and graceful steps. She was exquisite, her blond hair swept up in a bun, bare shoulders exposed, and her face flawless. She reminded Diego of a statue, a form carved of a single slab of marble, each curve of her body, each angle, clearly defined, smooth and untouched.

"You're one lucky guy," Nick leaned in and said to Diego.

Georgie made her way down next, the long train of her dress trailing behind as her father, an overweight man with a balding head who walked with big, cumbersome steps, held her by the arm. The exchanging of rings and vows was slow and predictable, and Diego felt Fiona's eyes on him. Several times he glanced over to find her smiling knowingly at him, a glimmer in her eye. He wished only to glance back, to see Cage in the audience, to yank the woman from his side away and take her place. He was so lost in thought, he didn't even hear the priest present to the crowd Mr. and Mrs. Nicholas Wexler, didn't remember his and Fiona's march down the aisle, a few steps behind the newly married couple. Next thing he knew they were all outside, in the glaring white light, standing along the sidewalk, throwing rice at the couple.

"So wonderful," Fiona said, dabbing the tears from her face with a handkerchief. "So . . . so romantic."

Through the dinner, the awkward speeches, the cutting of the cake, the bride and groom's first dance, Diego drank. Cocktail after cocktail.

"Slow it down, will you or you'll pass out," Fiona whispered to him at one point.

He couldn't help it. He was seething. Bill sat there with the woman, his arm around her shoulder. She tossed her hair about and batted her eyelashes excessively as she engaged the people sitting at their table in conversation. Bill took her out to dance a couple of times, and Diego saw him whisper in her ear from time to time, even kiss her neck, and caress her cheek. Toward the end of the evening, when Nick and Georgie had snuck away inside the house and the few remaining guests milled about, Diego walked over to the bar and asked the server for one more. He drank the whiskey and was smoking cigarettes when he saw Bill approach.

"I've been watching you all night," he said. "Don't you think you've had enough?"

Diego chuckled. "What do you care? You better go before your little harlot wonders where you've traipsed off. Does she know about your proclivities? The ones you keep so secret?"

"Please," Cage said. "Don't make a spectacle. She's my date. That's all. Nothing more."

Diego laughed and stumbled forward. Bill caught him. He grabbed him by the arms and led him away. He walked him down a gravel path behind the tables, and they found a bench and he sat him down.

"I'm sorry," Diego muttered. "I'm so sorry. I just. I feel so confused."

"It's all right," Bill said as he sat beside him. He reached into his pocket, pulled a handkerchief out and used it to dab Diego's face. "There's no reason to apologize. No reason to be jealous. She's just my date. From time to time I have to be seen with women like her. That's all."

Diego rested his hand on Bill's thigh and placed his head on his shoulder.

"Careful," Bill whispered, glancing around.

"Why?" Diego asked. "I thought you said—"

"You know why."

Diego stood now, swaying, his head swirling. "I'm going to find that girl of yours and tell her."

"Tell her what?" Bill rose, trying to get him to sit back down.

"About—" And as he walked away, Bill reached out, took Diego in his arms, and hugged him.

"Stop it. Come now," Bill pleaded. "Get ahold of yourself."

Diego collapsed, gripping his shoulders, sobbing. "I'll tell them. Please let me tell them," he said. "I can't stand it. I want to tell them who we really are."

"What's happening?" Fiona stood near the hedges, holding Georgie's bouquet, the flowers still fresh and fragrant. "What's going on?" She looked at him then at Bill. "Mister Cage?"

"Your friend here's had a little too much," he said. Bill removed Diego's arms from around his neck.

"I'll tell her," Diego said. "I'll tell them all."

"Tell them all what?" Fiona asked.

Diego collapsed on the bench.

"I should run along," Bill said. "Toni must be wondering what happened to me." He said good-bye to Fiona, turned, and left without saying a word to Diego.

"Hey," Fiona said, sitting down now, holding him up. "What's going on here? Tell me, please. What's happening?"

He took a deep breath and stood now. He cleared his head and focused. "Nothing," he told her.

The moon was full that night, the blue light eerie and incandescent. It bathed her face in a sickly pallor. She sat there, beautiful, lonely, her bare shoulders slender and elegant. No strand of her hair was unraveled, her makeup was still perfect, her dress just as smooth and pristine as it had been at the wedding ceremony. He repeated these words to Fiona again and again. There was nothing going on. Nothing. But he could see, even in that weak moonlight, the look of worry and doubt that he had cast upon her knowing face.

5

April 1932

FOR TWO MONTHS AFTER the wedding, he tried calling Fiona but was met with only silence. He didn't run into her around the studio, and when he asked any of the other makeup girls, they would shrug their shoulders and say they hadn't seen or heard from her. Georgie was gone, so he couldn't ask her.

"Where's your little gal?" Rose asked one day while he passed the front desk. "On you like glue then she's gone. What gives?"

"I think she's mad at me," he said, but he knew it was more than that. He remembered his behavior at the wedding and shuddered.

"Send her flowers," said Rose. "Chocolate. Give her some tickle." She winked. "That always cheers a girl up."

He sent her a box of chocolates and a bouquet of roses with a note that read: "My dearest Fi, I miss you." Near the end of April, Rose handed him a note.

"Guess it worked," she said and giggled.

It read:

We need to talk.
Fi

She showed up and was calm and polite when he answered the door. He led her in, and when he tried to kiss her, Fiona gave him a slight push and shook her head. She looked flushed and sat down, explaining that she was feeling ill.

"I've been a tad queasy and have had slight headaches," she said.

"Anything to drink?" he asked. "I could run down to the drugstore for some Bromo-Seltzer. I'm fresh out but could always use more." He pointed to the empty blue glass bottle on the table.

"No, thank you," she said. Fiona sat, removed her hat, and placed her hands in her lap.

"Look," he said. "I haven't been entirely honest about my feelings and—"

"I talked to Mister Cage the other day," she interrupted.

"Oh?" He tried containing the nervous tone in his voice. "Why?"

"I'm leaving Frontier. He didn't tell you?"

He paused, took a deep breath. "Why would he tell me, of all people?"

She remained quiet.

He cleared his throat. "What will you do?"

"I'm going to Sunrise Pictures. They've offered me a position as head of makeup. A step up."

Fiona would work on a series of high-budget films Sunrise would be shooting over the next few years. The first was to be called *Columbus*, about the famous explorer who found the New World. Much of the filming would be done overseas, in Italy and Spain. She would have to agree to be gone for at least six months. She said it was a great chance, and that she would be getting paid almost twice as much as she was making now.

"You didn't know?" she asked again. "He never mentioned any of this to you?"

"No," he insisted. "Why in the world would he have?"

"I just thought that the two of you were—you know?—close. You're his protégé. All that. Then at the wedding I found you two—"

He interjected. "I was drunk. I didn't know what I was saying."

She looked up at him now, and there was a deep sympathy in her eyes, a pain, an anguish he had never known before. "I think you knew."

"So you're taking it?" he asked.

"Of course. I'd be a fool not to," she said, shrugging her shoulders. "It's good money. A chance to spread my wings."

"Fi," he said. "What about us?" He reached out and took her hand.

"Don't," she said, removing his hand. "It was fun. But there's nothing between us. I should've realized that a long time ago. A guy like you has other interests."

"What do you mean?"

"Your career. Your ambitions. Your hopes. They aren't mine. And you still have to figure out who you are. I can't help you with that. I thought I could."

"But—"

"Good-bye. I'll see you around."

She walked out the door, and he didn't try to stop her.

Her departure left him reeling. Diego hadn't known just how much he needed Fiona—her company, her love for him. And now that she was gone, he came to realize that she was the only person who knew who Diego really was. He longed for home, for Mexico, even his grandparents. But he found now that his memories came in weak, sporadic fragments: wide green fields, the smell of loamy earth in the countryside, the sound of cornstalks rustling in the breeze. He thought about his mother and father, wondered about Javier, Carolina. His teacher, the only mother he had ever known. Their faces were obscured when he tried conjuring them up, as if he were seeing them through gauze. In his dreams, when he tried to reach out, to touch them, they would evaporate or turn to ash, which would frighten him, and he'd wake up panting, sweating, terrified, alone in his bed.

Bill kept busy around the clock, dealing with a series of pressing issues around the studio—threats of strike, financial strife, disagreements with R. J., temperamental actors—and canceled several outings and dates with Diego. When he did finally call and invite him out, it was business. They met at a crowded restaurant off Wilshire

Boulevard, and he found Bill sitting at a booth with a stack of papers before him. He looked tired and disheveled.

"We've got a picture for you," he said. He pushed the forms aside and rubbed his eyes. He took a sip from his drink then continued: "A real unique opportunity to help launch you." He slid a script across the table.

Diego took it and read the title. It was in Spanish. *La novia de sangre*, it read. He was confused. "What's this?"

"A script." Bill chuckled.

"But it's in Spanish. I thought I'd do English-language movies. Like I have been."

Bill said the talkies made selling films to foreign audiences who didn't speak English a little trickier. They had to now worry about words, about actual dialogues. Many studios had taken to filming two versions of films they hoped to pitch to international audiences or immigrants residing in the United States. In this case, they would be filming two versions of the film, one called *The Bride of Blood* for American audiences with an English-speaking director and actors; the other would have a Spanish-speaking director and actors.

"And the English version?" Diego asked him. "Why can't I do that one?"

"Not yet," he said. "Not quite yet. We have to work up to that. Be patient."

"But—"

"Trust me," he said. "I know what I'm doing. Do you accept the part or not? I need to know in the next 24 hours."

Diego took the script. "I'll tell you tomorrow then."

"Very well." Bill gathered his things and rose. "I'm sorry. I have to go. Please order whatever you like and put it on my account."

"You're not staying?"

"I'm afraid I can't," he said. "I'll make it up to you. I promise. All of it. I know we haven't spent much time together, but things have been stressful. Order anything you like on me." Bill grabbed his coat and hat and left.

Diego was angry so he ordered the most expensive thing on the menu: filet mignon in red wine sauce, and a bottle of merlot. After his meal, he read the script. The movie was about a blood-sucking female vampire terrorizing a remote town high in the Hungarian mountains. Diego knew he had little choice in the matter, and realized he didn't want to wait until tomorrow to decide. He asked the waiter to bring him a telephone.

He dialed Bill's number. Lawrence answered. "Please tell Bill I said I'll take the part," he said.

"Very well," Lawrence responded.

He hung up then finished the wine and ordered another bottle and a crème brûlée for dessert.

He couldn't remember the last time he had been as nervous as he was before this screen test. It would be in Spanish. The last few years had required him to speak more and more English so that, by the time the script for *La novia de sangre* came his way, Diego felt unsure about his ability to deliver the lines, to pronounce the words properly, to carry the language. He felt like an outsider, a stranger, as he flipped through the sheets, breaking down the scene he was to perform for the test. That morning, he found it hard to focus. He forgot his lines. His hands trembled, and he felt his heartbeat quicken. Nevertheless, when time came for him to leave for the studio, he put his jacket and hat on, took a deep breath, and marched toward the trolley stop, focusing, rehearsing his lines over and over.

At the test, he met his costar. Alicia Prado came from a line of impressive stock. Her father was a nationally recognized stage actor who toured throughout Argentina, Latin America, and Europe. Now an acting coach with his own theater troupe in Buenos Aires, where Alicia first got her start, he had been singlehandedly responsible for producing some of the country's most regarded actors and actresses, such as Olga Bermundes and Fernando Alaniz. Alicia had gone on to star in a number of successful films back in Argentina. She was in Hollywood now, she said, hoping to "make it big."

Alicia was young and radiant, with bobbed hair and an animated way about her. "I've heard so much about you," Alicia said when he walked up and introduced himself. She sat in front of a large mirror with lights running along its edges and was adjusting her outfit, a long blue and yellow dress.

"It's a pleasure," he said.

She smiled and rose. "My, but you are so tall." Her English, despite a strong accent, was understandable, her voice beautiful and melodious, and she immediately put him at ease with her affection, her kind face and jovial attitude. "I'll need lifts to reach you," she said, chuckling.

"They do that to some actors or actresses," he responded. "You know? Lifts."

"Oh, I don't mind if I have to," she said. "I'm just so excited to be here on the Frontier lot working on a movie. You know, the director is such a veteran of the film scene in Latin America. I do hope it's a fun experience."

"Have you worked with him?"

"No," she said. "But plenty of my friends have."

They watched the film crew get the lights and microphones in position. They darted around, back and forth, moving cameras into position, adjusting lenses, marking the slates with chalk. Alicia nodded to the director, who sat off to one side, flipping through the script, muttering to himself.

Alicia turned to him and asked, her tone serious, heavy, "Tell me, are you nervous? Are you scared?"

"No," he said, feigning confidence. Bill once told him that a leading man would never show his insecurities.

"Where did you study? What school?"

"None," he told her. "I have no formal training."

"Well," she said. "That's quite all right. I'm not a snob."

She said everything she learned about acting she got from her father. He trained her to perform from the time she was old enough to stand. And, when she officially joined his theater troupe at the age of 10, she had already accumulated an impressive amount of experience playing in the most prestigious and impressive theater houses in Argentina. It's been a lot of hard work, Alicia explained, and from the theater there eventually came offers from the film studios that were starting to emerge around Buenos Aires and throughout the rest of the country. They stood behind the cameras watching the crew prepare the set. He was in a version of one of the costumes his character was required to wear—a basic suit and tie—and the director had instructed the makeup people and stylists to do what they could to make Diego appear a few years older. But not too old, he had stressed. So they combed his hair to the side, put him in a different set of clothes, and gave him sideburns. They called him forward then, and Alicia stayed behind. He stood on the set, which was the interior of a courtyard where he and Mary, his character's young wife in the film, would meet and talk. The courtyard consisted of flower beds, a stone bench, and a gurgling fountain.

"We'll do some very basic poses, okay, son?" said the director. Then he asked him to stand by the fountain. "Here." He pointed to the small X on the floor, and Diego was annoyed; he knew where his mark was.

Carolina had sent him a few letters over the years. She had gotten his address from his grandparents and wrote him from time to time, filling Diego in on all that was going on in Morelia and her life. And, though he had rarely written her over the years, her correspondence had remained consistent. She had written at least once a month. He had told her, early on, about the rift between himself and his grandparents, his breakup with Paloma, his intention of someday returning but not until he had acquired at least a semblance of success. "So that years from now, my children could have real proof that I had lived," he wrote once.

She mentioned his grandparents in passing, a few lines scattered here and there throughout her letters: Doroteo was no longer working; they sold the house and business and moved out of the city. Where to, she never said. He also learned that Javier had returned back to Morelia after having traveled throughout the country, organizing rallies and protests, first against the church, then the government. For a time he lived in remote villages in the states of Oaxaca and Chiapas, helping the local indigenous people to build schools and clinics. "He's well," she had written. "Passionate as ever about his politics. Idealistic." In her last letter, she told him that Javier had gotten serious with a girl named Lucía Martínez, someone he had met in a class at the university. This class, taught by a professor named Juan Aragón, a man known to be a staunch Communist with radical ideals, a man who had made a name for himself by criticizing the corrupt government and political powers in Mexico, had apparently taken a liking to Javier and was grooming him to be his young protégé. But then Aragón died mysteriously. Some suspected it was murder. Javier had dropped out of school and taken up the man's cause.

It was well past nine in the morning now. He had overslept and needed to be at the studio by 10:30 for the last round of costume fittings before the company was to begin production of the film when there came a knock on the door.

"Yes?"

"You got a call," one of the other tenants shouted through the door.

"Thank you." He stepped out of his room, his shirt unbuttoned, shoes unlaced, as he went to the phone at the end of the hall. "Yes?" he said. "This is Diego."

"Hello," a young man's voice said. "Brother, it's so wonderful to hear your voice again."

"Who is this?" he asked.

There was a pause and then he spoke, "It's Javier," he said. "Javier. From Morelia. Brother, it's so good to be talking with you. So, so good."

"Javier?" He was stunned. Diego felt hot blood rush up to his face. "Javier?" He held the wall. "How did you get this number?"

"I called the studio. Pretended to be your brother," he said.

"You're calling me from Morelia? Why? What's happened?"

"Everything's fine. I'm in San Bernardino, actually." Javier sounded enthusiastic. He took many breaths and talked rapidly. "I should be in Los Angeles next month."

"What?" he asked. "Why?"

Javier said he was traveling through the United States with a group of his associates, visiting with union leaders and leftists throughout the country. Now that the left was in power in Mexico, Javier explained, there was very little to rally against, since the elites and their sympathizers had been ousted, so they set their sights on the United States. They would be stopping in Los Angeles then San Francisco, Chicago, and eventually New York—to shore up support for trade unions, workers' rights, to raise money for "the cause," as Javier put it.

"We'll be staying for a few weeks," he said now. "We're meeting with some directors, producers, and actors. We've gotten much support from Hollywood folks. I'd like to see you while we're there. There's a lot I need to tell you about. Can we? Will you be terribly busy?"

"I'm to begin filming a movie," he said, glancing at his watch. "I'm very late. I can't talk at the moment."

"It's fine," he said. "I understand. I want to see you when I arrive, brother. I must run, but I'll messenger you when we're there."

"Very well. I'd like to see you, too."

"Good," he said, then hung up.

He had no time to dwell on it. He finished dressing, combed his hair, and ran down the stairs and into the street to catch the next trolley to the studio.

A few days later, both *The Bride of Blood* and *La novia de sangre* began production with little attention in the media, only a few articles here and there in the trade journals about the happenings around Studio 18 on the Frontier lot as "the oldest movie company in Hollywood films the same movie in two languages." The articles told of the two separate crews. "While the English crew films in the morning, the Spanish cast and crew," one article wrote, "are at home, taking their much-needed siestas during the day. At around four o'clock, Dalton Perry and his crew bid a fond 'Adiós' to the studio. Then, an hour later, Señor Salazar and his troupe of bleary-eyed and sleepy Latin stars stumble in to film during the long hours of the night while the entire Frontier studios, and Hollywood, sleeps after a hard day of filming." Diego still couldn't believe his film was now being talked about in the magazines he had once so religiously read.

They were shadows, he thought on the first night of shooting. The studios shut down, lay silent, unmoving. The offices emptied out, and the clerks and secretaries and typists, the switchboard operators and messengers, the accountants and payroll staff, the makeup and wardrobe people, the set designers and architects, the directors and their assistants, Mr. Levitt and Mr. Cage, everyone, everyone just left. The scouts and reporters, the grips and lighting technicians, the carpenters and truck drivers, and the extras and talent agents, they all rose, straightened their backs, dropped their hammers or microphones, their blunted swords or wooden pistols, their pens or staple guns, and they marched en masse out of the iron gates of Frontier Pictures, "Where Stars Are Born," to families and dinner and a drink, to a hot bath or shower, to rest and regroup. They left it behind for the night, and they breathed and were grateful. With the offices and soundstages emptied, with the hallways and waiting lobbies and trailers hushed, with everything still, all activity stopped, when the great empires of the world—China, Egypt, England, Ancient Rome—ceased moving, ceased being, a new group took over, claimed the spaces, claimed the libraries and chambers and cathedrals of wise men and refined women, the battlefields of warriors and soldiers, the hallways and classrooms of learned men, the prairies of farmers, the oil fields of barons and tycoons, the countries of kings and dictators. They claimed this all, armed with feather dusters and cleaning solvents, metal carts with wheels they toted back and forth across the great canyons of the studio, their uniforms simple and forgettable. They washed the steps where a notorious gangster had been shot that morning, dusted the crib where a newborn had slept, straightened the office of an executive who had just launched the careers of some of the biggest film actors in history, polished the furniture in the waiting room where hundreds of extras had milled about, hoping and praying that today they would get their big chance, the break they were looking for, hoping for.

And the film crew of the first all-Spanish production ever to be shot on the Frontier Pictures lot joined that secret society, that underground citizenry who slept during the day and claimed the night for their own. Diego watched them with great interest—those silent, unseen Americans—watched with greater interest as he himself joined that segment of the population. For the next six to seven months, Studio 18 on the Frontier Pictures lot would be in operation 22 hours a day. The hours from five in the morning until four in the afternoon would belong to Perry and his all-English crew, and the hours from five in the evening until four in the morning were Salazar's and his group's.

Production began, then, simply, uneventfully, without much excitement, as the Spanish crew took the lead, shooting first. And it was a strange feeling to be sleeping during the day and passing through the gates of the Frontier Pictures lot at night, while the large domed soundstages lay empty and abandoned and dark. They had the entire place to themselves, and he and Alicia took time off between takes to drive around in the studio trams to visit the soundstages, to drop in on the sets of the other films under production at the same time as theirs. They scaled the Great Wall of China, marveled at fake icebergs, and danced around the mirrored walls on the set of *The Lady Sings*.

It was fun, and they played and drove through the lots and back roads, over sand dunes and a castle's moat, across the American prairie and around the Chilean Atacama Desert. Over the next few weeks, he found himself spending his free time with Alicia. Her spunk, her zest, made him laugh and remember what it was like to have fun again. She was so different from Fiona, and he loved how impressed she was with him, marveling at how well he spoke English. On the weekends and on days when they weren't filming, he took her around town, showing her the sights—the Egyptian Theatre, the Brown Derby, Sardi's—and they traveled all over the southland. The studio's media hounds leaked information to reporters, and their pictures appeared in all the publicity rags with captions that said things like "Frontier's Latin Heartthrob Seen with Leading Señorita," or "As Hopping as Two Mexican Jumping Beans."

A little over two weeks into shooting, Dalton Perry ran into some trouble on the English set. The article in the gossip section of *Snapshots* was vague, vague in the way such stories—carefully controlled by the publicity machine that was Frontier Pictures and its alliances with publications such as *Reel News, Screen Test,* and *Snapshots* itself—always were. It seemed that Jerome Hunt, who had taken the role of Peter in the English-language version, had been involved in an unfortunate and embarrassing scandal. The article mentioned an arrest, an "unidentified female entertainer," and a bottle of prescription drugs. Jerome's doctor, the article went on to say, was recommending the actor be pulled immediately from all current and upcoming projects to rest, for he was suffering from "mental fatigue and was not in the right frame of mind to make sound decisions."

Diego had read enough of these reports to know that the phrase "female entertainer" was a thinly veiled word for a prostitute, and that the prescription drugs were likely not at all given to Hunt by his physician but acquired illegally. This scandal would surely spell the end of Jerome Hunt's career. The actor had been a problem for the studio for years. Frontier had been looking for a reason to get rid of Jerome Hunt, whose antics and bad behavior had irked studio executives for some time, and this proved to be the perfect opportunity. He was immediately pulled from filming *The Bride of Blood*, and production on the English-language version came to a loud and grinding halt. With no one to play Peter, there weren't many choices left for Perry to rectify the situation. Diego wondered what solution would be presented, what the English-speaking crew would have to do to solve the problem. He wasn't surprised to find Perry there at the set when Diego walked in. He had made it a habit to arrive a few minutes early and sit in his small trailer to rehearse his lines while smoking cigarettes. The English company had vacated and his fellow Spanish actors and actresses had yet to arrive. Perry was anguished, Diego could tell, for he was pacing back and forth and talking with Salazar.

"I don't know," he overheard Perry say to Salazar. "I guess I'll have to look for a replacement. Audition everyone in the city. That'll take time. We'll be way off schedule. The producers won't be thrilled. We'll be over budget."

"Surely you will take the blame," Salazar said, sighing.

"Indubitably," he said. Dalton's face wore a look of anguish as he passed Diego. "Hey, there," he said, putting his hat on.

"Hey, Dalt," Diego said.

"Poor guy," Salazar told Diego when they were alone. "Poor, poor guy. What a headache."

6

June 1932

WHEN JAVIER AND HIS entourage arrived, Diego read about it in *La Opinión*. "Mexican radicals, led by their young and charismatic leader," the article stated, "have descended upon Hollywood." While in Los Angeles, the group would visit "local ethnic barrios." They would address the unfair treatment of Mexicans by the police and by civic leaders who were allegedly targeting and harassing those they'd been unable to drive out of the city. The papers printed stories about cholera and tuberculosis outbreaks among the Mexican barrios and claimed that if these people were not removed, Los Angeles would face an epidemic as widespread and lethal as the influenza outbreak of 1918.

He agreed to meet Javier at a diner. Diego arrived early and ordered a strong cup of coffee, which he drank quickly. The shoots had made him disoriented and groggy and, after nearly two months of filming, the long nights and sleeping during the day were disrupting his eating and resting pattern. Sitting in the café that morning, he found the bright lights glaring and intrusive and painful. His skin looked pale, his face a little more sallow, not as robust and full as it was before. He was yawning and rubbing his eyes when Javier approached.

Diego hardly recognized his friend, and even though it was only five years since he left Morelia, it seemed as though an eternity had passed. Javier wore a tan jacket and a black beret. He removed these and placed them on a hook near the front entrance. He had grown a thin mustache, and his sideburns were long and trimmed short. He was taller, more filled out, and when he walked over, he took long strides, as though he were marching. Diego rose and Javier hugged him, clamping his shoulders with his large hands.

"Look at you," Javier said, patting Diego's back. Javier touched his face and kissed him twice—once on the left cheek, then on the right. "Brother, what a pleasure it is to see you."

Diego felt Javier's arms, taut, muscular, and he shut his eyes and recalled once more the closeness of his friend, a feeling he had missed, had craved all this time. He remembered now what this had been, and he felt like crying because there it was again: the thing that had been lacking in his life. His reverie was interrupted by the sound of someone clearing their throat. Diego opened his eyes, and Javier let him go. He turned now and gestured to a young woman with light brown hair and bright lips, her grin wide, her eyes beaming.

"This is Lucía," said Javier. "My—"

"Partner," Lucía interjected. Lucía was tiny, thin, yet when she hugged Diego, he felt an assuredness and confidence within her that surprised him. "It is a pleasure to meet you, Diego. Though we met once before. A long time ago."

"Oh?" he asked, curious.

"Yes," she said as they sat in the booth. She removed her gloves and placed them inside her purse. "You came to one of our rallies. In a huge warehouse on the outskirts on Morelia. Have you forgotten?"

He thought about it for a moment. He remembered now. Following Javier and Esteban that day years before. "Of course," he said. "Yes, now I recall."

A waitress came over and they ordered more coffee and a basket of cinnamon rolls.

"I've been keeping up with all your news," Javier said. "I heard about the film you're working on. The one being shot entirely in Spanish."

Diego yawned again. "Yes, the schedule has me all out of sorts.

Filming throughout the night has its advantages but drawbacks as well." He sighed deeply. "Still, I wouldn't change it for anything."

"Imagine us sitting here with a real film star," Lucía said.

"Yes." Javier smiled as the waitress brought the rolls and coffee over. "Diego's certainly made a name for himself, though it would be nice if he used his sway to shed light on some injustices, get behind a cause."

Lucía took a sip of coffee and smirked. "Must you always be on a crusade?" To Diego, she said, "Never mind his diatribe, I think what you're doing is wonderful."

"Thank you," Diego said, then lit a cigarette.

"Look, all I meant was—" Javier started to say when she cut him off.

"Enough," Lucía exclaimed. "We're sitting here with one of your dearest friends. Someone I heard you talk about so often. Let's not waste time bickering. Let's catch up."

"And your mother?" Diego asked Javier. "She wrote me from time to time. How's she? Your father?"

His father cheated on Carolina. A woman appeared on their doorstep carrying a baby she claimed was his. A young girl, Javier said. Barely sixteen. A dancer he met at a hall one night. Manuel denied it, of course, but his mother, Javier insisted, knew the truth.

"So, she left him," he said.

"And my grandparents?" he asked. "What news do you have of them?"

"Not much. You know that they sold the house and business and left Morelia, right?"

He nodded.

"They're living just outside of Guadalajara, renting a small place owned by Emmanuel Pacheco."

"Renting?" Diego asked.

"Your grandfather lost a lot of money. Emmanuel Pacheco must have—"

"And Paloma?" he interjected.

"I don't know."

"Your fiancée?" Lucía asked. "I heard she married a man from Bolivia. Lives there on a farm with him." She took another sip of coffee before continuing. "Your grandparents. Last time we saw them, they looked so, so *meek*. Javier pointed them out to me. He said they were heartbroken over your departure."

"What was I supposed to do?" he asked. He ground his cigarette into the ashtray and lit another.

"I didn't mean to upset you," Lucía said. "Forgive me, please."

They were quiet for a while then Diego spoke. "It's fine. It's just, I sometimes feel so conflicted. Like maybe I should return. But I have a real chance here."

"Then stay," Lucía said. "Return only when you're ready."

"That's what I intend to do," he said to them both.

Javier and Lucía told Diego all about their plans to travel to San Francisco, Detroit, Chicago, New York City, visiting factories, steel plants, assembly lines, helping workers organize and strike if need be. There remained, they said, a great deal of inequality in the United States. People were still starving and out of work and desperate. He listened to them with great curiosity, almost baffled by the things they talked about, the ideals they proclaimed and espoused, things he knew very little about.

"Javier says you two were very close." Lucía stirred her coffee.

The two eyed each other. "We were," Diego said. "But then . . ."

Lucía asked, "Then what? Javier speaks of you with such great fondness, such tenderness. Yet he has never told me why you two had that falling-out."

"It was just one of those things," Diego said.

"Yes," insisted Javier. "Our lives went in different directions."

Diego looked at his watch. "I should go." He rose and put his jacket on.

"Our friend's throwing a party this weekend," Lucía said. "You should come. There will be many show business people."

"I don't think he'll be able to make it," Javier said. "He's much too busy. Aren't you, Diego?"

"What do you say?" Lucía asked. "We'll be leaving the following Monday. We won't see you again for who knows how long. Besides, I have a feeling you and Javier have a lot to talk about."

"Very well," he said.

She wrote the address on a napkin and handed it to him. He placed it in his pocket, then left the diner.

Not wanting to go alone, he invited Alicia. "Imagine it," she said, as they sat getting their makeup done before the day's shooting. "Me at a party with such radical people. And some show business folks thrown in, too? I wonder if any Hollywood bigwigs will be there. That's what I need," she said, turning to look at Diego as a makeup assistant glued the long and bushy sideburns along both sides of his face. The adhesive he used smelled awful and irritated his skin.

"I just bought this dress," Alicia said when he picked her up that night. "I was saving it for something special. I think this party might be it."

They had dinner first and took a taxi to the address Lucía had provided. The streets curved and climbed up and up as the car made its way. It was too dark to see anything. It had been gusty all day, the hot breeze bending the palm trees until it looked as though they were made of rubber, but now the winds had calmed some, so everything was quiet and still. He adjusted his tie as he walked up a stone path toward the house with a wide green lawn and shrubs shaped like giant eggs. Upon closer inspection, he could see lights flickering inside and could hear the chatter of voices and tinkling glasses. Several automobiles were parked in the gravel driveway to the side.

The party had been going on for several hours by the time they arrived. Inside, there was noise and women in feathered boas and short skirts and men with drunken red faces and sloppy hair. Jazz music blared from a room to one side of the foyer, and a couple stood at the foot of the stairs, kissing. There were people scattered about, chatting in pockets here and there, no one he fully recognized. A man he didn't know said hello to Diego by name as he passed, entering a room where a group of three women in dresses decked with small tassels stood barefoot atop a large wooden dining table, dancing wildly and giggling. They roamed about, and Alicia found the bar and had several drinks.

They watched people waltzing under a large chandelier to the music coming from the gramophone.

Alicia slurred when she spoke. "Can you believe all the people with him? I can't wait until I'm famous enough to have my own entourage. My parents sent me along with just one single chaperone, some old lady who never speaks to me and could care less if I stay out all night while I'm here." She stopped now, fanned herself with her hand and said, "I'm hot. Let's get some air, shall we?"

They found Lucía outside sitting at a table. Diego introduced her to Alicia, who smiled and told her, in an excited voice, what a roaring party it was.

"Where's Javier?" Diego asked.

"Over there." Lucía pointed.

Javier held court to one side of the large concrete patio, yelling and talking to a group of young men and women with agitated looks on their faces. "Tell me," he shouted to one as Alicia and Diego approached with Lucía, "how crooked do you think the LAPD is?"

"They must be stopped," one from the group said. "But how? The corruption here runs deep. Very deep."

"Every day there are more and more accounts of beatings," said a woman. "Of people disappearing. And the police do nothing whenever a report is filed. The chief is corrupt. The city politicians are corrupt. Everything here is based on lies and cover-ups."

The argument grew louder as they watched. Javier managed to tear himself away when a group of reporters with a small independent newspaper began to argue. He walked over to them and introduced himself to Alicia.

"It's a pleasure," said Alicia, bowing her head.

"Charmed," said Javier. "Your support means a lot. Actors are such visible personalities. They can do a lot to raise awareness."

"For your cause?" Diego asked.

"Yes," Javier said. "The cause."

"Always the cause," Diego said, his tone bitter and sarcastic.

Alicia gripped his arm.

Lucía cleared her throat. "Don't start, you two."

"You sound hostile," Javier said. "Are you not for social reform? The rights of workers? Their desire to be treated fairly?"

"Perhaps I am," Diego said. "Perhaps I'm not."

Javier shook his head. "A person with such contradictory views should be careful. That kind of gullibility can get you into some sticky situations. It's important to know which side you're on."

Diego knew which side he was on: his own. He was about to say this when Lucía announced she was going inside for a drink and

Alicia followed her, leaving Javier and Diego alone on the patio. Giant potted plants overflowing with vegetation lined the stone railing along the perimeter, and people stood next to them, smoking and flicking their ashes inside the pots.

"That was a bit rude, didn't you think?" Javier asked.

"I call it being honest," Diego said.

"So, is that what you've learned here? How to be honest?"

"Yes. That and how to survive."

The full moon cast enough light, turning the color of the grass from green to a deep jade. Several oddly shaped shadows stalked across the yard. They were low to the ground, with heavy, round bodies supported by pairs of skinny legs. The birds came into view, and he saw that they were peacocks. They had long and elegant necks, their plumage a fan of turquoise and indigo, glossy black and bright yellow. They stopped just a few feet from the perimeter of the patio, poking their beaks into the wet grass.

"Aren't they beautiful?" Javier said.

"They are," Diego replied. He placed his hand on the railing and watched as Javier stepped up to it. He stood beside Diego, very close. He was drawn to him and, in the silver glow of the moonlight, he watched his own fingers stretching out, saw his hand reaching. Diego squeezed it, and Javier's warmth soothed and calmed him.

"What are you doing?" Javier asked, startled, yet he didn't move his hand.

"I've missed you," Diego said. "Terribly."

"Brother, I don't know what—" he began to say when Lucía called Javier's name from the house. Quickly, he pulled his hand back and stepped away.

"Coming," he shouted to her. Javier adjusted his jacket and straightened his shoulders.

"You and Esteban," Diego said. "That time I saw you both. I always dreamed you'd—"

"That was a mistake," Javier said. "I was young. Confused. I was experimenting. That's all."

"Don't you ever think about us? How close we used to be? Do you ever think that we—"

"No. I have Lucía now," Javier said, his tone tense. "We're friends, Diego. Nothing more."

"But I thought just now when we held hands that—"

Javier interrupted him again. He walked over, placed his arm around Diego, and led him back inside. "What you think happened didn't. Do you understand?"

Diego didn't know what to say. He remained quiet as they walked into that crowded house, Javier's arm protectively around his shoulder.

The following Monday they were gone, but Diego had no time to dwell on what had happened that night. That week there came a message that Dalton Perry wanted to meet with him. When Diego arrived at his office, Bill was there.

"How are you?" Cage asked.

"Good," he said.

"Sit, sit," Perry implored them both. "Make yourselves comfortable." He took a seat behind his desk, leaned back, and asked Diego how things were going on the set at night.

"Fine," he responded. "A very good crew. A good movie." He looked over at Cage. "Am I being fired?"

Both men laughed. "No," said Cage. "We're giving you an opportunity. A very special one. Though, I must say I'm a little apprehensive."

They asked if he heard about what was happening with Jerome Hunt, with the scandal, and his being fired from the film.

"Sure I know," Diego said. "But what does this have to do with me?"

"I thought and thought and thought," Perry said, rising now and going to the window. He opened it up; a fresh breeze blew through the stifling room. "And nothing. Then it hit me. Wham!"

"Time is money," Cage said. "Scrapping the thing is out of the question because we've already invested too much. We could hire another actor to fill the role," Cage said. "But *that* would take time. We're on a tight schedule."

Diego knew what they had in mind. He remained quiet, though, listening as attentively as he could.

"I need someone, an actor who already knows the part, someone who's already rehearsed the lines," Perry said.

"We want you to consider performing both." Cage said.

"You speak *both* languages," said Perry. "I think you can do this. It's a very unique opportunity."

Cage said, short of canning the film, there was no other way. Recasting an entirely new actor for the role of Peter, he said, would set them back. They would have to conduct a search, the actor would have to memorize the story, the lines. "Frontier needs you," Bill said.

"Jacques, Fay, and Margaret will carry the film," Dalton Perry said.

"You'll just be along to play support," Bill added.

"Most of the character's role in the film requires that he lie in bed, semiconscious, after the countess bites him anyway," stressed Dalton.

"Plus, think of the exposure. Isn't this what you've always wanted?" asked Bill.

"And Salazar?" Diego asked.

"I'll speak with him and, with some cooperation, we'll swing it," Perry said. "We can do this, but we need to know if you're on board. It'll be a lot of work, a lot of readjusting."

Bill said, "It's all riding on you. We need to know if you're committed today. Before we all walk out that door. The entire production is resting on this decision."

He couldn't say no to Bill, not then. It was the opportunity he had been waiting for. He replied without hesitation.

"Yes," he said. "I'll do it. Of course I will."

The next day, Perry introduced Diego to the English cast. Fay Carmichael, in the role of Mary, and Margaret Dillon, Countess Carmilla, both had large personalities but managed to keep those in line. They got along quite well, laughing and joking with one another. Margaret Dillon was tall and statuesque, with fine features and a smooth complexion. She was definitely giving a very different take on the character than Veronica Flores, who had won the part in the Spanish version. Dillon was too overpowering in the role, Diego thought, and her personality acted to blunt the mystique and allure the countess needed to possess. Flores, though smaller and more energetic, could easily slip into the character's skin, transforming herself into the evil vixen in an uncanny way. Fay Carmichael was right for the part of Mary, for the actress had a very stern, very focused, and versatile way about her. She inherently possessed the bold and assertive attitude Mary had, especially once Doctor Von Karnston is introduced and she aids him in the investigation regarding her husband's illness and the strange puncture wounds on his chest. In the role of Lucretius Von Karnston, the eccentric doctor and professor of the occult and the dark arts, Jacques Fantin, a Frenchman and one of the studio's cadres of actors discovered by Cage, had been cast. Fantin's star had fizzled out at some point during its initial birth, and he was reduced to acting in less known, weaker films such as *Alarm* and *The Liberty Boy*. It was rumored that Frontier Pictures had no intention of renewing his contract after *The Bride of Blood* was completed. Such a promising career had turned into a rather disappointing one as, over and over, Fantin was either horribly miscast or criticized by studio executives when his films failed to bring in any profit. As Diego watched the scene play itself out on the set, he didn't notice when Jacques sauntered in and stood just a few feet away from him.

Perry looked over, nodded at both of them, and when Jacques noticed that Diego waved at the director, he glanced at him and asked who he was.

"I'm working on the Spanish version of the film," Diego responded.

"Ah," Jacques said. "You're the one who's going to burn the candle at both ends then, huh?"

"Yes," he started to say when Perry yelled "Cut!" and summoned both Fay and Margaret over. They and a group of various technicians and stagehands gathered around Jacques and Diego.

"Everyone," Perry said, holding a clipboard in his hand, "You all know that Diego will be taking over Jerome's role as of today. He's performing the part of Peter in the Spanish production. I consulted with Mister Cage, who agreed that, in light of recent problems with the picture, this would be the most logical and speediest solution."

"This is like something straight out of a movie itself," said Fay, putting a hand on her hip. "The actor drops out mysteriously and the hopeful apprentice waiting patiently gets his chance." She laughed and shook her head. "Seriously, some bozo should write this down, turn it into a script or something." Fay leaned in, gave Diego a pat on the shoulder and said, "Welcome aboard, kid," then turned and walked to her trailer.

"But does he speak English?" asked Margaret.

"Yes of course," said Diego. "I speak both."

"Well, there's that," said Margaret. "Fine. Welcome."

"She likes to think she's a real bitch," said Jacques. "Likes playing the whole diva role. But, in all honesty, she's a pussycat."

"They're an interesting bunch," Diego said to Perry, who was on his way out.

"That's one way of putting it," said Perry.

¶

July–October 1932

HE WAS EXHAUSTED. In between productions, once the English crew vacated the soundstage and before the Spanish crew came in, he remained there on the set and rested his head for a moment. Diego was tired, so tired, and everything fell silent, and all movement ceased. And he was no longer on a soundstage in Hollywood but at an inn tucked away in the remote town of Corovia in the Carpathian Mountains of Romania. And he plunged into that great chasm now, that crack in time, a moment that was neither day nor night but somewhere in between, a gray space, formless, ambiguous. He no longer walked among them, among the living. Diego felt himself separate from his body, his spirit hovering like black mist over his flesh, apart from and not a part of this life. He dreamed of terrifying specters with pale skin and sharp teeth, of hellish beasts with bristly hair and damp snouts and eyes as red as burning embers. He saw crosses and cemeteries—decrepit and decaying—dotting a dark and icy landscape of gnarled trees and derelict buildings, the sharp and thorny peaks of mountains, plains and valleys laid waste by the trampling of thousands of feet, of battles and bombs and guns and pestilence and plague, where nothing grew, no animals grazed. It smelled everywhere. And there was nobody. All the people had left the land, tired of the evil that thwarted good intentions, that made living impossible, unbearable. Inside the churches, plaster statues of the saints cried tears of blood. And Christ, nailed there to his cross, lifted his head, opened his mouth, and cried out in agony, his screams the screams of thousands, his cry not human at all, but more like an animal's, a sound so awful it separated the flesh from bone, shook the core, made the hair fall out, laid waste to the body, the soul, the anima.

The sets became real now, no longer props made of wood or foam. He saw the eerie twilight, the dusty, cobwebbed castles and churches, perpetually drafty, the extras in black and somber clothing, the old women with glassy, tear-filled eyes, holding candles, the beads of rosaries laced between arthritic fingers as the funeral procession wound down the narrow and cobblestoned streets of Corovia, the simple coffin hoisted on the shoulders of burly men with somber faces. It was all real, and it filled him with anger, with a rage so strong he could think of only to bring harm, to maim and kill and destroy all the evil, vile, and corrupt of the world, those who prey on the weak and poor, who feed off their blood, who draw strength from their misery, who ruin their lives for generations and generations.

In his dream, he watched as they lowered the casket into the ground. They gathered fistfuls of dirt and threw it down where it mixed with the moist earth the men scooped up with large shovels. The women stood huddled under an oak tree and prayed in hushed and sibilant voices. Children with pale faces and wide eyes ran between the crooked and splintered crosses jutting out from the ground marking the graves of their ancestors. The fake crows sat perched on the iron fence lining the perimeter of the cemetery, and soon they came to life, picking their feathers, squawking incessantly, waiting to feast on the rotting flesh of a field mouse or a beetle. Diego watched the backdrop of steel gray clouds, painted on the taut canvas by an artist in splattered overalls, roll by. He felt the cold wind blowing in from the blades of whirring fans against his skin. He felt the presence of a great, ancient evil watching him, waiting for the right moment to claim him, to devour them all.

They prayed.

They nailed crosses to their doors. They sprinkled holy water in the dark corners of their houses, where it was said sin festered. They kept their children away from the windows, for the evil roaming the streets could see them and snatch them away.

They prayed.

Yet still she came. Bathed in black. White skin. Sharp teeth. A thirst for blood, human blood. That which kept her alive, preserved. She drew strength from their fear, preyed off this, and the more they cried out, the more they screamed, the more she craved them. And she would come to claim dominion over the land, over the corrupt and immoral souls of the people. He felt his resistance waning and the temptation was too strong, the lust too enticing, the power too erotic, the taste of flesh too hard to resist.

He prayed. Who was he becoming?

Diego prayed.

He woke to the voice of an old man speaking to him in Spanish.

"¡Levántense, joven! Levántense," said the voice. "Que ya llegan."

Diego woke now. The old man's hand on his shoulder, a smile on his face.

"I fell asleep," he told him in Spanish. "I had an awful dream."

The old man looked around, regarding the eerie sets—the old cemetery, the dark church, the dark castle, the wooden coffins and crucifixes piercing the ground—and nodded.

"I can see why," he said.

He slept very little, only a few hours here and there, as they pushed on. Perry was a fine director, though, and never shied away from pulling Diego aside to coach him, provoking him to dig deep inside his own self to bring out emotions he never knew he had to complicate Peter.

"Characters need depth," he would say. "You must remember what is at stake for this man and why it is so important for him to fight for his life."

He pushed and nudged Diego along, scolded him kindly when he wasn't performing a scene just right, when the delivery of lines sounded "wooden," he'd say, or "overly fraught." There was a balance that needed striking, he would often comment, between true emotion and fabricated melodrama. The line between the character and the actor was thin, he said, very thin. Use moments in your own life—heartache, happiness, confusion—to augment and refine the role. Dalt was full of energy, almost maniacal, and would often take his tie and hat off, fling them across the studio, untuck his shirt and run around, exhausting himself, when a scene was performed without a hitch.

"It must be great," said an actress on the set one day when she stood in line near Diego at the craft service tables. The young woman was broad-shouldered with an angular face and sharp cheekbones. She was dressed as a barmaid, and Diego knew she had a small part in the film. Her scenes mainly involved serving drinks to some of the other characters and occasionally delivering a few lines of dialogue.

"Great?" he asked. "What?"

"Working that closely with a man like Dalton Perry," said the woman. "I'd kill to be in your shoes."

"Well, maybe someday you will be able to," he said. Diego stuck his hand out. "I'm—"

"Oh, I know who you are," she said, shaking his hand. "It's an honor, Mister León. I'm Gayle. Gayle Turney."

A month after the final scenes were shot, the editing of both *The Bride of Blood* and *La novia de sangre* were finally finished, the films ready to be premiered, both in October of 1932. The premiere of *La novia de sangre* was first, and it was held at the California Theatre on South Main Street in downtown Los Angeles, one of a handful solely devoted to running Spanish-language films. The initial screening was well attended, with a modest number of publicity reporters and photographers present, standing behind the ropes flanking the red carpet and shouting questions.

"Mr. León, what was it like working on this Spanish film?"

"Mr. León, tell us if you plan on making more movies in your native tongue."

"Diego, who did you like better? The English-speaking crew or the Spanish?"

He answered each question as Perry and Cage had taught him to, standing before the flashing bulbs of photographers and waving. *It was a rare opportunity to work on the Spanish film. Everyone on the set was kind and professional. Mr. Salazar was a fine director. There are currently no plans to star in another Spanish-language film. Working with both crews was an equal joy.*

"What do you make of the mass deportations the LAPD is conducting throughout the Mexican neighborhoods in the city?" asked one reporter from *La Opinión*.

"Politics don't concern me much," he said, an air of indifference in his voice, and let his thoughts trail off. He continued to smile, continued to wave, as the reporter waited, his microphone a few inches from Diego's mouth. When in doubt, he had been told to just smile, nod, and wave, then move on. And that's what he did, leaving the reporter behind, a confused look on his face.

"Repatriation, they're calling it," Salazar said once they were past the reporters and inside the lobby of the theater. "It's illegal. It's immoral."

"You're damn right," said a man standing near Salazar. "Everyone is suspicious. Mexicans with leftist affiliations are being rounded up and sent back. No questions asked, some of them even born here," the man said, stomping his foot on the ground, his shoe leaving an impression in the plush carpeting.

He didn't know why, but Diego leaned in, spoke up, and the small circle of studio executives and the ladies with them turned to look at him when he said, "The newspapers say they spread disease, that they're infected. I read there was a typhoid outbreak in one of the sections where a bunch of them live in shacks with no running water, no toilets."

Salazar shook his head. "Lies," he said. "All lies carefully planted by the LAPD to justify their cause. Here, the media, the police, the politicians are skilled in the art of deceit and fabrication. Never forget that."

He was grateful when Alicia and the rest of the cast showed up. She kissed him on the cheek and squeezed his arm. The lights dimmed and they strolled into the theater and took their seats. There, in the darkness, with the film reel beginning, and the opening credits flashing up, he forgot about it all, felt a wild thing stir inside his chest, a pang, a flutter, the first real taste of success.

Alicia wasn't going to return to Argentina. She wanted to try and make a go at acting in Hollywood. Who knows, Alicia said. There might be another opportunity waiting just around the corner. The one compromise Alicia had to contend with was that her chaperone, Blanca, would remain, at least until Alicia got settled in a more permanent place of her own.

The English-language premiere, which would be held at Grauman's Chinese Theatre just a few days after the Spanish one, was another event entirely. He wasn't ready for it, and it was Alicia who reminded Diego to make sure to look as good as possible, to draw as much attention to himself as necessary.

"What you wear is just as important as who is on your arm," she said.

"Do you want me to ask you to be my date?"

"I'm already going," she said, rolling her eyes.

Perry made sure to invite everyone from the Spanish crew, but only Alicia had said yes to the invitation, and he was grateful that she was going. As for Jacques, Diego had not seen him since the last day of shooting, and his guess was that he wouldn't be there because it had been made public by then that Frontier Pictures decided to go ahead and not renew his contract.

"Though I'm already going, it would be silly of me to show up alone," Alicia explained. "I will *accompany* you. How's that?" They were inside his apartment, and she went into his bedroom and rummaged through his closet and began pulling things out. "But what will you wear?"

"Oh, I'll find something."

"You can't wear what you did to the premiere of our production."

"Why not? It was a brand-new suit."

"It'll be the end of you if a photographer who was there that one night is at this premiere and snaps a picture of you wearing the same getup. No, we need something impressive."

"Like what?"

"A tuxedo," she said, still rummaging through his closet.

"But I haven't got one," he told her.

"Yes, I can see that. So we'll just have to get you one."

"Now?"

"Now. Come on." She reached out and took his hand. "There's time to do the alterations before the premiere."

¤

When they pulled up and stood in the long line of cars inching toward the front entrance to the Chinese Theatre, he couldn't help but recall Fiona, the date they'd had at the Pig 'n Whistle next door. He looked through the glass, trying to peer past the mobs of spectators and cameramen and reporters assembled there, hoping to catch a glimpse of the restaurant's sign, but couldn't for there were already too many people.

"Look at that!" Alicia said as they stopped. The driver got out and walked around the car, and they emerged and were standing on the red carpet leading all the way from the street curb to the entrance of the theater. Photographers took pictures, their cameras poised along the edge of the carpet, standing on wooden tripods, and the flashbulbs popped and hissed when they passed, the filaments littering the concrete like thin copper webs. There were hundred of fans and admirers behind velvet ropes. They waved at him, yelled things he couldn't hear or make out. Several reporters shouted, and it took him a while to realize that they were calling Diego by name. Alicia nudged him forward.

"Here," shouted a short man in a driver's cap, holding a microphone. "Sir," he told Diego. "Just a few questions."

"Certainly," Diego said, Alicia's grip on his arm firm.

"Bruce Bodine for KKGE Radio," the man said, holding the microphone. "We're live," he said, "broadcasting on all frequencies. The entire West Coast. With us now," the reporter continued, "is one of Hollywood's newest finds: Frontier's Latin Romeo. Mister Diego León. Now, what would you like to tell our listeners?"

He leaned in and spoke: "Hello, everyone out there. It's a beautiful evening in Hollywood, under the stars, and among them. We wish you were all here enjoying the premiere of this fabulous movie with us."

"I understand you worked on both the Englishand Spanish language production," the man said, holding the microphone out.

"Yes," he said. "I did. It kept me busy, but it was a joy, an utter joy."

"It must have been quite an experience. What was your favorite part?"

"Working alongside people like my costar here," he said, nudging Alicia forward.

"And who is joining us?" Bruce Bodine asked, beckoning toward the red cord separating them from the mob of reporters.

"Alicia Prado," she said. "I starred with Diego in the Spanish version of the film. I was Mary."

"Can you tell the audience a little about the mood out here this evening?"

"Electrifying," Alicia said. "Like Diego said, we wish you could all be with us."

"Any more pictures planned for you, Miss Prado?" Bruce asked.

"Yes, but I'm not at liberty to discuss them."

"Real secret, huh?" Bruce said. Then he brought the microphone up to his mouth and said, "You heard it here first, folks. We can't wait."

Then Bruce turned and nodded at the man, who now switched the console off.

"Thanks," said Bruce. "Enjoy the premiere."

They walked along, and when Diego was sure they were no longer within earshot, he asked Alicia why she lied.

"What do you mean?" she asked.

"Back there. All that about your upcoming plans. You're not doing any pictures, are you?"

"No," she said. "But it's good to say things like that. It builds mystique, I understand."

"Mystique, huh?"

"Yes," she said. "My new favorite English word." She scanned the area as they made their way toward the front of the entrance. "Speaking of, how were my pronunciations?"

"Fine," he said. "Your accent is much more subdued."

It was hard for him to discern who anyone was because they were all dressed so fancy, so lavish. Standing at the entrance of that massive building, its bright red and gold exterior, the Chinese dragons and circular gongs, he was beyond overwhelmed. The searchlights darted across the sky in dizzying patterns, there was chatter everywhere, and the walls were covered with posters featuring Fay Carmichael, Margaret Dillon, and Jacques Fantin in different scenes from the movie. Inside the theater lobby, Carole Lombard talked with Stu Berk and Tod Duren. Irving Thalberg of MGM was having what appeared to be a very heated conversation with Dalton Perry. He saw Claudette Colbert, Greta Garbo, and John Barrymore, who tipped his hat to Diego and raised his glass.

Alicia, he realized, was cunningly radiant, and all eyes turned to her as they circled the room. She wore a white gown with a bold floral design. The front of the neckline was cut very low, exposing a good deal of her upper chest. Even though it was warm enough that night, she carried with her a shawl. Her hair was swept up in a bun and she was all graceful neck and shoulders.

"Don't get starry-eyed, dear," he said as they walked about the large lobby, filled with studio people in tuxedos and fancy dresses.

"Who's getting starry-eyed?" she asked. "I've done premieres before."

"But not a *Hollywood* premiere."

"You have a point. But I think you're more nervous than I am."

"Oh nonsense," he muttered under his breath as they roamed around. "Act like you belong," he said as the crowd broke for them.

"Oh, but I *do* belong," she said.

The lobby was an impressive sight, with chandeliers hanging from the gilded ceilings, an ornate railing with inlays of Chinese writings and symbols, and scrolls made of imitation rice paper with drawings of temples and fountains. There were large gold dragon heads, and two lions flanked the main entrance to the theater, with its red carpeting and thick gold curtains. Everyone was there—Fay Carmichael and Margaret Dillon, Perry and Salazar—and he was surprised to see Jacques Fantin standing at the foot of the steps leading up to the second floor balcony.

"Relax," Diego said, "Have fun. Enjoy."

At this, Alicia smiled. When she saw Dalton Perry chatting with Margaret Dillon, she stopped, her gaze fixed on them.

"Would you like to meet her?" he asked.

"I don't think—"

"You have to be ready," he said. "Come on."

He introduced her to both of them, Alicia remaining quiet, nodding attentively, listening to Dalton talk about a new dog he'd purchased, a greyhound.

"I adore greyhounds," Margaret said, smiling at both of them, nodding at Alicia.

Diego jabbed her side, trying to provoke Alicia to speak. He cleared his throat.

"My father used to breed and raise greyhounds," she said.

They all looked at her and began asking about her family, her upbringing.

Confident that Alicia could handle herself, he snuck away. He headed toward Jacques.

"Why, hello," Jacques said. "You're looking rather smashing, I must say."

"You don't look so bad yourself, either."

"Well," he said, smiling. "I do clean up mighty nice now, don't I?"

"I'm surprised to see you here," he said.

"I know there are a lot of people who probably feel the same way, my friend."

He said he didn't want to give those in charge the pleasure of not seeing him there for one last time. After all, Fantin explained, he worked harder on the film than he had on any other during his time at Frontier.

"Well," Diego said. "I'm glad you're here."

"And who is the little señorita with you tonight?" he asked.

"Alicia Prado. Did the Mary role in the Spanish."

"Ah," he said. "I see. Well, she's a looker, I'd say. And she's working the room quite well, isn't she?"

Diego saw how Alicia moved from group to group now, talking with people, smiling and gesturing emphatically.

"Somebody's hoping to launch their American film career tonight, it appears to me," said Fantin. "Poor kid. She's trying too hard. She's not subtle."

"I disagree," he said. "She seems to be holding her own quite well."

Then there came a murmur from the crowd, and they watched as William Cage himself, accompanied by a brunette woman in a gold dress, came in. He went straight to where Perry and Salazar stood, talking with a man whom Diego knew to be one of the studio's film producers.

"Oh," said Fantin. "Look who just arrived. It's Billy the Kid himself. This should be real interesting. Tell me," Jacques said, leaning in. "Did he ever try the funny business with you?"

Diego cleared his throat. "What do you mean?"

"You know? Tried getting you in bed?"

"No," Diego said, adjusting his tuxedo jacket. "Absolutely not."

"I'm surprised. He's slept with every young attractive actor at Frontier at least once. Oh, everyone knows about him. When he tried to have a go with me and I respectfully refused, I saw my career at the studio hit the bottom. No leading parts. No big hits. Typical, isn't it?" Fantin said. "This industry's full of skirt chasers, closeted queers, all of them over-sexed and crazy with power. Why can't anyone be normal?"

Diego lit a cigarette. "Sometimes I just don't understand this place," he said.

He watched Bill standing in the center of the lobby, the beautiful woman clutching his arm. Was she in love with him, he wondered? What did they do when they were together? Diego tried not to imagine it. He couldn't help it, though, and he realized what was happening: he was jealous of her. His hands trembled. He felt himself perspiring. Diego wanted nothing more than to be the one on his arm, by his side, Bill's partner, his lover.

It was the greatest night of his life, and he was standing there on the balcony of the theater's lobby. Below, he watched them move about in beautiful dresses and sharp tuxedos. The biggest stars in the movie industry had come out to the premiere of a movie he was starring in, his American film debut. He should have felt proud, accomplished. Yet he was anything but that, and so much was still so far away.

ACT V

SCREENING

Fault Line (1974)

Director: Russ Mulligan

Cast: Meg Jeffries, Manuel Cardenas, Tom West, Amy Adamson, and Ben Hunter

After a 9.0 magnitude earthquake strikes the greater Los Angeles area, a disparate group of residents fight to stay alive amidst chaos of epic proportions. Diego León stars as police officer Sal Cruz.

SCREENING

The Butterfly Princess (1990)

Director: Martin Engel and Fernando Logan

Cast: Paulina "Lil P" Murillo, Alicia Prado, and Victor del Canto

In 1530, Princess Erendira of the P'urepécha people of western Mexico must train an army to do battle against the invading Spanish Conquistadors after they overthrow her father, King Tangaxuan II. In this dazzling animated musical, Diego León is the voice of Tarasco the talking turtle.

SCREENING

The Hungry Earth (1994)

Director: Mateo Ruiz

Cast: Ernesto Rey, Pilar Marez-Sullivan, and Carmen al-Hasim

Based on Tomás Rivera's 1971 novel ...*And the Earth Did Not Devour Him*, this experimental 1994 Chicano film explores the struggles of a group of Mexican-American farm workers in post-World War II Texas. In this, his final role before his death, Diego León plays "El Hablador."

1

April 1933–May 1935

Dashing Latin Actor Has Hollywood Abuzz
by Marty Morgan
SNAPSHOTS, *Spring/Summer Issue 1933*

Would-be hopefuls with stars in their eyes have been flocking to Tinseltown for as long as anyone can remember. It seems these budding thespians are as natural a part of the landscape as the palm and citrus trees that line the streets and avenues of our fair city. One such person arrived, like so many others, in Hollywood in 1927, at the tender age of 19 with only a few dollars in his pocket and the hope of someday seeing his name flashing on a marquee or on a billboard along Sunset Boulevard. Frontier Pictures' Diego Cortez dreamed of the day when the stardom he's currently experiencing would come but never thought it would take so much time and perseverance as it has.

Known best for his roles in such films as *The Bride of Blood*, *Far from Home*, and *Two to Tango*, the actor, humble and gracious, admitted to us from his Hollywood bungalow that the road to fame was paved with some tough choices, especially when he contemplated walking away from his career to return to Mexico to care for his aging grandparents. "That was difficult," he confessed, a slight quiver in his voice, as we sat in his bright and airy living room. "But these are the choices we're given. The journey's been a long one, but I'm glad to be here, glad to have the support of so many adoring fans over time."

And what times they have been for this young man, whose star is only getting brighter and brighter. "I started out so far away from here and am lucky and grateful to have finally arrived." With a family history ripe with loss and death, it's little more than a miracle that he is with us today. Diego was the direct descendant of a mighty king, the last ruler of the great Tarascan people who inhabited much of western Mexico before the Spaniards arrived. Born into an affluent family in the cosmopolitan city of Morelia, in the lush and fertile state of Michoacán, Diego, an only child, was a precocious baby and showed early signs of having an adventurous spirit when his negligent nanny turned away and he crawled off and got himself lost in a cornfield while on an outing with the family. In his first year, the family's simple life was turned upside down when an influenza outbreak that swept through the city claimed the life of his father, a successful businessman. His grieving mother raised the young Diego with the help of her parents, who doted on the boy. Diego grew into a handsome and charming young man. He was bright and quick, curious and charismatic, was loyal to his mother and obedient and polite and very devoted to God and his church. But, alas, tragedy struck again when an infection claimed the life of his beautiful mother. As he grew, his grandfather, a shrewd businessman, groomed Diego to work in his office, notarizing forms and documents.

"It was my grandfather's hope that I take over the business," he told me. "But that life was not for me. I had a calling. A desire to be something else."

Diego came in contact with his first silent movie when a picture house opened around the corner from his grandfather's business. From that moment on, the young man developed a love and fascination with Hollywood movies and all things American. Early one morning, while the grandparents slept, Diego, clutching only a duffel bag and with a few pesos to his name, snuck away and caught a train bound for the United States. His final destination:

Hollywood. His early years in Los Angeles were a struggle; he held down a number of jobs that included street newspaper vendor, a farmhand, and a ditchdigger. Underneath the rugged exterior, there is a genial sensitivity about the man, a curiosity akin to that of a young boy, ever quizzical and full of a pervasive nostalgia that is at once wistful as it is endearing. But there is also a chivalry within him, much like those possessed by the courageous and valiant matadors down in Old Mexico, a strict adherence to and devotion for his church, his God, and his family. Single, good-looking, a talented singer and dancer, Diego loves to entertain anyone from Zippo the Clown to Margaret Dillon and Frontier top man William Cage. Diego Cortez is truly a "man's man," a close friend any guy would hope for. Years of manual work have yielded a trim and muscular physique for the six foot one, 175 pound actor. With a healthy mane of dark chestnut hair that shines ever so brightly in the sun, a smile that beams confidence and wit, broad shoulders and a sturdy chest held up by muscular legs and arms, Diego is, without a doubt, every man's ideal companion and every lady's comely dream.

"It's the fans that keep me going, Marty," he confessed when asked what inspires him.

Diego Cortez is here to stay, according to his fans near and far. And we couldn't agree more!

After the *Bride of Blood* premiere, it was clear Diego had been noticed. Mr. Levitt himself urged Cage to do everything to get Diego into more of Frontier's major projects after his private viewing of *The Bride of Blood*. "This Latin kid's going to be big." In 1933, Diego became known as "Frontier Pictures' answer to Valentino." Bill suggested they change his last name from León to Cortez. More regal, he said. Makes one think of a manly man, like the great conquistador Hernan Cortez. It's adventurous, he insisted. Noble. R. J. liked Diego Cortez, and so did a handful of studio secretaries Bill went around asking, so it stuck. Diego hated it, but he had no choice.

There came new clothes and a new look to go with the new persona. A team of press agents was put in charge of reinventing him. A fictitious biography was written and fed to the media, who, in turn, ran with it and printed this whenever they wrote about

"Frontier's Latin Valentino." In this version of himself, he wasn't born into poverty. Diego Cortez had never lived through the hardships of the revolution, had never seen hunger, the cold, had never known the fear of despair and loss. He had been born into privilege, and this, the press agents said, was important to stress.

"Why?" he had asked. "Don't people like a rags-to-riches story?"

The agent, slow-talking, methodical, said that, under normal circumstances, this would be true. "But what we want to do is emphasize a cultured and sophisticated upbringing. We want to paint you as an educated, learned Mexican." He moved his pale, thin fingers across the wide boardroom table where they met.

"So many people in the press see the word 'Mexican' and think certain unfavorable things," said a female press agent sitting nearby. "We don't want them associating you with that."

And so it was. Diego held the *Snapshots* article written by the effeminate young reporter who had spent several weeks with him, smoking cigarettes with Diego, dining with him, staying the night several times and sleeping in the guest bedroom. The *Snapshots* article would be the first of many to feature his new biography. He would just have to accept that this was who he was now. He had gone from being one person to another almost overnight.

"Are you sure this is for the best?" Diego asked Bill one evening as they lay on Bill's bed. Diego held the magazine, his eyes focusing on his new last name. Cortez. "I still don't think I like Diego Cortez."

"It's good," Bill insisted. "I like it. It rolls off the tongue. It's very mysterious, exotic." He leaned over, pushed Diego down on the bed, and pressed his body on top of his. He reached for the *Snapshots* magazine and tossed it across the room. He kissed his neck and stroked his chest. Diego could feel Bill's hardness.

"It just doesn't feel right to me," Diego said. "My fans like me. Why can't I just be who I am? Why can't I just be Diego León?" He remembered what his father told him many years before, about being the last of the Leóns, about carrying on the family name.

"American audiences will mispronounce León. Plus there's the matter with the little accent over the O. It's too exotic-sounding."

"But my father—"

"Enough," Bill interjected. "You're being childish. People change things all the fucking time in this business. It's just a name." He stopped and calmed down before speaking again. "Isn't this what you hoped for? What you always wanted? Aren't you happy?"

"Yes," Diego said, kissing Bill on the lips. "I'm sorry. I don't mean to sound ungrateful for all your help. And I've really enjoyed this. Us together," he said.

"Me too."

"That makes me happy," Diego said just as Bill leaned in closer and took him in his arms. They kissed and caressed one another for some time before Bill penetrated him.

"I'll take good care of you. Just make sure to do exactly as I say," Bill said.

"I will. I promise."

Diego tried to focus but all he could think about was what Jacques Fantin told him at the premiere. He could feel Bill inside of him now, pushing deeper and deeper. He clenched his teeth and moaned.

Bill soon ordered more changes for Diego.

"What else?" he asked him.

"You need a car. Stop riding the trolley to work like some common dope." Bill reminded him that he was paying him enough money to afford such luxuries, so one Sunday afternoon, they went car shopping, and Diego purchased a two-toned 1934 Nash LaFayette Coupe with whitewalled tires and sleek running boards along either side. Inside, the interior was plush and soft, and when he drove up to the studio gates in it and showed it to Bill, Bill pointed to the car's registration on the neck of the steering wheel. "That there says it's registered to you. I don't want to hear about you riding that public trolley. You've got your own car now. And move out of the Ruby Rose. It's a real dive."

Diego spent the rest of the day driving around quiet neighborhoods, looking for the right place to live.

"I knew it, saw it coming" was what Rose said when Diego told her and Ruby that he would be moving.

"I'm sorry," he said. "Really, I am. It's just that, well, the studio thinks I should be somewhere else."

They were standing in the lobby. Ruby sighed and set a stack of receipts down. "Hey, look," she said. "We're glad for you. We don't mean to make you feel bad. It's just that, well, nobody can afford to live here anymore."

"We lower the rent," Rose replied, "and they still don't bite."

"Hard times." Ruby shook her head.

"Hard times indeed," said Rose.

Diego said, "Maybe I could talk to some people at the studio, see if anyone needs a—"

"No." Ruby raised her hand. "Please don't, honey. We'll be fine. Just fine. We'll figure something out. My sister and I are happy for you. Truly happy."

"Thanks," he said. "I'll keep in touch."

They smiled and nodded in a way that told them all he never, ever would.

Diego spent 1934 working on picture after picture. There was *Far from Home* with Eloise Kendall and Lester Frank, who showed up to the set every day without his lines rehearsed and reeking of booze. After *Far from Home*, there was *Two to Tango*, again with Eloise and where he had to learn tricky tango steps and wear tight outfits. After that there was *The Lost Years*, with Constance Gardner and Jacques Fantin, on loan from Empire Pictures, who had contracted him after Frontier let him go. Poetic justice, Jacques would say each time he showed up on the set. There was *The Penny Wish*, with Nivia Gaynor, a disastrous melodrama with a bad script and a horrible director. He played a college quarterback star in *The Touchdown Kid*, and would have to ice the bruises he received from being tackled again and again.

He was a powerful Chinese emperor in *The Silk Road* and spent hours in front of a mirror while the makeup artists applied adhesive strips on the corners of his eyes to pull them back so that he looked "Oriental." He was an Arab sheik in *Desert Nights*, a poor immigrant who comes to America to strike it big only to be met with failure in *Ashes to Ashes*. In between the films, there were shorts and serials, radio commercials and interviews, dates with new Frontier starlets, fundraisers and trips. The year 1934 was one of endless scripts and screen tests, of costume fittings and makeup sessions, of fake wigs and prosthetic noses and moles and scars and wounds, of epic battles and fancy balls, of births and deaths, of tragedy and celebration. It was dizzying, grueling, demanding in ways he never imagined. But it was what he wanted, what he had always wanted, he reminded himself. On the day he met R. J. Levitt at the Frontier Pictures New Year's Eve Ball of 1934, he remembered the first time he set foot on the studio lot with Charlie. When he shook R. J.'s hand, and when R. J. placed his arm, so firm, so loyal, so loving, around Diego's shoulder, and when he thanked Diego for his "years of dedication and service to this fine studio," Diego wanted nothing more than to hug the man, to profess his loyalty, to tell him just how much he and Frontier meant to him. But he remained assured and steady.

"This is your home," R. J. said kindly. "Understand, son? This is your home."

"Yes," Diego said. "Thank you, sir."

"Call me R. J." He smiled, his eyes beaming from behind his spectacles. "Not sir or Mr. Levitt," he said, chuckling. "Think of me not as your boss or the head of this big place. Think of me as a father figure. And may 1935 prove to be an even bigger success for you, son."

Diego belonged. For the first time in his life. He belonged. He had a place in the world.

With the help of a studio set designer, he made important decisions about furniture and artwork for his home: he bought a dining table and chairs, hand-carved and ornate with plush seat cushions; paintings in beautiful frames by artists whose names were exotic and fun to pronounce, which he hung on the walls; thick curtains and tapestries; new dishes and silverware and lamps; books, mainly for show, the set designer stressed, on religion and philosophy, heavy tomes written by men with intelligent and moving thoughts. The house was quiet, and the trees surrounding the property offered an abundance of shade. A gardener from the studio planted aromatic flowers near the kitchen and bedroom windows, pointing their names out— sage, heather, and lavender. The breeze that blew in from both sides of the house always carried a sweet and perfumed scent, relaxed him while he sat in a cushioned lounge in his library, sipping wine, his eyes glancing from one end of the room to the other.

This was home, Diego repeated to himself on mornings when he awoke, staring up at the beamed ceiling of his bedroom, in that hour's weak light. If his mother and father could see, he wondered if they would be proud of him there, in that new house with walls still damp and sticky from the fresh coats of paint someone else had chosen, lying on a bed with clean linens someone else had laundered. This place, and everything housed within it, was immaculate, untouched. The pages of his books weren't soft and tattered from use, the spines not wrinkled, but smooth and rigid and erect. No seat cushions were worn in, no thinning and wasted fabrics. No chips or cracks in his plates and drinking glasses. Nothing was mismatched. Every set of two things still had its pair and his towels had no frayed edges, no loose and errant threads. He wanted more than anything in that brief moment to keep it all new, undisturbed, unblemished. Everything in its place. Nothing strayed or lost or forgotten.

In the three years following their work on *La novia de sangre*, Alicia had thrown herself fully into pursuing stardom with zest, moxie, and a great deal of nerve. Alicia had invested in acting and dance lessons. She had studied voice and music and worked with an expert elocutionist to help her eliminate her accent. There were diet regimens. A stylist had moved her hairline back a few inches because wide foreheads were more "American-looking," and she had dyed her hair platinum blond, which Diego had to admit looked odd and clashed with her skin color. Alicia attended parties and premieres, schmoozing with directors and producers and other stars.

He knew it had been a struggle for Alicia following filming of *La novia de sangre*. She had worked steadily, taking parts in English language movies, but the films were low-budget productions with bad scripts and third-rate actors, the sort of stuff nobody ever saw, the sort of stuff Diego did when he first arrived. The big break never came no matter how much she poured into it and her career languished there, stuck in that perpetual rut. She was a creature laid waste after only a brief time in the business.

"Call me Alice," she told Diego when she ran into him at a fundraising benefit one day. "Not Alicia."

"Okay," he said. "Call me Cortez."

She laughed and gripped his arm. "Isn't it so much fun? We both have new identities."

In early 1935, Alicia Prado had given up on any hope of making it big in Hollywood. She decided to pack up her bags and leave. On hearing this, Diego drove out to the house she had been renting. He found Blanca sitting in the living room, folding clothes and placing them in a large trunk. He had never talked to her much throughout the years. She had always remained Alicia's chaperone, a chubby woman with dark skin and intense black hair, perpetually in the background, like a shadow or a smudge, always present but lacking any real form. He looked at her there now, her hands moving quickly, and he remembered Elva, her own brittle hands, the quiet way in which she had looked after him, raised him. Was she even still alive, he wondered? Would she recognize him? He removed his hat, cleared his throat, and Blanca looked up, startled.

"Señor León," she said and bowed her head slightly. "Cortez," she corrected herself. "Miss Prado's upstairs."

He handed her his hat and climbed the carpeted stairs. He never knew who owned the house, but it felt very cold and uninviting. The furniture was horribly mismatched, the wooden pieces chipped and simple, the glass windowpanes dusty and filthy, and the sunlight streaming in from the outside appeared sickly and weak as he walked down the short corridor. The door was slightly ajar, and he could see through the crack that Alicia sat on her bed, a stack of photographs beside her. She looked at them carefully, and she clutched a handkerchief. He could see that she was crying as she took each photo, regarded it, and then placed it gently in a cloth box on her lap. Diego knocked before entering, and there was a pause as she composed herself and rose before answering.

"Come in," she said.

He opened the door slowly, and entered. She stood at the foot of the bed, arms folded, eyes puffy but not full of tears. "Hope I didn't inconvenience you."

"Never." She hugged him.

They had bumped into one another at a party a few weeks before. Alicia was there with a young man whom she introduced as Paul, the son of a studio producer. When Paul skulked away, Alicia told him she had already purchased two tickets—one for her and one for Blanca—on a steamship headed for Valparaiso, Chile. From there, they would board a train to Buenos Aires.

"So you're really doing this?" he asked her now, looking around the bare room. Everything was packed away in a large valise in the corner. The bed had been stripped of its sheets, and the armoire and dressers were covered in large tarps.

"I am," she said, sighing. Alicia took the remaining pictures she had been thumbing through and placed them in the photo box then closed it. "I was feeling a bit nostalgic, looking at all these pictures." She led him out of the bedroom and into a small library at the end of a hall. "Come here," she said, walking toward a chaise near a window with cracked glass. "Sit next to me, my friend."

He removed his jacket, and sat. He lit a cigarette.

She reached for the pack and said, "May I have one?"

"Of course." He handed her one and lit it.

"My father frowns on women who smoke. Says it's not ladylike. But I don't care. Soon enough I'll be back home. Soon enough he and my mother will be running my life again. I don't want to leave."

"What'll you do? Once you're back?" They sat in that yellowing and sick light, in that drafty house with its stained walls and fractured glass windowpanes. He felt her hopelessness, her defeat.

"Continue working." Alicia puffed vigorously on her cigarette. "Hollywood isn't the center of the movie industry, you know? There are directors, producers, writers, and studios in Argentina, too." Alicia put her cigarette out. "It's fine. Really. I don't feel defeated. Nostalgic, yes, but not defeated." She took his hand and pressed it between both of hers. "You must remain true to yourself, dear friend. All those things that make you who you are. You mustn't forget it. Promise me you won't."

He placed his cigarette in the ashtray and rose now. "I know who I am, Alicia."

"Do you?" She rose, walked over, and hugged him. "Take care of yourself." She leaned in, kissed him on the cheek, and then walked out the door.

Downstairs, Blanca was gone. He found his hat, grabbed it, and left. He sat in his car, the engine idling softly. He put the car in gear, gripped the steering wheel and pulled away from the curb, letting the roar of the rushing wind erase her words.

In 10 years, Alicia Prado would return once again to Hollywood, a very different woman than the one he had just left. In that time, she would meet and marry a man named Francesco Arnoldi, a respected Italian director and filmmaker. Alicia would become his muse, starring in a number of films he would direct, each of them hugely successful abroad. They would have a child, a boy named Franco. Alicia would return to Hollywood in 1945 a mother, happily married, an international star with a string of hit movies to her credit. Every studio would be clamoring to sign her, and she would eventually end up at American Pictures and enjoy the kind of success and longevity most actors and actresses would simply never know.

May of 1935 began with filming on *Crazy for Miss Cavendish*, in which he played a lovelorn Spanish teacher at an all-girls prep school in New England. Though he was glad to be back in the studio, working again, this did little to satisfy him, and he felt lonely and distracted without Alicia. On the car drive home from the studio, he passed endless blocks of homes, shaded under the verdant green leaves of eucalyptus and ash trees. He drove slowly, peering into opened windows, hoping to catch sight of a family sitting down to dinner, together, their faces warm and glowing. Back at his house, he poured himself a strong drink and listened to the radio. There was a program on, a variety show featuring amateurs performing comedy skits and singing songs. It was all so maddening, so tedious, that he rose and turned the damn thing off. He drifted into the kitchen, opened the icebox for no other reason than to open it. In his office, he signed photographs of himself for fans then tore them up. He walked to the library, picked up the phone, and dialed Bill.

"Can I come by?" Diego asked.

"Now?" He sounded irritated. "I'm busy."

"Just for a little bit," Diego said. "I'm lonely. I really need some—"

"Okay," he said, his voice softening. "Come over."

Their meetings as of late consisted of brief sexual interludes that usually ended with the two of them dressing in a rush, Bill explaining that he had a lot of work to do, a whole lot, and Diego being hastily led to the door. Bill would give him a quick peck on the cheek and say he'd call him soon and they'd have dinner, just the two of them. "I promise you, my love. I promise." But they never did. The phone would ring. Diego would drive over. They would have sex, and that would be the end.

He knew their relationship was evolving into one of convenience, one where Diego satisfied him and William Cage, in turn, protected Diego's interests in and around the studio. It was because of Cage that he was being cast in film after film, receiving billing, not *top* billing, not yet, but billing nonetheless.

Diego sped down the winding road skirting the Hollywood Hills, toward Bel Air. He rolled the window down, caught the faint scent of blooming flowers, damp earth, and orange blossoms. He looked below, deep into the narrow ravines cutting through the canyon, the chasms netted with the green and waxy leaves of juniper, ash, and eucalyptus trees, and the occasional palm fronds—ratty, frayed, their edges wind-whipped and battered and singed by the hot Santa Ana winds that blew in each October. He gripped the steering wheel, his hands hot, damp. *Because of Bill*, he told himself.

He found Bill in his library that night, sitting in a wingback chair, a lit pipe in his mouth. He wore his smoking jacket and black loafers. His hair was glistening, wet with pomade, and neatly parted and combed. He was reading a script and hardly looked up to greet him as Diego walked in.

"Would you like a drink?" Bill asked him. He rose and poured one for himself.

"Sure," Diego said.

He handed the glass to Diego and took a sip from his, regarding him. "Is everything all right?"

Diego shrugged his shoulders. "Yeah. It's just that ... I've missed you. We haven't been ... together much lately."

"I've been busy," he said. "You understand."

Diego said nothing.

"Are you sore at me?" Bill asked. "What have I done?"

Diego took a long drink and felt the alcohol burn as it traveled down his throat. "I've just been lonely. It's been a hectic week on the set. Dalton's keeping us busy."

"A quick turnaround for this film," said Bill.

"For this film and for all the others I've done and will do."

Productivity, Bill explained, was the goal. Like an assembly line, movies needed to be shot quickly, edited, and shipped out to the theaters. It was the only way to stay ahead of the game. They were running a business, Bill said, and Diego needed to remember that. Efficiency and profit were important, and it was necessary, he said now, for Diego to remember his part in all of it.

"Which is what?" Diego asked him.

"To act," he said. "To play your roles as best as you can. To be as lucrative and as profitable for the studio as possible."

"Is that all I am?"

Bill took a long drink and poured himself another. He threw his head back and laughed. "That's all any of us are."

"What do you mean?"

Bill walked to the library entrance. He closed and locked the doors. He took Diego by the hand and led him to the couch and they sat. When Diego tried to kiss him, Bill looked away. He gripped Diego by the back of his head and, with his left hand, untied the sash of his smoking jacket and pulled his pants down.

"Go on," he said, his voice forceful and assured.

"Stop it, Bill," he said. "You're being disgusting."

"Come on," he said. "It's what you came for, isn't it? Would it help if I said please?"

Diego relented and kneeled before Bill. What else was there to do? Diego realized what he was: nothing more than a cog. Bill could take this all away so easily, if he wanted to. He closed his eyes and took him in.

When Bill finished, he rose quickly, adjusted himself, and smoothed back his hair. There came a knock on the door, and he walked over and unlatched it. Lawrence announced that Bill's company had arrived.

"Mister Tod Duren is waiting for you in the foyer."

"Thank you," said Bill. He turned to Diego and smiled. "Lawrence, please escort Mister Cortez to the door and tell Tod I'll be with him shortly."

"Yes, sir."

Without saying a word to Bill, Diego turned and followed Lawrence out. Standing in the foyer was a young man in an argyle sweater and tweed trousers. He smiled, almost beamed, as Diego approached with Lawrence.

"Please wait for Mister Cage in the sitting room," Lawrence told him. "He'll join you shortly."

The young man nodded slightly. He had clear blue eyes, handsome features, and broad shoulders. He was muscular and fit and exuded an air of confidence. "Thank you, Lawrence," Tod said. His voice was soft, clear, and he seemed to move with grace and fluidity as he walked toward the sitting room to wait for his host.

2

August 1935

AS SUDDENLY AS DIEGO'S success had come, it seemed in peril. In August of 1935, they speculated that Frontier Pictures was sinking fast. Executives were on edge. You could feel the tension, the restlessness, the uncertainty running all throughout the studio.

Financial backers had pulled their money, and the studio was deep in the red and there was no way to save it. Diego followed the reports in the trade magazines carefully. There were rumors of a takeover by a group of European investors. German. French. No, British. One day there were reports that Levitt would be fired. Then William Cage would be the one to go. Or they would both be going and a new head of Frontier would take the helm.

"It doesn't matter one bit," he heard a handful of extras talking one afternoon on the set of *Crazy for Miss Cavendish* as they were wrapping up the movie, shooting some final scenes before postproduction. They stood near Diego's trailer. He listened from inside, smoking a cigarette and practicing his lines. "Whoever takes over's gonna fire a whole lotta people."

"You're right," said another, a woman in a houndstooth dress and jacket.

The women were posing as secretaries and schoolteachers or any of the multitudes of other nameless people in the background of the film. They wore tight dresses and skirts, their hair neatly coiffed, their faces freshly powdered. They were perfect and looked like mannequins or dolls, Diego thought.

"The suits shuffle in then out," said the first.

"Players change, but the game remains the same," said a third.

"Yeah, and we're the ones stuck here," said the woman in the houndstooth suit. "Hustling from one studio to the next. The ones at the bottom always get it in the end."

The powers-that-be would eventually dictate their lives, Diego understood, with little input or regard from them. It was no different in Hollywood than anywhere else. Whoever took over would make changes, call it progress, and herald it a better and more equitable approach. But it would just be more of the same, he knew. Some things would be lost, and some things would be gained. All in the name of progress. All in the name of efficiency.

The speculations continued all throughout the rest of the month and into September. There were rumors about clandestine meetings around Frontier with wealthy financiers, talks involving Cage, Levitt, both of them, then neither of them. He gave up trying to decipher what it all meant for the studio, for himself, his career. Bill was busier than ever and certainly wasn't going to tell him anything, and Diego needed to focus on his acting now more than ever.

Diego flipped through the magazine, his eyes glossing over the same old reports and articles. But he stopped when he saw the writeup. It seemed Bill had been spotted around town recently with a "fresh-faced all-American-looking boy" who was described as handsome, tall, and with blond hair, blue eyes, and a great smile. He was apparently a new actor the studio was "grooming." The article also included a photo of the two men sitting at a table, Bill's arm around the actor's shoulder. The photo identified him as "Tod Duren: Frontier's next big thing."

A few weeks later, he received word that Bill wanted to see him in his office. He took his time driving over that morning, his heart beating fast, his stomach queasy.

"Am I being let go?" he asked Bill when he arrived.

"No," he said. Bill sat behind his desk. He lit a cigarette. Diego noticed that his hands trembled slightly. There were bags under his eyes, and he looked tired and worn out.

"Are you okay?" Diego asked.

"Of course. Just a case of the jitters. We're meeting with the board. Going over the finances. It always makes me uneasy."

"But things are good. There's nothing to worry about, correct?" Diego asked, gesturing around them. Outside, the lot was busy. Through the opened windows, he watched technicians move back and forth between the stages. Loud trucks hauled props around. Cranes lifted walls and painted backdrops. Extras in costumes and uniforms paraded up and down the road. "The gossip rags. Talking about a takeover."

Bill waved his hand. "Don't pay attention to that garbage. There's nothing to worry about."

"And Tod Duren?" he asked. "Who's he?"

He sighed. "Tod's none of your concern, okay? There's nothing for you to worry about." Bill sat back in his chair. "I didn't invite you over to fire or replace you. I have a script for you, a part in it I think was made for you."

"Oh?" he asked, relieved.

"Yes. A real good one."

It was, he explained, a script based on a novel called *The Underdogs* by a Mexican writer named Mariano Azuela.

"Yes, I know it," Diego said. "I mean I've never read it, but of course I've heard of it." From what Diego recalled, it was the story of a lowly peasant who gets into some hot water with a local powerful hacienda owner in the early days of the Mexican revolution. The peasant, Demetrio Macías, must flee his village when the Federales come looking for him. He leaves his wife and child behind and ends up leading a battalion of ragtag fighters against Porfirio Díaz's troops. He has adventures along the way, including an affair with a young woman named Camila, but ultimately grows disillusioned with the revolution, and he and his men forget who or what they're fighting for. In the end, Macías returns home, broken and defeated. It seemed the script was written about a year ago and had been passed around and around, but no one expressed interest, so it sat on the shelf until one of Bill's assistants was rummaging through things and found it.

"When I read it," Bill said, "I immediately thought of you."

"You did?" he asked, a hint of pride swelling inside of him.

"I did."

Diego sighed and smiled. "I'm touched."

"Well, who else, right? Anyway, this movie has all the makings of a hit. There's action, adventure, romance, and an exotic locale. This'll really sell you, kid."

"You think so?"

"So what do you say?" Bill asked.

He felt resistant. He didn't know why, but there was something about it that made Diego uneasy. He knew he had little choice in the matter. A contracted star was almost always given a script, assigned a role, and told to play the part. Few of them—with the exception of Fay Carmichael, Stu Berk, Margaret Dillon, and Lester Frank—had the luxury of deciding what role to take and which one to pass on. Diego wasn't quite there yet.

"Do you really think it's good?" he asked

"Yes," Bill said, puffing on a cigarette. He stood now and lit another one then paced back and forth across the office. "Let me level with you."

"Okay. Level with me."

"We're all under pressure. Everyone. Every facet of the studio, from the technicians and prop designers, to the directors and bigname actors and actresses. Belts are tightening everywhere, and we're all being required to produce more successful pictures. Frontier's in big trouble," he admitted.

"But how could this happen?" Diego asked.

He shrugged. "It happens," he said. "What's important is that the studio needs you. We need you to do this picture. If it's big enough, it might very well save us."

It was Bill's vulnerability that made Diego say yes. Finally, Diego thought, here was proof. He saw just how much Bill needed him.

"Okay, Bill," he said. "I'll do it. I'll do the picture. What are we calling it?"

"*The Revolutionists*."

"Very well," Diego said, moving toward the door.

"I'm counting on your discretion, Diego," Bill added. "What I said. Keep it to yourself, please."

"Of course."

Bill hugged Diego and gave him a gentle kiss on the cheek before opening the door to show him out.

They went into production quickly on *The Revolutionists*, billing it as an epic adventure story. There would be gun battles and violence, swelling music and romance. Lots and lots of romance between the brave and noble Macías and his peasant mistress, Camila, whom he ultimately rejects in order to remain faithful to his wife in the end.

Aside from a few film projects she had done for the studio over the years, Diego wasn't too familiar with the work of the actress they picked to play the peasant Camila, a young woman named Gayle Turney. He couldn't figure out why she seemed so familiar until he met her on the set for their first screen test.

"We worked together," Gayle said. "Well, not really. I had a small part in a film you starred in a few years ago. *The Bride of Blood*. I was the bar matron, remember?"

"Yes," Diego said. "I think I recall. We met by the craft service table, correct?"

Gayle smiled now, her grin wide, her teeth bright white, straight. "Exactly. You were quite kind. When I talked of how envious I was of you getting to work so closely with Dalton Perry, you told me I just might someday get to do the same. Little did I know that I would have that chance. Look at me now."

"Well, I'm happy to be here with you."

But he wasn't. From the beginning, he felt the pairing off. Despite favorable reactions by casting directors, Perry, and recent fan polls demanding to see more of Gayle Turney in major pictures, Diego felt their chemistry wrong.

"She's a different kind of actor," Dalton said when Diego expressed concern about the decision to go with Gayle.

"Different how?"

Dalton shrugged his shoulders and sighed. "She's savvier. Tougher. Opinionated. She's intelligent. Experienced. Educated. They're saying she's the shape of things to come."

"She's almost as tall as me," he protested.

"I like her. She's not your typical female actress. A breath of fresh air."

"I'm not convinced," Diego told him.

"Just you wait and see. Trust me."

Gayle was too overpowering, too serious. She always showed up on time, always had her lines memorized, and never shied away from expressing an opinion about a specific scene or some dialogue. She was courteous to Diego, always professional, and very guarded.

Dalton seemed to enjoy the way she questioned his directorial choices, even the script. She challenged him, he confessed to Diego one evening. Her curiosity made him examine his choices, his "mode of expression." It all seemed like hogwash to Diego, and he grew more and more tired of her constant interferences, her intellectualizing and rationalizing. It was tedious, and he felt disenchanted, uninspired.

A month into the shooting, he was feeling pushed out of the film. All of the attention both on the set and off seemed to focus more and more on Gayle and her character. Slowly, Gayle took center stage, and Camila was written into more scenes, her story line was given more heft, and her role in the film was augmented in such a way so that it became an absolutely essential element in the plot. It was aggravating him, and he began to wish he'd had the strength to turn down the project.

Meanwhile, he did everything he could to make working on the picture more tolerable. Even when, in between takes, she gave him pointers, he managed to be gracious and considerate toward her.

"I really appreciate your help," he'd say. "Honestly."

"It's nothing." She stood before a large mirror, removing her makeup with a towel. "I just remember that day when you took the time to speak to me. I was intimidated, and you made me feel so at ease, such a part of the production."

"It was nothing," he said.

"Oh, but it wasn't. You were kind. I'll remember it always."

The truth of the matter was that he didn't resent her. Gayle Turney was a kind human being, ever gracious and fair, intelligent and generous. She brought gifts—bags of oranges and lemon marmalade made with her very own hands from the citrus trees that lined her property—to everyone on the set, from lighting technicians to carpenters, producers to random extras. She always stopped to chat with her fans and sign autographs, volunteered her time to charities and donated money and clothing to the Red Cross and the Salvation Army. He envied her. She was talented, confident, assured, and when she spoke, others listened. She came from a simple background and made herself into a success bit by bit because she had chosen wisely, called her own shots, and had never given in. Gayle had remained in complete control of her career and would do so for many years to come.

3

September 1935

THE SPECULATIONS ABOUT FRONTIER in the papers and trade columns only worsened throughout the early fall of 1935. "It's not looking good for the Old Girl," they said. More financial backers had pulled their support, claiming the economic woes left them with little choice as the Depression continued on, leaving the studio vulnerable for a hostile takeover. Meanwhile, there were more rumors circulating throughout Hollywood about Bill and Tod Duren. They were seen everywhere together—the racetracks, the polo field, parties, and dance clubs. At times it was just the two of them, and other times they were escorting starlets or fashion models. They called him "Tod Duren: America's Guy" or "The Guy Next Door," with his "down-home good looks" and his "old-fashioned charm." Bill told reporters that the studio had big plans for Tod. He would begin work on a movie next month, a melodrama titled *The Violent Hour*. It would be his first major role. As a leading man.

"Aren't you taking a gamble?" the reporter asked. "Putting such a green actor in a leading role in a big motion picture? Up until now, he's been support."

"I'm confident that Tod will pull this off," Bill said. "So confident that he'll be sharing top billing with his leading lady, Fay Carmichael."

It was unheard of, Bill admitted, but he believed in Tod Duren's abilities. Diego couldn't help but feel jealous and spiteful of the "golden boy's" opportunity but also, and maybe more than that, his place at Bill's side.

One morning, Javier called Diego to say that, after many hours of train travel and a series of delays, he was in Los Angeles again. Diego was excited; maybe this visit would allow him the opportunity to focus on something else besides the upheaval surrounding the studio and Bill and Tod Duren.

"I imagine you're busy with your new film," he said. "But I'd like to talk before I leave."

"Of course," he said. "Tell Lucía I look forward to seeing her again."

"She's not with me, hermano. She left me for another man."

"Oh," he said. "I'm sorry."

"Meet me at Olvera Street," Javier said. "There's a rally planned."

Dalton Perry had phoned him at four a.m. on the day he was to see Javier. An unexpected delay and word from up top to speed up production meant that they would have to film that day after all.

"Sorry," Perry said. "I know you haven't had a day off in a long time. But, such is business. I can send a car for you."

"No," he told him. "I'll drive myself there."

Hours of filming under a hot sun—with countless extras, a cavalry of temperamental horses, one of which had bucked a trainer off its back when he tried mounting it, sending him flying into the air where he landed on top of a craft service table and had to be rushed to the hospital, of buzzing flies and a chorus of shouts and curses as Perry tried orchestrating a complex scene—had left Diego drained and overwhelmed. He barely had enough time to rush home, bathe and change, before rushing out again. Now, well past noon, he drove on, his foot pressing down on the gas pedal as the car continued toward downtown Los Angeles.

Olvera Street, a former dilapidated alley near downtown, had been reconstructed back in 1925 to look like a quaint Mexican bazaar. The old adobe and brick structures were renovated. Along its walkway, lined with trees and fountains, tourists shopped for serapes, toys, clay pots, cacti, candles, sweets, and candies. The female merchants of these shops donned frilly costumes and lace skirts, their hair in thick braided ponytails. The men wore vaquero pants with pointed boots, embroidered shirts and large sombreros. It was almost like a movie set. It was more like Mexico than the Mexico Diego remembered.

He'd gained increasing popularity among Mexican-American movie audiences, and he didn't feel like being recognized today, so he hid behind dark sunglasses, his hat pulled down low, as he weaved in and out under the brightly colored cloth tarps, brushing past groups of tourists huddled together whispering and pointing at the paper piñatas, the wooden whistles, the bags hanging from hooks on posts. The air was heavy with the scent of cinnamon, corn, refried beans, and leather. Boys in overalls and wool driver's caps darted about, polishing the shoes of old men who sat on benches reading the paper. The shops and eateries facing the narrow, cobblestone avenue were crowded with people. Mariachi musicians strolled from table to table, singing songs for money. Diego stretched and craned his neck, past the heads of the pedestrians, toward the front entrance. The street spilled out into the principal plaza, a large concrete square with Main Street to its west and Alameda to its east. Up ahead, City Hall loomed large and bright white in the afternoon sun, and he remembered the day he first arrived in Los Angeles, remembered men scaling up the metal beams like ants.

In the plaza a modest crowd of people had assembled around a raised wooden platform. They carried banners in various sizes and colors: *International Brotherhood of Workers, IFC, Ejército Mexicanos Unidos.* There were members of the Communist and Socialist parties, trade union representatives, and other activist groups. Diego searched the crowd and saw Javier standing with a few others, looking out across the square to a group of police officers standing, shoulder to shoulder, along the perimeter of the plaza near Alameda Street.

"What's happening?" Diego asked once he reached Javier.

Javier shook his head. "It seems that the police are here as well." He said something to the group, and he led Diego away from the crowd and toward the vendor stalls along the avenue. "Just like being back home, isn't it?"

"Almost." Diego laughed. "But not quite."

"Do you ever think about returning?"

"Sometimes," Diego said. "But I'm not sure my grandparents would have me. Anyway, I think this is my home now."

He looked back. He could see that the crowd had grown some; more men and women had joined the mass, waving banners and flags in the air, their chants growing louder and louder, mixing with the guitar strums of the mariachi musicians strolling through the street.

Javier placed his arm around Diego's shoulder. "Come back," he said. "With me."

"What are you talking about?"

"I'm talking about quitting your work here. I'm talking about returning with me. Helping me in the fight."

"Fight for what?"

"For workers' rights. Men like your father. Campesinos. The poor. The people you once were like."

He said Diego was famous in Mexico. His face, his name, could do a lot to further the cause, to help Javier shore up support. Things, he admitted, had not gone as well as he hoped in the United States. America, he said, chuckling, had its hands full, had its own hungry and destitute people.

"Lucía left me," Javier said. "Even she got . . . disillusioned. Met an artist in New York City. Fell in love with him." They found a bench and sat down. Pigeons dotted the alleyway, and Diego watched them pick the ground and fight over bits of bread and seeds someone had scattered on the ground.

"What do you say?" Javier told him. "We could move to Mexico City. Start a newspaper or something. Just the two of us. Like we used to talk about."

"Javier, I can't just—"

"Come on, hermano," he pleaded. "I need you. I need your help."

Diego stood and took a few steps forward, startling the pigeons. They fluttered away in a panic, and he watched them fly off, past the branches and telephone poles, their wings beating fast.

"No," he said. "I can't."

Javier only wanted Diego to help him further the cause. That wasn't friendship or loyalty or love, he understood. It was to keep the cause alive, to keep the fight going, to simply survive.

Javier sighed. "There's nothing here for you, Diego. Anyone can see that. You're alone. In exile. No one respects you or your work. Back there, you're known. You're loved and you're missed in Mexico."

"I'm not missed." Diego laughed.

"Oh, but you are," Javier urged him, his eyes moist. "You are, Diego."

"No one misses me."

"They do," he said. "My mother, your grandparents, even I—"

"Enough," Diego told him. "I'm not going back, Javier. I'm simply not."

"Very well," he said. "I'm disappointed. I guess I should go then. The rally's about to start." Javier stood and gave Diego a hug and a kiss on the cheek. "I admire you," he said. "Your conviction. Your belief in yourself."

"It's all I have left," Diego said. "It's all that I am now."

"It's all any of us are," Javier said.

Diego wanted to be with him, but he knew such a thing was impossible now, more so than it had been years before. He watched his old friend walk past the street vendors and stalls to the rally, a group of people shouting and chanting, their fists puncturing the sky above them.

4

March 1936

THERE WERE SEVERAL DELAYS—threats of strike, injuries, disagreements—so filming on *The Revolutionists* dragged into the following year. One day, a girl in a gray tweed skirt came to the set and handed Diego a slip of paper.

"What's this?" he asked.

"Message from Mister Cage," she said, then turned and left.

He opened it and read:

Please come and see me this afternoon.
Three p.m.
WC

He found him in his office, rifling through a stack of papers. "Sit," he urged, and didn't look up as he pointed to the chair across from his desk.

"You wanted to see me?" Diego asked.

"I did," he said.

"What about?"

Bill leaned back in his chair, and sighed. He stared intently at Diego, removed his glasses and scratched the bridge of his nose.

"Your contract's up," he said. "After you finish this project. I'm sorry to tell you that we won't be renewing it."

"Come again?" Diego asked, stunned.

Bill shook his head. "I'm sorry. There's nothing I can do. Frontier's having to make a lot of tough calls right now and, to put it bluntly, you're no longer considered a viable commodity."

"What do you mean I'm not viable? What about this film I'm about to finish up? I thought you said it was big, that it would save the studio?"

"That may be, but polls show your popularity slipping, and your other projects haven't made us much money, and we, the studio, just don't feel it's fiscally sound to be investing in you anymore."

Diego stopped listening. He felt his skin grow hot, his limbs tingle. He rose and walked over to the window and loosened his tie. Everything spun, and he gripped the wall to keep from losing his balance. Bill went on, explaining the details of what releasing him from his contract would mean in a noncommittal tone, as if he were rattling off a list of instructions.

"The Latin thing's over," he said. "It's no longer exotic, it doesn't sell." Trends changed, he went on. Tastes were different now. "Audiences are fickle. They want a fresh face. The 'boy-next-door' type."

"Like Tod Duren?" Diego asked. He walked over to a cart in the corner of the office where Bill kept his liquor and poured himself some whiskey. He reached for the cigar box and plucked one out.

"Excuse me, but those are . . ." Bill started to say.

Diego ignored him and lit it anyway.

"Yes. Tod Duren. We feel—"

"And who is 'we'?"

The investors, Bill explained. The new investors who had their eyes on different faces, he told Diego. "Their approach is different from R. J.'s, and I welcome it."

"And what about R. J.?" he asked.

Bill sighed and shook his head. "R. J. He didn't see things the way we did."

"You sold him out, you mean," Diego said.

"We had a difference of opinion, and he was a gentleman about it." R. J. understood, Bill claimed, that this was business, and that this was how things went sometimes. "Diego," Bill said now, his voice softening, "I wish to God it were different, but it's not. You're not what we're looking for anymore. You're not what anybody wants."

"Is that meant to make me feel better?"

"What do you *want* me to say?" He tapped his palm against his desk; a set of pens and an ink bottle trembled. "This isn't easy for me."

"What now?" Diego asked himself, asked Bill, puffing on the cigar, taking a drink of whiskey, and pouring himself more.

"That's very expensive whiskey. I would really appreciate it if you didn't—"

Diego ignored him, drank, and poured himself another glass.

Bill sighed. "Very well," he said. "If it'll make you feel better, finish it all."

Cage told him that he would fulfill the rest of his contract by completing his work on *The Revolutionists*, by performing any publicity associated with the picture, and attending the premiere. After that point, he would be released.

"Released?" Diego asked. "What a beautiful word for such a horrible thing."

He slammed his drink down and headed for the door, but Bill stopped him.

"You may find this hard to believe," he said, "but I did care for you. Very much. And I'll continue to. In a different life, you and me would be together. We'd be happy."

Through the opened windows there came the sound of shouts and car horns honking, of ringing bells and whistles. All the work at the studio continued, moved forward, but there, in William Cage's office, the air and everything around it remained still, suspended in time.

"I have to go now, Bill," Diego said. "Thank you for the opportunity."

"Diego, I'm really sorr . . ." Bill started to say, but Diego didn't let him finish. He opened the door and walked out. He didn't want to hear it.

He took a long drive up the highway skirting the ocean. He watched the tan cliffs unfold, the water lapping the edge of the shore, the seagulls drifting on currents of air. Diego pulled the car off the main road and followed a narrow trail up a winding bluff. He parked and got out. He couldn't feel anything but light passing through him, not through his physical body, but his soul, his being. He felt alert, cognizant yet without any real physical form, without any physical features. That wonderful sensation of warmth, of serenity, of at long last being at peace, was all he knew he had ever wanted. He stood at the edge of the earth, overlooking that vast and ever present ocean. Behind him, in the far distance, was a chain of green hills. Beneath the chain of hills, he imagined a fertile valley filled with fruit trees which people picked, tossing the harvest into large wicker baskets. The men sported strong arms that worked to lift children up to the trees to pick apples and oranges that tumbled down onto the ground when the slightest gust of ocean breeze fanned the branches. He felt the breeze, smelled the salt and brine. Below, the waves crashed against the rocks along the seashore. Far off, toward the horizon, the sun floated there, suspended, refusing to set, lighting everything up at once, and the land was golden and peaceful and the people were happy.

He wanted to sprout wings and fly off and away. Maybe he should have listened to Javier. Maybe he should have followed him back to Mexico. Things might have been different. They might have had a life together. What would he do now? he wondered. Who would he become?

As filming on *The Revolutionists* neared completion, along with his contract with Frontier, Diego was finding it harder and harder to summon up the energy to be there. It was exhausting, having to pretend, and he wanted to sleep more than anything in the world. To close his eyes for a good, long time and shut all the voices out until . . . until what? He went from days where he was hopeful, reminding himself that it wasn't the end, that Frontier wasn't the only studio in the business, to moments of fear and regret, moments when he looked back at the decisions he had made that led him here to this, this lonely life, this life where he truly had nothing at all left. It made him sick, this back-and-forth, this constant tugging and pulling. When would it end? How had he arrived here?

He was dressed in costume—frayed cotton trousers, a heavy wool jacket adorned with embroidered galloons, boots, a large sombrero, and a fake mustache—when he arrived. He grabbed a pistol and placed it in his leather holster. The set designers had arranged several props—a fiberglass horse, a whiskey barrel, a pitaya cactus—and they would be shooting a series of movie stills, he was told, by a group of fidgety photographers, then some headshots.

"The studio hired a new photographer," one of the casting assistants told Diego while they watched the set designers arrange the props. A piece of the wooden barrel had been chipped, a large hunk of wood missing from one side when it was dropped while it was being moved, and they had to call in a carpenter.

The casting assistant told Diego, "Why don't you go inside the trailer." She pointed to a white Airstream parked behind the stage. "Mister Apple can take your headshots, and when he's done we should be ready out here."

"Very well," he said, and walked to the camper.

He opened the door and stepped inside. A chair was positioned in front of a black velvet curtain. In front of the chair was a camera on a tripod, the wooden stilts gleaming new and smooth. A large lamp sat atop a stack of crates, the light pointing directly at the chair.

"Hello?" he said. "Anyone here?"

"Coming," said a voice from behind a narrow door. Soon it opened and the photographer stepped from behind the trailer's kitchenette that seemed to double as the dark room. He wore a white apron and thick, black glasses.

"Why, hello!"

The man's voice was familiar, but from where? "Hello," Diego said, feeling uneasy.

The photographer came closer and removed his glasses. "Don't you recognize me?"

Diego continued to stare. It was none other than Charlie Applebaum. "Charlie?" he asked, stunned.

"It's me," he said, laughing, slapping his knee. "What a surprise. I knew you worked here. But I didn't know you were on this picture." He laughed and gave Diego a quick pat on the back. "Why, it's been a while since I saw you. Thought you were sore at me."

"Sore? Why would I be sore, Charlie?" Diego smiled.

He placed his hands in his pockets and shrugged. "I dunno. After I was evicted from the Ruby Rose, I never saw you around the diner."

"I got busy. My life," he stammered, "became a little occupied."

He looked around, said, "Wow. You're a photographer now?"

"Can you believe it?" Charlie said. "Been enjoying my work. Better than I could have ever imagined." Charlie walked over and handed Diego a book. Inside, the pages were filled with head-shots of faces he recognized—Lester Frank, Ada Daniels, Margaret Dillon, Clark Gable, Greta Garbo—each personally autographed by the actors themselves to Charlie.

"You took all of these?" Diego asked, thumbing through the book. The pages went on and on. "Every single actor in Hollywood must be here."

"They are," he said. Charlie said it took him spending a few weeks thinking about his life, about the choices he'd made, about his career in pictures. He was taken in by a preacher, he said, right after he left the Ruby Rose. This preacher was a great man named Brother Earl. He preached the word of God with his daughter, Rebecca. They made me see, Charlie said, that a career in pictures wasn't for me. So, he said, he started attending services more and more, grew closer to Brother Earl and Rebecca.

"They made me see the error of my ways. Now, I'm much happi-er. Changed my name. I'm Charlie Apple. I attend services regular-ly, and I just bought a studio. I'm still getting settled, but I already got customers flocking there. Girls wanting their headshots, guys like you, like I once was, needing their photos to pass around at the studios." He folded his arms and leaned up against a chair.

"That's great," said Diego. There was an awkward pause, and they stood there, quietly, Charlie playing with his glasses and Diego jiggling his hands in his pockets. "Well," Diego said. "Where shall I sit?"

"Here," he said, pointing to a chair.

"Very well." Diego sat.

Charlie positioned himself behind the camera, fiddled with dif-ferent glass plates, adjusting the lens and the lamp. He covered his head under the camera's cloth and held the flashbulb up. "Good," he said, his voice muffled. "Stay there. Just like that. Don't move. Stay quiet and still."

He snapped several pictures, the flashbulbs exploding, the black smoke dissolving into the hot air. Charlie said nothing for a while then spoke again. "I know what you did. I know it was you who took my spot."

"What are you talking about?" Diego asked. He felt Charlie's eye on him, magnified, behind the large glass plate of the camera. "Spot? What spot?"

"When the studio called that morning. It was you. You intercepted the message."

"What are you talking about? I . . . that's absurd." The lamp's light glared in his face. He squinted and began to sweat.

"I had a friend who worked on that picture. I ran into her a few days after I was evicted. She told me a guy showed up claiming to be me. Only it wasn't me. She recognized you from a photo in the paper."

"Charlie, look—"

"The thing is that I'm not sore," he said. "I really and truly am not sore at you. Because if you hadn't done that, who knows where I'd be right now, who I'd be. The whole show business stuff. Why, I never had the chops for it."

"Hey," Diego said. "Look, I'm sorry. I needed a break. I needed to make it here. I was desperate."

"I was too," Charlie explained. He stopped now, removed the cloth, and stood straight. "I too was once lost, but now I'm found." He approached and placed his hand on Diego's shoulder. He looked into his eyes, and Charlie's gaze was penetrating, sharp and frigid as ice. "I know you. The real you. What you're capable of. Why you do what you do. What you're running from. I know who you truly are."

"You don't," Diego said, standing now. "You don't know *anything* about me."

He turned toward the door, trying to erase Charlie's words from his memory, trying to erase his own guilt that felt heavier now more than ever before.

He didn't need prayers from the likes of Charlie Applebaum, or Apple, to help him gain clarity. What he needed were the things he had depended on that got him this far: determination, opportunities, luck, and talent. Yes, sir, he told himself. I'll be fine and dandy. Something will give. It's not the end of me. A minor setback. A small wrinkle in an otherwise smooth plan. Diego had read a few days before an article about Thomas Edison and how many times he had to redesign, redraft, and reimagine all of his inventions before getting them just right. He admired the man's tenacity and told himself he would go forth from that day forward and try to emulate it. Diego would allow himself to think only successful thoughts. He would forget the past. He would work harder. He would eventually triumph.

Diego was feeling chipper for the first time in weeks. Though apprehensive about his next move once work on the picture was over, he walked around that day—the sun shining brightly, a cool breeze blowing in from the coast—at Frontier and reminded himself that, though he would miss it, there were other games in town. Another studio will pick him up. He walked with a slight skip in his step, whistling, as he strolled around the studio, killing time between takes, when he ran into Georgie Wexler. She was coming out of the studio diner with a group of girls, all of them seamstresses in the costume department.

"Well, look at you!" she said, running up to give him a hug.

"Georgie?" He hugged her back and said, "What a surprise. How's tricks?"

She waved good-bye to her friends. "It's good to see another familiar face. I was just having coffee with the girls. How I miss them."

"Are you visiting?"

"For a few days," she said, leaning up against the diner's wall. Georgie unbuttoned her coat, and he looked down and saw her belly.

"You're pregnant?" he asked.

"Four months," she said, out of breath, fanning herself with her hand. "My, but the little bugger tuckers me out."

"What have you and Nick been up to these last few years?"

She told him how, after their honeymoon, they moved to Connecticut where Nick attended law school at Yale, how he finished up the year before and was now working in Manhattan for a friend of his father's. They bought a house in the suburbs and Nick commutes into the city.

"Just like we planned it," she said, smiling and pointing to her belly. "Now, all we have to do is wait for the little one to pop out, and we'll be complete. I've seen your movies," she told Diego now. "My, how you've changed."

"Yes, well," he said. "It's show business."

She looked at her wristwatch now and buttoned her jacket up. "I have to meet my mother for tea," she said. "Dear, look at the time." Georgie leaned in and kissed Diego. "Did you know Fiona's back? Living in Pasadena."

He was surprised. Fiona. He hadn't thought of her for so long. "Really?"

"Yes," Georgie said. "She has a son. Cutest little thing."

"Where does she live?" Diego asked. "I must go see her!"

The houses on Serenata Street were modest bungalows with small yards and large porches. The car crept along, and he counted the numbers until he came to 156. He had picked up the telephone book, thumbed through it, and there she was. She would remember him as he *was*. That notion made something inside of him tremble. Something inside of him said he should start the engine and turn around, to forget about this. But he stepped forward, walked up the paved path lined on either side with blooming yellow poppies, climbed the wooden steps to the porch, and stood there, by the door, peering through the screen at the inside of a small living room furnished with a sofa and coffee table and bookshelves, all of them modest pieces, nothing fancy or expensive-looking at all. They were arrogant in their simplicity, in their imperfection, and this put him at ease. So he took a deep breath and knocked until he heard a set of footsteps approach. The screen was dirty, and all he could make out was the silhouette of a figure, a featureless face, ambivalent and unclear.

"Yes?" she said.

He took his glasses off and removed his hat. "It's me," he said. "Fi, it's me."

The screen door opened, and she stood there at the threshold, in a pair of loose-fitting trousers with mud caked on the knees, a white blouse, and a checkered scarf tied around her head. She wore no makeup, sweat glistening in the crease above her lip, and yet she looked just as adorable as ever. She put her hand on her hip and said in a voice that was loud and direct, "Well, I'll be a son of a bitch!" And she laughed and threw her arms around him and kissed him on the cheeks.

She was a different person, a whole other woman. He regarded her still beautiful bright blond hair, the traces of freckles on her face, and the voice and the smile and the unmistakable flicker in her eyes.

"What happened to you?" he asked.

She smirked, patted him on the shoulder. "Motherhood happened, doll."

"Yes, but—"

"It makes you practical. Makes you respond to the world differently. No more revealing dresses." She stopped, batted her eyes in an exaggerated way, cocked her head to one side, coyly, and then there she was, the Fiona he remembered, and then she vanished. "No need for wild parties and bathtub gin and running with film stars. I have a son to look out for. Got to take care of him on my own. I'm all he's got."

"Where is he now?"

"Inside. Napping."

She grew vegetables out back. They were in low boxes throughout the yard, their leaves green and healthy and robust. Still some weren't doing so well. Snails, she said, leading him out. She was having so many problems with snails.

"They crawl up and devour my tomatoes." Fiona bent down, broke a stem off, and showed it to him. She pointed to the tiny holes on the leaves, and they looked like the burns from a lit cigarette when pressed against a sheet of paper. "Would you look at that?"

After showing him the garden, she led him around and up to the front, and they sat on the swing in the porch that let out a series of low creaks as they rocked back and forth.

"Been meaning to take some oil to that," she said. "So?" She turned to him now, smiling. "A real-life movie star. That's exciting."

"Why, it sure is," he said. "Who would have thought, huh?"

"I would have. You were a natural. Driven."

"And you? Tell me about you." Diego didn't want to talk about Frontier. He wasn't ready to tell Fiona the truth.

She folded her arms, and they were flecked with mud, her fingernails coated with dirt and grit. "Where to begin?" She shook her head. "Where to begin?"

She said Europe was fun, and working on the set of that picture had been the best experience of her life. The cast was amazing, the director a real sweetheart, and the location was to die for. She rented an apartment in a building owned by an old woman with a blind cat.

"Things went sour when work on the movie was done, but the eventual project was shelved along with the other ones I was told I'd be on. I gave up after that."

Out of a job and pregnant, it was hard finding work, and she lived hand to mouth, barely able to pay for her apartment. When the baby came, the old woman kicked her out, said the boy wasn't letting the other tenants sleep with his incessant crying. So she left, had a string of low-end jobs—waitress, newsstand worker, clerk— most with flexible hours. She left the boy with various people she knew and trusted, sometimes women she worked with, with a lady she befriended who looked after other kids, other times even taking him with her to work. Eventually, she came back to the States and borrowed money from her parents, who also helped her find a place to live in Pasadena.

"I'm a bit of a shame to my family." Fiona shook her head. "They hate that I had a baby out of wedlock, that there's no father."

"And who is the father?"

"Someone," she said, placing her hand on his. "A nice young man I met one day. An actor."

Diego pulled his hand back. He was beginning to understand. "Fiona, am I the—?"

"My boy's real smart," she said, her eyes filling with tears. "The best kid around. I love him so."

He hugged her close. What if he were to leave it all behind— the acting, the schedules, the public scrutiny, all of it—like so many others had. He could be here with her and the boy, he insisted, live a simpler life.

She laughed, shrugged her shoulders. "This life's anything but simple."

"Let me back in, Fiona," he said. "Please."

"I can't. I'm sorry. We've been down there before, you and me. We're different people. There's no way we could ever make it work now that I am who I am."

"And who are you?" he asked.

"I'm a mother who gardens, whose knees are scraped and who goes to bed exhausted, happy but exhausted. You're a star now."

"Who knows for how long." He smirked. "Fi, my contract is up. Frontier doesn't plan on renewing it."

"I'm sorry," she said. "Oh, I'm so sorry, angel."

"You see? I have few choices now. Let me back in. Please," he said. "I love you."

"You don't love me," she said. "You can't."

"I'll prove it. Let's get married."

"No." Here she paused. "You have other . . . interests. I know. I've always known."

"I'll change. I'll be different."

She pulled Diego away. "No. You'll grow to resent me." Fiona held his hand and said, "I see the real you. And I accept him. It's time you stop denying it and start doing the same thing, angel. You have to."

"I can't," he said. "I'm not strong enough."

"Oh, but you are. You always have been."

She kissed him on the cheek, said she needed to get back inside. Her son would be waking from his nap soon and would be wondering where she was. Fiona didn't invite him in. She walked inside and closed the screen door.

"I'll tell him," she said.

"What?" he asked. "Tell him what?"

She was once again a shadow, a silhouette framed by the screen door's edge. "About you. When he sees your movies he'll know you. I promise."

"What is the little bugger's name?" he asked, smiling, tears welling up in his eyes.

"I named him after his daddy," she said, folding her arms, nodding triumphantly.

He wiped the tears away with the back of his hand. "That's good. It's a great name." He smiled. "I love you," Diego said. "I mean it. I do. I always have."

"Thank you. I really did need to hear that after all these years. Thank you."

He could see that she was smiling as she closed the front door and locked it.

It was amazing. What they could make. What they could do with wood and concrete, metal and glass. How they could turn day into night, a summer breeze into a blizzard, a barren wasteland into a fertile valley. *Amazing*, Diego thought. *Truly amazing.*

The entire south side of the soundstage had been converted into a quaint Mexican village, nestled among the hills and valleys of that nation. This was Demetrio Macías's home, the one he returns to at the end of the book, where his wife and child are waiting for him. The carpenters had cobbled the street, setting each stone in place individually, one after the other, by hand. The shacks lining either side of the road were constructed of actual bricks, not foam, and truckloads of straw and palm fronds had been brought in to make the roofs of each dwelling. The hens and roosters, the goats and pigs, the horse and mules were all real. The extras playing the village residents stoked real fires, and the women ground real corn on actual stone metates. One extra gossiped with a lighting technician as she practiced patting tortillas. Another smoked a cigarette and read a copy of *Screenshots*. Two men dressed as campesinos in tattered trousers and frayed huaraches played poker and used a stack of film reel canisters to shuffle their decks and lay their hands down. Behind them, the set designers hung a large canvas with large and billowy thunderclouds painted on its surface. They climbed up ladders and used pulleys and cranks to stretch it out, covering the studio's metal walls.

"Over here! Mr. Cortez," shouted a makeup assistant. "Over here." The girl took him by the arm. "We have to hurry," she said, leading him to a chair where he sat.

He was nervous, and a queasy feeling filled his stomach. His mouth watered as he sat at the makeup table while the girl dabbed his forehead.

"My, but you're perspiring a lot," she said, fanning him with her hand as she worked.

"Sorry," he told her. A copy of the script lay opened on his lap, and he was trying to focus, trying to go over his lines, just words, he reminded himself, when Dalton approached.

"I'm sorry to hear the bad news," he said, sighing. "Why didn't you say anything sooner?"

Diego shrugged his shoulders. "Guess I was hoping it was a lie."

"If it helps at all, I think they're making a big mistake letting you go like that."

"Thanks." He nodded. "I appreciate it."

"You're a great actor, a great guy to work with. I know you'll land on your feet."

"Thanks a lot."

After 30 minutes, Diego was called onto the set. The extras still milled about. Two girls gossiped about rumors on the set of another film. A little boy and a girl fought, and the boy was scolded by one of the supervisors when he pulled the girl's pigtails and she began to cry. The actress playing Demetrio Macías's wife walked onto the set. She wore a ruffled skirt and a white embroidered blouse with a rebozo draped over her shoulders. Her hair was in two pigtails that were adorned with brightly colored ribbons, tied at ends in two big bows. She wore red pumps, and a costume assistant walked over and handed the actress a pair of leather huaraches.

"Where do you want me?" the actress asked Dalton, placing the sandals on.

"Over there, Judy," he said, pointing to the small shack at the very end of the row. He turned to Diego and asked, "Your son? Where's your son?"

"What?" he asked, stunned, confused. "What are you—?"

"I'm right here! I'm *right* here!" the young boy who had been scolded earlier shouted, bursting through the crowd of extras, technicians, the costume and makeup assistants clustered around the set. He was about seven years old, Diego figured. Everyone took his or her mark when Dalton gave the order. The actress playing Demetrio's wife walked to the end of the row of houses, the boy trailing behind her, as the remaining extras took positions throughout the village.

"Very well," Dalton said, walking over to his chair, a copy of the script resting on his lap. "Macías has been away for a long time now," he shouted to Diego.

"How long?" He stood in between the cameras and the very edge of the set.

Dalton looked down at his script. "Two years."

"No," Diego said. "It was longer than that. He was gone longer."

"Who?" Dalton asked. He removed his glasses and scratched his forehead.

"Gabriel."

"You mean Demetrio?"

"Yes," Diego said. "Right. Him. Me. Demetrio."

Judy looked at Diego, her eyebrows furrowed. "What's the hold-up?" she asked.

"Look, that doesn't matter," Dalton explained to Diego. "What does matter is that he comes back after years of fighting. He comes back disillusioned, defeated."

"Why?" Diego asked.

"Why what?"

Diego remained quiet.

Dalton rose suddenly and walked over to him. He shouted, "Give us 10 minutes alone!"

A chorus of voices came from the dark shouting, "10 minutes," again and again until they faded away. All of them—the stagehands and extras, script supervisors, sound engineers, Judy, the young boy—rose and walked out at once, leaving him and Dalton alone.

"Why are you doing this?"

"Doing what?"

Dalton placed his arm around Diego's shoulder. "Asking all these questions, delaying things."

"I'm not. I'm just trying to figure this out, just trying to understand it all."

"I appreciate that. I really do. And I've admired every single thing you've done to make this picture good, but it's over. Let's just end it and move on, okay?"

But he didn't want to move on. To what? Where? Diego chuckled and said, "And this is how we go? This is how it ends?"

"Are you okay? Did you bump your head?"

"No," he said. "I'm fine."

"Let's continue then, shall we?"

"Very well."

They all marched back inside now, the multitude of faces and arms and torsos, assuming their rightful positions behind cameras and scaffolds, next to makeup tables and floodlights. The extras went to their marks. Judy strode in, passed him, and stood in front of the small house that was their home. The young boy took his mark beside her and Dalton Perry told him to grab hold of his mother's skirt, see? Like this. He looked over to Diego now.

"When you see Macías coming from over there," Dalton told Judy, pointing to where Diego stood, "you and the boy walk toward him and you all converge there." He pointed to a yellow mark in the middle of the street.

The lights dimmed now, and the crew stood a few feet from the set holding tin cans with long and pointed nozzles puffing out threads of white smoke. A set of large fans with sleek metal blades near them remained off. These would be switched on, and the crew would stand to one side, pointing the nozzles to the current of air, and they would pump out clouds of smoke caused by the small fires the other villagers gathered around.

The makeup assistant walked over to Diego to touch up his face, applying more layers of foundation. She scooped it out of small metal trays with a spatula. It looked more like putty or clay than makeup, Diego thought. It was flesh colored and frightening. She used a series of brushes and sponges to dab and smear it on, again and again, until it felt heavy and thick on his face, and it dried the skin underneath and caused it to itch.

"You got a lot of that stuff on you, and I managed to get your skin to look a few shades darker," she explained. "Let's hope it's good enough, though."

It was caked on, like varnish, and he felt it penetrating his pores, invading the fibers of his own skin, his own flesh, hardening it like a shell, changing its color and appearance as it worked its way deeper and deeper inside, bonding with his flesh. When the makeup people and crewmembers, when the lighting and sound technicians, when they all receded back behind, into the darkness that swallowed everything around the stage whole, just before Dalton was about to yell action, Diego raised his hand and asked a question.

"What is it now?" Dalton said.

"The boy," he said, pointing at him. "What's his name? What's his character's name?"

"It's irrelevant," said Dalton.

"No. It's not."

"It's irrelevant. Now, let's get on with it. We have a busy schedule today."

"Yeah," said Judy. "I got another shoot in an hour. Let's go. Who cares about a stinking name?" She held the boy's hand now.

The whole crew moved out from behind the shadows, out from behind the edges of the darkness circling the set, and they watched him.

"Yes." Dalton rubbed his eyes. "His name's not necessary. Please. Let's get on."

"But—" he shouted.

Judy gave him a curious look. "Are you sauced?" she asked, chuckling.

"He's supposed to be me," Diego insisted.

"He's not you," Dalton shouted. "You're you. What are you talking about?"

At the moment when the stories crossed, his own and that of the book and the movie, Diego León went from being to not being, to being again. He was back in Mexico, and he wasn't. The walls of the adobe homes that had been built and assembled a few hours before were stained to look aged and weathered, as though they had been there for generations. The sound of thunder was a record-ed disk. The dark storm clouds were merely painted on, and they rolled by on the long and continuous strip of canvas. Two men used handheld cranks and pulleys to mimic motion, to mimic the sensation of them moving through the painted hills and fake valleys of a country, of a place he once knew, of a home he once lived in, of a family who once loved him. Diego thought only about history and memory, about the places where they all begin. Somehow, among all that lawlessness, among the feuds and poverty, beneath a great and ancient sky, in the green mountains of a village in Michoacán, along the banks of a wide lake filled with fish whose skins were whiter than ghosts, lived his ancestors. And though Elva recounted this story hundreds and thousands of times, it was only now, once he reached the end of all things, that he chose to remember. He was born of a people versed in the art of storytelling, versed in the art of artifice, in make-believe, in obfuscation. And now he searched in all of that light and untruth and half-truth for something to give him back that which he knew he was missing, that lost feeling, that unspoken thought, that trace of the shadow, that fragment of the bone, fossilized, and forever preserved which held the key to his salvation, to his knowing who he was and who he would become.

Who would be left to remember them once they faded away into obscurity, into nothingness, like the countless before them and all of those yet to come?

Then Dalton called "action," and Diego wound up the crooked street of that village now, and his wife saw him, and she walked on, toward him, stunned, unbelieving.

"You're back," she said. "Please tell me you'll stay now. For me. For your son." She said to the boy, "Look. It's your father."

Diego reached out, tried hugging him, but the child recoiled, hiding between his mother's legs.

"Don't be frightened," his mother said. "It's your father!"

Diego looked at the boy, and in his face he saw his own, still forming, on the verge of becoming what it would eventually turn into. He saw Fiona's face and his child's face and knew this to be his own. And he finally understood, finally knew what they'd lost, and knew what they'd done to find themselves here, in a vague place, a shadow on a map. He could hear his thoughts now, his and this strange boy's and Fiona's child's, all of them mixing together, ringing so loud in his head. He would not let the boy inherit that legacy of hardship and death, of humiliation and hunger carved into his skin and his father's own skin.

He reaches down and picks his son up, his mother pleading with his father to stay this time, to stop fighting, to stop searching. Diego cradles his son in his arms, the boy's sobs growing louder and louder. He knows he's home. *I'm here,* he tells him, this stranger, this boy, this child, his. His. *I see you. I remember you now. I won't let you go.*

There's no need to go back, he thinks. There's nothing left to fight for but this.

Only this.

EPILOGUE

OBITUARIES

Diego León, Actor, is Dead at 90; Career Spanned Nearly 6 Decades

Hollywood, Calif., March 10, 1998 (AP)—Diego León, the suave and debonair character actor, died at his Santa Monica, California home. From 1929 to 1994, the Mexican-American actor was in close to 100 films and, later in his life, appeared in many television shows. Heart failure was the official cause of death, said Dr. William Chi, Mr. León's personal physician. He was 90.

León was born in a remote village in Michoacán, Mexico in 1908. His grandparents raised him after León's parents died when he was a child. In 1927, at the age of 19, he arrived in Los Angeles and never returned to Mexico. León moved into an apartment in Hollywood and began working as an extra at Frontier Pictures. "He was very ambitious," said Kristof Meyers in a phone interview from his Colorado home. "His only desire was fame and attention. He craved it, up until his death, I imagine." Meyers lived next door to the actor for a brief period. From 1930-32, he took on extra work to make ends meet. It was around this time that the actor began going by his more recognized name of Diego León.

His first major role was that of Emile in *The Bride of Blood* (1932). The next year, he was a misunderstood Italian youth in *Far From Home* and followed this up with *Two to Tango* (1934), where he played an Argentinian tango dancer. He was a bumbling lovelorn teacher in 1935's *Crazy For Miss Cavendish* and a journalist in *The Other Strange* the following year. He played a sultry nightclub owner in *Panamania* (1940). 1947's *Sequoya's Talking Leaves*, where León starred as the Native American credited with inventing the Cherokee alphabet, was the last film in which he worked with longtime friend and director Dalton Perry. The split followed an eventual break between the two and they never spoke again.

He was a wealthy Spaniard in 1941's *Hot Tamales*, and a street boxer in 1942's *Down For the Count*. Later in his career, León was determined to take on more challenging roles, but found them hard to come by. He was a scientist in the sci-fi B movie classic *Attack!* (1955), an inner-city high school teacher in *Uptown, Downtown* (1956), and a Hungarian immigrant in the hardscrabble Nebraska plains in 1958's *My Antonia*. After his role in the 1969 spy thriller *Destination: Diamondhead*, León shifted his attention to television. He had recurring roles in the television drama *Two If By Sea*, and in *Visitors* as well as regular appearances in the sketch comedy show *Laugh Central* and the variety show *Here's Bee Kelley*. It was his role as saloon bartender Chico Miranda in the television western *Dry Gulch*, and as Dr. Tripp in the science fiction cult classic *Orion 7* that he is most remembered by. León returned to films in the epic disaster *Fault Line* (1974), followed by *The Hungry Earth* (1990). His last role was that of Tarasco the talking turtle in the animated musical *The Butterfly Princess* (1994).

Professor Marco Antonio Saldino, a Diego León film scholar, said, "Ramon Novarro, Gilbert Roland, Ricardo Montalbán, and Anthony Quinn were great actors who contributed significantly to the legacy of Latinos in Hollywood, but it was Diego León whose work remains the most lasting, the most complex." He says León was the first Chicano actor in the film industry. "Like many minority actors at the time, Diego León was constantly being cast in roles that reinforced the image most Americans had of Mexicans," he explained. "The greaser, the sultry lover, the hot blooded boyfriend. What set León apart from his contemporaries was the sometimes deliberate way he exaggerated these stereotypes, almost as if he were calling attention to them in order to show how myopic Hollywood was, and is, when it comes to race."

Alex Espinoza is the author of *Still Water Saints*, *The Five Acts of Diego León*, and *Cruising: An Intimate History of a Radical Pastime*. He's written for the *Los Angeles Times*, the *New York Times Magazine*, *Virginia Quarterly Review*, *LitHub*, and for *NPR's All Things Considered*. The recipient of fellowships from the NEA and MacDowell as well as an American Book Award, he lives in Los Angeles and is the Tomás Rivera Endowed Chair of Creative Writing at UC Riverside.

LARB
LIBROS

LARB Libros highlights emerging Latinx talent. Each new title published in this new series will be the winner of the Tomás Rivera Book Prize, a unique partnership between UC Riverside and the Los Angeles Review of Books. Open to any author writing in English about the Chicanx/Latinx experience, the Rivera Book Prize is committed to the discovery and fostering of extraordinary writing by a first-time or early career author whose work examines the long and varied contributions of Chicanx/Latinx in the US. The Rivera Book Prize aims to provide a platform that showcases the emerging literary talent of the Chicanx/Latinx community, to cultivate the next generation of Chicanx/Latinx writers, and to continue the rich literary memory of Tomás Rivera, Chicano author, poet, activist, and educator. Known for his seminal collection of stories, ...*And the Earth Did Not Devour Him*, Rivera was the first Latino Chancellor of the UC system and a champion of higher education and social justice. The Rivera Book Prize honors his legacy and his belief in the power of education, activism, and stories to change lives.

The inaugural title is *The Five Acts of Diego León* by Alex Espinoza.